Cheating Truth

Keith Mullins

Copyright © 2014 Keith Mullins
All rights reserved.
ISBN: 1499267746
ISBN-13: 978-1499267747

Cover photo: Natasha Bos

In memory of my mother

Prologue

The music had finished some time ago, likewise the rapturous, slightly drunken, applause. Now the only sounds were the voices of the picnickers, calling out to each other cheerfully as they began to make their way home along the darkened paths, their cries softened by the midsummer lushness of the shrubberies. Occasionally one or two would stray closer, giggling as they stumbled through the azaleas and rhododendrons.

But none of this disturbed the body.

The rain fell gently at first, misty, barely distinguishable from the dampness already hanging in the night air. A light shower, the lingering picnickers said, best pack more quickly, but no need to panic. Then the droplets grew larger as the storm gathered its strength, and faster, until the picnickers' cries became tinged with urgency, and the laughter turned to irritation. But soon all other sound was drowned out by the relentless drumming of the rain on the leaves. The body was alone in the night with the dark, and the rain, and the azaleas.

The body had fallen face down, and the head, with its strange, bowl-shaped indentation at the back, was lying almost under one of the bushes, affording it some initial protection from the rain. The force of the downpour was too great for the canopy to withstand for long, however, and the occasional drip landing on the head became a steady stream. Slowly, very slowly, the water began to gather in the hole at the back of the head, blending with the blood that was already congealing there to form a small, rose-red, puddle.

PART I

Chapter 1

A few weeks earlier

Jake Chester sat in the tiny room in the Battersea, South London, flat that served as his office, staring at a computer screen. As he clicked on yet another link he felt a slight twinge in his arm, causing him to wince. Could you get RSI from too much surfing the internet, he wondered? Or maybe it was tennis elbow?

Quickly he clicked open another window and started Googling. 'Tennis elbow' produced nearly five million hits. Might take a bit of time. On the other hand, anything would be better than researching this article he was supposed to be writing. What had ever persuaded him to accept a commission on tree houses anyway?

Oh yeah, he needed the money. That was it. Or rather, Isabella had persuaded him - if that was the right description for a screaming match, liberally smattered with snatches of her mother's native Italian - that he needed the money. Not that she didn't earn enough for both of them. Never mind that wasting his time on this sort of crap was preventing him concentrating on his real work, the type of material that would one day win him a Pulitzer Prize. He was expected to 'pay his way'. Bloody bourgeois concept.

The phone rang. It was Isabella. Checking up on him as usual.

She sounded harassed.

"I'm going to be tied up in meetings for the rest of the day," she said without preamble. Tell me something new, he thought. "And I'm going to be late, so we're going to have to leave the moment I get in. I just wanted to check that you've remembered to pay those bills and chase up that bloody plumber."

"Leave?" he repeated, puzzled. "Are we going out tonight? I didn't know."

A theatrical sigh. "Of course you know, I reminded you this morning. Peter's quiz night. Or were you asleep?"

Jake did remember. Now. "Oh yeah. Yeah, should be fun. What time was it again? Eight?"

"No, it's not eight, it's seven thirty. And I won't be back before seven at the earliest. So everything has to be ready. Now, have you done those things I asked you?"

The pause while he thought of a suitably elegant evasion was enough for her. He realised he'd left it too late and braced himself for the onslaught.

"You haven't, have you? Can I ask what you actually have been doing all morning? While I'm working like a dog to keep you in booze? Do you know what time I got into the office today?"

She paused for breath and he heard a voice in the background. It sounded amused. All right for some – they weren't on the other end of her tirade. On second thoughts, though, if they worked with Isabella they probably had been. More than once.

When she resumed she just sounded tired. "I've got to go now. Just make sure it all gets done." And she hung up.

*

Isabella leaned back in her chair and rubbed her eyes. She felt a small stab of guilt. She wasn't actually tied up in meetings for the entire day – she was about to sneak off for a quick lunch with her best friend from university, Felicity Guthrie. But sod it – she had been working since before seven. It wouldn't do Jake any harm to do something useful for once.

She slipped out of the offices of the City law firm where she was a junior partner. She seemed to spend most of her waking hours there, and stepping out on to the pavement, even for a half hour break, was a relief – she seemed to breathe more easily and felt half a stone lighter.

She wished.

They were meeting at a trendy Japanese restaurant a couple of streets away, all pale wood and glass. Felicity was already there, sitting at a table in the window studying a menu. She looked up with a smile as Isabella slid into the seat opposite her.

"Sorry," said Isabella. "Have you been waiting long?"

"No problem – I've only been here a couple of minutes. So how are you? You're looking well."

Isabella laughed. "Liar. I must look as if I've been dragged through a hedge backwards. I didn't even have time to put any lipstick on."

Felicity, in contrast, was her usual exquisite self. She had the knack of appearing to have thrown on whatever garments had come to hand – in this instance, jeans and a black cashmere polo-neck – that just happened to be absolutely perfect for the occasion. Her long blonde hair was tied back in a neat ponytail and her make-up was flawless.

There was a lot to be said for being a trophy wife.

"Anyway," continued Isabella. "How was the dentist?"

Felicity waved a dismissive hand. "Oh, it was only a check up. All clear, thank God."

The waiter appeared at their table. "Shall we just share the large sashimi?" suggested Isabella. "And what do you want to drink? I'm sticking to mineral water, I'm afraid. Heavy meeting this afternoon."

Felicity wrinkled her nose, a characteristic gesture she'd had as long as Isabella had known her. "What the hell – I'll have a glass of white wine."

Isabella raised her eyebrows. "Still no luck then?"

Felicity shook her head. "Nope. We're thinking of going to a specialist later in the year if nothing happens." She looked at her friend solemnly. "Don't leave it too late, Bella. These things are never as simple as you think."

Isabella sighed. "I know. But I'm so busy at work – and one of us has to earn some money."

Felicity laughed. "That's what you get for marrying Jake, the handsome rogue. Me, I went sensible. A nice, rich, older advertising executive."

"Poor Hugh. Though you do actually adore him."

Felicity said nothing. A small smile played around her lips.

"Come on – don't give me all that bollocks," said Isabella, waving a chopstick at her. "You know you do."

"Oh, of course I do. It's just – sometimes I wish there was a bit more excitement in my life."

"You should try being married to Jake if you want excitement."

It came out with more resentment than she had intended, and she saw a quick look of concern cross Felicity's face.

"Problems?" she asked.

Isabella shrugged and ran her fingers through her thick, dark, hair, uncomfortably aware that she hadn't had time to wash it that morning. "Oh, nothing new. I just get fed up with having to think of everything all the time – as well as doing the work and bringing in the money. I know he has his own things – his writing and so on – and that they're important to him, but I wish he'd show a bit more consideration for me sometimes. I don't want gratitude – just some appreciation would be nice."

"How's his work going?"

Isabella shook her head. "That's the whole problem. He's so frustrated. He was going to be the great writer. Not just a journalist, but a columnist, opinion former, whatever. And while everyone else has been getting on in their own way, he's just been stuck. That's why I encourage him to keep at it – because I know, if he does have some success, I'll get the old Jake back. But Jesus, it's hard work." She grinned. "So don't knock that boringly successful advertising executive of yours too much, okay?"

Felicity didn't return the grin. She was silent for a long moment. "Do you think the grass is always greener?" she said eventually.

Isabella looked fondly at her friend. Most people on the planet would think she had the most perfect life imaginable. "Probably," she said.

Their food arrived, and for a few minutes they busied themselves dividing up the slices of raw fish.

"It'll be fun to see the others tonight," said Isabella after a while. "We don't get together anything like as much as we should."

Felicity nodded. "Absolutely. When I think about all the time the four of us used to spend together…"

"Mainly lying around Peter and Simon's house doing bugger all," interrupted Isabella. "What did we find to talk about? There were times when we never even got to bed, for Christ's sake – just did some bacon for breakfast and crashed later. I couldn't do that now if I tried."

"It's age, darling, age. That and work. But students are another species, anyway. They're on a different time zone and still fondly imagine that they can make the world a better place. Sweet, really."

"I suppose you're right," said Isabella. "People do change."

"Except us."

"Except us, obviously. Do you realise I've known you almost exactly half of my life now?"

"God – how depressing! Sorry, I didn't mean it to sound quite like that. I just had a sudden vision of me in another seventeen years time. Not a pretty sight."

Isabella smiled. "I don't know. Techniques in plastic surgery are advancing at a rate of knots, I hear. Anyway," she continued, dodging a napkin. "It's not just that we change inside – it's all the people we gather along the way. I mean, fond as I am of Hugh, if you, me, Simon and Peter went out now the dynamics would be completely different to, say, this evening, with all the other halves in tow. Come to think of it, that's not a bad idea – why don't we do it some time?"

Felicity laughed. "It's a great idea, but can you see the lovely Abi agreeing to it? She's convinced that I'm going to jump into bed with her precious Peter the first chance we get."

"Well, you did before, didn't you?"

Felicity tossed her head. "Ancient history, darling. As you say, people change. For one thing, Peter was a lot more fun then."

"True."

One of the subjects that could always keep the rest of their group entertained for hours was the subject of why Peter had married the homely, religious, Abi. There was nothing really wrong with her, they always concluded – she was just, well – not very likeable. Worse, she had absolutely no sense of humour. "Poor Peter. She hasn't really been a positive influence on him."

"That's the understatement of the century," said Felicity.

"But you still love him, don't you?"

Felicity leaned across the table and patted her friend's arm. "Of course I do, darling, I love all of you. You're my best friends in the whole world. It's just that I don't love Peter in quite the way that he'd like me to."

"Whereas I'd say that Lin has actually been quite good for Simon," continued Iasbella. "Brought him out of himself a bit – made him less uptight. You remember what he used to be like – really nerdy and prudish."

"Again true," acknowledged Felicity. "I don't think he ever had a girlfriend even, before he went off to Thailand and came back with the lovely Lin."

"Too damned right! I always used to get stuck with him when you and Peter were being all lovey-dovey, which was a bit awkward as I didn't fancy him in the slightest. Long, lanky – a chest that was nearly concave – and those awful tortoiseshell glasses. And don't get me started on his record collection."

Felicity nearly choked with laughter. "Oh God – poor you. Thank Heavens for Lin. I have to say that I do like her. But I still don't really feel that I know her, do you? I mean, I know it's a cliché to say about an oriental person, but she is pretty inscrutable, don't you think?"

"Possibly," agreed Isabella. "Though I think it may have something to do with the accent. Her English is pretty near perfect now, but there's still something about intonation, isn't there?"

"Maybe," said Felicity. "I think I meant more like when you look into someone's eyes – whether you feel you're seeing the real them?"

Isabella laughed. "So that's what inscrutable means, is it? I've often wondered. It's a funny word, don't you think? I mean, you never say that someone is scrutable, do you?"

"Now you're sounding like a lawyer. Try and remember that you're talking to a simple housewife."

"Yeah, right. Nobody changes that much."

But they did of course. Simon, the geeky, awkward medical student, had turned into a successful doctor with a beautiful wife, whereas the witty, amusing Peter, who at one stage seemed to have the world at his feet, was a bitter, unhappy and underpaid schoolteacher. And as for Jake – well – she preferred not to think about that.

"Nor are we going to," she continued firmly. "We'll stay friends for ever." She grabbed her glass and raised it in a toast. "To us!"

"To us," echoed Felicity. "And all who sail in us."

Isabella giggled. "Come on," she said. "I've got to get back. Some of us have work to do, you know."

*

For a while after Isabella had hung up Jake just sat at his desk, scowling at the telephone. Who the hell did she think she was, talking to him like he was her fucking servant?

He'd lost interest in tennis elbow. And tree houses. He got up and went into the box room across the corridor and opened the old wardrobe standing by the window. He took out a laptop computer and returned to his desk. Then he switched on the new machine and sat down to wait.

This was where he did his other surfing, the stuff that Isabella would not approve of. To put it mildly.

Soon he was skimming through some of his favourite websites, allowing the flow of images first to soothe, then erase, the memory of his wife's voice. These women – degraded, submissive – didn't nag him about plumbers. Here they were put to their proper use. And here he could forget, and lose himself – sometimes did in fact, realising with a start that two, maybe three hours had passed without him noticing. He'd thought several times it was the sort of thing that should worry him.

Except that he couldn't really be bothered.

He was just about to close the window filling the screen when he suddenly froze, his arm poised in mid-air.

"What the fuck…"

He leaned forward, getting as close as he could before the image blurred and faded into a mass of separate, meaningless, pixels.

Frowning now, he clicked back to the main site menu. He copied the address into a folder, then carefully scrolled through each image in turn. Finally he selected one and saved it into his pictures file, where he proceeded to enlarge and rotate the image until he could clearly see what he wanted.

Satisfied at last, he leaned back in his chair, put his feet on the desk and gazed thoughtfully at the screen.

"Interesting. How very interesting," he told the laptop. "Yet another victory for investigative journalism."

The internet was a truly wonderful thing.

*

Hugh Guthrie slammed the door closed behind him and tossed his keys onto the hall table. He stood listening for a moment before his wife's voice drifted down the stairwell in front of him.

"I'm up here, darling."

He picked up the handful of letters piled neatly on the table and idly flicked through them. Bills, more bills - and then his stomach took a lurch.

It was one of them. Another letter.

He stared at the envelope, with its neatly typed name and address. It could theoretically be from anywhere, but he knew. He'd seen them often enough to know.

Later. He'd open it later. For now he'd enjoy the early summer evening.

He took his time mounting the broad staircase, his feet making no sound on the thick wool carpet. It was an impractically pale shade of cream that Felicity had insisted on, despite his warnings that both their Polish cleaners would probably resign in protest. They hadn't, of course, but only because Felicity had given them a stonking pay rise. Bless her.

She was in the bath, covered in bubbles. She looked like the woman in the old Imperial Leather adverts. He bent over and kissed her lightly on the forehead, taking the opportunity to slide his hand down from her shoulder to the breast undulating gently under its protective layer of foam. She splashed him and he jerked back.

"Watch out, you've drenched my cuff!"

She giggled. "Diddums. Serves you right. Anyway, you've got time to change if you want. We're not due there for an hour. For once you're actually home when you said you'd be."

Hugh moved over to the window seat on the opposite side of the bathroom, opening the window before he sat down. He glanced outside at the quarter acre of the prosperous inner-London suburb Putney that was their garden. It was particularly beautiful this year. Pity he didn't get to spend more time in it.

He yawned and turned back to face his wife. "Don't think I can be bothered to dress up for a school quiz evening. A G and T might hit the spot though."

"Sound good to me - you couldn't make it two, could you darling?" she said. "I wasn't thinking of you dressing up though – rather the opposite."

He shook his head, noting the 'you'. The notion of Felicity not dressing up for any social event, however minor, was pretty unthinkable.

She shrugged. "Your call. So - how's the big wide world of the international advertising executive?"

"Manic. This work for Anderson's is driving everyone round the bend – no one seems to be able to make a decision there. Anyway, there's nothing more I can do until the morning. How was your day?"

She wrinkled her nose. "Oh, nothing special – dentist, lunch with Isabella, then I needed a new pair of boots so I went up to Selfridges. Not very exciting really."

If it's that boring, he thought, you could always try doing something useful with your life. But there was no point in saying anything. Felicity was Felicity. Being beautiful was her career.

Instead he said, "I've got to go to the States all next week, try and get this Anderson mess sorted. That okay with you?"

She smiled. "I daresay I'll manage."

Not that Hugh had expected her to object. He rather suspected that she enjoyed the occasional break from him. It was not that there was anything wrong with their marriage, other than the inevitable boredom, and their time apart was never used for anything untoward. At least he didn't think so. And they still had feelings for each other, each in their own way. Like, he completely adored her, and she – he hoped he wasn't deluding himself – was still quite fond of him. It was just that - after ten years – perhaps even he could accept that you could have too much of a good thing.

He got to his feet and went to lean over her again. "Of course you will."

He set off back downstairs, her voice following him after a few seconds. "Don't forget my drink."

*

He prepared their drinks, put his in his study and took Felicity's up to the bathroom. She was standing in a towelling dressing gown dabbing something beige onto her forehead. She saw the look on his face and turned.

"What?"

He feigned innocence. "Nothing. I know you always like to look your best for dear Peter."

She grimaced. "Please. I'm not sure I can cope with too many more of those puppy dog looks he gives me. You'd think he'd have grown out of it by now." She sighed and started dusting her face with a brush. "No, I thought you'd have realised by now that women don't dress for men – at least most of the time - they dress for other women. So I'm certainly not going out without making a bit of an effort. Can you just imagine the look of satisfaction on Abi's sour little face?"

Hugh laughed. "Why not say what you really think? And what about poor Lin? Surely you've got something nice to say about her?"

She turned to face him and folded her arms. "How about, her skin is so perfect she doesn't need make-up. That nice enough for you?"

*

Funny how a woman could turn what should be a compliment into something that sounded like an accusation, Hugh mused as he returned to his study. But then, he'd never felt he understood women. And it was surely too late to imagine he was going to start doing so now.

He'd married comparatively late, nearly forty, when Felicity was in her mid twenties. By then he'd spent so much of his energy, and put so much of himself into building up his advertising agency, he'd begun to suppose that he'd have no passion left for falling in love. Lust, yes, but life had by that stage instilled in him a fair degree of cynicism about grand romances. So when he'd met Felicity - and fallen for her so completely - there was always a part of him, looking in from the outside, as it were, that felt little more than surprise.

But it had worked out well. Many of his friends had said to him – privately, of course – that they suspected Felicity of being a gold-digger. He had always hoped that there was more to their relationship than that, but he had to acknowledge a kernel of truth in the accusation. Her main problem was that she was lazy. She wanted the good things in life, and though she was quite capable of getting them for herself, it was so, so much easier if someone else was prepared to give them to her.

They had, if not exactly a marriage of convenience, a marriage that was highly convenient for both of them. They'd started trying for a family, but it wasn't proving as easy as he'd imagined, and while both of them were playing it cool for now, he suspected that Felicity was less relaxed about it than she was letting on. For the time being, though, there was nothing untoward to disturb the placid tempo of their comfortable suburban existence.

Except for the letters. Hugh held this one in his hand, unopened, as he sat in his favourite old leather armchair, sipping his gin.

He resented it even being here. This was his favourite room, indeed the only room that could be described as *his,* the only space that he'd refused to allow Felicity to have 'interior designed.' With its unfashionable dark wood, leather furniture, and faded prints of country pursuits, it was his haven, his den, his refuge.

Until the letters had started arriving last year, waiting for him on his desk when he returned from the office. Not often, maybe once a month. At first he'd assumed that they would develop into some sort of demand, or at least threat, but they hadn't. Just the same old accusation, or a variant on the theme, sometimes spelt out, sometimes merely hinted at.

He put down his drink and ripped open the bland, white envelope. As usual, just the one sheet of paper, ordinary printer stuff. This time the message was even less imaginative than usual. Pure melodrama, as if the author watched too many bad movies.

"I know what you did!"

*

A few miles across London, a mouse clattered off a computer screen and fell in pieces. Cursing under his breath, Peter Willis fought the temptation to pound it into yet smaller fragments. That would really have got the kids howling. Not to mention Abi.

He pulled the scattered bits of plastic towards him and gingerly began to reassemble them. The casing had come apart but nothing seemed actually broken. Thank God.

The cursor started moving across the screen again and he ventured an experimental click. Nothing. The damned thing was still frozen.

"Peter?" Abi's voice echoed up to his attic eyrie. She sounded irritated. "What are you doing? You said you'd help with the boys' homework."

He sighed and heaved himself out of the chair.

"Just coming."

The kitchen was stifling, thick with steam and the smells of fish and cooked cheese. Abi, red-faced and tense, was putting plates in front of Sammy and Tom, their two sons.

She saw him come into the room and shook her head in exasperation. "It's too late now – it's their teatime."

Sammy pulled a face. "What is it?"

Peter inspected his son's plate. "At a guess, it, as you call it, is fish pie and green beans, lovingly hand-cooked by your devoted mother."

"Smells horrible. Why can't we have sausages or burgers or something like anyone else?"

"Because fish is good for you and that rubbish isn't," said Abi. Her voice was weary. "It helps the brain to grow. You'll thank me when you're older."

"When all your friends are drivelling retards," said Peter, helping himself to a biscuit.

The boys sniggered and Abi glared at him.

"Well really – all kids like a bit of junk food once in a while. Why can't you cut them a bit of slack sometimes?"

Her face grew even redder. "When I've seen you lift even one finger to help with their upbringing then maybe I'll start taking advice from you on nutrition. Until then I'll do it my way, if you don't mind."

There seemed no good answer to that.

"What's a retard?" asked Tom, pushing a piece of fish around his plate.

No-one answered that either.

Peter wandered over to the back door and pushed it open, breathing in the fresh air. He looked at the small square of grass that was their back garden. Beyond it he could see a half dozen other identical patches, and he knew that beyond them were hundreds, thousands, more.

New Malden – heaven on earth.

Not.

"What were you doing up there all that time, anyway? You were over an hour."

He affected nonchalance. "Nothing much. Just doing some stuff on the computer. Or trying to, anyway. Damned thing's crashed again."

The sound of a casserole being slammed down with unnecessary force made him jump. He turned round.

"What?"

She didn't look up. "I'll thank you not to use language like that in front of the children."

It was her nanny-knows-best voice.

He sighed. "Abi, do you really think they don't hear far worse than that in the playground every day? And use it, for that matter. I'm a teacher, if you remember – I do know these things."

"Well you ought to know how to set a better example then, didn't you?"

Peter looked at her without enthusiasm. Her straw coloured hair was scrunched back into an untidy bun and she was wearing a shapeless cotton print frock. Baby pink at her age, for God's sake.

There had been quite a good figure in there once, he recalled. Not that you'd know it now. Yet all you ever read about these days, it seemed, was how women were obsessed by their looks, and keeping in shape. Just his luck to marry one of the ones that let themselves go.

She was continuing.

"Anyway, what's the matter with the computer? It was fine this morning."

He shrugged. "I don't know. It just froze on me. Overloaded maybe." He turned to the two boys picking unhappily at their food. "You two haven't been cluttering it up again with downloads have you?"

Sammy shot him a resentful glance. "We're not allowed, remember? It's just a crap computer. I don't know why we can't have an iPad like everyone else."

"I've told you, next Christmas..." he began, but his reply was drowned out by the sound of the casserole being slammed down again.

"Sammy! You will not use words like that in my house!"

Sammy slid back in his chair, a mutinous expression on his face. "He does. "

Abi fired an I-told-you-so look at him. He thought of pointing out that the boy would probably have come out with exactly the same thing whatever his father had said, or that he possibly might not have done if his mother hadn't made such a big deal of it. But he decided against. He was too tired for another pointless argument.

He raised his hands in surrender.

"Okay," he said. "But what's the big panic? It's only the school quiz evening and it doesn't even start until seven thirty. We've got ages."

She opened her mouth to speak, then glanced at the boys and thought better of whatever it was she was about to say. "I told you this morning, if you'd been listening. I'm helping with the food. So while you've been faffing about with goodness knows what I've been trying to get the boys' homework done, feed them, and prepare a rice salad for your wretched quiz evening. Then, if I have time, I might try to have a shower and change. That enough of a panic for you?"

He turned back to the garden. "Bloody martyr," he muttered under his breath. But he made sure she didn't hear him.

"Anyway," he continued in a normal voice. "Why is it my quiz evening? It's the boys' school. And you're always on at me to be more involved in their *educashun*?"

He exaggerated the syllables of the last word and the boys giggled. Abi ignored them.

"Because you were the one who insisted on going – you know I hate that sort of thing. But you wanted to go out with your friends, so off we're going."

He spun round to face her. "Oh, so they're my friends, are they? I'd rather thought that they were our friends. Or have I missed something?"

She gave a short laugh and started loading crockery into the dishwasher. Noisily. "Oh, please. Of course they're your friends. Your precious little gang from university. And all the rest of us just have to tag along."

He stared at her, genuinely surprised. "Is that how you think of them? But you've known them for years now – almost as long as I have. You get on with them all right don't you?"

She straightened. "Is that what you think? Really?" She shook her head in disbelief. "I've always known you were delusional but that really takes the biscuit."

"What are you talking about?"

She turned to the boys. "Sammy, Tom, take your food into the front room. You can watch a DVD while you finish."

With exclamations of delighted surprise they rushed out of the room, leaving their parents in a temporary void of silence. All too temporary, thought Peter.

Abi wiped her hands on a towel, then smiled. Not a friendly smile.

"So there's Isabella and Jake. What can I say? She is obsessed, materialistic, self-absorbed…"

"A typical lawyer then." He couldn't resist the interruption.

She continued as if he hadn't spoken. "Too selfish to have a family, has an nasty temper and worse language. While he's a drunken, lazy, good-for-nothing who thinks he can charm his way out of everything. They both seem to have complete contempt for everything I stand for and are quite happy to show it – and do you ever stand up for me? Do you hell."

He gaped at her in astonishment.

She laughed at his expression. "Then there's Simon and Lin – I suppose he's fine in his way. Though what possesses a man to take a woman like that for his wife I don't know – or rather I suspect I know all too well. And Hugh – I suppose he's okay, though I can't remember him ever saying more than two words to me."

"And finally - Felicity. The beautiful Felicity, drifting through life, smiling graciously at all the simpering idiots falling over themselves to do her bidding." He turned away again so that she wouldn't see his face darken, but she was too quick for him.

Her eyes narrowed. "Oh yes, I've seen the way you look at her. I know about you two. Lust's a sin, Peter. A deadly one. I hope you haven't forgotten that."

"Oh for God's sake! What do you know? That we went out together as students? That was fifteen years ago. We're both married now." One of us, happily so, he might have added. But he didn't.

She gazed at him for a long moment. He stared her down, daring her to say more. Then her eyes dropped, and he released the breath he hadn't realised he was holding.

Only to be sucker-punched from another direction.

"So come on then, tell me what you were really doing upstairs. I can always tell when you're lying to me."

I sincerely hope not, he thought. But he might as well tell her. She'd find out soon enough.

"I was doing some work on my business plan. You know, the one I told you about. I'm going to speak to Simon tonight – see if he's interested in backing me."

Her hands, which had been busy spooning rice from a saucepan into a large plastic container, suddenly became motionless. He braced himself for the onslaught to come. But her voice when she spoke was reasonable.

"I thought we'd agreed that you wouldn't do that?"

Peter took a deep breath. "No, we didn't agree that. You expressed some reservations, but we never agreed that I shouldn't."

"Reservations?" she flared. "You want to humiliate yourself by going cap in hand to your – sorry, *our* friends, be even more humiliated by being turned down, or even worse be ruined by running up huge debts to people we know, for some failed business venture. If that's what you call reservations, then yes, I've got them!"

"Why are you always so negative?" He started pacing up and down the tiny kitchen like a tiger in its cage. "Why should he turn me down? And why shouldn't it succeed? There's a huge market out there for this kind of online educational material. All it takes is the right ideas, presented in the right sort of way, the right person running things…"

"Exactly," she interrupted him, grabbed his arm and held him in front of her, forcing him to meet her gaze. "The right person. You're not a businessman, Peter. Look at yourself – successful businessmen have drive, they work all hours, don't take no for an answer, don't quit on things. Be honest, Peter, is that you? And do you really think that Simon is going to think so?"

He eyed her steadily for a few seconds then pulled himself free.

"Sod you," he said, and walked out the door into the small garden.

She followed him. "Why can't you be content, Peter? Why can't you just accept things the way they are? You've got us, we have our home, you're a good teacher in a decent school. Why can't you be happy with what you've got?"

He turned, and she recoiled at the expression on his face.

"Happy? Content? With this?" he flung his arms wide, just missing her face. "A job I hate, a mortgage so crippling that it won't be paid off if I work until I'm seventy, all to live crammed in this damned shoebox?"

The 'with you' hung unspoken in the air. For a brief moment they just stared at each other, neither quite able to believe what he had said. Then he shook his head.

"And you ask why I can't be happy."

*

She watched him march back into the house, heard him tramping upstairs and then the attic door slam. Then she wiped away the tear that had started running down her cheek.

Chapter 2

The car inched forward towards the temporary traffic light and Dr. Simon Rayner stole a glance at his wife Lin. She was leant back against the headrest, eyes closed, her head slightly to one side, her black hair tumbling over her shoulders. She was, he thought, just as he had when she'd placed that first cocktail in front of him in the Bangkok restaurant ten years ago, quite the most perfect, most beautiful creature he had ever seen.

Sensing his gaze she turned towards him and smiled. Then her eyes registered the line of traffic stretching in front of them and the smile turned to a frown.

"God!" she muttered. "Are we still only here? We're going to be late, aren't we?"

"Maybe. A few minutes at most though. These things never start on time anyway." He stopped talking as the light changed and concentrated on following the car in front – a Belgian registered BMW- as closely as possible without causing an international incident. Miraculously, they squeezed through on amber.

"There we are," he said triumphantly. "We should be fine now." He glanced at his wife and smiled. "Wouldn't want you to miss the quiz now, would we?"

She grimaced. "Well, now you come to mention it. It's all right for you but I always feel so useless at these things. What do I know about sixties pop music or your English football players?"

"A lot more than I know about Thai culture. But it's only a bit of fun. It's a social thing really – a chance to see everyone. We haven't had a get-together like this for ages."

She yawned. "I know – everyone's so busy. Who's idea was this, though – Abi's?"

"Actually, no – it was Peter's."

She shot a surprised look at him. "Peter? That's a first. I've never seen him organise anything successfully. I didn't think he was capable of it."

He laughed. "That's a little unfair. At uni he was a real social animal – always setting up impromptu parties and things. Anyway, here we are – bang on time."

The car turned into the school playground turned car park for the evening and Lin sighed. "I just hope that Jake doesn't get drunk and start picking fights with everyone."

He laughed. "Who, Jake? You must have the wrong guy. Come on, a bit of fireworks never hurt anyone."

He locked the car and she took his hand as they walked across the tarmac. "Maybe. But isn't there some English expression about playing with fire?"

*

The quiz was being held in the cavernous, echoing, hall that doubled as the school's gym. With its grey plastic tiled floor and featureless walls, brightly lit by fluorescent strips, it was the sort of room that took Simon straight back to his schooldays. And never failed to depress him.

It was clear that most of the other parents were also taking the view that the quiz was unlikely to start at its appointed time. A couple of dozen people were milling around, holding wine glasses and chatting in a desultory fashion, while at the far end of the hall a small group of women, Abi among them, were busy over pots and bowls.

He spotted Peter, sitting alone at a table and nursing a glass of red wine. With his tweed jacket and untidy brown hair he looked liked everybody's stereotype of a schoolteacher. He was staring moodily across the room. Simon followed his gaze and saw Felicity and Hugh talking to a couple that he didn't recognise.

Hugh looked as if he'd come straight from work. He was still in his daytime suit, leaning close to the other man and listening attentively to whatever he was saying. Simon guessed it did not concern primary school quiz evenings. Felicity, like her husband, was listening to the animated chatter of the short, mousy, woman next to her. Unlike him, however, she looked totally, utterly, bored.

Simon walked across to Peter, who seemed to brighten at his approach. He jumped to his feet with a smile and clapped a hand on Simon's shoulder.

"Simon, mate, glad you could make it. How's it going? Not lost too many patients recently, I trust?"

"Only the ones beaten up by your pupils. But yeah, it's going well. We're expanding the practice but thanks to my beautiful receptionist here we seem to be coping."

Peter grinned at Lin. "Well, I hope he's paying you properly." He leaned over and kissed her lightly on the cheek. "Good to see you."

"You too. We were only just saying it's been too long."

Peter shrugged. "I know. Everyone's so busy now, that's the trouble. Anyway, what do you guys want to drink?"

"I'll get it," said Simon. He gestured towards Peter's now empty glass. "Top up?"

Peter grinned. "If you twist my arm."

Simon moved away towards the bar. Lin grabbed his hand and walked beside him.

"So far so good," she said.

He smiled down at her. "I told you it would be all right. Don't you trust your husband?"

She smiled back and squeezed his hand. "Ask me again at the end of the evening."

*

Simon and Lin got back with their lukewarm white wine just as Isabella and Jake were arriving. Jake greeted them cheerily.

"Simon, great to see you. And Lin, more gorgeous than ever – come here and give me a kiss."

He ran a hand through his wavy blond hair (which Simon thought he probably dyed) and held out his arms towards her.

She presented a cheek, pulling away before he could actually touch her. Simon turned his attention to Isabella.

She was a striking looking woman. Not conventionally pretty, but men's heads turned when she was around. Her Italian ancestry was obvious from her lustrous, dark hair, and strongly featured, olive complexioned face. When they had been students together, and Peter and Felicity had been a couple (how long ago that seemed now) he had often wondered whether he should make some sort of play for her, but at the time he had been too shy. He still sometimes wondered what her response would have been. Not that it mattered now – not now he had Lin.

Isabella seemed a lot less relaxed than her husband. She was obviously still in her work clothes. She looked like she'd managed to run a brush through her hair, but her make-up didn't look as if it had been touched since the morning. From her expression, attending a quiz evening in a grimly clinical school hall had not been top of her 'must do' list.

He gave her a peck on the cheek. "Hi Bella – how's tricks? Busy at work?"

Her reply, whatever it might have been, was cut off by her husband's laughter. "Busy? That's a good one. If she came home any later she'd meet herself going off the next morning."

She gave a tired smile. "Please don't take any notice of my husband – he has no idea how long I work. He's normally curled up drunk by the time I get home, and still sleeping it off when I leave again. It's something to do with having a creative mind, apparently."

She turned to Peter and gave him a big hug. "Hello, Peter, how are you?"

He returned the hug. "All the better for seeing you. Thanks for coming. I know how busy you are."

"There's always time for friends, as my mother used to say. Among other things."

Jake seemed unconcerned by his wife's comments. He flashed a smile in Simon's direction. "Actually, I'm doing rather well at the moment. I've got several quite lucrative little pieces coming up. One of them I wanted to talk to you about, as it happens."

He pulled both Simon and Lin to one side. "I've been commissioned to do an article about multi-cultural London – you know, mixed-race marriages, pressures and prejudices, cultural differences, that sort of thing. I wondered if you two would be prepared to be interviewed, share your experiences with the readers?" He grinned at them both.

Simon looked at Lin, who shrugged. "Don't see why not."

He nodded to Jake. "You're on. Anything to help a pal."

Jake clapped him on the shoulder. "Brilliant – thanks a bundle. I'll give you a call next week then, to arrange a suitable time." He grinned again. "And a suitable pub."

*

Felicity arrived at the table in a haze of Chanel, closely followed by Hugh.

"Darlings," she cooed, air-kissing all of them in turn. "How wonderful to see someone civilised. Hugh managed to find one of his clients and I've just had a ghastly quarter of an hour with the wife going on about her bloody fundraiser for deaf Guyanans."

Hugh rolled his eyes. "Ghanaians, actually darling. And they're blind."

Simon smiled to himself. He couldn't quite remember at what stage Felicity had started speaking like a Home Counties version of Greta Garbo. He wasn't sure she even realised she was doing it any more.

Peter rubbed his hands enthusiastically. "Well, at least we're all here now."

Felicity turned to Isabella. "I was just talking to Peter earlier, saying how nice it was to see old friends again. I was talking about his jacket, of course. I'd swear he had the same one at university, didn't he?"

Peter adopted a virtuous expression. "At least I'm keeping my carbon footprint down," he said. "Unlike, I suspect, you."

Felicity looked down at her outfit, crisp white trousers and a powder blue jacket, and frowned.

"You're not seriously suggesting that a girl should wear the same clothes more than once, are you?"

Everyone laughed.

Felicity looked around. "Where's Abi then?"

Peter gestured towards the end of the hall. "Over there," he said. "Doing her domestic goddess thing."

Jake guffawed in appreciation. "Good old Abi – you can always rely on her to be in the kitchen at parties."

Felicity raised an eyebrow. "That's a bit rough, isn't it? Biting the hand that feeds you and all that? Without her and her little friends you'd have rather a hungry evening."

"Wouldn't do him any harm," said Isabella. "He could do with losing a few pounds."

This time Jake did look discomfited, Simon was amused to see. Any adverse comment regarding his appearance obviously hit him where it hurt.

Simon felt a light touch on his arm and he turned to see Lin.

"I think I need another drink," she whispered.

*

There was some delay and it was another twenty minutes before the quiz actually got under way. By then Simon estimated that all of them were on their third glass of wine except for Peter, who was on his fifth. Although at the rate Jake was going, he would be catching up pretty soon.

There were about a dozen tables in the hall, each, like them, constituting a team of eight people. Peter, as their host, assumed the role of team leader.

"The first round is numerical," announced the quizmaster, a short, excessively jovial man with untidy ginger hair who had taken nearly five minutes to explain the perfectly simple rules. "Needs to get out more," Jake had muttered to general agreement.

"First question: we all know that the Earth is roughly 93 million miles from the sun, but how far – to the nearest ten million – is Jupiter. How far, to the nearest ten million miles, is Jupiter from the sun."

The silent hall was immediately filled with urgent whisperings. Simon looked around the room; at every table heads were bent towards each other, shaking, nodding, listening attentively.

"Just my luck," said Peter. "I've got to take a bunch of bloody school kids up to the Planetarium next week. The one use that could have been to me, and the timing's wrong. Anyone else got any ideas?"

Heads were shaken all around the table.

"Come on, Simon, you were a scientist," said Felicity.

He shrugged. "Sorry," he said.

Then Lin spoke. "I think," she said slowly. "It's something like 480 million miles."

The others looked at her in mild surprise, and Simon felt a small surge of irritation. His perfect angel, his Lin. Just because she was beautiful and spoke with a foreign accent people always assumed that she had a brain the size of a sparrow's. It had been her misfortune to be born into a poor family in a poor part of the world, but lack of education did not imply lack of intellect, Simon would tell people. Not that they listened.

"Are you sure?" asked Peter.

She shook her head. "No. I don't even know why I think that. It just sort of popped into my head."

Peter still looked dubious and Simon rolled his eyes. "Oh for God's sake!" he said, ignoring Lin's gentle shushes. "Have you got a better guess? Has anyone?"

No one spoke.

"Well, it sounds the right sort of ballpark," said Hugh. "So I suggest we go for it."

He pulled the answer sheet away from Peter and duly wrote down 480 million.

"The second question will take you all back to Sunday school," said the quizmaster, beaming around the room. The woman sitting next to him whispered something to him and he reddened. "Those of you with a Christian upbringing, that is."

Jake gave a sigh. "Just bloody get on with it," he said too loudly.

People at neighbouring tables shot him meaningful looks and the quizmaster peered around uncertainly.

He raised his voice. "So the second question is, what is the eighth, the eighth, book of the Bible?"

Jake gave a short laugh and nudged Abi with his elbow. "One for you, babe. None of the rest of us knows any of that nonsense." He picked up his glass and took a large gulp of wine.

There was silence and he looked around the table in surprise. "What? What have I said? I mean what's the point of having a God-botherer in the party if she can't get that sort of thing right?"

"I don't think that's quite the point," began Lin, but before she could finish Abi had grabbed the answer sheet and scribbled something down.

Jake pulled it over, muttering, "See? I told you so," then in a slightly louder voice, "Ruth? Are you sure? I've never heard of it."

"Shhh! Keep your voice down!" Peter sounded annoyed. "Of course she's sure. Aren't you?" he asked, turning to his wife.

She frowned. "Yes, of course I'm sure. It's one of the shorter books, but it's definitely there. Straight after Judges." She turned a sullen gaze on Jake. "I thought journalists were supposed to have good general knowledge?"

"Ruth's good enough for me," said Hugh. "Might even get us one over the competition."

"Or it would have done if Jake hadn't gone and told everybody else," muttered Isabella. Jake glared at her.

The quizmaster cleared his throat loudly. "Next question, for all you old rockers out there, in which year did Elvis Presley die? In which year did Elvis die?"

Hugh whispered something to Felicity, who shrugged.

"If he's dead, of course," said Jake.

Hugh paused in the middle of writing down his answer and looked at him, a baffled expression on his face.

"What did you say?" he asked.

"I said *if* he's dead. There's quite a respectable body of opinion out there thinks the whole thing was staged."

Felicity hooted with laughter. "Oh yes, I'd forgot, he's flipping burgers on a UFO, isn't he?"

Isabella joined in. "Don't be silly – don't you remember he was working at the chip shop by the union building?"

Hugh continued to stare at Jake. "A not so respectable body of complete lunatics, you mean."

Jake rolled his eyes. "You people," he said. "So fucking gullible. You believe everything you read in the papers, take it as gospel."

"That's hardly likely, given the calibre of journalist they know," said Isabella, still laughing.

Jake was about to reply but Peter interrupted. "Shut up you lot – here comes the next question."

*

By the time the food break came round their team was lying third, with only a few points separating them from the joint leaders, tables 4 and 11. Peter had become both more excitable and more voluble as the levels in the wine bottles on their table had gone down. As the occupants of the leading tables walked past on their way to the buffet he examined each of them minutely.

Isabella was watching him, looking bemused. "Peter, what exactly are you doing?" she asked.

"Checking out the competition, of course," he said, craning his neck to get a better view of a skeletally thin blonde. "Looking for weaknesses. We've got a real chance here, you know."

"That's all right then. I thought you were checking out that girls's bum." She turned to Felicity, ignoring Abi's glare. "What were we saying earlier, about people not changing?"

But Peter was not to be distracted. "I'm worried about Table 6 – they've got the Dentons, who both work at the BBC, and Jeremy Boyle, who's some sort of professor. I don't know the other couples."

"Peter, darling, it's only a game," said Felicity gently. "Who gives a damn?"

Peter shook his head sorrowfully.

"That was always your problem, Felicity – no killer instinct. Except when it came to cadging fags."

"Now there's a thought," she replied. She grabbed her coat. "I'm off for a ciggy break." She headed towards the door. "Get me some food, darling, will you?" she called over her shoulder to her husband. "Something not too heavy."

Peter edged around the table to Simon. "Actually, Simon, I wanted a quick word with you if you've got a minute."

Something in his tone made Simon wary but he couldn't quite think of a reason to say no. "Sure – let's talk on the way to the bar."

Jake had obviously had exactly the same reaction to Peter's words. He laughed and called out after them. "If he tries to touch you for one of his hair-brained schemes

I'd be careful, Simon. Remember the school video library!"

Peter spun round to face him. "Why don't you just mind you own business?" he said, his face reddening.

Jake waved his hands in the air. "Ooh, scary!" He got to his feet. "Think I'll join Felicity."

*

As they walked across the hall Simon glanced at Peter apprehensively. He'd decided some time ago that the trouble with Peter was not that he wasn't bright enough to run a business, but that he was too bright. He loved thinking about the big picture – and had had some really inspired ideas, to be fair – but he just got bored with the little stuff. Unfortunately for him, it was the boring little things - like bills and cash flow - that made the difference between success and failure. Peter was one of Simon's best friends, but he really wasn't cut out to be a businessman.

Yet even allowing for the alcohol, his reaction to Jake's jibe about his business experience was over the top. His heart sinking, Simon concluded that Jake must be right. He was about to be offered the investment opportunity of a lifetime.

Peter took a deep breath. "Sorry about that," he said. "Jake just has that effect on me sometimes."

Simon chuckled in sympathy. "I know what you mean. Anyway, what did you want to talk to me about?"

Peter fumbled in his pocket and pulled out a rumpled wad of paper. "Well, I've got this idea for a business – online educational modules. I reckon it's an absolute banker but I need capital…"

"Hold on a second," Simon put out his hand. "Before you go any further – I don't want to waste your time. I'm sorry, but I've got absolutely no spare capital at the moment."

"But you've not even heard…"

"Peter, mate, I don't need to. Even if it was an oil well in your back garden I wouldn't be able to. Every penny I've got is being ploughed back into the practice at the moment."

Peter stopped dead and stared at him. "It's what Jake said, isn't it?" he said eventually.

Simon shook his head. "That's nothing to do with it – I've already told you, you know it's not you…"

"Well just have a look then. Come on – you're my oldest friend. I promise you won't be wasting your time."

Simon sighed. He had a feeling that Peter was not going to leave him alone until he agreed to look at whatever hair-brained scheme he'd come up with.

"Okay, I'll have a look. But I'm not promising anything, all right?"

*

Jake found Felicity standing under a tree on the far side of the schoolyard, gazing out across the playing fields. Without the glow from her cigarette he would probably have missed her. She turned at his approach.

"Oh, it's you." She turned back to the playing fields.

"Don't sound so enthusiastic. Thought you might appreciate a kindred spirit."

Her head snapped round. "Are you? I hadn't noticed."

He moved closer. "I think so. We both get impatient with people like them, even though they're our friends and we're actually quite fond of them. We both think that life is for living and enjoying, And we both get irritated when things – or people - get in the way of that. And neither of us have any compunction about going after what we want."

She raised her eyebrows. "Sounds rather a dangerous combination to me."

"Oh, it can be." He moved closer again, scenting her perfume over the cigarette smoke. "But that's part of the fun, don't you think?"

He had her full attention now. "And what is it you want, Jake?"

He laughed. "I think you know that, don't you Felicity?"

"You're drunk." She blew cigarette smoke in his face.

"Maybe. But in vino veritas and all that. I'm only saying what I've thought for a long while." He paused for a few seconds then continued. "And you're bored. I can tell. Why not have a bit of fun?"

He held her gaze. She returned his stare, unblinking, for a long moment, and then suddenly dropped the cigarette and stubbed it out with her foot.

"That rather depends on what you mean by fun, doesn't it?" She folded her arms and leaned back against the tree. "What exactly are you suggesting?"

He shrugged and propped himself next to her, trying to hide his surprise. He couldn't quite believe that they were actually having this conversation; that she hadn't simply laughed in his face.

"Oh nothing untoward." He grinned and turned towards her. Their faces were inches apart. "At least not yet. What about a spot of lunch one day? We'll go out to the country – find a nice little pub."

She stared at him. "I had lunch with your wife today."

He shrugged. "And?"

"And she's my best friend."

He nodded. "It's good to have lunch with your friends. That's all I'm suggesting we do."

Seconds passed, then she smiled. "Okay. Lunch."

He looked at her, slightly dazed that she had agreed. He had only followed her out of boredom, and it was only something in her manner, the way she was standing, that had prompted him, completely on impulse, to say what he had said. There were then those awful seconds, which had seemed like hours, wondering whether he'd made a terrible mistake and that she'd rush back into the hall proclaiming to her husband and his wife and everyone else what he had done.

But she hadn't.

He leant towards her. "How about a little something on account then?"

She slid away. "Come on," she said, "We'll be missed."

"So when shall we do this lunch?" he asked as he followed her back across the playground.

She shrugged. "Next week's good for me." She paused for a moment and then glanced up at the stars. "Hugh's away on business."

*

Amazingly enough, despite all the tantrums and varying degrees of inebriation, the second half of the evening went well for their table. By the end of the penultimate round they were lying second, only two points behind the leaders. All of them had contributed to some degree, Simon reflected, some more surprisingly than others. Isabella's knowledge of the classics and Hugh's expertise in more recent history were only to be expected, and his own scientific background came in useful on a number of occasions. Felicity's encyclopaedic knowledge of soap operas had, on the other hand, been a bit of an eye-opener – she scored ten out of ten in the relevant round, to their amusement and her mild embarrassment.

Peter had resorted to regular, slightly drunken, exhortations to his team to keep concentrating on the game.

"We can do this, guys! Two points is nothing. Especially on this round - it's the wipeout. There's always a big swing on the wipeout."

"What the hell is a wipeout?" asked Isabella, stifling a yawn. "God, I hope it finishes soon. I'm knackered."

"If you get one wrong you lose all the points for the whole round. So you mustn't guess – we only put down an answer if we're absolutely certain."

Felicity pulled a bored face. "That's us finished then – all we've been doing all evening is guessing."

"Speak for yourself," said Jake in a lofty voice. "I've had full confidence in myself all evening."

She raised her eyebrows. "Really? There is such a thing as being too confident, you know."

Peter shushed them. "Quit fooling around you two - it's starting!"

"What is the sea area – as in the shipping forecast – to the immediate north of Ireland?"

Peter's expression of disappointment was almost comical. Then Hugh pulled the answer sheet towards him and wrote something down. Peter craned forward. "Malin - are you sure?"

Hugh rolled his eyes. "Totally. I've been sailing since I was ten."

Peter seemed, if possible, to get even more excited as the round progressed. After nine questions they had got six correct, assuming that Lin was right about the northernmost of the major Japanese islands and that Abi was correct in asserting that Nicholas Brakspear was the only English pope (the others were all agreed by general consent).

"And now for the final question of tonight's quiz." The quizmaster mopped his brow. Even he seemed to have lost some of his joviality, worn down by the overheated atmosphere in the hall. Or perhaps more likely, by the endless stream of appeals and complaints emanating from the participants.

"Very suitable for tonight – in what year did St. Winifred's school choir have a Christmas number one with 'There's No-one Quite Like Grandma'."

Felicity actually laughed out loud. Simon smiled and glanced at Lin who pretended to think for a moment, furrowing her brow and pursing her lips before regretfully shaking her head. Peter cradled his head in his hands in despair. Only Abi and Jake seemed to be actively considering the question.

Suddenly Abi leaned across the table. "Eighty – nineteen eighty," she whispered.

Jake looked up. "No you're wrong. It was eighty one."

"I'm telling you, it was eighty!" Abi's voice was urgent. "I remember because that was when I was a bridesmaid."

Jake shook his head. "And I'm telling you, you're wrong! I was really into music at the time, and I remember how disgusted we were at school."

Hugh looked from one to the other. "Well, if we can't agree…"

Jake banged his hand on the table. "Sod that, I'm telling you. That one point could be the difference between winning and losing, and having sat here all evening being bored to tears I'm not going to lose just because she," he jabbed his finger violently at Abi, "Can't count!"

Simon looked at him in surprise. His normal, easygoing manner, veering between leering and sneering as Lin had once put it, seemed to have deserted him. His face had reddened and his words were slurred. He was obviously very drunk.

The others were all staring at him as well. Felicity looked amused, Isabella embarrassed. Abi was speechless with rage, Peter just seemed confused.

"I don't have a view," said Lin. "So I propose we put it to the vote."

Jake banged the table again. "We haven't got time. Why won't you people listen to me?"

Simon turned back to Peter. "You're the team captain – you decide."

Peter looked as if his insides were being put through a mangle. "Eventually he nodded at Jake. "Okay – we'll go with you – but you'd bloody better be right!"

Jake looked triumphant. Abi just shook her head in resigned disgust.

*

The wait for the results seemed endless. Peter's anxiety was contagious - even Felicity and Hugh appeared on edge, glancing nervously towards the podium. Or perhaps they were just dreading the inevitable bust-up if their team hadn't won.

At long last the quizmaster finished counting the scores and started reading out the answers. As predicted, they had six out of the first nine.

"And finally, the last question, and fittingly the one that proved decisive. St. Winifred's School Choir had a Christmas number one in – nineteen eighty!"

There were a few cheers from across the room, and rather more groans. Their own table sat in silence for a long moment, as if in suspended animation. Then Jake shrugged and laughed.

"Oh well, sorry guys. Just as well it's only a game."

Hugh shook his head in disapproval. "What was that Felicity said earlier about over confidence?"

For some reason Felicity seemed to find this terribly funny. She burst into loud shrieks of laughter, which eventually turned into a coughing fit. Hugh gave her a slightly puzzled look then handed her his handkerchief.

"You complete shit!"

All eyes turned to Peter. He was leaning forward over the table, his gaze fixed on Jake.

"You utterly moronic, cretinous wanker! Why the hell did I trust you? You cost us the game, you fucking shit – we would have won otherwise!"

Jake looked taken aback. "Steady on – I said I was sorry."

"You're nothing but a bloody loser, and never have been!"

Jake barked a short laugh. "Now that's rich, coming from you!"

Peter banged the table. "But why? Why did you say you knew if you didn't?"

Jake spoke slowly as if to a simpleton. "Because I thought I did know, didn't I? Anyway, it's not as if you covered yourself with glory tonight – I can't think of a single question you got right on your own."

This seemed only to inflame Peter further. He stood up, almost foaming with rage. "That is so not the point. The fact is, you cost us the game. You!" He pointed at Jake with a trembling arm. "And I'm not going to forget it."

He stormed off towards the door. Abi shrugged and followed.

When they'd gone there was silence for a moment or two. Then Jake whistled. "Talk about an overreaction."

Isabella shook her head angrily. "That is so you. You're now sitting here thinking that you're some sort of victim. You don't see that you brought it on yourself. But you did, Jake, you did. Just as you always do."

Simon and Hugh walked out to the cars together, Lin and Felicity following.

"So what did you make of all that?" asked Simon.

Hugh gave a wry smile.

"I make that men who can't hold their drink shouldn't drink so much." Then the smile faded. "But I am rather afraid that one day our friend Jake will end up going too far, one way or another."

Chapter 3

Felicity stood in the hotel lobby and watched Jake fumbling in his wallet with growing impatience.

"For God's sake get a move on – I've got to get back." She glanced out at the street outside. "And now it's starting to rain. Christ! What a disaster."

Jake turned to stare at her, a hurt look on his face. "What's that supposed to mean?"

"Nothing. Just get on with it."

Jake turned back to the hotel clerk and carried on counting out ten-pound notes. Felicity watched the girl behind the reception desk out of the corner of her eye, alert for the slightest sign of a smirk, but there was nothing. Just boredom.

But boredom could get you into trouble. More so even than lust. It was boredom that had taken her to that sweet little country pub near Guildford on Tuesday. And it was boredom that had brought her to this grotty little hotel off Baker Street today. With Jake.

The lunch had actually been quite fun. It had been a beautiful day, and they'd sat in the garden, almost the only people there as it was a weekday. They hadn't drunk much; just talked - about their lives, their partners, their frustrations.

She'd tried explaining to him how different they had all been as students, before he had known them – how bright and optimistic Peter had been, how lively and carefree Isabella was before she sold her soul to law school. He'd listened, asking the occasional question, laughing in the right places. Of course he'd heard lots of the stories before, but that was part of his charm, the way he could, if he chose, make you feel the most fascinating person in the world. She'd seen enough of him over the years to know that that wasn't the whole story by any means. There was another, darker side to him – the spiteful, clever Jake who used his wit to wound and diminish people, to compensate for his own inadequacies and frustrations, his own sense of failure. But on that rather enchanted June day, in the walled garden under the shade of the apple trees, she had chosen to forget that Jake. She allowed herself to fall for the charm.

"And what about you?" he'd asked.

"What about me?"

"How have you changed?"

She'd shrugged. "You'll have to ask the others about that. But I don't think I've changed very much."

She'd realised even before she'd finished the sentence that it was a ridiculous thing to say. Even since she'd been married to Hugh she'd probably changed out of all recognition, let alone since university. But he'd not said anything. Just smiled.

Then he'd tried a different tack. "So what do you think the twenty year old Felicity would make of the thirty five year old model? Would she be pleased? Would she be proud of what she achieved?"

It was not the most comfortable question to have to consider. Because actually, she knew the answer without even thinking about it. Her younger self might be wowed by the clothes, and the big house, and the luxury holidays, but when she learned that it was all provided by Hugh she would be a lot less impressed. In fact, she'd be downright appalled at how little she'd done with her life.

So she ducked the question. "Not very gallant to remind a girl of her age quite so bluntly." Wondering even as she said it why it seemed almost automatic these days for her to hide behind the façade of a blonde airhead.

But again he'd just smiled and said nothing.

Today had been very different. She'd entered into this affair, if it could be called that after one lunch and one shag, not because she had the slightest interest in Jake, but because she was bored. Bored with her life, bored with Hugh, but most of all bored with herself. Of course she was attracted to him, she wouldn't have entertained the idea for a second if she hadn't been. He was very good looking, in that slightly foppish, English way, and he made her laugh. And there was always that vague air of danger about him. She'd tried justifying it in her own mind as a sort of adventure, a mind broadening and hopefully amusing experience. But deep down she knew it was probably just curiosity. Curiosity and lust.

She had woken early that day, filled with the sort of restless anticipation you felt in the build up to a holiday as a child. It was not as if this was the sort of thing she did every day, after all. The morning had seemed to last an eternity, and she had ended up getting showered and dressed much earlier than she needed to.

It was in the taxi ride up from Putney that the doubts started to set in, and the excited butterflies in her stomach began to sink and turn into the sort of hollow trepidation you felt before an exam. She had tried analysing her thoughts. Was she feeling good old-fashioned guilt, a remnant from those church outings as a child? Abi would certainly suppose so. Eventually she decided that it was something much simpler — fear of getting caught and losing the secure, comfortable life she had organised for herself.

How mundane.

Well, she would just have to be careful. Nothing ventured, nothing gained, etc. It was going to be a bit of fun and that was that. She had sat back, closed her eyes, and tried to relax.

*

The first shock had been the hotel. From Jake's description she had been expecting the Cleopatra to be a trendy little boutique style establishment, and had visions of chic designer furnishings and chilled champagne brought in flutes by Armani clad flunkies. What she found was a rundown three star a few hundred yards from Madame Tussauds catering for low-budget package tourists - little better than a rooming house, really. She stood outside for a moment, gazing up at its grubby windows with the mean little curtains draped behind them, and her heart sank.

She made her way through the tiny reception area to the lift, relieved to see that there was no one in attendance. Jake had texted through the room number and the floor and a few moments later she was knocking on the door of room 16.

He'd opened the door and invited her inside with a broad grin. He gave her a chaste peck on the cheek then handed her a plastic glass filled with champagne. Warm champagne.

The spell was well and truly broken. The grotty hotel, the cramped room with its chintzy, mass-produced furniture, the plastic glasses. It was all so far removed from her idea of a romantic tryst that she felt as if she had just woken from a soft focus pastel dream into harsh, bright, reality.

But she was here now. She briefly contemplated leaving, before it was too late, but dismissed the idea. It was already too late. And part of her was still looking forward to the sex. She wondered if the seediness of the surroundings might even give it an extra frisson.

*

They'd sat on the edge of the bed and had a desultory conversation while sipping their champagne.

"How was your journey?" he'd asked.

She'd shrugged. "Fine. I came in a cab. You?"

He shook his head. "I came to Waterloo then took the tube."

It was hardly Pinter.

But the biggest disappointment of all was yet to come. Or not, so to speak. For all the twenty, sweaty minutes that they had spent tumbling under the cheap duvet, she felt nothing. It had been so strange; familiar activities but with unfamiliar sensations. It all seemed wrong, somehow - not morally, but just not right. The sounds weren't right, the smells weren't right, the flesh that her fingers touched wasn't right. It was hurried, urgent, not very relaxing.

Jake seemed to enjoy it though. It was obvious that he wasn't there because he was bored – there was no shortage of lust in Jake. It was also clear to Felicity that he fancied himself as a bit of a stud, making a performance out of everything. At times he reminded her of a randy pigeon, with all the rearing and arching and thrusting. It was presumably for her benefit, though he might as well not have bothered. But she must have made the right sort of noises, because when he eventually rolled off her he mistook her sigh of relief for one of satisfaction.

He'd grinned. "Pretty good, eh?"

She'd managed a weak smile. "Yeah."

She'd dressed quickly, ignoring his cheerful chatter about trips to the country and weekends in Paris. There would be time enough to deal with that later.

He'd wanted another drink, but she insisted that she had to get back. In reality though, she simply couldn't stand being with him a moment longer.

Eventually he finished paying the clerk and together they went through the squeaky revolving door onto the pavement outside.

It was now raining hard and Felicity scanned the street in vain for a taxi.

"If you're getting a taxi you could give me a lift and drop me off on the way," he said hopefully.

She turned on him in amazement. "You have got to be joking! You may not mind the thought of Isabella chewing you up into little bits but I have absolutely no intention of losing my marriage for this."

"You're being paranoid. Who's going to see us?"

"I don't know. But whoever it is I don't want them to. The less we're seen together the better. Damn! Where are all the cabs when you need one?"

He gave up. "Oh well, I suppose there's always next time." He turned and tried to make eye contact. "Felicity? There is going to be a next time, isn't there?"

She glanced at him impatiently. "Maybe. Possibly. I don't know. Look, we'll talk, okay?"

He gave a reluctant nod. "Okay. But..."

He broke off and peered through the rain. "How weird. That looks just like..."

"Taxi!" Felicity had spotted a cab at the next junction and sprinted off towards it, just pipping two aggrieved looking tourists to the prize.

She wound down the window as she passed him. "I'll call you."

Jake watched until she was out of sight, only then noticing quite how drenched he was. Then he turned and trudged off in the direction of the tube station.

*

"That's it?" asked Lin. "Are you sure?"

It was Saturday lunchtime, a bit over a week since the quiz evening. They'd agreed to meet Jake for a pub lunch to talk about his forthcoming article.

Simon glanced at the note in his hand. "Well this is Bingham Street, and that's the Imperial, so I suppose it must be."

Lin pulled the car in to the kerb and they both stared at the dingy pub across the street. It was an old-fashioned London boozer, with frosted windows made doubly obscure by generations of cigarette smoke, peeling green paint and a battered blackboard offering Sky sports. She could imagine all too well what it was like inside. It was the sort of place that had all but disappeared from the smarter parts of town, replaced by more modern, more welcoming bars and gastropubs. God knows how Jake had managed to find one in this corner of Clapham. Or more to the point, why. As far as she was concerned, she'd had to put up with several lifetimes worth of grotty bars back in Thailand. She certainly didn't need any more here.

She turned round the corner and parked, then they walked together back to the pub.

The interior was much as she had expected. Battered wooden tables and chairs stood on a worn carpet, its swirling pattern mercifully almost concealed by stains. At one end there was a mini-arcade of amusement machines, their garish display a lure to those with more money, or perhaps time, than they knew what to do with. At the other three men were seated, nursing their pints, watching a football game on the television. One of their number gave the newcomers a cursory glance before returning his attention to the screen in front of him. There was no one behind the bar. And no sign of Jake.

They went over to the bar and Simon coughed loudly. After a few seconds a painfully thin girl of about nineteen emerged, wearing jeans and a white tee-shirt, her long blonde hair pulled back into a pony tail. She smiled at them hopefully.

"Yes please? What would you like?"

She spoke with a pronounced accent. Lin couldn't place it exactly, something east European.

"A pint of Youngs for me, please. Lin?"

"Just a diet coke, thanks."

They looked around as the girl prepared their drinks. Lin pointed at a sign over a door in the corner. "Look," she whispered.

Simon followed her gaze. 'Toilets and beer garden' it said. He shrugged. "Let's take a look. It can't be worse than in here."

She giggled. "Want a bet?"

A few moments later, glasses in hand, they were standing in the doorway to the 'garden'. A pile of broken furniture fought for space with the weeds that choked the concrete yard, roughly twelve foot square. Simon turned.

"Okay, you win," he said.

They found a window seat where the cushions seemed a bit less soiled than most, and sat down to wait for Jake. After ten minutes Simon began to get cross.

"I really don't know what he's playing at," he said. "His very words were, 'it's a great little place, loads of character, you'll love it.' And look at it – it's just crap."

Lin nodded her agreement. "Probably his idea of a joke. I still haven't got the hang of the British sense of humour, I'm afraid."

He looked at her, unsure whether she was winding him up. "I can assure you this is not the British sense of humour. This is Jake's very own."

Just then the door slammed open and in marched Jake. He waved at them without speaking and went straight to the bar. When the barmaid came out from the back room again, rubbing her hands on a cloth, his face broke into what Lin could only describe as a leer.

"Hello, my dear – you're new, aren't you? What's your name?"

She smiled hesitantly. She's seen his type before, thought Lin.

"Karla," she said. "From Poland," pre-empting the inevitable next question.

"Well, Karla from Poland, you can get me a pint of bitter and then tell Barry that Jake is here."

He joined the other two. "You found it all right, then. Great little place, isn't it?" He took a long gulp of his beer and looked around approvingly.

"Quite unique," said Simon. "How do you know it?"

"Oh, an old pal of mine took it over quite recently. He's got great plans for it." He turned as a man emerged from behind the bar.

"Here he is now. Barry, how are you mate? Come and meet some friends of mine. Simon, who was at uni with Bella, and this is his wife, Lin."

He was, thought Lin, almost a caricature of a pub landlord. He was presumably roughly the same age as her husband, but looked at least ten years older. Untidy, wispy hair of an indeterminate sandy colour straggled down around a pasty face, while an ancient Status Quo tee shirt strained with the effort of trying to contain an industrial-sized paunch. She couldn't even see if he was wearing a belt.

He shook hands with them. "Pleased to meet you," he said.

His voice was surprising — soft, well-educated. The sort of voice, she imagined, that some of the pub's clientele would have thought just invited a slap.

He was continuing. "I don't know why Jake's brought you here now, quite frankly — it's a complete shit-hole at the moment." Another surprise. "But it'll be very different in six month's time, I promise you. It's got huge potential."

"I don't think it's that bad," said Jake, looking round again. He sounded as if he meant it, as well. Or perhaps he was just miffed at Barry's tone. "Anyway, the main reason we're here is for one of your famous lunches — I've told them how good a cook you are."

No you haven't, thought Lin. But Barry was just staring at him, frowning. "God, Jake, you are a dickhead. I told you when you called that the kitchen was out of action. It's completely unsanitary," he said, shooting a look of apology at Lin. She nodded, believing him.

Jake glared at him. "So we've come all this way for a pint of fucking Youngs? Fucking brilliant."

Barry shrugged. "I did tell you." He turned to Simon and Lin. "Sorry — have the next drink on the house. And I'll make sure you're invited to the grand reopening party." He returned to the bar, shaking his head as he went.

Jake downed the rest of his pint in one. "Oh well, a beer and crisps lunch — even more like uni than I expected. And free, too — how good is that?" He got to his feet. "Same again?"

He really was quite irrepressible, thought Lin. You could almost admire him for it. She watched him order the next round, flirting with the Polish girl, leaning right over the bar to get a better view when she bent down for their crisps.

"So," he said when he'd sat down again. "I think I told you what this article is about. We're examining the experiences of mixed-race couples in London, and I thought some first-hand stories would put a bit of flesh on the bones."

Simon shrugged. "Fire away. What do you want to know?"

"Let's start with how you met. Bangkok, wasn't it? What made you go out there?"

"I just fancied a change. I'd done a few years in a hospital in the Midlands, saw an advert for doctors in Thailand, and thought why not?"

"Must have been strange, being where no one knows who you are, or what you've done. Or was that part of the attraction?"

Simon looked blank. "I'm not quite sure what you mean. Why would that be attractive?"

Jake shrugged airily. "Oh, I don't know – fresh start, that sort of thing? No? Never mind. So - you were in Bangkok, and you met this beautiful girl."

"That's right. I was spending a couple of years out there working in the local clinics. I was out drinking with some friends one evening and we went into this bar. Then, suddenly, I saw this absolute vision." He turned to Lin who took up the story.

"He was so sweet." She smiled at the memory. "You get used to men staring at you, and coming on to you, but all Simon did was look at me like I was some sort of goddess or something. He couldn't even bring himself to speak to me – one of his friends had to do it."

"So how long had you been a bargirl at that point?"

Lin felt herself redden.

Simon scowled at him. "She was a waitress, not a bargirl, Jake. There is a bloody difference, you know."

Jake waved a dismissive hand. "Is there? I'm not an expert on these things I'm afraid. What's the difference then?"

"For Christ's sake, a bargirl's a prostitute, Jake! You don't imagine Lin would ever have done anything like that, do you?"

Jake gave a self-deprecating grin. "Sorry – no, of course not. Carry on, Lin – you were waitressing."

She shrugged. "What's to tell? I'd been in Bangkok for several years. I had to waitress for the money, obviously, but I was mainly trying to learn English. You can get much better jobs as an English speaker."

"What, waitressing in hotels and so on?" asked Jake.

She shook her head in exasperation. "Hardly. I mean decent jobs, in offices and so on. And then I'd be able to get some qualifications."

"But you'd be less likely to meet a rich husband in an office, surely?"

Simon started to interject again but she got there first. "Jesus, Jake, what's the matter with you? I wasn't trying to meet a rich foreigner, I was trying to better myself." She saw him grin, unfazed. "Anyway, shouldn't you be taking notes?"

He shook his head. "Perfect memory, me. Don't need notes. So tell me about how your life changed after meeting Simon. Did you carry on waitressing or did you move straight in with him?"

This time Simon got in first. "What the hell has that got to do with anything? I thought we were supposed to be talking about life in London, not Bangkok?"

Jake shrugged again. "Just background. Humour me a little."

After a shaky start the interview seemed to settle down somewhat after that. Jake always had the ability to turn on the charm when it suited him. He soon had them laughing and sharing stories of their life in London, although even then it seemed to Lin that he wanted to focus on the negatives – people's prejudices and preconceptions – rather than what they'd achieved together. It was what made a good story, she supposed.

Jake had one more surprise up his sleeve though.

"I think that's about it then," he said, finishing his fourth pint. "Just one more thing, though – do you have any tattoos, Lin?"

She felt herself colour again. "What? Did you just say what I think you did?"

He nodded. "That's right. Tattoos."

Simon just stared at him. "What the fuck are you talking about, Jake?"

Jake waved an innocent hand. "Oh, nothing sinister. It's the sort of thing that can add to prejudice though. Make it more difficult to assimilate?"

Simon shook his head in amazement. "You're talking utter crap, Jake. How does it add to prejudice? Half the population has got tattoos."

Jake ignored him and smiled at Lin. "Anyway, do you?"

Suddenly she wanted the whole experience to be over. "If it matters, then yes, I do," she said wearily.

Jake looked triumphant. "I thought you might. Call it journalist's intuition. Can I see it? Assuming it's nowhere too private."

Simon jumped to his feet. "That's it – I've had enough of this. Come on Lin – we're going. And you can piss off, Jake."

He pulled Lin to her feet and started leading her to the door.

Suddenly Jake lunged forward and grabbed the hem of her tee shirt, wrenching it up to reveal her back.

Simon swung round. "What the fuck...?"

Too shocked to protest Lin craned her head over her shoulder and tried to pull away, but Jake's grip was too strong. He was gazing at her lower back, a look of rapt attention on his face.

Then he released her and she backed away, still too stunned to speak. He looked up at her and grinned broadly.

"Thanks," he said. "That's just what I wanted to see."

*

The phone went just as Abi was wrapping the last of the sandwiches. She let it ring for a moment just in case Peter was going to answer it, but there was no sound of movement from upstairs. As had been the case for almost the whole morning.

Muttering to herself she grabbed the receiver, trying to wipe her hands on a dishcloth at the same time. It was her friend Sonia.

"Abi? You sound a bit flustered. Is this a bad time?"

She gave a tired laugh. "No more than usual. It's just that it's the church fete this afternoon and I said I'd bring lunch for everyone who's helping set it up."

There was a pause on the end of the phone. "Damn, you'd told me that. What am I going to do now?"

"Why, what's the matter?" Her heart suddenly lurched. "It's not the boys, is it?"

Both of her sons and Sonia's two played football at a recreation centre a few miles away in Streatham every Sunday, Abi taking them in the morning and Sonia picking them up afterwards. Abi would have preferred somewhere closer, but the boys loved it there. And at least it got them out of the house and away from the TV. Today was a big day; the annual tournament.

But it wasn't anything wrong with the boys, thank God. Mandy, Sonia's youngest, was a bit under the weather and Sonia didn't like to leave her. Meanwhile Derek, Sonia's husband, was working today, so Sonia was wondering if Abi could pick them up just this once.

"I would do, but I've really got to be at this fete, I'm afraid," she said. "I seem to be organising about half a dozen different stalls." She thought for a moment. "I suppose I could get Peter to do it."

Sonia sounded dubious. "Would he? That would be great if he could."

"Of course he will," she said with a confidence she didn't feel. "Now you go and look after Mandy and leave it all to me."

*

"Peter? What on earth are you up to all this time?"

Abi marched into the attic room and stopped dead. Her husband was seated in his desk chair, his head turned towards the window, apparently transfixed by the roofs of the houses across the street. The computer screensaver was on, playing out its endless pattern of coloured pipes. e ignored her.

"Peter!" she repeated, this time more loudly.

Slowly he turned, his eyes focussing on her gradually as if he were coming out of a trance. Then he frowned. "What? What's the matter? Why are you shouting at me?"

She shook her head in exasperation. "I've been calling you for the last ten minutes. What have you been up to for the last two hours?"

He shrugged. "Just work. You know, marking – lesson preparation, that sort of thing. I do have a job to do you know."

She looked pointedly at the empty desk. "Oh really?"

"Yes. Really." And he turned his attention back to the houses opposite.

She waited a moment, but it was as if he'd forgotten she was there.

"Peter, what's the matter? These last couple of days? You don't seem to have been yourself."

"Myself? What's that supposed to mean? Do you know what myself really is? Or do I, for that matter?"

She persevered. "You've spent the entire time just sitting up here moping. Is there something wrong at work?"

He sighed. "No, there's nothing wrong at work."

"Well, what then?" She paused, but he continued to stare out of the window. "Is it Simon?"

"Simon?" He seemed genuinely puzzled. "Why should I be upset about Simon?"

She hesitated. "Well – I thought he might have come back to you – you know, about your business proposition?"

A curious look passed across his face. "No he hasn't come back to me, come to think of it. I'll call him now, in fact." He looked up at her. "Was there anything else?"

She met his gaze and tried to hold it, but it was she who broke away first. There was something, or rather a lack of something – an emptiness - in his eyes that frightened her. She felt like she was in the presence of a stranger.

"You're going to have to collect the boys later – Sonia can't make it, and I'm at the fete."

He waved her away. Dismissed her. "Whatever."

She turned away. Her only consolation was that whatever had upset him, it didn't seem to be anything to do with her.

Peter listened to her plod down the stairs with relief. The truth was, this time for once, it wasn't anything to do with Abi. But he could hardly tell her what the real problem was, nor of the rage and frustration that blanketed his mind like a cloud of acid rain, overwhelming him, gnawing away at his soul at the same time as obscuring everything else.

He was fairly sure she wouldn't be very sympathetic.

At least talking to Simon would take his mind off it. He pulled the phone towards him and dialled.

"Simon mate, how're you doing? It's Peter."

"Oh, hi Pete – good to hear from you. I've been meaning to call and thank you for the quiz evening the other day. It was fun."

He didn't quite manage to sound as if he meant it. Peter couldn't really blame him. "Yeah – it was. Just like the old days, the four of us sitting around a table like that. Drinks and arguments."

Then he paused. "Look, I'm sorry about the way it ended, though – I know I behaved like a bit of a prat."

"Hey, don't worry about it – it was fine, honestly."

"It's just that arsehole Jake – he's got the knack of really winding me up. I shouldn't let him get to me, I know, but…"

He heard a snort at the other end of the line.

"Tell me about it. Lin and I had lunch with him yesterday, for this article he's doing. He was a real pain then, as well. How the hell did Bella end up with a tosser like him?"

"I'm not exactly the one to ask, am I? But I'm telling you - you should be careful what you say to him – he's a nasty piece of work. I wouldn't trust him further than I could throw you."

Simon laughed. "And knowing what a weed you are… No, I reckon you're right. I wish now we hadn't agreed. Still, it's done now." He paused. "Anyway, was there anything in particular you were calling about? It's just we're going out any minute."

"No problem – I was only wondering if you'd had a chance to go over my business plan."

"Oh shit, I haven't got back to you, have I? Look, I'm sorry Pete but the answer's got to be no. It looks interesting, it really does, but it's like I said – I can't make any commitments like that at the moment."

Peter knew he shouldn't be surprised. His friend was only repeating what he'd said the other evening. And it was exactly what Abi had told him to expect.

Perhaps that was why it was so galling to hear.

He forced his voice to stay calm. "But why not? If it's really interesting, as you put it? What's wrong with it?"

He heard a sigh. "Peter, I told you the other night – it's not the plan that's the problem – I just don't have the spare cash at the moment. I'm not even putting in to my pension this year."

"Listen, Simon – we are not talking vast sums here – I can't believe you couldn't find that amount of cash if you wanted."

There was silence at the end of the phone so he continued. "Is it Jake? Christ, Simon, you're not taking his word over mine are you? After what we were just saying about him? For God's sake, you're my best mate!"

"Jake? What the hell has Jake got to with anything?" Peter could hear the impatience in his voice. "I've told you why I can't do it about five times now. Are you just not listening, or what?"

Peter felt all the frustrations of the last few days welling up, sensing the catalyst that would allow them release. "And you've waited a week to tell me this? Couldn't you have had the decency to call me yourself, instead of leaving me hanging around? Before leaving me in the lurch, that is?"

He knew he was being unreasonable, even irrational. And slagging off potential investors was not really a recipe for success, either. He just couldn't help himself.

He'd certainly succeeded in irritating Simon, though. "Peter, I haven't the first fucking idea what you're talking about. I gave you fair warning the other day that I wasn't likely to be interested - you can hardly tell me you were relying on me. If you were, you're even more screwed up than I thought."

Silence hung for a moment. "And what's that supposed to mean?"

"Oh for God's sake, you know what I mean." He sounded exasperated. "It means I don't know why you're approaching me in the first place – you must have more promising candidates. What about Hugh? He must have loads of spare cash."

"No!" He realised he'd shouted the word. "No," he said more quietly. "I won't be asking Hugh for money, thank you very much. Not now, not ever."

He could imagine Simon's face – shocked, puzzled, wary – as he spoke. "Well, I guess that's that then. Now I've got to go. Love to Abi." And he hung up.

*

Peter held the now silent receiver in his hand until the tone changed, then he slammed it back into its cradle.

"Well sod you, you bastard!"

For a while he sat, feeling the adrenaline coursing through his veins, nursing his resentment. Then suddenly the anger was gone. He simply felt drained.

He leaned forward, put his arms on the desk, and rested his head on his hands.

"Fuck you Jake," he said to himself in a low, muffled voice. "Fuck fuck fuck fuck fuck fuck fuck."

After a few minutes he straightened and drew the keyboard towards him. "All right," he muttered as he opened a new Word document. "So you think I'm going to let you get away with this, do you? Let's shake things up a little."

And he began to type.

Chapter 4

The next Monday morning Jake was at his desk early. For once he was enjoying his work. He was writing his article about Simon and Lin, and he was on a roll. It was a strange thing, writing, he thought – sometimes you could just stare at a blank screen for ages, waiting for inspiration, while at others the words just seemed to pour out, so fast that you could barely get them down quickly enough. At least that was what it was like for him. It was presumably one of the things that distinguished the true artist from the mere journeyman.

The phone rang and he looked at it, annoyed. Normally he welcomed any interruption to his work, but when the juices were flowing like this he knew from experience to make the most of it – the muse might not return fast.

The phone continued to ring. He glanced at the jumble of words on the screen in front of him and realised that the spell had already been broken. With a sigh he reached for the receiver.

It was Felicity.

"Jake? Can you talk?"

He leaned back in the swivel chair and smiled into the phone. "For you, babe? I've always got time."

"I meant, are you on your own?" She sounded tense and irritable. "But I presume that means that you are. I need to talk to you."

"Sure, we've got lots to talk about. Like, when do I get to see you again? Why didn't you reply to my texts by the way?"

A pause at the end of the line. "I needed time to think. Jake, this just isn't me. It was fun, it was interesting, but I don't want any more of it. It's over."

He was stunned. Completely lost for words as the message of what she'd just said sank in. Then he exploded. "Over? How can it be over? It's hardly even started. You're not making any sense."

He heard a sigh. "I know, I'm being unfair and I'm sorry, but I just can't do it. I'm sorry." She paused again and when she resumed her voice was stronger, more confident. "My mind is absolutely clear about this – clearer than it's been for a long time. I felt terrible last week, not because of what I was doing but because of what I wasn't doing. I wanted to be with Hugh and I wasn't. And I'm not going through that again."

"So what you're saying is that being with me made you realise that you'd rather be with Hugh. Great." He knew he was sounding petulant but he couldn't help it. "And don't give me all that love's young dream stuff – you're just worried about losing your lifestyle. Don't deny it – you said it yourself."

"I know I did, and that's what I thought at the time, but I was wrong. It was more than that. I know that now. I should thank you, really."

"Too bloody right you should. What about me? Led up the garden path and then dumped just when it was getting interesting."

"Oh, pull the other one, Jake." Her voice was scornful now. "Don't pretend you have any feelings for me at all. You can't complain – you got laid didn't you? Now just be grown up and move on."

He sensed he had lost the high ground and it enraged him. "And supposing I don't want to?"

Her voice grew guarded. "What do you mean?"

"Supposing I don't want to move on. Supposing once wasn't enough?"

"That's not an option for you, Jake, I've already told you. It's over."

"And I'm saying I'm not happy about it."

"Well, that's tough, isn't it?" He could hear the impatience in her voice. She had given her message; as far as she was concerned that was it. "What are you going to do? Blackmail me?" He said nothing and after a moment she continued. "My God, that is what you're thinking, isn't it? You utter bastard. How dare you!"

He let silence hang for several seconds. Once again it was Felicity who broke it.

"But you know what? I hadn't realised that you were stupid as well as a shit. Because if Hugh finds out, then Isabella finds out – and I reckon that leaves you in a far worse position than me. I'd think very carefully before you do something that's going to land you out on your ear – in the gutter where you belong."

She hung up.

He cursed loudly and fluently and stormed down the corridor to the living room, where he poured himself a large whisky. The infuriating thing was, she was right – he could never risk publicising the affair. Not that he would even call it that. One lousy shag. She wasn't even that good, uptight bitch.

But if she thought that it was over, that she could pick up him up and dump him at will, then she was going to be in for a nasty shock. He wasn't yet sure exactly how, but he'd make her pay. Somehow, and sometime soon. That was a given.

Calmer now, he returned to his study and tried to concentrate on his article, but his mind kept wandering. After a while he gave up and turned to the laptop sitting on a side table, the picture file he'd been working with earlier still open.

He stared at it as if seeing it for the first time. Then he laughed out loud.

"Why not? Why not indeed?"

*

That evening Isabella pulled her keys out of the front door and kicked it shut behind her. She could hear the television, the volume turned up high. From the noise of all the gunfire and shouting it sounded like Jake was watching an action movie of some sort. Either that or he'd invited the all the local drug dealers around for drinks.

She followed the sound of the television into the living room. Jake was slumped on the sofa, a nearly empty bottle of red wine in front of him. He hadn't noticed her arrival.

She dropped her briefcase with a loud thud just inside the door. He turned his head and raised a hand in greeting, then returned his attention to the television. With a sigh she marched over, picked up the remote control, and pressed the mute button.

In the sudden silence Jake turned to her, his face twisted into an ugly frown.

"What the hell did you do that for?"

His voice was slurred, his eyes just a little bit unfocussed as he stared at her.

"Because I wanted to talk to you, and I didn't fancy shouting loud enough for the entire block to hear."

He grabbed the remote control back and restored the sound at a lower volume. Then he turned back to her, his expression sullen. "Talk away, then."

She bit back the sarcastic response that her mouth was just itching to make. She was too tired for a row.

Tired and hungry.

"Well, for starters, I was wondering if you'd done anything about supper. It is nearly nine o'clock, you know."

She spoke with exaggerated patience, as if to a recalcitrant schoolchild, but it didn't seem to register on Jake. He looked at his watch in surprise. "Oh yeah, so it is. Anyway, it's not a problem – I thought we'd just get a pizza in."

She stood and stared at him. He stared back, oblivious to how close he was to being slapped.

A takeaway pizza. After over twelve hours working on the most tedious property deal imaginable. With what seemed like the most boring people in London.

In the end she just couldn't be bothered to make an issue of it. Later, perhaps, when she was feeling less like a zonked out zombie.

"Okay – I'm going to have a shower," she said. "I won't be long. You get the pizza in, okay?"

He nodded and returned his attention to the movie.

Fifteen minutes later she was feeling refreshed and somewhat more human. She put on a dressing gown, poured herself a glass of white wine from the bottle open in the fridge, and went and sat down with Jake. The film had finished and he was flicking aimlessly through the channels.

"Mmm, I'm starving," she said, taking a sip of wine. "What have you ordered?"

He glanced at her. "Oh, I haven't got round to it yet – I'll do it in a minute."

She froze. All the tension eased away by the shower came surging back.

She slammed her glass down on the table next to her chair.

"Jake, have you actually got round to doing anything today?"

He turned to her properly this time. "What? What are you talking about?"

"I ask merely because I left you in bed this morning, and I return to find you drunk on the sofa, with no obvious signs of activity anywhere around the place. So, I was just wondering – have you actually done anything at all today, or have you just loafed around getting pissed?"

It was a poor time to start a fight, with her exhausted and him drunk, but she couldn't help herself. She was near breaking point.

He was staring at her. His face, already suffused from the alcohol, was now redder still with anger.

"Why thanks for asking, Bella, actually I've had a pretty shitty day, as it happens." His voice was heavy with sarcasm. "Just who the fuck do you think you are, talking to me like that?"

Her adrenaline surged. "Who am I? I'm the person who pays for this flat, that wine you're drinking, the pizza you'll eat if ever get off your fat arse to order it. I keep you, Jake. Though God knows why."

"Oh really? That's how you see it, is it?"

"Yes, Jake. That is exactly how I see it."

There was silence for a moment, broken only by the twittering of the panellists and occasional forced laughter from the game show that Jake's channel hopping had arrived at.

"So that's it," he said eventually. "You're no different to all the others – you think I'm a failure, a loser. You think you're too good for me now."

It was the sort of thing that seemed to happen increasingly often when he was drunk these days - the mood swing from vicious, incoherent rage to maudlin self-pity. She wasn't sure which she found hardest to deal with.

She suddenly felt incredibly weary again.

"No, I don't think that you're a loser," she said with a sigh. "I just wish that you'd make something of yourself. You're wasting your life, and you're too good or that."

He rolled his eyes. "You think I like being dependent on you – knowing what everybody says about me? Do you think I deliberately avoid getting a decent break? It's not exactly easy out there, doing what I do, you know."

His voice was bitter, defeated, and she found herself speaking gently to him. "I know it's not easy – nothing worthwhile ever is. But if you really apply yourself, Jake, you can do it – I know you can. I've got faith in you."

An odd look came into his eyes. For some reason that she couldn't name she found it faintly disquieting.

"You're right, you know. If I really go for something I reckon I can get it." He grinned at her. "It's just a question of knowing what buttons to press."

Pleasantly surprised at the positive turn in the conversation but still feeling slightly uneasy, she nodded. "So – what sort of stuff are you up to at the moment?"

He grinned again and waggled a finger at her. "Actually, since you ask, I've got something quite big on. I can't say exactly what, yet – it's all under wraps. But I promise - you'd be very, very surprised if I told you what it was."

He sounded pretty pleased with himself. She, on the other hand, had heard about Jake's big projects before – ones that often turned into a car review, or something similar. She wasn't holding her breath for the Pulitzer just yet.

Her scepticism must have showed.

"What? My darling wife doesn't believe me? Trust me, Isabella, if you knew what I was working on the last thing you'd do was accuse me of sitting around doing nothing all day."

His smile was mocking now. She still didn't have the first idea of what he was talking about but she knew that she'd had enough of this conversation.

She downed the rest of her wine and got to her feet. "I'm not hungry anymore, and I'm shattered. I'm off to bed."

*

Hugh's bag was one of the first to appear on the carousel, a small pleasure after the monotony of the transatlantic flight. A pretty expensive pleasure, to be sure, given the amount his clients had paid for his first class ticket, but it gave him some satisfaction. And it was surely only his due since his return, originally scheduled for Friday so that he would be home for the weekend, had been delayed by five whole days because of the client's incompetence.

Even better, he would be away before the irritating American with the loud voice who'd spent most of the flight complaining.

He looked at his watch – just gone nine in the evening. Bang on time.

When he got to the arrivals hall he was surprised to see that Dave, the company driver, wasn't standing in his usual spot waiting for him. Most unlike the reliable Dave. Puzzled and slightly annoyed, he stopped and stared around the crowded concourse.

"Hugh!" A familiar voice but not the one he'd been expecting. "Hugh – I'm over here."

He turned to see Felicity waving at him. Still more surprised, he navigated his way through the stream of passenger trolleys towards her.

"Felicity! I wasn't expecting to see you here. Has something happened to Dave?" He kissed her lightly on the cheek.

"No, Dave's fine – I just thought I'd surprise you."

"Well, you have that. And just look at you."

His mind fuddled by the flight and lack of fresh air, he was only just noticing what she was wearing. The tiny black cocktail dress was new, he thought, at least he couldn't remember seeing it before. The diamond set had been a present for her last birthday. She looked ravishing, although when he looked more closely she looked tired beneath her make-up.

"Have I forgotten an anniversary or something?"

She laughed, slightly nervously he thought. "No. I've missed you, that's all. So I've organised a bit of a treat for us."

She sounded excited, like a child that couldn't wait to give a present to their parent. He couldn't help but smile back.

"Okay, so what's the deal? I'm guessing we're not going paintballing."

She smiled, more naturally this time. "Not exactly, no. But I've brought you some fresh clothes. You've got time for a very quick shower and change in your executive suite, or whatever it calls itself. Then Dave's going to whisk us into town for a romantic dinner. I'd assumed that since it's only tea time in New York you wouldn't be too tired?"

She arched her eyebrows inquiringly and the corner of her mouth turned up, dimpling her cheek.

"Tired?" repeated Hugh. "No, I don't think I'll be too tired."

*

"Is everything all right?" he asked as the car sped them along the M4 back into London. He couldn't shake the impression that there was another emotion behind his wife's high spirits this evening. She was tactile and flirtatious and had hardly stopped talking, and for a while he couldn't pin down what the problem was. Then it hit him. She was anxious about something.

She turned to him, startled, interrupted in full flow about her friend Lucy's problems finding a good stables for her horse.

"Of course. Why shouldn't it be?"

He shrugged. "I don't know. You just seem a bit – edgy, I suppose."

She looked out of the window. "Why should I be edgy? No, I'm just excited, that's all. And I suppose a bit nervous." She took his hand and squeezed it. "I want this to be fun for us and there's nothing worse than a surprise that goes wrong."

He leaned over and kissed her gently on the cheek, reassured.

*

Somehow she had got them a table at Le Caprice.

"Either you planned this months ago or you slept with the manager," he said as they sat down. He looked across at her with a smile. She seemed to be having difficulty getting her napkin exactly how she wanted it. "Felicity?"

She gave a quick laugh. "I was lucky – they had a cancellation at the last minute. We were originally booked in to sit at the bar."

He glanced around the restaurant, seeking familiar faces, noticing that his wife was doing the same. The difference being that she would be celebrity spotting, while he would be looking for business acquaintances. It probably said something about their respective characters, though he wasn't sure what.

He saw a couple of businessmen he vaguely knew, one out with a group of other suits, the other at what appeared to be a family party. No celebrities, or what passed for them these days. He saw Felicity frown in disappointment and guessed she'd come to the same conclusion.

She saw him looking at her and quickly smiled. "Anyway, we're here and that's all that counts. Champagne, I think, don't you?"

*

If it wasn't their anniversary, it certainly felt like it, or some similar celebration, he thought as they relaxed into their meal. Felicity had chosen carefully; he had taken her to Le Caprice for their first date all those years ago. Then she was so excited that she could barely eat, constantly glancing around at the - to her - impossibly glamorous crowd of fellow diners. The restaurant itself had hardly changed. The décor, the languid piano music, the buzz of conversation that made you feel that you were really where it was *at*, these were still there. Only they were different. And as he looked across the table at the still youthful beauty that was his wife, he could fool himself for a moment that those differences were not so very great.

But, magical though the evening was, he couldn't help wondering what had prompted Felicity to arrange it. Anxious not to break the spell, he chose his words with care.

"This was a brilliant idea – it was just what I needed. I feel ten years younger than I did on that plane. What made you think of it?"

Her reaction surprised him. She put down her glass and clasped her hands in front of her on the table. She stared at them for a few moments then looked up and met his eyes. When she spoke her tone was almost solemn.

"It was last week. It may sound ridiculous but I just realised that I missed you. And I got to thinking about what it would be like if I lost you."

Surprised but oddly touched, he leaned across the table and took her hands in his own. "But that's ridiculous. Of course you're not going to lose me. Why would you?"

She shrugged and looked at her hands again. "No reason. It's just that sometimes – I don't know – you don't really appreciate something until it's not there." She looked up. "And I just wanted you to know that I do appreciate you. I really do." She paused. "I suppose I'd forgotten how much I loved you."

They didn't speak much on the journey home, just held hands in the back of the car. It wasn't until they were safely in the house, in the dark of the hall, that she pulled him to her, kissing him fiercely, holding him so tightly that he could scarcely breathe. Then she released him, and still wordlessly, took his hand and led him upstairs.

So it wasn't until the next morning that he looked at his mail and opened the letter.

At first he was just bewildered, disoriented. He read the words but they made no sense. Then came the anger, burning slow at first but building until it was a torrent of fire, rushing through his veins.

The previous night was as if it had never been. It was simply a memory, no more substantial than the recollection of a summer mist.

*

Simon stood at the bottom of the stairs, the Saturday papers under his arm. Including one that they didn't normally read. The one with Jake's article in it.

"Breakfast," he called. "I've put it out in the conservatory."

"Down in a minute," came the muffled response.

He stood for a moment then moved back into the kitchen, a faint frown creasing his face.

Lin had been out of sorts for several days now. Whatever it was had come on suddenly. It had been the Tuesday. They had as usual driven to the surgery where he practiced as a GP and Lin acted as receptionist cum office manager. There hadn't seemed to be anything noteworthy about the morning and she'd been fine when he'd gone out for his short lunch break. But when he returned to the surgery he'd found her slumped on her chair at the reception desk, her face pale, staring blankly out of the window. When he'd asked her what was wrong she hadn't even heard him. He'd repeated the question and she'd shaken her head as if to clear it, murmuring something about a summer chill.

Since then there had been no sign of any cold or flu symptoms, just this strange lethargy and distractedness. He'd asked her if there was anything bothering her, if she was worried about anything, but all she did was say no, everything was fine, she was just a bit under the weather.

If she wasn't worried, he certainly was. It was probably nothing, but – if anything happened to Lin, he didn't know what he would do.

He had just sat down in the conservatory and was pouring himself some coffee when she appeared in the doorway in her bathrobe.

She gave him a wan smile. "Bit of a waste of a weekend to spend it in bed. Especially in this weather."

The hot spell had, in defiance of Sod's Law, continued into the weekend, and through the roof of the conservatory the sky was already a deep, cloudless, blue.

He smiled in return. "Sunshine – just what the doctor ordered. How are you feeling today?"

She nodded. "Better, thank you. And hungry."

"That's good." Whatever it was that had affected her had also ruined her appetite – she'd barely eaten in the last couple of days. But she was certainly looking better. Her natural colour had returned and she was holding herself more firmly, more positively.

She started buttering some toast then pointed at the gaudy tabloid lying on the table.

"Since when do we get that?"

Here we go, he thought. "I was going to tell you but I was waiting until you were feeling stronger. Jake called yesterday to tell me that his article was appearing in it today. Pretty pleased with himself, he sounded. And after what happened at the interview I didn't find that too reassuring."

The sight of the newspaper and the thought of Jake's article had exactly the effect that he had feared. The colour drained away from her face again and she hunched forward, pulling her robe around herself protectively.

"Have you looked at it?" she asked, a tremor in her voice.

He shook his head. "No. I thought we'd do it together. Make it a sort of family occasion." She didn't respond and he continued, with more confidence than he felt. "I'm sure it'll be fine, you know. After all, what can he say?"

She took a deep breath and nodded. "Let's do it."

They pulled the paper between them and quickly flicked through the pages until they came to Jake's article. With the headline 'I Crossed the World for Love', it wasn't hard to miss.

"He's got a photo of us!" gasped Lin. "How the hell did he get that? We never gave him one did we?"

Simon shook his head. "It's from our wedding, remember? Isabella would have taken some. What a nerve. And it makes a bit of a mockery of the 'names have been changed to protect the identity' bit."

"Bastard," she muttered. "What's he actually say?"

Jake had found four mixed race couples to interview, a 'cross-section of London society' as he put it. They were the only Anglo-Asians, and were dealt with last.

They read the half page or so of text with growing horror. Simon's hand instinctively felt for Lin's, and grasped it tight. When they had both finished reading he leaned back and looked at her anxiously, for a moment his concern for her outweighing his anger.

It was worse than they'd ever imagined. Jake had somehow managed to convey, without saying as much, that Simon had gone to the Far East to escape some kind of scandal, and that Lin was a sort of cross between a prostitute and a mail-order bride.

"You okay?" he asked gently.

She nodded, looking anything but. "Yeah – I sort of half expected something like this." Her mouth twisted in a parody of a smile. "I suppose it's our fault for being stupid enough to trust someone like Jake."

"But he's supposed to be our friend!" He slammed his fist down on the table, unable to contain himself any longer. "How could he?"

"I don't think you know our friend Jake quite as well as you think you do." There was bitterness in her tone. "He's a user. He uses people, and he doesn't care whether they're his friends or not."

"Well I'm not standing for it." He got to his feet. "I'm going to phone him now."

"No!" Her voice was sharp, and he looked at her in surprise. "No, Simon, there's no point. It's done now. That's what he'll expect, and all he'll do is laugh at you. And I couldn't stand that."

He stood, wavering, pulled by his angry need to do something but held back by the insistence in Lin's words. She had spoken with more force than he had ever heard from her, and now she was staring at him with an intensity that was almost alarming.

He sat down again. "But what do you want me to do?" he asked. "I can't just let him get away with it. I'd have thought you'd have wanted me to stick up for you."

She smiled, her face taut with strain, and took his hand. "Of course I do. But the fact is he has got away with it. There's nothing we can do about that – just take it with dignity."

Then the smile faded. "People like Jake are dangerous, Simon – you have to be careful how you deal with them. I'm not sure you realise that."

He shook his head, bewildered. This was so unlike Lin. One of the snide innuendoes that Jake had made in his article was that Western men married oriental women because they were passive and docile, submissive little dolls. Not Lin. She was never afraid to speak her mind – in fact he had never seen her afraid of anything. Yet here she was, behaving like Jake's caricature. "So we do nothing?"

She held his gaze. "For now."

Chapter 5

It was the following Saturday. Isabella sighed and dropped the document she was reading on the floor beside the sofa. Ten o'clock in the morning and here she was, sitting at home, still doing work that should have been completed by yesterday evening. Now, thanks to the inefficiency of the client's own legal team, she'd be lucky to get it done at all by Monday's lunchtime deadline. Well, if necessary she would work all day today and all day tomorrow. Except for this evening. She'd been looking forward to tonight's concert, and she was damned if she was going to miss it for some miserable property deal.

As she got up to refill her cup from the cafetiere she wondered, not for the first time, whether it was all worth it. The long hours, the stress, the sheer joylessness of a City career. Sure, the money was good – and would be way better yet in years to come if she really made it – but what was the point if you never had time to spend it? She thought with a shudder of one of the senior partners, who'd recently dropped dead of a heart attack months before a long-planned early retirement.

He was fifty-four.

She wanted some kind of life for herself before she died. Travel, new experiences, the feeling of achieving something other than a large bank balance. Maybe even children. Maybe even with Jake. Though sometimes she wondered.

She heard him stirring in the bedroom. There was someone untroubled by stress and overwork. He had the best of all possible worlds, everyone said – a job where you made your own hours and a well-paid wife who was never there to tell him what to do.

Sometimes her frustration with him grew almost too much to bear. He wasn't stupid, if he set his sights a little more realistically he could have a decent career and they could be a normal married couple. But no – he had to be the great artist.

The only thing that kept her sane was the knowledge that he hated the situation even more than she did. She knew that he bitterly resented being dependent on her, and loathed being regarded by everyone they knew as a failure. That, at the end of the day, was why she put up with his chippiness, and his laziness, and his occasional downright obnoxiousness. It was why she sometimes even felt sorry for him.

No wonder her mother accused her of being a martyr. Who else would work as hard as she did, contribute as much to the relationship while getting as little back as she did, and still feel guilty about it?

But for some while now he'd been acting very strangely. He was always up and down, but recently his moods seemed to have been swinging even more violently than usual. Since their conversation a couple of weeks ago in which he'd first mentioned that he had something big on the horizon he'd dropped several more hints, but still given her no more details. He'd been pretty excited for days now, though, and she couldn't help but hope that this time there was something with substance to it. Whether for his sake or for hers, she couldn't say.

He stumbled into the room, dressed in the shabby towelling dressing gown he always wore.

"Morning, my gorgeous – hard at work already?" He threw himself into an armchair and yawned broadly.

She pulled a face. "Only for the last two hours. And I'm going to be stuck with it for the rest of the day, too, if we're going to get to this concert this evening. Which reminds me, don't forget that you promised to take some booze along for the picnic."

He beamed. "Already done, already done. I popped down to the wine merchant yesterday. All is prepared – you don't have to worry your pretty head about a thing."

She stared at him. "Are you feeling all right, Jake? I know I've said it before but you're behaving very oddly, you know."

He laughed and came over to the sofa; bending over he planted a kiss on her forehead. "Of course I'm all right," he said. "I've already told you – I've got something on the go, that's all. I'll tell you what it is when the time's right."

His eyes were bright and mischievous, and she felt the now familiar faint trace of unease. She pulled away from him.

"I know that expression. You're not causing trouble, are you?"

He sat down in his chair again and raised his eyebrows loftily. "Making trouble is what journalists do, darling – you know that."

She shook her head impatiently and leaned down to pick up her discarded documents. "I hope you know what you're doing, Jake," she said. "One of these days I'm afraid you're going to go too far. Then neither I nor anyone else will be able to help you."

*

Simon tossed the newspaper back on the table. "Sunny at first, risk of thunderstorms later."

Lin glanced up through the conservatory roof at the cloudless blue sky. "I can see the sunny bit."

"No, but there's a sort of heaviness in the air. Can't you feel it - a kind of brooding feeling? Almost a sense of foreboding?"

She pulled a face. "I've got a sense of foreboding, all right. I didn't know it had anything to do with the weather though."

He knew what she meant. When he'd first got the email back in January, offering him priority booking for a series of open-air jazz concerts in Kew Gardens, the vast botanical gardens to the south west of London, it had seemed a great idea. A picnic on a summer's evening, listening to Jools Holland; it was an idyllic prospect - almost like old university times. The others had all jumped at the chance, and Abi had even offered to co-ordinate the catering.

That was then. In the months following, there had been that awful quiz evening, with Jake and Peter's drunken row, the embarrassment of having to turn down another of Peter's hair-brained business propositions, and last but by no means least, Jake's bloody newspaper article last weekend. His vision of a wine-soaked recreation of their student days now seemed destined to be more Abigail's Party than Brideshead Revisited.

He sighed. "Well, it's too late to get out of it now." Not that he hadn't thought about it.

"Who said anything about wanting to get out of it?"

He recoiled at the sharpness of her tone. "No-one - I just assumed…"

"That's the trouble, though, isn't it? People do just that. They make assumptions."

She got up and went into the kitchen, busying herself with her picnic preparations. Starters and nibbles, as allocated by Abi.

He stared at her back, rigid with some private emotion, wondering what he'd said wrong this time. She seemed to have got over what was physically wrong with her the previous week, a summer cold or whatever it was. But the piece in the newspaper, with its snide innuendoes and seemingly casual contempt for them and their feelings, appeared to have had a more lasting impact. She'd withdrawn into herself, spending more time alone with her thoughts. They'd not had a proper conversation since that day, he realised. It was as if ten years of loving relationship had suddenly been rolled back.

Jake, he thought bitterly. It was all bloody Jake's fault.

*

The day turned out even hotter than forecast. Simon and Lin spent the afternoon lounging in the garden, reading. He retired to the shade early on, but she remained stretched out on a sun bed, soaking up the rays, as she put it. The tensions of the morning seemed to be forgotten as she chattered away, teasing him about his old fashioned straw hat.

The sun must be good for her, he reflected – she was almost back to her old self. And she did look fantastic in a bikini.

Eventually he looked at his watch. "It's getting on for five – I suppose we should think about getting ready."

Lin stirred and opened one eye. "Guess so. I think I'd better have a shower first, though." She sat up, stretching her arms above her head.

"Shower sounds good," said Simon, watching her. "Don't suppose you want your back scrubbed, do you?"

She walked over to him and knelt down next to him, grinning. "You suppose right – we've not enough time. Now, if you'd suggested that half an hour ago…"

She stood up and walked into the house.

"Tease!" he called out after her.

The first blot on what was turning out to be a rather enjoyable day was when they arrived at the tube station. There was a whiteboard, on which was scrawled 'District Line Engineering Works. Reduced Service All Day Saturday And Sunday.'

"Bloody typical," said Simon, staring at it. "Pick one of the hottest days of the year, when loads of people are going to Kew for a concert, and decide to cut the number of trains."

"We could always get a cab," suggested Lin.

Simon glanced at his watch. "No – we're here now. It's not too long a journey. We'll manage."

They went down to the platform, where they took their places among the throng of hot, sweating, would be travellers.

"Are you sure about this?" asked Lin, looking around dubiously at the disgruntled faces. "Some of these people look as if they've already been here ages."

"So it's more likely that there'll be a train soon, isn't it? Come on - it'll be fine. We've got loads of time, anyway."

It was another fifteen minutes before the first train arrived, by which time the platform was becoming seriously crowded. Simon watched with dismay as the carriages passed by. Every one of them was absolutely packed.

"Jesus, how the hell are we supposed to get onto that?" he said.

Lin hoisted her backpack over her shoulder. "Sheer brute force, I guess. Come on – we'd better try – the next one's not likely to be any better."

Somehow, they, their packs and the cool box squeezed onto the train, where they stood, jammed against each other in a corner. It was obvious that quite a number of the other passengers were also headed for Kew, and any floor space not occupied by people's feet was taken up with picnic paraphernalia.

On top of everything else, it felt like it was about forty degrees.

"You realise that it's illegal to transport animals in these conditions, don't you?" said Lin. She winced as the train braked suddenly, driving somebody's elbow into her ribs. "This would constitute cruelty to sardines."

"It won't be long now," was all he could think of to say.

Suddenly her face convulsed in pain. "Shit!" she shouted. "What the fuck was that?" She craned down at her feet. "It feels like someone's stabbed me in the foot."

"Sorry, dear." An elderly woman was leaning down to retrieve her umbrella. She looked shocked at Lin's words. "It just slipped out of my hand."

"Well, can't you be a bit more careful? My foot is in agony, and I can't even reach to rub it."

"It was an accident, you know," said the woman, her mouth tightening in disapproval. "There's no call to go on like that."

Lin left the woman tutting to her companions and turned pointedly back to Simon. "Next time – taxi," she hissed.

They continued the journey in silence, although Lin's mutinous expression and the fact that she wouldn't meet his gaze spoke volumes.

The train continued its rattling, lurching progress. The humid atmosphere became increasingly rank, and whenever they drew up at a station everybody strained towards the doors, to catch a few precious wafts of fresh air. Nobody spoke; it was as much as they could do to stay upright. It was bad enough for them, thought Simon – God knows what it must be like for some of the more elderly, frail passengers.

At last the journey was over.

"Thank God for that!" said Lin, taking a deep breath as they fell onto the platform. "I never want to have to go through anything like that again."

They joined the procession of concertgoers making the short walk from the station to Kew Gardens itself. Soon they were standing in front of the main gate.

Lin stared at the queue that snaked away down the road as far as the eye could see, a look of disbelief on her face.

"I thought we were early. Some of this lot must have been here for hours." She pulled the backpack from her shoulders and dropped it in front of her.

Simon lowered the heavy cool box to the ground and started massaging his aching fingers one by one. "I told you there's always a bit of a dash for the best places. Come on - it'll move quickly enough once it gets going." He picked up the box and began walking towards the back of the line before realising that Lin wasn't with him. He turned to find her standing where he had left her, her arms folded obstinately. "Lin?"

"I've got a better idea. Why don't we go back to that café by the station and wait till the queue's gone?"

He put the box down again and adjusted the strap of his own backpack. The material of his shirt, drenched by sweat where it had been clamped against him by the weight of the pack, slid unpleasantly against his skin.

He took a deep breath and forced his voice to stay reasonable. "Because that would defeat the entire point of getting here early. Come on, Lin. The sooner we're inside the sooner we can sit down and have a drink."

She heaved a loud sigh, grabbed her backpack and marched off ahead of him. With a more discreet sigh of his own he picked up the box and followed.

*

Forty minutes later, sitting on a rug under the gentle shade of a spreading oak, a cold drink in his hand, Simon began to dare to hope that the evening might be a success after all. Peter and Abi had got there shortly after them, and while Peter was checking out the stalls selling everything from drinks to straw hats Abi was busying herself setting out the picnic. Hugh and Felicity had just phoned to say that they'd arrived and would be with them in a minute or two. Naturally there was no word yet from Jake and Isabella. The rest of them would probably have a collective heart attack if that particular couple were ever on time for anything.

While Abi's ample back was turned Lin leaned over to him and planted a small kiss on his forehead. Then she gave a wry smile and mouthed the single word - 'sorry'. He glanced quickly at Abi then leaned forward himself, pulled the back of his wife's head towards him and kissed her full on the lips. She giggled and pulled away, shaking her head in mock remonstration.

Peace was restored.

Hugh and Felicity arrived. He was carrying a large bag in each hand, his face flushed and damp with exertion, his checked shirt clinging to him. Felicity, in contrast, looked as fresh as if she had just walked out of an air-conditioned department store. The fact that all she was carrying was a handbag and a rolled up umbrella might have helped, of course.

"Darlings," she said, pecking Simon and Lin lightly on the cheek. "What a fabulous place. How clever of you to have organised it, Simon."

Hugh put the bags down heavily. "God, it's hot," he said, unnecessarily. "Any chance of a drink?"

Lin waved her can of lemonade apologetically. "Only soft at the moment, I'm afraid. Jake's supposed to be bringing the first batch of booze. Then we all chip in at the bar later, as necessary."

Simon felt something settle a little lower in his stomach. It was as if the mere mention of Jake was enough to cast a pall over the evening.

Hugh looked annoyed. "And of course he's not here yet. Bloody typical. Who on earth trusted him with something that important?"

"Actually, he volunteered." Abi's voice came unexpectedly from behind a stack of Tupperware pots. Simon had almost forgotten she was there. "Apparently Isabella wasn't very pleased." She looked up and saw the questioning looks on their faces. "Something about him always being happy to spend her money."

Hugh grunted. "Well, I'm not waiting for them all evening. I'll go and get some fizz."

He strode off towards the bar.

"How was your journey?" asked Simon. "We had a shocker – the tube was worse than a cattle truck."

"Really? Poor you," said Felicity. "Ours was fine - we had a car bring us. He's picking us up afterwards as well – we can give you a lift if you'd like."

"That would be brilliant, if it's not too much trouble. I'm not sure our marriage would survive a return journey like that." He smiled at Lin.

"Not a problem," said Felicity. She looked around. "This is a good spot you found," she said.

Simon followed her gaze. It was an extraordinary sight - a tribute to the seriousness with which the English middle classes took their picnics. While most were making do with a few blankets and some food and drink, many had brought folding chairs, even tables. Most bizarrely of all, he could see several parties who seemed to have brought the entire contents of their dining rooms - tables groaning under the weight of crystal glasses, real china and cutlery, even candelabra. He recalled the struggle of manhandling his own modest backpack and cool box and shook his head in incomprehension. Mad dogs and Englishmen indeed - even if it was only the late afternoon sun.

The stage for the concert had been set up directly in front of the Temperate House, a vast, ornate Victorian conservatory the size of a hotel that loomed over this section of the horticultural gardens. Simon had staked out their group's territory a couple of hundred yards or so back, on a small rise. Better still, there were no trees in front of the one they were seated under, so they would have completely unobstructed views. The nightmare of the tube journey, even his tribulations with Lin, all had been worth it in the end.

"Thanks," he said. "We're better off than them, at any rate." He gestured towards the mass of people occupying the open ground in front of the stage.

Felicity nodded. "Poor dears - they look sweltering."

They must be, he thought. Even under the tree the heat was oppressive - it seemed to have got hotter as the day progressed. It was now technically early evening and he still felt unpleasantly clammy. It was the humidity, he supposed. That and the fact that there was not even a breath of wind. Many of those sitting in the open were huddled under their umbrellas - they had obviously all read the same weather forecasts - makeshift parasols that only seemed to him more likely to trap the heat and make things worse.

A few minutes later Hugh returned with two bottles of champagne. He was accompanied by Peter, whom he'd bumped into at the bar.

"Peter, darling," said Felicity. She looked him up and down as Hugh set to work on the bottles. "Good of you to make an effort."

Simon grinned. Peter was wearing a pair of old khaki shorts and what seemed to be an even older white polo shirt. He looked like he'd just finished trekking across a desert.

Peter didn't seem to find the comment funny. He nodded coolly at Felicity, then downed his champagne Hugh passed him in one gulp. He held out his glass for a refill. "Still no Bella and Jake?" he asked "Shame."

"It will be if we've got nothing to drink," growled Hugh, half filling the glass this time. "It'll be your round next time."

"Not with champagne, it won't," said Abi, earning a glare from Peter. "Anyway, I wouldn't worry about Jake. People like him always turn up." The 'unfortunately' hung unspoken, but very much present in the air, thought Simon.

"Just like the proverbial," he finished instead.

As if on cue his phone rang, and a few minutes later the last of the couples made their appearance through the trees. For once it was Isabella, looking almost fresh in pale linen trousers and a white top, who seemed relaxed, while Jake, obviously struggling with two heavy cool bags, was showing signs of stress. Isabella had clearly extracted her pound of flesh for his profligacy.

"Christ!" he said, almost dropping the bags and throwing himself onto Felicity and Hugh's picnic rug. "Who the hell's idea was this anyway?"

Simon bit his tongue. Telling Jake to fuck off if he didn't like it would doubtless be very satisfying but hardly conducive to the congenial, harmonious party atmosphere he was hoping for.

As it was Isabella answered for him, while Hugh handed both the new arrivals drinks. "If your attention span really is too short to retain that sort of complicated information, you can thank Simon and Lin for organising, at some trouble and expense I believe, your evening's entertainment. So thank you," she said sweetly, raising her glass to the others. Jake took a swig himself and muttered something inaudible.

He picked up the now empty bottle. "Not bad. Not quite up to your usual standards, though Hugh, is it?"

"I got it from the bar," said Hugh through gritted teeth. "Because we were dying of thirst and the person who was supposed to be providing the booze failed to turn up with it."

Jake looked genuinely surprised. "I can hardly carry enough for eight people for the entire evening, can I? I thought we were just supposed to get the ball rolling."

Simon saw Hugh, who had got even redder, open his mouth to object further, and interrupted hastily. "Whatever. We're all here now so let's not spoil things by arguing about it. What have you brought, Jake?"

Jake plunged his hand into the cool bags and started pulling bottles out one by one. "We've got some fizz to kick off with, then some Sancerre, then some quite good Italian pink. Should last a while," he said proudly.

"As you can see, my husband decided to push the boat out for you all," said Isabella, acid in her voice.

There was a general murmur of slightly shame-faced appreciation.

Nothing like a public disagreement about money to stifle the English into tongue-tied embarrassment, thought Simon with amusement. Might be worth remembering for later.

"Food's ready," said Abi. "Starters here, mains over here. Lin, do you want to tell us what everything is?"

Lin had brought a sort of oriental buffet for starters, ranging from satay to dumplings to delicate little pancakes containing several different types of meat and vegetables.

"Mmm," said Jake, grabbing a satay stick. "Spicy. Delicious." He grinned at Lin then turned to Simon. "Nothing quite like a spicy oriental, is there Simon?"

All good intentions forgotten, the memory of the newspaper article still fresh in his mind, Simon felt his temper flare.

"Now look here, Jake, I'm warning you…"

"Simon!" Lin's voice was low, insistent. "Leave it. It's not worth it. Don't rise."

He stared at her for a few seconds. She held his gaze unblinkingly. Once again he wondered what was going through her mind, why she of all people was so determined to avoid getting into any sort of argument with Jake.

"Sod it," he said. "I need the loo."

As he left the shade of the tree the heat hit him like a slap. He could almost feel the electricity in the charged air. There was no doubt that the weather was ready to break, probably in spectacular fashion. At least the storm would clear the air. He just hoped that the rain and thunder would wait until after the concert was over.

And that their own particular storm wasn't going to break too spectacularly.

*

Felicity watched Jake pour the last of the champagne from Hugh's bottle into his glass.

"I take it you're not driving."

"Too right. My lovely lady wife has volunteered to do the honours. Haven't you, my sweet?" He beamed at Isabella.

She snorted. "Like I have a choice. It's drive or die."

"Do you ever have a day when you don't drink, Jake?" Felicity asked him. "I seem to remember reading that you're supposed to have at least two a week."

Jake appeared to think for a moment. "Not that I recall, no. But I did give it up altogether a while back." He paused and grinned around at their disbelieving faces. "Longest morning of my life."

Hugh muttered a sarcastic 'ha ha' under his breath, the others said nothing. Lin seemed to be staring at Jake as if he was some peculiar specimen of insect life.

Felicity turned away to hide a smile. She didn't want people thinking that she found Jake's ancient joke funny, and she wasn't smiling at that anyway. No, it was this whole situation. It was patently clear that quite a few of them would rather be somewhere else, or at the very least they would be a whole lot happier if one or two of the other members of the party were to miraculously disappear.

There were tensions everywhere, she could feel them. Some were obvious and out in the open; some others, like that between her and Jake after their ill-fated dalliance, she was aware of - but there were others, too, lurking just beneath the surface, she was sure of it. She would have to ask Isabella if she had the same impression when she got the chance.

The whole evening felt like a volcano - the longer the pressure kept building up inside, the harder it was going to blow. And the trouble was, this sort of thing always brought out her mischievous side. While the rest of them were all desperately trying to keep the lid on things, she was rather looking forward to the explosion.

So long as it didn't involve her, of course.

"Do you ever take anything seriously, Jake?"

All heads turned towards Abi.

"I mean, you just go through life, pleasing yourself, never giving a moment's thought to anyone else. Everything's just a big laugh to you, isn't it? But doesn't that ever bother you at all?"

Felicity stifled a giggle. She had obviously been wrong in her supposition that everybody else was anxious to avoid provoking a scene. The words 'light blue touch paper and stand well back' came to mind.

"What the fuck are you talking about?" Jake's face had screwed up into an ugly scowl. "What's wrong with having a good time? That's the trouble with you religious nuts - you want everyone to be as miserable as you are. Just because my arsehole gets more laughs than you do you think there's something wrong with me? Uptight bitch."

There was silence for a few moments, then Isabella spoke, putting on what Felicity presumed was her courtroom voice.

"I apologise for my husband's colourful, if somewhat inarticulate, answers to what I imagine you meant to be largely rhetorical questions. Yet I have to point out what in legal circles we call contributory negligence, ie you were rather asking for it."

As attempts to pour oil on terminally troubled waters went, it wasn't bad, thought Felicity.

Abi remained unmollified. She glowered at Isabella. "He's disgusting. I don't know how you put up with it. What you see in him."

Felicity saw Isabella's mouth harden. "Since you ask, about seven inches. When he's sober, at any rate. Though it's hard to remember that far back."

Felicity, whose own memories in that respect were a bit too recent for comfort, was mildly shocked. She supposed that they had all become accustomed to Isabella being the respectable face of her marriage - if she wasn't arguing with Jake she was wearily apologising for him. They'd forgotten that she was as liable as any of them to get fed up with Peter's boorishness, or Abi's self-righteousness.

Peter. She shot a curious glance at him. She wasn't particularly surprised that he hadn't leapt to his wife's defence, but now she came to think of it he'd seemed oddly subdued the whole evening. Normally he couldn't resist the odd dig at Jake or the opportunity to remind them how hard up he was compared to her and Hugh. But tonight he'd hardly said a word.

As if sensing her gaze he turned to her. He looked as if he wanted to say something, but all he did was stare at her. Flustered and disconcerted, she looked quickly away.

Perhaps it was the weather that was making everyone behave so oddly. She looked up at the sky where it was visible beyond the shade of the tree. Within the last half hour the sun had disappeared, the blue canopy replaced by a heavy grey, brooding and ominous.

Not long now.

*

When Simon returned a few minutes later he found the group sitting in silence, the atmosphere if anything even more oppressive than before. He shot an enquiring look at Lin, but she merely shrugged.

He was saved from further enquiry by the arrival on stage of the first support act, a female singer he'd never heard of. She sang the sort of bland, easy listening stuff that offended no-one but was totally unmemorable - certainly not worth crossing London in a cattle truck and enduring an evening with Jake for, he thought. But by tacit consent they all settled down and listened as attentively as if Lennon had come back from the dead and the Beatles reformed. Perhaps they were all just grateful for the truce, the opportunity to relax without the necessity to bite each other's heads off.

The truce lasted until the interval. Somehow over the course of the three, all equally forgettable, support acts, they had managed to drink all the booze that Hugh, Jake and Simon had either brought with them or bought at the bar. Logically, therefore, it was Peter's round.

Still feeling slightly guilty about his rejection of Peter's business proposition, Simon would have been happy to overlook this, and take care of the next few bottles himself. Although they all got fed up with him going on about it all the time, Peter did have a point - a teacher with two kids was simply not in the same financial league as a doctor, a City lawyer, or a senior advertising executive. Jake was being bloody minded though, and for once Hugh, normally happy to stump up for everyone, supported him. So with an ill grace Peter tramped off to the bar, ostentatiously leafing through his wallet as he picked his way through the rugs and tables.

It was nearly ten minutes later that he returned, hot and irritable, carrying three bottles of what Simon recognised as the cheapest Italian plonk on sale there.

"God, the queues here. You'd think they'd at least staff the bloody bars properly."

"What do you expect?" Hugh inspected the label on one of the bottles with thinly-disguised distaste. "It's the interval."

Peter looked around for some sympathy, at first surprised, then annoyed when none seemed forthcoming. After a while a malicious gleam appeared in his eye.

"So," he said, drawing the word out in an exaggerated fashion. "Working on any good articles are we, Jake? Any more grand exposes?"

Involuntarily Simon felt his hands clench into fists.

"Peter!" protested Felicity.

But Jake chose to take the question at face value. "Not really. I've got a few interesting research projects going, but nothing really important at the moment."

"Research!" laughed Isabella. "Is that what you call it? Trawling around the internet all day for God knows what."

"That is because, my darling, you fail to understand the true nature of being an investigative journalist." He struggled with the word 'investigative' and Simon suddenly realised that Jake was actually quite drunk. "A reporter must persevere - he must follow his hunches, and even when things aren't going his way he must persevere. Only then will he get results."

He looked around expectantly, though what reaction he thought he was due was unclear to Simon. Most of them just looked baffled, though for some reason Felicity had reddened slightly.

Their silence seemed to annoy Jake. He dropped his oratorical tone and resumed his normal voice.

"Results," he repeated. Then he turned to Lin. "I'm sorry if I offended you earlier, my dear. But I'm afraid that's me - I always say what I think. And, of course, it follows that I always mean what I say."

Everyone stared at Lin, wondering how she would react to this strange outburst. For a moment Simon thought she was going to ignore Jake, as in fact she had done for most of the evening, but then she shrugged and looked him square in the eye.

"So do I, Jake. So do I."

The silence that followed seemed somehow equally loaded with unspoken yet significant meaning. Eventually it was broken by Felicity, who, Simon had noticed, was the only one of them who seemed to be finding the whole evening highly amusing.

"So Jake, give us an example of some interesting material you've turned up during your research. If there's anything suitable for mixed company, of course," she said, patting Abi lightly on the shoulder. Abi ignored her.

Jake shook his head. "No can do, I'm afraid. Confidential, you see – got to keep it under wraps until it's ready for publication. Reveal your secrets too early and…" He waggled his finger at them.

Pompous git, thought Simon.

"But how about this?" Jake continued, oblivious. "It's not really news but it's fascinating stuff. I found this link to a website for this performance artist. Basically, if you're having a party, she'll come along and erect this contraption, sort of a lounger it must be, with a huge black velvet curtain down the middle, so the room's sort of divided in two. She lies on it, her top half clothed, sitting up, her bottom half naked, legs spread."

"I'm not sure I want to hear the rest of this," interrupted Isabella.

"No, hear me out - it's art, nothing more," said Jake.

"Yeah, right," muttered Peter. "Like pole-dancing's just aerobics for people who don't want to get too hot."

Jake cocked his head. "Bit of an expert on pole-dancing, are we? Anyway, where was I? Oh yes - so the top half of her is like, just a normal party guest, drink in her hand, chatting away about house prices and speed bumps and other crap, while her lower half is being felt up by anyone who wants to."

"And shagged?" interjected Felicity, all polite interest.

"No! I told you, it's art. But listen, the whole point is that nobody in one half of the room can see, though they obviously know, what is going on in the other part."

"But how exactly is that art?" Felicity spoke as if to a very young child.

"It's all about making explicit the extent to which we depersonalise sex." Both his expression and his voice were so earnest that Simon wanted to laugh. "The person and her genitalia become two totally distinct elements, and are experienced as such. Implicitly we do that all the time - some people are just friends, we don't think about them sexually at all, others we are only really interested in for their bodies. This is just highlighting that. That's why it's art."

Felicity finally broke into peals of laughter. "Jake, you are priceless. That is the most unbelievable crap. Where on earth did you get it from?"

"It was on the website." He seemed taken aback by her reaction.

"Jake, you don't think it just may, possibly, have been a spoof?" asked Isabella, also laughing.

"No I don't!" he snapped. "God – you people – you have such sheltered little lives. You don't have the first idea of what's really out there. You just have no idea."

There was real venom in his voice now. It struck Simon that the one thing Jake couldn't stand was being laughed at.

"Sounds to me like it's simply an advert for an overly imaginative prostitute," said Abi.

Jake sneered at her. "And what the fuck would you know about anything?" he said.

Abi bridled and opened her mouth to speak, but Peter got in first.

"Jake – don't speak to my wife like that, okay?"

Everyone seemed surprised to hear Peter actually sticking up for his wife for once. Even Jake appeared taken aback.

Then he laughed. "How sweet – Sir Galahad rides to the rescue of his beloved. Bit late for that sort of act, isn't it?"

Peter reddened.

Isabella looked sharply at her husband. "For God's sake, Jake, why don't you just shut up for a bit? Give everyone a rest."

Hugh propped himself up on his elbows and grinned. "Well, personally, I think it would be a shame if your performance artist or whatever you call her weren't genuine. I think it's an absolutely brilliant idea for my next birthday party."

He ducked as Felicity threw a grape at him.

"You wish. Only if you want it to be your last," she said.

The laughter and banter that followed seemed to lift some of the tension from the group. Only Jake sat, a petulant expression on his face, staring pointedly into the middle distance. He really is like the playground bully, thought Simon – happy to pick on the smaller kids when he gets the chance, utterly unable to handle it when the tables are turned. But at least everyone else appeared to be having a good time now.

Then Jake leaned over to Felicity, pushing up close to her face, fixing her gaze with his. "And you – you think my work is crap, do you? Let me tell you, there's some stuff that I've got that could make no end of trouble if it got out. You do realise that, don't you?"

She held her ground. "Is that so? Then you'd better be careful, hadn't you? Because my understanding is that people who know things that they shouldn't do quite often come to a bad end."

She spoke coolly enough. But Simon couldn't help noticing that the hand that held her glass was trembling slightly, and he wondered why.

*

At last Jools Holland came on, to a rapturous welcome from the slightly tipsy audience. Many rose to their feet and started streaming towards the stage for a better view. Felicity jumped up.

"I love this song - I'm going up to the front. Anyone coming with me?"

"Sounds good to me." Lin clambered to her feet and the two of them joined the throng manoeuvring their way through the now largely deserted picnic sites.

Isabella watched them for a while but soon lost sight of them in the crowds milling round the stage. She yawned and stretched her legs into the newly vacant space around her.

"I'm quite comfortable here, actually."

"Quite so," said Jake. "Why exert yourself when you can relax, that's my motto."

She looked across at his prone figure, finding the sight deeply depressing. That Jake preferred relaxation to exertion was all too apparent, and a dozen possible replies to that effect, of varying degrees of acerbity, suggested themselves. But what was the point? There were times for a serious conversation with her husband about his career -though God knows she hadn't found one yet that made any difference. But when he was drunk in front of a group of their friends, most of whom he'd managed to offend already, definitely wasn't one of them. Why spoil the evening just when it was becoming enjoyable?

Suddenly he rolled over and scrambled awkwardly upright. "Need the loo," he mumbled, and wandered off between the trees.

She settled back to listen to the music. This was the life, she thought. No email, no phone, no hundred page documents or clients screaming for them to be finished yesterday. Just friends, good food, drink, music and a summer evening. It was what she imagined a weekend party at a country house would be like. Right down to the rows.

She tried to put from her mind the fact that most, if not all, of those seemed to involve Jake. He was always argumentative and provocative, but when he was sober he was at least sometimes entertaining with it. When he got pissed, though, he was just boring and embarrassing. Like tonight.

And maybe it was just because she losing patience with him, but it seemed to her that he was getting worse. He got drunk more often, and when he did he was even ruder and more aggressive. It was another thing that she would have to have out with him at some stage, she thought wearily. But not tonight. She deserved one decent evening.

Although it was a curious evening. The dynamics of their group were always fluid and changeable, but on this occasion the mix seemed even more volatile than usual. There were strange undercurrents; things going on that she didn't understand. An unexpected turn of phrase here, a surprising silence there. The whole atmosphere was heavy and portentous, like this sultry, tropical, night itself.

The song came to its triumphant climax, and the five of them joined in the applause and cheering. She glanced around at them. It made a pleasant change to have a few minutes without any squabbling or back-biting, though she couldn't avoid registering that it coincided with Jake's absence. Then she saw that Simon seemed to be peering anxiously into the crowds, craning his neck to see better.

"Something wrong?" she asked.

He started almost guiltily, she thought. "No," he said. "Just seeing if I could spot Lin." Then he frowned. "Think I might go and try and find her, stretch my legs for a bit."

She shrugged. "Go for it."

He trotted off, soon disappearing into the amorphous mass of fans.

The music started again, this time a slower, more lyrical piece, almost a ballad. Isabella lay back on the rug, watching the leaves above her against the darkening sky. Still not a breath of wind stirred them. She allowed the soft, dreamy rhythms to lull her. Her eyelids drooped, and she found herself drifting, drifting…

"Is Felicity not here then?"

Lin's voice jerked her awake and she struggled up onto her elbows.

"I thought she was with you," said Hugh.

Lin shook her head. "We got separated ages ago. It's a real scrum at the front. I assumed she'd come back here. Where's Simon?"

"He went off to look for you," said Peter. "Christ, it's getting like a French farce here."

Hugh got to his feet. "I'll go and find her - I could do with a stroll myself."

Lin turned to follow him. "I'll come with you. I'd better see if I can find Simon." She sighed. "He'll probably start panicking if he can't find me."

Isabella looked at Peter and Abi. "And then there were three." Then she looked up at the sky, now almost completely dark, and frowned. "Actually, Jake's been gone a hell of a long time now. I hope he's all right."

"Probably propping up the bar, or sulking. Or both," said Peter. He saw the look on Isabella's face. "What? You're not really worried, are you? Jake's got years of practice at being lashed. At worst he's going to be throwing up somewhere."

"I'd just like to know he's okay, all right? I think I'll go and see if I can find him."

Peter shrugged and scratched his backside. "Suit yourself." Then he looked at Isabella again. "Christ, you really are worried, aren't you? Look, I need a pee - I'll come with you and check in the loo for you, all right?"

*

Abi watched them disappear with mixed feelings. The French farce was rapidly turning into that Agatha Christie story, Ten Little Indians, or whatever it was called. She felt a surge of resentment. Here she was, being taken for granted again. Good old Abi could look after things while everyone else went traipsing around, suiting themselves. Never mind that she'd done most of the work for this blessed picnic. And of course nobody thought to ask whether or not she needed to go to the ladies.

Then she remembered the anxious look on Isabella's face. The poor woman really did seem worried about her worthless husband, and it was un-Christian not to feel concerned for her. Even though the disappearance of probably the most unpleasant man she had ever met was the best thing that had happened to her all evening.

*

Isabella and Peter threaded their way across the grass.

"Are you okay?" she asked after a moment.

He shot a look of surprise at her. "Me? Of course I am – why shouldn't I be?"

She shrugged. "I don't know – you just seem a bit out of sorts, I suppose. As if you haven't been enjoying yourself much."

He shook his head. "No, I'm fine. I always enjoy these reunions, you know that. It's just – I sometimes think about what might have been, you know?"

Isabella just avoided tripping over someone's umbrella. "Not really, actually."

He stopped and turned to her. "Yes you do. You know how it used to be – just the four of us? Me and Felicity – and I always thought how great it would be if you and Simon got it together as well. Just think what a brilliant time we'd have had."

She stared at him, not sure whether to be touched by his sentimentality or exasperated at his choice of time to start such a conversation. "But that was never going to happen, Peter. I never thought of Simon that way."

"Why not? You always got on really well. And he fancied you, I know he did."

"Yes, but I never fancied him. Don't get me wrong, he's a great bloke – one of my best friends – but there was never that sort of spark."

Peter set off again. "There's more to a relationship than just fancying someone, you know. It's what's inside that counts."

She waited for the inevitable reference to Jake, but it didn't come. Perhaps he knew that it didn't need to be said. "In any event, it's just as well - Simon is completely besotted with Lin. And Felicity with Hugh," she added for good measure.

He snorted. "You reckon? I don't know what to think any more. Anyway," he continued, sounding moody. "I don't suppose I could have afforded to keep Felicity, the way she's turned out."

She laughed. "You've probably got a point there."

He continued. "Everything seemed so much simpler then, so much easier. Why has it all got so complicated?"

He sounded so disconsolate that she put her arm around his shoulders as they walked. "It's called nostalgia, and growing old. It was less complicated then, you're right about that – all any of us had to worry about was ourselves, and now we've all got other commitments. But it wasn't easy. You've just forgotten."

He shook his head. "This isn't how I imagined it would be."

"Things never turn out as we plan, Peter. We just have to make the best of them as they are. If all you do is live in the past, or the might have been, you never live at all."

Which is exactly what you're doing, she thought. But she suspected that Peter didn't need to be told that either.

*

Simon and Lin eventually caught up with each other near the front of the crowd and decided to stay there together for the last few songs of Holland's act. Now he was there himself he better understood the compulsion that led many of the audience to leave their comfortable chairs and blankets and stand, cramped and jostled by strangers practising barely-remembered dance moves. It was a totally different atmosphere; the music louder, the rhythms more urgent, all discomfort, all other thoughts blocked out by the euphoria. It reminded him of his youth, then caught himself. He was only thirty-six - why was he sounding like his Grandad?

They remained there until the end, clapping and cheering with the rest of the crowd until they got their encore, and it was only when the lights came on and the roadies began clearing the stage that they reluctantly started to make their way back.

It came as something of a shock to turn from the brightly-lit stage and realise that it was now fully dark, and it took their eyes some time to adjust. In any indoor concert there would be house lights, and possibly aisles to guide them back to their places. Here there was just the faint illumination from the food and drink stalls to the side. From the conversations around them they were not the only ones with the same problem.

They stood and stared at the vague outlines of the trees against the night sky, now rendered indistinguishable from one another.

"I think it's over there," said Simon, pointing at a grey mass.

Lin shrugged. "Let's try that then. It's going to be the right general direction, anyway." She took his hand and gave it a squeeze.

As soon as they found the others it was obvious that something was wrong. Peter was standing with a worried expression on his face, while Felicity and Hugh were peering out into the darkness, trying to find familiar faces in the shadows. Abi looked as if she was guarding the stack of packed up picnic equipment.

"What's up?" asked Simon. "Where are Jake and Isabella?"

"Jake's disappeared," said Felicity. "He's not been seen for ages. Isabella's beside herself. She's out looking for him."

"And we've got to get back for the babysitter," chimed in Abi. "Not that anyone seems to care." Everyone ignored her.

The six of them stood there, unsure what to do. Suddenly Simon became aware of a change in the tenor of the chatter around them; the low, cheerful background hum became interspersed with shrieks and cries of annoyance. And then the first raindrops made their way through the leafy canopy above them.

"Now that's all we need," grumbled Hugh, reaching for his umbrella. The others did likewise.

At that moment Isabella reappeared. Even in the gloom Simon could make out the wild expression on her face.

"Has he come back yet? Simon, Lin - have you seen him?"

They shook their heads apologetically.

Peter kicked a tree root. "I've already told you, he's probably lying drunk under a bush somewhere. He'll turn up."

"Shut up, Peter," said Felicity.

The rain gradually increased in intensity, drumming on their umbrellas, all but drowning out the sounds of the rapidly departing picnickers.

"So. What do we do now?" asked Peter eventually.

And that was when they heard the scream.

PART II

Chapter 6

A year later

Isabella pulled into the lay-by and checked the directions Hugh had emailed her. Stay on the A38 after the M5 ends just beyond Exeter, and eventually follow signs for Bovey Tracey. That sounded easy enough. It was once she was off the main road that things looked like they might get a bit complicated.

She took the opportunity to get out of the car and stretch her cramped limbs. It was taking far longer than she had realised in the July traffic. Hugh had offered to give her a lift down from London but she had decided to drive herself and visit a friend in Wiltshire overnight, breaking the journey. She valued the independence having her own car gave her.

After a minute or two she eased out into the traffic again and resumed her progress westwards. The Devon Expressway, as it was called, was a pleasant dual carriageway that meandered through the green fields and gently rolling hills of South Devon. Now she was off the motorway she felt she could relax and enjoy the drive a bit more. Despite years of living in London, there still was some fundamental part of her that was drawn to the country.

Hugh and Felicity had organised this trip away for the seven of them. It was largely, she suspected, for her benefit, as she knew for a fact that Hugh and Felicity themselves were going on their regular visit to the South of France later in the summer, while Peter and Abi were taking the boys to Greece. Assuming that Simon and Lin also had their own plans, it seemed obvious that the idea of renting a house on the beautiful but wild National Park of Dartmoor for a week was undertaken solely to ensure that she wouldn't be on her own for the anniversary of Jake's death.

Her initial reaction had been that the whole notion seemed a bit ghoulish. It would be like attending some bizarre sort of college reunion– exactly the same group that had been at Kew that fateful night, except for one difference. One person would be missing.

But then he would always be missing.

Felicity had talked her into it, though. We're your best friends in the world, she'd said – we're the ones who should be with you. It's not going to make anything better avoiding us.

That's what she'd thought, of course – that's what they'd all have thought – that, she, Isabella, was avoiding them, as if she blamed them for not having somehow prevented Jake's death. It wasn't the case, though. It was just that the whole thing - her own grief, the long, exhausting police investigation, those awful days when it had seemed that she was a suspect, and then finally the pain and frustration of coming to realise that they were giving up on finding the person that had bludgeoned her husband to death with a bottle – all this had left her utterly drained. Drained, hopeless – and completely unfit for human companionship. The fact that she'd responded, after the first numbness had worn off, in true Isabella fashion by throwing herself even harder into her work didn't help, of course. Although she'd heard people - kindly people, well-meaning – say that anything that took her mind off things had to be good. As if anything could take your mind off the death of a partner.

Particularly such a brutal, violent death.

That was then though. In recent months she'd started to feel things differently. She couldn't say she was over it – would she ever be able to say that? – but she did feel that she wanted to move forward in her life. And to do that, she'd decided, she had to stop hiding from what had happened.

In many ways, that was what was behind the book. The book wasn't going to be about Jake, or even about them as a couple – not factually, anyway. Apart from anything else, such a thing wouldn't be very interesting to anyone else, so what would be the point of writing it? She didn't need that sort of simplistic catharsis. But it was about a widow, and the way she copes with the death of her husband from cancer. And to write the book she wanted to write, she would have to look at her own life honestly and penetratingly, drawing what insights she could. Her own experiences and emotions would be the raw material for her fiction, even if they were then crafted into something unrecognisable as her life.

In such a project there could be no running away from the truth.

It was the same harsh logic that made her agree to Hugh and Felicity's plan. Of course being with them all reminded her of that night. And of course it was painful. But it was something that had to be faced. It was either that, or spend the rest of her life hiding from the shadows.

All of them, Hugh and Felicity, Simon and Lin, Peter, and even Abi, had been wonderfully supportive over the last twelve months. They hadn't pressured her, or criticised her, or told her what she should or shouldn't be doing, but she'd always been made aware that they were there for her when she needed them. And naturally the seven of them had met before as a group– at the funeral, at New Year, and at the rare parties that she could be persuaded to attend.

But there had never been any occasion where she would have spent such a long time with them, or so undiluted by other people. She wondered whether she was taking on too much, too soon.

She shook her head, willing herself to be more positive. This was her first proper holiday in over a year. She would be spending it with some of the people she loved most in the world. It would give her the opportunity to start her book – she'd brought an old laptop of Jake's that she'd found hidden away in a cupboard for the purpose. She would be able to go walking on Dartmoor, a part of the country that she'd always liked the sound of but never got round to visiting.

And it would get her through the anniversary.

It was going to be a good week.

*

Half an hour later she was turning between a pair of improbably grand wrought iron gates onto an overgrown gravel drive that wound away through densely packed shrubs. She felt a shiver run down her spine as she realised what they were. Would she ever, she wondered, ever be able to see rhododendrons again without also visualising Jake's drenched, damaged body?

The last stage of the journey had, as she had feared, been hard work. She'd had to negotiate tiny, impossibly twee villages of whitewashed stone and thatched roofs, and single track roads with high walls on either side and wafer thin passing places that had rattled her Londoner's nerves. But now she was here, only minutes away from a gin and tonic.

Suddenly she was out of the gloom of the bushes, with the late afternoon sun spreading across a wide lawn, bathing the house beyond in a creamy glow. She slowed the car to take a proper look at it.

So this was Harracombe Lodge. It was much more imposing than anything else she had seen on the way down here. Two storeys of seemingly solid granite, topped by steep gables and a slate roof. Broad steps led up to a pillared entrance, with wide bay windows on either side. Today it looked charming and welcoming, but she suspected that on a gloomy winter's afternoon its grey stone walls would take on an altogether more forbidding aspect.

She drew up at the side of the house and clambered out of the car. Hugh's Mercedes was there, as was Simon's Audi, plus a battered Clio that she didn't recognise.

"Isabella, darling!" Felicity was swooping down the weathered stone steps in a cloud of her trademark Chanel, arms wide in welcome. "Welcome to Harracombe Lodge. You found it all right then?"

Isabella also opened her arms and was surprised to receive, rather than the normal air kiss, a full-bodied bear hug. She was even more surprised to find it oddly reassuring.

"Just about," she said, recovering her breath. "They don't want any casual visitors though, do they?"

"Value their privacy." Hugh came down the steps, grinning. He was clutching a fishing rod in one hand. "Sensible chaps. Let go of her now, darling, and take her in for a drink. She looks shattered. I'll get her bags in a minute."

Felicity led her into what Isabella supposed the owners would call the drawing room. She threw herself onto a sofa with a sigh of relief.

Given the grandeur of the exterior, she had imagined the house to be full of the sort of brittle-looking antiques that people paid a fortune for in auctions and then were afraid to sit on. In reality though it seemed that the owners were far more concerned with comfort than looks. While the faded chintz upholstery wasn't exactly her style, it look far more cosy than she had expected.

"Sorry it's all a bit shabby," said Felicity.

"No, it's perfect," said Isabella. "Really homely. How did you find it?"

"It belongs to some friends of Hugh's. I think their ancestors used it for various unmentionable country sports. They rent it out most of the summer, but it was free this week so we thought it would be fun. Now, more importantly, would you like a cup of tea or a proper drink?"

Isabella looked at her watch. It was a quarter past six. "A proper drink, I think – it would be rude not to. And go easy on the tonic."

*

Minutes later, she and Felicity were seated on the stone-flagged terrace at the back of the house. They'd left Hugh sorting out his fishing tackle and taken their drinks out to catch the last of the sun.

Isabella eased back on her chair.

"This is the life," she said, stretching her legs out and admiring the view.

The terrace, set with clusters of ancient wooden tables and chairs, as well as a number of incongruously modern sun loungers, sat above a broad lawn that descended steeply to the floor of the valley. There it gave way to woods that rose, equally steeply, the hillside opposite. Beyond the woods, at the very top of the hill, she could see the beginning of Dartmoor proper.

"Isn't it?" Felicity smiled at her friend. "Just like the old days – us all in a house together – nothing to do except slob around. I even brought a bundle of eighties cds to get the proper atmosphere going."

She paused, then continued in a conspiratorial whisper. "I did think of asking Peter to get a few spliffs, but thought better of it."

"God!" Isabella almost choked on an almond. "Can you imagine Abi's face? It would have been worth it just for that."

"I know - she'd probably never speak to any of us again."

"And your point is?"

Felicity waggled a finger. "Now, now. We mustn't be unkind."

Isabella smiled and took a sip of her gin and tonic. "I know. But you can't say it's not tempting. She does rather ask for it."

But of course Felicity was right. Much as you might like to keep your friends as they were, it was one of the facts of life – people changed. Peter wasn't a carefree student anymore – he was a schoolteacher married to a religious nut. If you pretended otherwise you just got grief. You had to take people as they were now. You couldn't turn the clock back.

She realised she was in danger of getting maudlin. She pulled herself up and gazed around the grounds. "So – where actually is everyone?"

Felicity shrugged. "Oh, out there somewhere. Simon and Lin went off to explore the grounds. There are acres and acres of it – it goes right up to the edge of the moor, and supposedly there's a private gate so you can walk straight onto it. And Peter and Abi took Sammy and Tom out for a hike to work off some of the energy from the drive."

Isabella nodded. "It's beautiful. I'm looking forward to exploring it myself."

"Well you'll have plenty of time. We thought we'd discuss plans over dinner, see what people fancied. Have you got any thoughts?"

Isabella shook her head. "Nothing beyond getting some fresh air and exercise. And starting my book, of course."

A shadow seemed to cross Felicity's face. "Your book? But are you quite sure...?"

Isabella finished the sentence for her. "That it's a good idea? Why shouldn't it be? I can't run away for ever, you know."

Felicity frowned but whatever she was going to say was lost when a loud, slightly braying voice cut across the terrace.

"Aha – our last guest."

Isabella turned and saw a short, rather plump girl of about twenty five approaching, a cheerful expression on her round, somewhat red face. She wiped her hand on the back of her jeans and held it out to Isabella.

Felicity rose to her feet, her sangfroid apparently restored. "Isabella, this is Sophia, who will be cooking for us."

Isabella shook hands. "Pleased to meet you."

"Call me Bubs – everyone does."

Isabella raised an eyebrow. "Bubs?"

"That's it. Apparently it's because I had such a bubbly personality as a baby, and it sort of stuck. Just as well I'm not, like, flat chested, eh?"

She bounced back into the house.

"Quite a character, isn't she?" said Felicity, not with complete approval.

Isabella smiled. "She's cool."

*

Somewhat later, bathed and changed, Isabella came downstairs for pre-dinner cocktails. The staircase, a graceful, curving affair, reminded her of those old films where the heroine made a spectacular entrance to the ball. With no one to laugh at her she tried gliding down in the approved way, and thought she did pretty well. Mind you, it was probably easier in jeans than in a full crinoline.

Felicity, her mind clearly set on creating the perfect traditional country house weekend, had insisted on the cocktails. Isabella would hardly have been surprised if she'd also insisted on black tie for dinner.

She was the last one down, and as she entered the drawing room she was greeted by a chorus of welcome, with Peter, Simon, Lin and even Abi all jumping to their feet and rushing forward to hug her. Even if the whole thing was, as she suspected, stage-managed by Felicity, she couldn't help feeling touched.

Felicity herself was wearing a slinky black cocktail dress, but Isabella was relieved to see that most of the others hadn't bothered to dress up either. Hugh and Simon had both gone native, it seemed, with check shirts and tweedy trousers, an effect magnified by a healthy-looking ruddiness around their faces. Lin wore a red silk blouse over black jeans, while Abi was in one of her retro Laura Ashley style frocks. And if she was in any danger of feeling underdressed there was always Peter, in a faded blue tee-shirt and ripped jeans.

"What would you like?" asked Hugh from his position next to the well-stocked drinks table. "We've got just about anything, I think."

"Just a glass of white wine for now, thanks."

She took her drink and relaxed into one of the deep armchairs next to the stone fireplace.

"Cheers," she said.

"To holidays," replied Simon.

"Mm. Absolutely. I don't feel as if I've had a proper break in God knows how long. I'm so looking forward to just sitting around doing nothing."

Peter laughed. "You've got a hope. Sergeant Major Felicity here has got the whole week organised like a military operation. Walks, excursions, and anyone falling down on the job gets put on washing up duty. Isn't that right, Hugh?"

"Most unfair," said Felicity, pulling a face. "Just because none of you are capable of organising anything, If it wasn't for me you wouldn't even be able to find your way down to breakfast."

"Just as well I like walking then," said Isabella. She smiled at her friend and turned to Simon. "Talking of which, how are the grounds? You both look like you've had plenty of fresh air."

Lin made a show of scrutinising her husband. "He always goes red when he takes a bit of exercise. It's because he's so unfit. Oi!" She ducked away from Simon's elbow. "But the grounds are amazing. There's this wonderful old wood, like an enchanted forest, you can't hear a sound except for the birds and so on, and then you follow this river along and you come to a lake, with a boathouse and everything."

"Apparently there are trout," interjected Hugh. "I'm intending to have a go there later in the week."

"Sounds fun, if you like killing things," said Peter.

There was an uncomfortable silence. Out of the corner of her eye Isabella saw Felicity glaring at him.

"Seriously, though," said Lin. "It's just a magical place, and there's loads still to explore. Perhaps we could do it together?"

Isabella nodded. "I'd like that."

She glanced out of the window. The sky was turning a rich shade of pink over the moors. The perfect sunset in the perfect setting.

She turned back to the others. "So, what are we going to do in the evenings?" she asked. "Felicity's brought some music, so we can party, but is there anything else to do here?"

Simon slapped his thigh. "Damn! I knew I'd forgotten something. I was going to bring my iPod – I've put all my old stuff on it."

"Thank God you didn't then," said Felicity. "Lin, really, I don't know how you put up with it."

Lin shrugged. "Earplugs," she said succinctly. "Either that or leave the house."

Everyone laughed.

"Bella's got a point, though," said Peter. "What are we going to do in the evenings? There's nowhere to go out to. Now, personally, I think it would be a great house for those old-fashioned party games. I mean, don't you think we should be playing charades, or sardines, or something like that?"

There was a sudden uncomfortable silence. Isabella wondered if everyone else was thinking, like her, of the last time they'd all played a game together – at the school quiz evening.

Hugh shifted in his seat. "Never been much for that sort of thing myself."

Felicity shook her head firmly. "Nor me," she said.

Peter looked disappointed.

Abi suddenly leant forward. "Guess what? Peter's getting a promotion," she said.

There was a murmur of congratulation, tinged possibly with relief at the change of subject. "That's great," said Isabella. "What to – deputy head or something?"

Peter shook his head. "Nothing that grand. Just head of department. Still, a step in the right direction. And a bit more money, of course."

"Terrific," said Simon, raising his glass. "And well overdue."

Isabella took a sip of wine and leaned further back in the chair. She studied the ceiling, an extraordinarily complex pattern of plaster tracery that she had not really noticed earlier. She tried to follow one particular branch, a vine that seemed to wind through other branches and squares of trellis across the whole room, wrapping itself around different objects along its way. She had the sudden illusion that if that one branch were taken out, the whole ceiling would come crashing down.

Were people like that, she wondered? If one individual were removed from any group, the nature of the group would inevitably change, but would it necessarily be the weaker for it?

Or were there some people whose departure served to strengthen those that remained? On the surface it certainly seemed so. But that too could be an illusion.

*

The next morning Isabella settled down with her laptop in what estate agents would probably call the library. It was in fact a tiny room, tucked away in a corner of the ground floor containing just a couple of bookshelves, a battered armchair and a small desk. It was quiet though, and the view from the window, of a narrow strip of grass giving way to woodland, was dull enough not be distracting. At least she wouldn't be forced to look at rhododendrons all day.

When she'd announced her plans at dinner the previous evening, she was greeted by an awkward silence. The others had agreed, subject to the weather, on an early start and an easy stroll on the moors up to the vast rocky outcrop of Haytor, and plainly they felt that she should join them. Felicity had tried to persuade her.

"But darling, the whole point of being down here is to explore the moors and get some fresh air. You can't sit here cooped up on your own the whole time."

"It won't be the whole time. Just the mornings. You're coming back for lunch aren't you? I'll catch up with you then, and share the afternoons."

"But what if we want to go out for the whole day? Do a really proper hike?"

"Then I'll probably come with you. But surely we don't have to map the whole week out in advance?"

They'd continued for a while, increasingly half-hearted protestations. But they knew her well enough to know that when her mind was made up she wasn't going to be budged.

It wasn't even as if they were going to miss her company — it was only for a few hours after all, and she was prepared to bet that by the end of the week they'd all be gagging for some space from one another. It was that they thought it was somehow unhealthy for her to be on her own, as if she were going to be brooding, wallowing in self-pity. To them, jolly hikes on the moor with so many people that you didn't have time to think was part of the process of 'moving on'.

They didn't realise, and for some reason she was reluctant to explain to them, although she was certain of it, that this period of being alone with her thoughts - facing up to her demons, almost – was absolutely key to her being able to move on.

Whatever that entailed.

She wasn't intending to do any serious writing this morning. Her first task was to sort the jumble of ideas swirling around in her head into something resembling a coherent story. To that end she had set herself the target of completing a plot outline, however sketchy, by lunchtime. Once that was in place she could start the fun part.

She assumed the laptop battery would be flat so she plugged it in and turned it on, scribbling a few notes in an old notebook while she was waiting for it to power up.

Then she stopped and stared at the machine in puzzlement.

Jake had bought the laptop about a year before his death so that he could work away from home. But to the best of her knowledge he'd never done such a thing; the only work he ever did, if you could call it that, was on the pc in his study. So the laptop had languished in a cupboard in the spare room, unloved and forgotten, and, she had believed, unused. But here it was with a username programmed in – JC.

Jake's initials - and his excuse for behaving like God almighty. Jake had used the laptop.

Her finger trembling slightly, she moved the cursor over the JC icon and clicked. A password request came up.

Not only had he used the machine, but he'd gone to the trouble of setting up a password protected user identity.

She tried typing in a few names that he might have thought of for a password – his own, hers, his pet dog when he was a child, even old girlfriends – but all came up blank.

Frustrated, she shook her head and abandoned the task. She was wasting valuable time. And for all she knew, there might be nothing inside – it might simply be that Jake had set the account up when he had first got his new toy, and never actually used the computer for anything serious at all.

*

Felicity rubbed the goose bumps on her arms and shivered. "God, this wind," she said.

"I told you you should bring a jumper," said Hugh. "Here – take mine."

"Thanks," she said, pulling it over her head. "My silly fault – I thought it was supposed to be summer."

"It's just very exposed up here, that's all. Look, it's worse on top. Those boys can hardly stand up."

She followed his gaze. Sammy and Tom, conspicuous in their bright red jackets against the grey of the stone, were clambering up the side of Haytor rocks. Even from here she could hear their excited cries and those of their mother, impotently shouting that they should take the path.

She and Hugh, together with Peter and Simon, had stopped for a rest, leaning against a cluster of weathered granite rocks a little to the side of the summit. Despite the wind, it was a gloriously sunny day, and they had clear views in all directions.

Hugh was now peering south. "I suppose that must be the Teign estuary," he said, pointing at a river valley in the distance.

She shrugged. "If you say so," she said.

She turned back towards the summit. Abi seemed to have given up haranguing the boys and was deep in discussion with Lin.

"I wonder what they're talking about."

Peter glanced at the two women with little interest. "Probably the same as we are."

"Which is?"

"Isabella. And Jake."

"But we aren't."

"No, but I bet we're going to."

Of course he was right. It was all but inevitable that they would end up talking about Jake and Isabella.

She sighed. "It is weird, though."

Peter turned to her. "What?"

"Us – the seven of us – without Jake. It's only the second time, you know, on our own."

Simon settled back and folded his arms behind his head. "I know what you mean. Last night at dinner – well, you know I'm not the superstitious type – but you could feel there was something missing."

"But perhaps he wasn't missing," broke in Peter. "Perhaps he was there, like Banquo – you know, the spectre at the feast."

"Not funny," said Felicity.

Peter's face darkened. "I hope you're not expecting me to pretend to miss him."

Hugh raised an eyebrow. "Didn't anyone ever teach you that it's not done to speak ill of the dead?"

"What, after the way I was grilled by the police, just because we had an argument at that stupid quiz evening?"

"We were all grilled, as you put it, even Isabella. It was hardly Jake's fault."

"Oh, come on! Bella's not here, let's at least be honest amongst ourselves. He was a creep, a nasty piece of work who made trouble wherever he went. Bella's better off without him and if we're truthful, none of us really care that he's gone."

Felicity stared at him. "Peter, that's an appalling thing to say."

She was genuinely outraged, even though part of her knew he was right. Or perhaps because of that. "If you hadn't noticed, poor Bella was absolutely devastated by the whole thing. Just because you couldn't get on with him."

"Oh yeah, and we all know how well you got on with him."

There was something in the way he spoke the words - almost as if he knew.

But he couldn't.

She felt herself beginning to blush. "What the hell do you mean by that?" She knew her voice sounded aggressive but she couldn't help herself.

Peter looked sullen. "Nothing."

Hugh was staring at him strangely.

"What?" said Peter, reddening himself.

Hugh spoke very slowly and deliberately. "I think we should all be very careful about what we say. For Bella's sake."

*

Suddenly they heard their names being shouted and the tension was broken. They looked over to see Abi gesturing that they should start returning to the cars. They got up and started ambling back down the hill, Peter lagging behind, still sulking.

"So how do you reckon it's going?" asked Simon. "With Bella, I mean."

Felicity shrugged. "Not bad, I suppose, as well as can be expected in the circumstances. Tomorrow, the actual anniversary is going to be difficult. I think we should make sure she doesn't spend all day sitting around moping on her own."

"Doing this book, I suppose. What's it about?"

She shook her head. "Not really sure – something autobiographical, I think. She's a bit cagey about it, with me at least. I think she thinks that I disapprove."

"Why shouldn't she write a book?" Peter's tone was belligerent. "It's supposed to be cathartic, that sort of thing, isn't it?"

"What, raking up the past? What's done is done." She paused, and when she resumed her voice was soft, almost contemplative. "Perhaps that's something you should bear in mind more often, Peter. For any number of reasons."

"Hear, hear," muttered Hugh.

Peter rounded on him angrily. "That would suit you very well, wouldn't it? The last thing you want is anyone digging around too much, disrupting your cosy little world. Keep a stiff upper lip, turn a blind eye, preserve the status quo at all costs, is that it?"

Hugh stopped in his tracks and turned round to face Peter, forcing the other man to stop as well. The others stood to one side, watching the confrontation with apprehension.

"Peter, I haven't the faintest idea what you're going on about, but I don't like the sound of it. And I also don't like the way you look at my wife. So get out of my face before I do or say something I'll regret. Okay?"

Peter glared at him and stepped round him to carry on down the hill. After a second the others followed, walking in an uneasy silence.

"I think you're all missing the point completely," said Simon eventually. "It's nothing to do with us - Bella's got to do what's right for Bella. If she wants to write this book then she has my full support. I mean, what harm can it do?"

Hugh shook his head. "You sound very sure of that, Simon. But I wonder if you've really thought it through?"

"Shut up, the lot of you!" Felicity stamped her foot in exasperation. "Just listen to yourselves. Let's just concentrate on why we're here, which is to help Bella get over this. And squabbling and accusations and muckraking isn't going to help anyone. So let's forget the past and let whatever sleeping dogs there may be lie in peace. For Bella's sake."

Then she added under her breath, "For all our sakes."

*

Isabella had become absorbed in her work, and was surprised to find when she looked at her watch that over an hour and a half had passed. She glanced back through the notebook over what she had done. It was a good start – you could hardly call it a proper plot outline yet, but the bare bones were there. At least when she came to sit down and actually write tomorrow morning she wouldn't be looking at a blank page with a totally blank mind as well.

She deserved a coffee.

She wandered into the kitchen. Bubs was preparing lunch, seated on one of the wooden benches, worn glossy with years of use, that ran on either side of the massive pine table that sat in the centre of the room. She looked up with a smile.

"Hi there – I'd heard you hadn't gone out with the others. What have you been doing, just chilling?"

Isabella shook her head. "Actually, I'm trying to write a book. I just thought I'd allow myself a bit of a coffee break."

She went to put the kettle on but Bubs stopped her. "No need for that, I'll make some proper stuff."

Isabella sat down at the table and looked around. "Thanks."

The kitchen was a strange mixture of old and new. The walls were lined with ancient cupboards, their doors cracked and warped with age, while two massive porcelain sinks took up nearly an entire wall. On another stood the inevitable Aga. Yet the wooden work surfaces were covered with state of the art equipment; microwave, blender, espresso machine, the works.

She peered into the bowl that Bubs had been working on. "Mm, this salad looks delicious. Where did you learn to cook like this? Last night's lasagne was just unbelievable."

"I did a cordon bleu course in my gap year. Are you into cooking?"

"When I have time. My mother's Italian so I suppose it's sort of in the blood. So what did you study at uni?"

"Psychology. Then I did a ski instructors' course between my degree and my masters."

Isabella found herself re-evaluating Bubs. "A woman of many talents. So what brings you to our table?"

She shrugged. "Just filling in. What I really enjoy is the skiing, but that's obviously a winter thing. Then what I think I ought to be doing is something in clinical psychology." She paused while she diced an onion. "And of course what my parents want me to do is find a rich husband, preferably in the City." She looked up and gave Isabella a conspiratorial smile. "They think this is some sort of huntin' shootin' fishin' chalet, and that there'll be loads of eligible stockbrokers here. So everyone wins."

Isabella smiled wryly. "I suppose there's a first time for everything."

Bubs gave her a shrewd look. "So what's your story then? Everyone seems great mates here but – well, I can't help noticing there seems to be something in the background. Something people aren't talking about?"

Isabella said nothing, and she continued quickly. "Sorry, just tell me to shut up if I'm butting in where I'm not wanted – I know I'm bloody nosy. It's just that you seem so – well - sad."

Isabella shook her head. "No, it's all right – and you're right – there is something." She took a deep breath. "Basically, my husband died. A year ago tomorrow, to be precise."

Bubs put the knife down, a look of concern on her face. "Shit, that's terrible. What was it, cancer or something, or an accident?"

"Nothing like that. He was murdered."

The look of concern changed to one of horror. "Christ, you're kidding. That's unbelievable. Do you – I mean, can you talk about it?"

She hesitated, and realised that she never really talked about Jake's death. Somehow the story had always gone before her, people warned lest they say the wrong thing or show the wrong emotion. She had never actually had to explain to a stranger what had happened. It felt strange having to do so now, with this cheerful young girl who knew nothing of her or of Jake, or of any of the rest of them.

Strange, but appropriate, today of all days.

So she sat down and told her tale, beginning with the concert at Kew, her frantic search, and how the young couple had stumbled over his body in the bushes. Then the police investigation - the futile quest for any forensic evidence on the sodden, trampled, ground, the endless interviews of her and the others, and the fruitless trawling through his papers and computer records. The inevitable spotlight of suspicion falling on her and the rest of their party, and all the other false leads. Finally the gradual waning of interest, first from the media, and then from the police, as other, more pressing cases came along, cases that might actually get solved.

Bubs sat listening with rapt attention, eyes wide in sympathy. "So you still don't know who did it?" she asked when Isabella finally fell silent.

Isabella shook her head. "No. Officially the case is still open, but they haven't got any new leads to follow. Apparently they think it was some sort of random mugging that went wrong. Though his wallet wasn't taken. I don't know."

She sighed. "The problem is, he was so drunk, and he always became a complete tosser when he was like that. He could easily have picked a fight with the wrong person. I don't suppose I'll ever know now though."

Bubs frowned. "But that's terrible. It's awful for you, and it's also really bad for you, psychologically I mean. It, like, keeps the wound open."

Isabella laughed bitterly. "Tell me something I don't know. But there's not much I can do, is there? I've tried pulling every string I can with the police, but they seem to have lost interest completely. The original guy in charge of the case has retired and I don't think they've even bothered to put someone else onto it. And there's not much I can do on my own is there?"

"I guess not. Poor you, though."

She hesitated, then continued. "Well, if there's anything I can do – I don't suppose there is, but sometimes it helps to talk to a stranger, you know, someone who's not been involved…"

Isabella gave her a tired smile. She was a good kid. "Thanks - it's a kind thought. But I think it's something I can only really deal with on my own."

Chapter 7

There was at least an hour until lunch, but she seemed to have lost her appetite for writing. It was as if the effort of recounting all the details of Jake's murder and the subsequent investigation had drained her of all her energy. Instead she curled up on the bed with one of the trashy novels she had brought with her. This was her idea of a holiday, she thought, kicking off her shoes and stretching her toes luxuriantly across the bedspread. No responsibilities, no pressures, just pleasing herself. For now, at any rate. She was uneasily aware that she had promised to go out with the others that afternoon. Some duties you couldn't escape.

Lunch itself was an untidy, boisterous, affair. Sammy and Tom were trying to outdo each other with tales of daring on the rocky slopes of Haytor. Though Peter seemed to be in one of his moods, all the other adults appeared cheerful and relaxed, energised perhaps by the unaccustomed freshness of the Dartmoor air. If anyone noticed that Isabella was more subdued they didn't say anything.

She found herself sitting between Simon and Lin.

"Sounds like a good morning," she said.

Simon nodded between mouthfuls of tuna and pasta salad. "Fantastic. I'm really stiff now, though. Out of condition. How about you, Lin?"

Lin shrugged. "Not too bad, actually. Tired, I suppose, but good tired. Not really stiff."

Simon gave a rueful smile. "The advantage of going to the gym three times a week. How about you, Bella – how was your morning?"

"Not bad," she said. "I made a start on my book and then had a coffee with Bubs. Then I read for a while. Very restful."

"Bubs," said Lin. "What sort of a name is that?"

Isabella shook her head. "I know – weird."

"It's a sort of English upper class thing," said Simon. "A lot of posh girls have got nicknames that sound like insults – Bumbles or Bubs, or Podge, or Pookie. Ask Felicity – she'll know."

"Actually, Felicity seemed a bit disapproving of it," said Isabella. "I think she'd rather call her Sophia."

"Perhaps that's because she's not really upper class," said Lin.

"Miaow!" said Simon.

Isabella, taken aback, looked at her. She hadn't spoken to Lin much since they'd got down here – come to think of it she hadn't had a proper conversation with her in months. She seemed different, somehow – harder, perhaps. Or perhaps it was she, Isabella, who was in fact different – noticing now for the first time things that had always been there.

As if sensing her gaze Lin suddenly turned to her and looked her straight, disconcertingly so, in the eyes.

"How are you, Bella? I know it's been a horrid time for you – are you feeling – well, you know..?"

Her voice was low, her face full of concern. She really cares, thought Isabella with mild surprise. She'd had many enquiries into her well being over the last twelve months, some embarrassed and awkward, some oleaginous with false sympathy. She reckoned she was pretty well placed to recognise the real thing.

"Better?" she finished. "Yes and no. The pain hasn't gone away, but it somehow feels further away, if you know what I mean. And some of the numbness has gone, as well, which is a good thing."

Lin hesitated before speaking. "You really loved him, didn't you?"

Once again Isabella was taken aback by her directness. "Yes, actually, I did. He wasn't perfect – he drove me mad sometimes, and I know he upset a lot of people." She paused. "I don't think I've ever apologised for that newspaper article."

Lin shrugged. "What's past is past. And it was hardly your fault, was it?"

"No, but... Well, anyway, we had our ups and downs, like everyone. But at the end of the day, he wasn't a bad husband. He liked to flirt but I genuinely believe he was always faithful to me."

An odd expression passed over Lin's face. For a moment Isabella thought she was going to say something, but before she had a chance Felicity's voice boomed down the table.

"Okay everyone, here's the plan. By general consent, everyone's knackered by that pathetic little stroll this morning, bunch of townies that you are, and we're planning a big all-dayer tomorrow, so we're going to take it easy this afternoon. So we're going to the twee little village of Widecombe, as in the fair. Sightseeing, shops, and a cream tea for those who want a heart attack. How's that sound?"

There was a general murmur of approval.

"What about you, Bella? Are you up for the tourist trail?"

Isabella shrugged and smiled gamely. Traipsing round a tourist trap was about the last thing she wanted to do. "Guess so. I haven't had a cream tea in years."

They got up to leave table and Isabella caught Lin by the arm.

"What was it you were going to say back then? Before Felicity interrupted us?"

Lin's face was blank. "Say? Nothing. I wasn't going to say anything."

*

Despite her misgivings Isabella enjoyed her trip to Widecombe, the small village in the centre of the moor whose annual Fair had become immortalised in the popular folksong of the same name. The village itself seemed overrated, she thought, nothing much but a handful of tourist shops scattered around a moderately attractive church. But the drive there, over the open moor, was magical. The colours and the textures, and the sheer size of it all, took her breath away.

On the way back she excused herself from Hugh and Felicity's small talk and leaned back into the corner of her rear seat, just watching the countryside roll past. It had been a long afternoon and she was pleasantly tired, and in normal circumstances she could easily have dozed off. But she was still vaguely unsettled by the discovery that Jake had possibly used the laptop.

They arrived back at the house and she trailed up the steps behind the other two.

"I don't know about you but I'm going to have a drink before I have a very long, very hot, bath," declared Felicity. Hugh grunted his assent.

Isabella looked at her watch and wrinkled her nose in thought. It was five thirty. "Actually, you know what? I think I'd rather have a cup of tea."

She ambled in to the kitchen and found Bubs preparing vegetables.

"Hiya," she said when she saw Isabella. "Good trip?"

Isabella shrugged as she put the kettle on. "If you like trashy souvenirs and fat American tourists. But no, it was quite fun actually. It's just that now I've started this book, I want to get on with it, and I hate wasting time."

Bubs nodded as she tipped a pile of sliced carrots into a pan. "Oh yeah, you said. What's it about?"

Isabella felt herself colouring. "It's about a woman whose husband dies of cancer, and how it changes her whole life – changes her, in fact." She saw Bubs' face and added hastily. "It's not autobiographical in any way. It's just something I think I can do."

Bubs shrugged. "Sounds good to me. So you've actually made a start, have you?"

"Not on the writing as such – just the plot outline. It's a bit annoying, actually. I brought an old laptop of Jake's down, meaning to do it on that. But I can't get into it."

Bubs looked puzzled. "How do you mean?"

"It's weird. It wasn't a machine that he actually ever used, or at least I thought he hadn't. But when I logged on I found that he'd set up a username for himself. Password protected. I tried a few obvious things, but none of them worked. It's all a bit of a mystery. Anyway, I mustn't keep you – I only popped in to get a cup of tea." She turned to go.

"Hang on a minute. Let's get this straight."

Isabella looked at her in surprise.

"You said earlier that the police had checked all his work and his computer records for leads, but that they all ended up as blanks, right?"

"Right."

"But did they check this laptop?"

Something cold seemed to slither down Isabella's spine. "No. They never saw it. And I never said anything because frankly I'd forgotten all about it. It wasn't with his other things." She sank back down on to the bench.

"Don't you see what this means? There could be something important in there – something that might help us find out what happened to him."

Isabella wondered slightly at the 'us' but put the thought aside for later.

Bubs was continuing. "I mean, perhaps he had enemies. Did you ever think of anyone who might have wanted him dead?"

Did Jake have any enemies? Was the Pope a Catholic?

"Look, Jake was an investigative journalist. He sometimes put people's noses out of joint. But the police went through all his published articles, and his pc, checking up on any likely candidates."

"But not his laptop. Maybe it was something to do with his personal life instead, that's why he didn't put it on the pc? Did he ever upset people in ways other than through his writing?"

Isabella was beginning to feel uncomfortable with the direction the conversation was taking. "I've already told you, Jake was no saint. He got pissed, he got into arguments, and yes, people got pissed off with him. But not enough to kill him, for Christ's sake."

"But someone did, didn't they? Kill him, I mean?"

Isabella suddenly felt incredibly tired. "Just where are you going with this? What are you getting at?"

Bubs looked at her hands. "Nowhere, honestly. All I'm saying is that you should look in the laptop. If there's nothing there, at least you won't have to worry about it any more. And if there is – well – you want to know, don't you?"

Isabella shook her head wearily. "Obviously. But I can't get in, remember? I suppose I could give it to the police. They have experts for that sort of thing."

"Maybe you'll have to, but I think it would be better to see if we can crack it ourselves first. I mean, you're probably right, and there's nothing in there that's any of their business. So let's at least try. What was the thing most precious to him that you can think of?"

"The most precious thing in Jake's life was Jake. And I've tried that, and all the permutations I could think of." Then, feeling she sounded mean, she added, "I also tried my name. And about all the family and friends I could think of."

"Damn!" Bubs shoved her face in her hands.

She appeared to be thinking furiously, but what about Isabella couldn't imagine. If she couldn't think of any keywords that her own husband might dream up she didn't see that a complete stranger could do any better.

Suddenly Bubs looked up. "People are much less random and more predictable about these things than you'd think. There are always patterns. What about work? Did he have any role models there, any people that he particularly looked up to?"

Isabella shook her head. "He was a freelance investigative journalist, I told you. He worked alone, he didn't even work for the same people all the time. And he was pretty contemptuous of most other journalists."

"Investigative journalists." Bubs got to her feet and started pacing up and down the room. "There must be some."

Suddenly she clicked her fingers. "I know – what about those guys who exposed Watergate? They got a Nobel Prize for it, didn't they? Surely Jake must have rated them?"

"Pulitzer Prize," said Isabella absently. "But yes, you're right, he did." She felt a surge of excitement. "But what were their names? God, I ought to know that."

"No idea, I'm afraid. If I was at home I'd get it off Google in a second, but out here in the sticks…"

They racked their brains for several minutes. Finally Isabella shook her head.

"It's no good," she said. "How annoying."

"Maybe one of the others will know?" suggested Bubs.

Isabella got to her feet. "It's worth a try. But I'd better not tell them why I'm asking. God knows what sort of lecture I'd get if they knew what we were up to."

Again, that strange 'we'. Now she was doing it. How did that happen?

*

She found Hugh, Felicity, Simon and Lin in the drawing room, drinks in hand, the women discussing the next day's outing, the men immersed in magazines.

"There you are, darling. There's some white wine open, or…"

"I'll be along properly in a minute, but I just need to check something," she interrupted. "For my book," she added, seeing the look of curiosity on her friend's face. "Can any of you remember the names of those two journalists who won a Pulitzer for Watergate?"

"What's this, another pub quiz?" asked Peter.

She flashed him a quick smile that she hoped didn't look too impatient.

"Bob Woodward and Carl Bernstein," said Hugh magisterially, looking up from his copy of Country Life. "Thought you of all people would know that."

"Thanks. Sorry. Just forgot."

She dashed out of the room, leaving the others staring at each other in bewilderment tinged with unease.

*

She grabbed Bubs from the kitchen and dragged her into the tiny library, shutting the door behind her.

"Woodward and Bernstein," she whispered.

"Well, what are you waiting for?" came the return whisper.

The laptop seemed to take an age to boot up but finally there was the login page. Isabella tried Woodward first, and was asked whether she had forgotten her password. Fingers trembling, she typed in 'Bernstein'.

The message flashed up immediately.

'Welcome JC.'

They stared at the screen. On the face of it there seemed nothing other than the usual icons, indicating the standard programmes that every computer came with.

"It doesn't look like he did use it," said Isabella. She didn't know whether she was relieved or disappointed.

"Try the 'My documents' folder."

The page popped up and Isabella felt the hairs on the back of her neck stand on end. There were the normal subfolders – My Music, My Pictures and so on – but there were also others that could only have been put there by Jake. Some of them seemed the obvious things that a journalist would work on - there was one called Politics, one called Sex Scandals, one called Conspiracies – but there was also one labelled Adultery, and a whole range identified only by a single capital letter. She clicked on Conspiracies, and the screen filled with lists of files – Dodi/Di, 9/11, TWA 800 – dozens of them.

"What's with the thing about conspiracies?" asked Bubs. "This lot reads like the index for wacko central."

Isabella shook her head. "Jake loved this stuff. Sometimes I used to think he was a complete fantasist. He was always seeing sinister goings on when there was nothing there."

"Except maybe he once saw something that was there."

Isabella clicked on one of the files at random. Page after page of clippings, jottings, references jumped out at her. "God, it's going to take for ever to go through this lot."

Bubs looked at her watch. "And I've got to get the boys' tea and then your dinner. Let's just see what else there is in general and look properly when we've got more time. Try the pictures folder – see if he kept anything there."

Isabella obediently clicked the folder open.

"Shit!" said Bubs.

Both women stared in shocked silence at the screen.

"Sorry, maybe you'd rather I wasn't here?" said Bubs after a while. She sounded embarrassed.

Isabella shrugged uncomfortably. "It's a bit late to worry about that now." She scrolled down. "Christ, how much of this stuff is there?"

"I'm guessing he wasn't gay, anyway. Did you know he was into this stuff?"

Slowly Isabella shook her head. "Not like this. I mean, he was always eyeing up women, but this… No wonder he never seemed to get any work done. Where did they all come from?"

"The internet, of course. Get his Favourites up."

After the galleries of naked women in the Pictures folder the list of Jake's favourite internet sites came as little surprise. You didn't need a diploma in technology to guess what Asianxxx.com might contain.

"I can't say I'm actually familiar with any of these but I think I get the general idea," said Bubs. She put her arm around Isabella's shoulders in an awkward gesture of sympathy. "I'm really sorry. This must be an awful shock for you."

Isabella wondered what she did feel. Disgust, nausea, embarrassment – but shock?

"I don't know," she said. "I mean, yes, I am shocked, I suppose, but in a way I'm not really surprised. If you knew Jake…"

Her voice tailed off. Bubs looked at her with concern.

"Look, perhaps this is all too much at one go? We can always carry on in the morning."

Isabella shook her head firmly. "No. I need to see what's there. I know you've got to go, but…"

"No, I've still got a few minutes. Let's try some of these single letter files then."

Not sure whether she was relieved to have the support or annoyed at Bubs's persistence, Isabella opened one at random labelled 'H'. It seemed to involve a doctor.

1995 – H. leaves after incident at N. general. Child died while under his care – negligence? Query: other participants? Exact position? BMA inquiry?

Isabella stared at it in bewilderment. "So what's this then? Who's H when he's at home?"

"Hugh?" suggested Bubs.

Isabella glanced at her in surprise. "No – Hugh's not a doctor. Simon is – but he's not an H. Anyway, what made you think of Hugh? There are millions of people who's name begins with an H."

Bubs said nothing for a few seconds. When she spoke her voice was very quiet and studiedly level.

It's simply that – well – it's a fact, isn't it? Most murders – I think it's supposed to be over 70 per cent -

are committed by people who knew their victims. And the only people who were there and knew Jake that night, apart from you, were your friends." She looked up at Isabella, her face solemn. "The ones in the drawing room."

Isabella stood up so suddenly that her chair toppled over backwards. As the other woman's words sunk in she felt rage course through her and she struggled for control.

"How dare you?" she breathed. "How bloody dare you? Those are my friends you're talking about. My best fucking friends in the whole world. Have you any idea what you're saying?"

Bubs was also on her feet. "I'm sorry – I didn't mean..."

"Just shut up! Shut the fuck up! The subject is closed. I don't want to hear you ever say anything like that again. Do you hear me? Never!"

*

Jake used to describe his wife's temper as like a summer storm – arising from nowhere, raging ferociously for a short while, then disappearing as quickly as it had arrived. That was in the days when they'd still spoken of such things.

Isabella reflected on this while she mounted the stairs to her room, already feeling guilty about her outburst towards a harmless girl who only meant well. Talk about an overreaction. But it had been an outrageous thing to suggest. Or at least that's what she told herself.

She ran herself a bath and settled herself into it, savouring the heat and fragrance, and went over the conversation again in her mind. She had, she decided, most definitely overreacted to what was, in reality, simply tactless thinking out loud. Bubs was, after all, just a young girl who did not know her friends as she did.

It was the porn that had got to her. The conspiracy theories and the rest were no more and no less than she would have expected from Jake, but what they had found in that pictures folder had really shaken her up.

But that was not really an excuse for her outburst. She needed to apologise.

On her way to the mandatory pre-dinner drinks she popped her head round the kitchen door.

Bubs was working at the table. She looked nervous when she saw who the visitor was.

"Hi," she said.

Isabella was never one to beat around the bush. "Look, I've just come to say I'm sorry. I was completely out of order. You were just trying to be helpful, and I – well, I shouldn't have talked to you like that."

Bubs looked relieved. "Oh, that's okay. I thought afterwards I'd been a bit out of order myself. They are your friends, after all – you know them infinitely better than I do. I'm afraid I do that sometimes – speak first and think later. And what I didn't tell you is that crime was sort of my thing at uni – I did a criminology module as part of my course? So I'm sort of interested." She paused, suddenly looking anxious again. "You don't mind? It's obviously…"

"It's not a problem," Isabella interrupted her. "Don't worry about it."

She lowered herself onto one of the benches. "The silly thing is that of course the same thing occurred to me. It did to the police, too. You wouldn't believe the number of motives they managed to drag up – everyone one of us had at least one, according to them. Me, because we argued a lot. Peter, because they always rubbed each other up the wrong way. Simon and Lin because he wrote a pretty shitty article about them. But you can't allow yourself to go thinking like that, looking at everyone with suspicion forever. It's not a question of loyalty even – it's just that you'd go mad thinking that way."

Bubs shrugged. "Of course. I understand. It was stupid of me to think that no one else would have thought of those things." She hesitated. "So, are you going to carry on going through that stuff on the laptop?"

Isabella nodded. "Absolutely. You were right about that at least – I'll never be able to relax if I'm always wondering what's in it. I'll carry on tomorrow morning."

Bubs nodded. "Cool."

Isabella got up to leave, then paused. She still felt bad about her earlier outburst, and wanted to make it up to the girl in some way.

It was obvious that Bubs was fascinated by the whole situation. She was already involved whether Isabella liked it or not. And surely there couldn't be anything in the laptop more shocking than the pictures they'd already seen.

"Do you want to help?" she asked, still not sure even as she said the words whether she was doing the right thing.

Bubs turned to her and smiled for the first time in the conversation. "Really? Are you sure? I'd love to if you don't feel I'd be in the way."

"Of course you won't. In the morning then."

*

The fresh air had taken its toll on those who had been out walking on the moors, and after dinner that evening almost all of the party expressed a desire for an early night.

Felicity and Hugh bid the others good night at the top of the staircase and went into their room.

She flung herself onto the bed and groaned.

"God, I'm exhausted. What an evening."

Hugh drew the curtains and sat down in an armchair facing her.

"It was certainly strange," he agreed.

On their arrival at the house they had asserted their 'droit de organisers', as Felicity had put it, and appropriated the master bedroom for themselves. It was far and away the best of the six bedrooms, beautifully proportioned, with a bay window overlooking the rear lawns and a huge four-poster bed. Earlier Felicity had used the Jacuzzi bath in the en suite to ease away the aches and strains of her first proper hike in years.

If only it had a minibar as well.

"Strange! That's one word for it. This morning she'd agreed to go out with us all tomorrow – she seemed quite keen on the idea, in fact. Then this evening she announces that she thinks she'd like to stay here on her own, if that's all right with us. Not very sociable, is it?"

Hugh shrugged. "It's probably the stress of the anniversary. It's obviously a difficult time for her."

She shook her head in exasperation. "Do you think I don't know that? That's why we're here, after all." She paused. "Why, do you think I was too hard on her?"

Hugh laughed. "No, not really. She knows you mean well. Anyway, she agreed in the end, didn't she? Once she realised that you weren't going to let her mope around on her own."

She thought for a moment. "But the odd thing was, I didn't get the impression that she wanted to be on her own – at least it wasn't the negative thing of not wanting our company. It was more as if she actively wanted to be here, rather than there."

Hugh considered that for a moment then nodded. "I know what you mean. But perhaps she's just getting into this book of hers."

He got up and started undressing for bed.

Felicity forced herself off the bed and started doing the same.

"I hope we're doing the right thing," she said after a while.

He looked at her. "What do you mean?"

"All this. It's so beautiful, and away from London, I thought we'd all be able to forget about everything down here, or at least that it'd be less in your face. But I've a horrid feeling that things are going to keep getting stirred up."

He went over to her and put his arms around her, stroking her hair and back. "Listen, things will settle down. It's all just very emotional for everybody just now. The main thing is to stay calm."

"You can talk, after this morning."

"I know – I just got provoked. I shouldn't have risen." He kissed her lightly. "It won't happen again - promise."

He went into the bathroom. She finished getting undressed and pulled on her dressing gown, then followed him.

"You were a bit harsh on poor Peter."

He snorted. "Poor Peter my arse."

"Oh, come on. He hates his job, he's got an unhappy marriage – he's been pretty unlucky. Don't you feel at all sorry for him?"

He rounded on her. "No, I don't, because it's not about luck. Everything that's happened to him is a result of his own choices. He chose to be a teacher, because it seemed like an easy option, and he liked the idea of the long holidays. And it was his decision to marry Abi. He could have chosen differently. If he'd really wanted you he had his chances, rather than hanging around whinging about it now."

She recoiled at the vehemence in his voice. After five years of marriage she had got used to his laid-back calmness, understated in a very English way. She knew of course that he got stressed, or rattled by things, just like anyone else, but he rarely showed it. To have him expressing his feelings so rawly was new – and faintly unsettling.

She shook her head. "I was never an option for Peter."

Not that he had realised that. Or did now, for that matter.

She steeled herself to ask the question that had been bothering her for most of the day.

"Why did you say what you said to Simon?"

He paused in cleaning his teeth. "I've already told you – I shouldn't have."

"But you did. Why?"

He sighed and turned to face her. She was surprised to see how serious his expression was.

"Felicity, has it occurred to you that Simon might have killed Jake?"

She wasn't sure what answer she had been expecting, or fearing, but this certainly wasn't it. She felt her jaw drop. "Simon? What on earth are you talking about?"

"Don't get me wrong, I don't know anything. But he was pretty upset about that article – especially the effect it had on Lin. And I reckon our Simon has hidden depths. He had the opportunity too."

"So did several thousand other people. Including us."

"True. But most of them had no motive."

She thought about that for a moment.

"Why haven't you said anything before?"

"What would be the point? There's no evidence, and I could be completely wrong. As you said earlier, what's done is done. Why stir things up?"

She sat down on a bath stool and laughed. "How funny."

He looked puzzled. "What's funny?"

She shook her head. "Nothing. I'm surprised you don't suspect Peter."

"Doesn't have the balls. Or a motive." He paused. "Has he?"

He spoke lightly, but something in his tone made Felicity feel that it was not a rhetorical question.

"He disliked Jake. Even resented him."

"A lot of people disliked Jake. And Peter resents everyone."

"Anyone would think that you don't like Peter."

He sighed. "I don't dislike him. I just get impatient with him."

They finished in the bathroom and went to bed. Felicity waited until he had turned the bedside lamp off.

"You haven't had any of those letters for a while, have you?"

She felt him tense beside her.

"No. Not since Jake died, actually."

"Coincidence?"

"Maybe. Maybe not. Who knows?"

"Very true." She snuggled up to him. "But all the same, I think it might be another one of those little things that it's best not to mention."

*

Isabella had lingered downstairs after the others had gone up to bed on the pretext of needing to get a drink of water. Once the goodnights were over and she had heard all their bedroom doors shut safely behind them she rushed into the library.

She'd anticipated opposition to her plan to stay in the next day, of course, but she hadn't expected Felicity to be so implacable about it. She probably could have stood her ground and won, but only at the expense of arousing altogether more interest than she wanted in what she was doing. And a part of her felt guilty – she knew that this whole trip had been planned for her benefit, and she didn't want to seem ungrateful. So she'd given in, with as good a grace as she could muster.

But the thought of waiting another twenty-four hours to see what secrets the laptop contained was too much. She would give herself a couple of hours tonight to see what there was, and if necessary carry on when they returned the next day. At least that way she might actually enjoy the walk, rather than being on tenterhooks the whole way round.

And this way she could do the preliminary work on her own. She liked Bubs, and in many ways it was refreshing to have someone to talk to who wasn't connected with Jake and the events of that terrible night. She felt bad about excluding her now. But she regretted that impulsive offer to let her help. She had the feeling that whatever lay in that laptop was between her and Jake, at least in the first instance. Anyone else would be an intruder.

She turned on the desk lamp and settled down in front of the laptop. Before her the window, so bright yet tranquil earlier in the day, loomed, a mass of impenetrable blackness. She shuddered and rose to pull the curtains, shutting out the night.

She heard a noise behind her and turned to see Bubs standing in the doorway, a look of surprise on her face.

"I thought I heard a noise in here," she said. "Are you starting now? I thought we were going to do it in the morning."

Isabella hid her frustration. "Change of plan. You heard them in there; there was no way in a million years that I was going to get out of that walk tomorrow. And I couldn't bear to wait another day."

Bubs came into the room and shut the door gently behind her. "Why didn't you tell me?" Then she saw the look on the other woman's face. "You want to do this on your own – is that it?"

Isabella felt awful. "I just feel – there's going to be private stuff in there. It doesn't seem right to have someone else here. Not now, anyway – maybe later."

Bubs shrugged. "That's fine, it really is. I mean, this is nothing to do with me, I know. But all I would say is that now is exactly the time when you might need some company. Let's face it - from what we've seen already, there might be some pretty nasty things on that computer. You might be in for a bit of a shock."

"After the last year, I think I can handle shock okay." But inside she was wondering whether Bubs might not be right. The thought of being on her own in the small hours in this room, with its deep shadows and almost palpable silence, was a lot less appealing than it had appeared in the warm, brightly lit dining room earlier in the evening. Most of her and Jake's privacy had been shot to pieces by the police investigation anyway. And she wouldn't even have got into the computer without Bubs' help.

"Oh, go on then. As you say, I might be glad of the company."

Bubs beamed. "Great. We'll need something to keep us going, though. What do you reckon – coffee, or I've just corked up a nearly full bottle of white wine?"

Isabella grinned. Bubs' enthusiasm was infectious. "The wine, definitely."

*

"There's no point in just clicking around randomly, we need some sort of plan," said Isabella, staring at the mass of folders on the screen in front of her. A tight knot had developed in her stomach.

Bubs nodded her agreement. "Why don't we get rid of the easy stuff first? These conspiracies, for example – most of them look like publicly available information, nothing to get anyone worked up about. Let's just check them and then we can concentrate on the more obscure stuff."

They started working their way through the files one by one. Bubs had been right, none of them seemed to contain anything very contentious, and they made rapid progress.

"I suppose if he really had found proof that the palace had ordered Princess Diana's murder or something he would have been in danger," said Bubs after a while. "But was he actually a good enough journalist to be able to do that sort of thing? No offence, but there doesn't seem to be anything very original here at all."

Isabella sighed. "He thought he was. But the realistic answer is no. He was too lazy, for one thing."

She ought to feel disloyal saying that sort of thing about Jake, she thought. For months that would have been the case. But here, in the intimacy of the tiny room, sitting in the small puddle of light created by the desk lamp, honesty seemed the only option. There was no more point in lying to Bubs than there was in doing so to herself.

After nearly two hours they had scanned all the Conspiracy, Politics and Sex Scandal files. And found nothing that even remotely indicated a potential motive for murder.

Isabella stretched back in her chair and yawned. Suddenly she started.

"What is it?" asked Bubs.

"I thought I heard something." Both women listened for a few seconds, then Bubs shook her head.

"I can't hear anything."

"Probably my imagination. All these conspiracies. Have you noticed how much more silent it is in the country? It's absolute silence – not a sound. It makes you realise that in London it's never really quiet. You think it is, but there's always a background hum of something. But here there's nothing."

Bubs yawned and rubbed her eyes. "I'm a country girl myself – I can't get on with London. Anyway, are we going to carry on? I can't stay awake much longer."

Isabella looked at her in amusement. "I thought you youngsters were supposed to be able to stay up all night clubbing?"

"Not when we've been up since seven getting your meals."

"Touché. Okay, let's just try a few of these anonymous files. If we can work out what at least some of them are about it'll give me something to think about while I'm striding through the bracken tomorrow."

They were much less easy to make sense of than the conspiracy files. Isabella clicked open one that concerned someone identified only as 'Y', and what might have been a dodgy property deal. There were several newspaper and web references, and a handful of dates and initials.

She stared at the few lines of script doubtfully. "I just don't see the point of this. If I understand what he's suggesting correctly, there was no crime or serious wrongdoing committed at all. There just isn't a story here."

"Perhaps it was work in progress."

Isabella shrugged. "Maybe. I don't know. Of course, we would be stuck in the middle of nowhere without the internet. Otherwise these links might give us an idea what this was all about."

"We can always pop into a town and find an internet café," said Bubs. "But why was he so secretive? After all, this was his private computer, and it was password protected as well."

"That's Jake for you, I'm afraid." She yawned and looked at her watch. "God, nearly two. I suppose we ought to turn in. Otherwise we'll get so tired we'll miss whatever it is we're looking for. Trouble is, I don't like leaving the job half done."

"I could always carry on tomorrow while you're out," said Bubs. "Only if you're happy about it, obviously."

Isabella's initial instinct was to say no. "I'm not sure about that," she said. "I sort of think I want to be there if anything's found."

Bubs nodded. "Fair enough, but it's all anonymous – even if I find anything interesting I won't know who it refers to. But what I can do is catalogue what's here – summarise it for you. Then when you look at it you'll be able to scan through it quickly and see if anything strikes a chord, or looks worth following up."

Isabella came to a decision. Bubs was right – it would save time, and on the strength of what they had seen so far, she was hardly likely to arrive home and find the solution to Jake's murder lying neatly on a plate.

"Okay," she said. "Go for it. You can go through all the document files and summarise them if you've got time. I don't think you need to go through the pictures, though."

They represented a different part of Jake's life. One that she didn't want to dwell on.

Chapter 8

Isabella woke the next morning to a persistent tapping. Her head felt thick and for a moment she couldn't remember where she was.

"Isabella? Are you awake?" Bubs' voice brought her up to date with a jolt. "They asked me to bring you some tea."

"Come in." She forced herself up onto one elbow as the other woman put a steaming mug on the bedside table. "Thanks. What's the weather like?"

Bubs crossed the room and drew the curtains. She pulled a face. "A bit grey, I'm afraid. Nothing like as good as yesterday. Looks like it might even rain."

"Brilliant. I have to go on a long hike that I don't want to do and I'm going to get drenched into the bargain."

"I thought you said you liked hiking."

Isabella took a gulp of tea. "You know what I mean. Am I the last one up?"

"'Fraid so. And you'd better get a move on – I'm about to serve breakfast."

*

Isabella felt like a schoolchild again as Felicity fussed over her, checking that her socks were suitable for her walking boots and that she had the right waterproofs. She knew, and appreciated, that her friends wanted to look after her, but this was ridiculous.

"For God's sake, Felicity, you must be getting broody. You're treating me like a toddler. Why don't you help Abi with Sammy and Tom if you need to get it out of your system?"

Felicity looked affronted. "I'm just trying to make sure we don't get to the middle of the moor and then find you've forgotten something crucial - you don't exactly look switched on this morning. Anyway, you know what Abi's like. She'd probably think I was going to do something unspeakable to her precious boys, and shoo me away."

Isabella giggled. After the misery of the last year, she had almost forgotten what fun her friends were.

That was one of the problems with getting older – people's lives diverged, and everyone was too busy with their own concerns. They just didn't make enough time for each other. Until, sometimes, it was too late. She resolved to make sure she had a good, long, gossip with Felicity at some point during the hike.

Unaware of her friend's slightly depressing musings, Felicity was continuing. "Seriously though, what's the matter? You seem completely in neutral this morning. Didn't you sleep well or something? Both of us crashed out immediately."

Isabella could hardly tell her the truth. "No, well actually I woke up in the night and couldn't get off again. You know – thinking about things."

Felicity patted her arm. "What you need is a fifteen mile hike through some bogs. That'll tire you out."

She went off to pester Bubs about the picnic.

"Bogs?" called Isabella after her retreating back. "What bogs? No-one said anything about bogs."

*

They set off in a convoy of three cars, Isabella travelling with Hugh and Felicity again. Once again they quickly climbed onto the high moor, leaving the trees and fields of South Devon behind them.

"Isn't this the way we went yesterday?" she asked from the back seat.

"To begin with," said Hugh. "We could go a different way but it's much further on the map. Not too many roads over the moor."

"In fact, we're not too sure that there are many in this direction at all," added Felicity. "After Widecombe this one looks as if it'll turn into a succession of dirt tracks."

"We'll be fine," said Hugh. "Where's your sense of adventure?"

Isabella settled back to enjoy the ride. However much they might all laugh at Felicity's tendency to over-organise, there was something very relaxing about being driven somewhere, for an excursion that she'd had no hand in planning, with a picnic that she had no hand in preparing. Some people – Jake in particular - had called her controlling, but she was only like that when she felt it was necessary, when no one else seemed in control. She loved the sensation of being looked after, of surrendering her time to someone she trusted. She didn't get the opportunity to do that very often these days.

Felicity's voice broke into her thoughts. "What do you think about the idea of us all doing the same sort of thing at New Year? Not here necessarily, though it might be fun, but somewhere with log fires and things, where there might even be snow."

Her immediate thought was 'let's see how this week goes first, shall we?' but that seemed churlish. Instead she hedged her bets.

"Might be fun. I'd have to let you know though. My mother is talking about a possible family reunion in Italy over Christmas."

It was only a small white lie. Her mother had talked about the possibility of such a reunion for as long as she could remember.

She could only see the back of Hugh's head but his face had obviously shown his reaction to the idea.

"Hugh is less keen," said Felicity. "Aren't you darling?"

He didn't answer for a moment as he manoeuvred the car past a tractor in a passing point on the single-track road.

"All I said was that I wasn't sure the dynamics of the whole group were as good as they might be with just some of us. I don't mean you, of course, Bella – we'd love to see you any time – but…"

"What he means is he'd do it if Peter and Abi weren't there," interrupted Felicity. "But we couldn't simply not invite them – it would be too unkind."

"But would it?" argued Hugh. "Let's face it, they have different priorities to the rest of us – the boys, for one thing. They wouldn't normally go on the same sort of holidays as us."

"That's because they haven't got the money we have," said Felicity, a hint of petulance in her voice. "Why does money have to dictate everything all the time?"

"Because that's the real bloody world," said Hugh, sounding exasperated himself. "People grow apart, Felicity. Their lives change for lots of reasons, money being one of them. Okay, you were great mates with Peter at uni, but what do you really have in common with him now, apart from shared history? If you met him now, do you think you would be friends?"

Felicity said nothing.

Hugh was right, thought Isabella, but he was wrong as well. Of course they had all gone their different ways, but that shared history would always be there, and it couldn't be replicated. Friendship was about more than just liking and being able to afford the same sort of holidays. And weren't people who surrounded themselves with exactly the same type of person generally pretty dull; unchallenged, secure in their own certainties, semi-comatose within their own little comfort zone?

She remembered the look on Peter's face as he had come up to give her a hug that first evening. Awkward, yes, embarrassed, but also genuinely warm.

"I think we're like family, us lot," she said. "We may not always agree, or even like each other all the time, but there's something between us that you can never take away. I think we're the stronger for it."

Hugh raised his eyebrows. "Maybe," he said. "And maybe not. You'd know better than me about that. But it wasn't really Peter I meant, anyway – it's Abi. You've got to admit that none of us have a lot in common with her."

"True," admitted Isabella. "I can't see her skinny dipping at midnight, can you Felicity?"

Felicity giggled. "I'd completely forgotten about that. No, I can't see that being her sort of thing at all. Or that she'd be that impressed if Peter suggested it."

"Forgotten what?" said Hugh, glancing at his wife. "More undergraduate high jinks? You've never mentioned this before."

"There's not much to tell. It was one summer vac – the four of us were hiking in Scotland," said Felicity. "One evening we all got pissed and Peter came up with the bright idea of going for a nude swim in the local loch. So we did."

"And?" asked Hugh.

"And what?"

"What happened?"

"Everything got cold and shrivelled, that's what happened," said Isabella. "Most unappealing."

Felicity turned and gave her an arch look. "Really? How interesting. Personally, I wasn't looking."

Isabella returned the look. "Actually, darling, I was talking about you."

Hugh laughed. "Touche! Not much chance for that sort of thing here, sadly. Not unless you fancy the river Dart by moonlight, or heading south to the coast."

Isabella sighed. "That's the awful thing, though, isn't it – everything has already headed south. If we tried it now it would be, so long water nymphs, hello walruses."

"Nonsense, darling," said Felicity. "We're both in perfect shape. Aren't we Hugh?"

"Absolutely," he said, winking at Isabella. "As is Lin."

Felicity punched him. "That was *not* necessary," she said. "Complimenting the two of us would have been quite adequate, thank you."

No one mentioned Abi, thought Isabella. No one needed to.

She felt an unaccustomed stirring of sympathy for her. Poor Abi – even in something as mundane as this she was the odd one out.

They continued to wind their way across the moors. Felicity had been right; the road was little more than a track. At least not many other people were mad enough to take it. The most serious hazards were the sheep and ponies that seemed to live out here. They appeared to have no road sense whatsoever; in fact the reverse – Isabella could have sworn that on several occasions an animal had deliberately stepped out right in front of the car.

At last they turned back on to what passed for a main road on the moor.

"Not far now," said Hugh. "We'll be there in a couple of minutes."

"Where exactly are we going?" asked Isabella. "You did tell me but I've forgotten."

"We're basically going to follow the river. There's a good footpath at first, though it'll probably get a bit rougher later."

"The theory being, that if we're walking along next to a large river, even we can't get lost," said Felicity.

"You may laugh, but that's a real consideration," said Hugh. "Especially if the mist gets up."

"I'm not laughing," said Isabella.

*

The convoy pulled into the car park. Isabella got out of the car and stretched, glancing up at the sky. It was a solid blanket of grey. Low clouds swirled around the tops of hills, obscuring the pattern of the landscape. She shivered.

"Are we sure about this?" she asked.

Hugh looked up from lacing his walking boots. "It'll be fine. We'll just have to make sure we stay below the clouds. Trust me."

Abi was reading the notice board with information for tourists.

"Hugh," she said, sounding alarmed. "There's an army firing range out there. It talks here about Danger Areas. Are you sure this is the right place?"

Hugh's rolled his eyes.

"The range is miles away, Abi. There's no chance we'll get that far. And if we did, it's well signposted. We'll be fine."

He spoke with exaggerated patience, as if to a child. Abi reddened but said nothing.

Personally, Isabella thought he was being a bit unfair on her. It was a perfectly reasonable question to ask, or at least it would have been if it hadn't been in that dreadful hectoring tone of hers. She wasn't that thrilled about the prospect of walking into a firing range herself. In the fog.

The first part of the hike was easy enough; a level path running parallel with but some distance away from the broad river. Sammy and Tom sprinted on ahead, hopping on the stones that littered the way, ignoring their mother's admonitions not to wear themselves out. The steady rhythm of the walking was soothing, and Isabella found herself thinking about the conversation with Hugh in the car. The reality was that there were many people who were important in anyone's life, but at any one time there were some whose importance was more in focus than others.

Take her mother, for instance. Like many Italian families they'd always been close – both her brothers still lived only a short drive away from their parents' home in Ipswich – but for some years now her visits home had been getting less and less frequent. Her life with Jake and the pressures of her job, often having to work at weekends, had left her with little spare time – or so she had justified it, both to her mother and herself.

All that had changed with Jake's death. Her immediate instinct had been to return to the home of her childhood – and stay there. It was several weeks before she could bear to visit her flat on her own – weeks more before she was confident enough about spending the night there to move back in properly. And all the time, there was her mother; never fussing, never asking anything in return, just a source of strength and security when she needed it most.

And then there were the others. Like the guy in the office who she used to have the occasional drink with after work. They were both married, and there was never any real danger of anything serious developing between them. But there had been a real frisson, and she had always felt that if things had somehow turned out differently, they could have been genuine soul mates.

But once again, that had all changed with Jake's death. At first she had put his sudden awkwardness down to embarrassment, the modern Englishman's inability to accept the cold realities of death and bereavement. She had seen it the faces of so many people, the overwhelming fear of saying the wrong thing stifling all attempts at anything but the most banal expressions of sympathy.

Then his awkwardness turned to avoidance and distance, and by the time her other friends had realised with relief that she was still a real person, and that they could stop treating her like an infinitely fragile piece of crystal, he'd become a stranger.

For a while, naturally, she was hurt and bewildered. Then she came to realise that what he felt for her was not dislike, or distaste, or disdain, or any of the other things it felt like at different times, but fear. Probably not consciously, but he was afraid, not of her as a person, but of her new status as a single female, a potential threat to his own domestic composure. Happy to flirt when he knew there would be no consequences, he was now unable to go back to a normal relationship (whatever that might be), for fear, presumably, that given any sign of encouragement she would remember his previous whimsy and take it at face value.

What she couldn't work out was whether this behaviour displayed colossal insecurity or colossal arrogance. Perhaps it was both. Either way it was yet another interesting module in her crash course on life.

*

Felicity watched her friend trudge along, head down, absorbed in her own thoughts. She itched to go and talk to her, bring her out of herself, but she managed to restrain the impulse. It was going to be a long day, and Isabella would be ready to chat at some point.

The path, having climbed away from the river and run along the side of a ridge for some while, now started to fall away again towards a stream that merged with the main confluence some hundreds of yards ahead of them. Hugh stopped and peered at his map.

"We've got to bear left a bit, I think, cross the stream, then there's a path that follows the river again."

Felicity looked where he was pointing. "Are you sure we can get across that?" she asked. "It looks like a swamp. That bright green always means trouble, even at this time of year."

"We'll be fine. A bit of water never did anyone any harm. That's why we've got boots on."

Isabella joined Felicity. "I hope he knows what he's talking about," she whispered. "A bit of water might not do you any harm, but a lot of water can. And that looks like a hell of a lot of water to me."

Felicity squeezed her arm. "He's normally quite good at that sort of thing," she said. "But why don't we stick together for a while? Then we can pull each other out of the boggy bits if necessary."

Hugh set off again and the party followed in single file, picking their way through the increasingly soggy grassland as best they could, occasionally calling out warnings or giggling as one or another of them looked like losing their balance. Felicity and Isabella brought up the rear.

"God, it's years since we did anything like this together," said Isabella as she grabbed hold of Felicity for support for the dozenth time. "How come you're finding this so much easier than me?"

Felicity smiled. "About the only advantage of all those damp weekends I used to spend with Hugh shooting, I suppose. I don't bother any more, of course. I let him go off and then I let my hair down. A girl can have so much more fun on her own."

Then her smile faded as she remembered one particular occasion when she'd attempted having fun without Hugh.

Isabella, concentrating on not losing her footing, was oblivious. "We should go off and have some fun together some time – you know, a girls' outing. We used to – why don't we any more?"

There was an obvious answer to give the widow of one year as to why she didn't seem to go out on the town much, but Felicity sensed that she didn't need telling that. Instead she said, "Well, those thirteen hour days of yours, six days a week, don't help, I should think."

Isabella sighed. "I know. I think that's one thing that's got to change. Something like – well, you know – it sort of puts things into perspective. It's just knowing what to do about it."

Felicity was surprised. "What, you mean you're thinking about quitting the law?"

"Maybe. Or maybe just doing something less full on – leaving the City perhaps. I'm not sure. It's something to think about." She frowned. "Anyway, I don't want to think about work now. Let's just enjoy the walk."

They continued in silence for some time. They eventually managed to cross the stream, a deep, winding tributary, far more vigorous than it had seemed from a distance. The path then narrowed and climbed again, until it ran below the summit of the ridge, occasionally dipping down towards the river below them. They saw people on the other side of the river, struggling along a track that seemed to alternate between thick gorse and barely passable bog. She was glad she was on this side.

Eventually the path broadened out sufficiently for them to walk side by side again.

"It's odd," said Felicity, panting slightly from the exertion. "It seems so peaceful, but it's hardly quiet. You can always hear the river, and when you get close it's almost deafening."

"I know what you mean," said Isabella. "I think it's something to do with it being natural. I've always found it strange that I can be lulled to sleep by waves on the seashore, even if they're crashing really loudly, but a dripping tap will drive me berserk."

Felicity suddenly giggled.

"What?" said Isabella. "What have I said?"

"Nothing. I was just thinking about that time we went to Brighton and Peter fell into the sea."

"Oh God, yes! What happened? I remember us all having to give him our sweaters and coats but I can't remember why."

"My fault, I'm afraid. I decided I simply must have a particular stone which was only visible when the tide went out. I persuaded poor Peter to try and get it for me, and he tripped and couldn't get out of the way in time."

"That's right. And it must have been freezing, too. It was the Christmas vac, wasn't it?" She smiled mischievously. "Poor Peter. You were always able to twist him around your little finger – he'd do anything for you. Still would, I expect."

Felicity didn't want to think about that. "Who were you with, anyway – some complete loser. Roger, was it, or Rufus?"

"Rupert."

"Oh yes, Rupert." She remembered now. Handsome but a complete dickhead. Just how Isabella had always liked them. "I wonder what happened to him."

"He's a barrister. Doing quite well for himself, apparently."

Felicity nodded. "Funny how things turn out – who does well, who doesn't, who you keep up with, who you don't."

Isabella looked up, surprised. "How weird. I was only thinking the same thing myself, earlier. And how some people are there for you when you need them, and how others you don't see for dust." She put an arm around her friend's shoulders. "But you - you've been such a good friend, Felicity."

"Well, that's what friends are for. Anyone would do the same."

Isabella shook her head. "Not like you. I've never found it easy to trust people but somehow I know you'll always be there. I can't tell you how grateful I am."

Felicity turned away. She didn't want Isabella to see the look of anguish on her face.

*

They'd fallen some way behind the others and when they rounded the next turn they found them sitting around the edge of the path on rocks or waterproofs. Hugh, Simon and Abi were pulling bottles and plastic cups from the rucksacks. Hugh looked up when he heard them.

"Thought this would be a good spot for a refreshment break – just a few minutes rest, have a drink. It's quite a view."

Isabella looked around her. He was right – the view was spectacular. They had followed the river round a huge arc, so the road and the village where they'd parked the cars were completely screened by the hills on the opposite side of the valley. The only signs of civilisation visible at all were a few sheep huts. Below them the ground fell away steeply, grass and gorse interspersed with jagged granite slabs. And far below, the river, black and silver, meandering its way along the floor of the valley.

But it was the view ahead that really took her breath away. She could see the path continuing to climb, up and up, until it disappeared, swallowed up into the swirling grey of the cloud. And in the same way, the cloud seemed to disgorge the river, which appeared as if from nowhere, snaking its way towards them, tumbling riotously over jumbled piles of rocks into the relatively peaceful pools beneath.

She stared. "I thought you said we needed to stay below the clouds?"

He frowned. "I know. I'm hoping that it's just a sort of passing mist – you know, the sort that comes and goes. We may even be able to get above it, like when you're skiing. In any event though, we'll be all right – we can't get lost so long as we stick to the river."

She looked up. It seemed to her that they would have to climb a hell of a long way to get above the cloud cover. It was broken, to be fair – every now and then a patch would clear to reveal a bleak stretch of rock strewn hillside, or occasionally one of the vast hilltop outcrops known as tors. But she could see nothing even resembling clear blue sky.

She shivered. "It's spooky. You can almost imagine that those are buildings up there. Monstrous, misshapen buildings, lived in by monstrous, misshapen beings."

He looked amused. "I'd never got you down as having an overactive imagination, Bella," he said. "Most unlike a lawyer. But in a way you're right. Apparently there used to be settlements up there – Iron Age or something."

She suddenly made a decision. "I'll tell you what, while you're having your rest, I want to pop up to that little tor just there. It won't take me a minute."

There was a chorus of protest. She batted it aside impatiently. "For goodness' sake, I'm not a child. I won't even be out of your sight. And if the mist does come down all I've got to do is come down slowly until I hit the path. I can hardly miss that."

"I'll come with you," said Felicity.

"No!" she said, more sharply than she'd intended. "Sorry, I'd just like to be on my own for a few minutes. I won't be long."

*

She started to scramble up the rocky slope. It was harder going than she'd imagined, and predictably enough, her chosen tor was further away than she'd thought. Eventually, though, she made it, and stood beneath the grey stone monolith with something approaching awe.

It was much bigger than it had seemed from below. A stack of huge granite steps jutting out from the hillside, it looked like a giant's pack of cards, petrified in the act of being shuffled. Occasional tendrils of mist reached down like fingers from the clouds, adding to the illusion.

Earlier in the day she had seen some small yellow flowers, and now she looked around for them again, but at this height on the moors only the hardiest plants survived; gorse and heather, bracken, and some strange spiky thing that looked like a sea anemone. Changing tack, she gathered an armful of small stones instead, and began to clamber up the side of the tor.

The mist had made the granite damp and slick, and she struggled to keep her balance with the added inconvenience of the stones. Then she was on the highest slab, fifteen feet across and flat as a tabletop.

She stood and looked around at the panorama unfolded in front of her, trying to catch her breath. The tor would make an ideal picnic spot on a more clement day. Today, however, she had a different purpose in mind. She carefully arranged the stones in a little pile in the exact centre, then she got down on to her knees and began to pray to her mother's God.

The stones were for Jake; a memorial, on this, the anniversary of his death. In memory of the good times, the Jake that she'd met and fallen in love with, rather than the flawed character he became, and never had the chance to change back from.

The prayers were for her.

She wasn't really sure what she was praying for. Some sort of release, perhaps, an ability to move on and get on with her own life, but she realised now that she would never be able to that while she was still haunted by not knowing how Jake's life had ended. She would never be able to forget the events of a year ago, any more than she would be able (or want) to forget Jake himself. But she had to be able to consign them to where they belonged, in the past. And that meant, perversely, confronting them – objectively and without emotion.

She'd been guilty, she realised, of beginning to idealise her husband. Though she'd always loved him, she had always been realistic about what sort of man he was. But without the daily reminder of what he was really like she'd chosen, consciously or unconsciously, to forget the more unpalatable aspects of the complex mosaic that made up Jake.

That was why the porn on the laptop had been such a shock. A year ago the discovery would have upset her, for sure, but she suspected that she would have greeted it more with weary resignation – as well as being angry, of course – than disbelief. But those carefully stored images of exploitation and degradation didn't fit at all with the image she had chosen to keep of her husband.

Now that the crude reality had been thrust so starkly in front of her she had no choice but to abandon her rose-hued spectacles, and face the truth and whatever consequences that followed.

But to face the truth, you first had to find it.

*

By the time she got down to the path again the mist was noticeably thicker. She found what sounded like a heated debate in progress.

"Oh come on," Peter was saying. "We've come all this way. We can't just give up now."

"It's not giving up, it's just being practical," said Felicity. "There's nothing brave or clever about being lost on the moor."

"We can't get lost as long as we follow the river, that's the whole point." He turned to Hugh. "Come on, Hugh – back me up here."

Hugh shrugged. "So long as we stay on the path it should be all right. But the path may get a bit vague later on – you know how it is on the moors."

Felicity tossed her head in exasperation. "But what's the point – you won't be able to see anything anyway."

"It may clear higher up – you said so yourselves earlier," said Peter.

"Let's ask Isabella," suggested Simon. "Any sign of it thinning out up there?"

She shook her head. "Just the opposite. I lost sight of you altogether for a few moments. Not the most reassuring experience."

"That settles it for me then," murmured Lin to no one in particular.

"Why don't we take a vote on it," said Hugh. "All those who want to carry on and see if it gets any better…"

He put his hand up, as did Peter, looking pleased. A moment later Simon followed suit.

"And us, and us," chanted Sammy, jumping up and down with excitement. "We want to go, don't we Tom?"

"Shh!" their mother urged. "This is something for the grown-ups to decide."

Felicity had folded her arms in disgust. "Men!" she said. "Those against…"

She jabbed at the air defiantly. Isabella and Lin contented themselves with a raised forefinger each.

"A dead heat," said Peter, turning to his wife and putting his arm around her. "So you've got the casting vote, love."

Isabella stared at him. He actually sounded excited by the whole thing.

And she thought she didn't get out enough.

Abi was looking embarrassed. "I really don't mind," she said. "I'll just fall in with you."

Peter looked triumphant.

"No bloody way," said Felicity before he could speak. "If you lot want to wander off into the mist you can do so, but I certainly am not. I'll stay here."

"You can't do that," protested Hugh. "If we do get above the cloud we'll want to go on. We could be ages."

"If," she said, with a heavy emphasis on the word. "If that happens, I'm sure one of the boys won't mind popping back to get us. But otherwise I'm staying put. What about you - Lin, Bella? You staying with me?"

Lin shrugged. "Why not?"

Why not indeed, thought Isabella? She nodded her agreement.

Then it occurred to her that this was the first time since – well, for a year - that she had seen the party get even close to a proper, full blooded row. Not that it meant that they hadn't been at each other's throats when she wasn't there, of course. But it was perhaps another sign of returning normality.

It was a funny thing to be pleased about.

*

The men set off, accompanied by Abi and the boys. Isabella, Lin and Felicity made themselves as comfortable as they could, sitting on waterproofs and using the rucksacks as back rests.

"Well if you ever wanted conclusive proof of women's superior intelligence, this is it," said Felicity, settling back and taking a bite out of an apple. "Mind you, I don't quite understand why Abi felt she had to go with them – she could have stayed here with us. I'm sure she'd have enjoyed it more."

"I expect it's her religion," said Isabella. "Something to do with the man being the head of the household and her having to respect him. She explained it to me once – headship, it's called."

Felicity looked surprised. "Respect? That's a good one. Only when it suits her, I'd say. I've heard her be really vicious to that poor husband of hers."

Isabella shrugged. She thought that if she were married to Peter she'd be a lot less tolerant of him than Abi was. But then Felicity had always had a bit of soft spot for Peter. Even if it was only from pity. Or perhaps guilt.

"I hope that's it, anyway," she said.

"Why?" asked Felicity, looking puzzled.

"I think she means that it's quite obvious that Abi doesn't really want to go tramping around in the mist with her babies," said Lin, leaning back and peering into the clouds overhead. "So if it wasn't the headship thing the only other possible explanation would be that she simply doesn't like us and didn't want to be with us."

Isabella grinned. Lin was normally so quiet that it was easy to forget that she could have such a sharp tongue. Easy to forget - and sometimes quite unnerving to be reminded of.

"Got it in one," she said. "Do you think she does like us?"

Lin laughed. "You've got to be kidding. Not that I can say it bothers me especially."

"Doesn't sound as if you care much for her. But I think it's just her manner, you know. Her heart's in the right place."

Lin turned to her and stared at her for a moment, her expression unreadable. "Maybe," she said. "But you don't see the way she looks at me."

Isabella was intrigued. "What do you mean?"

Lin shook her head. "You probably think I'm paranoid, but you don't know what it's like. Wherever Simon and I go, you can see people looking at us, looking at me like I'm some sort of cheap hooker. And then you see the surprise on their faces when I open my mouth and they find that I know words of more than one syllable. So they reassess, decide maybe I'm a high-class call girl instead. But Abi – she takes the biscuit. She just oozes disapproval from every miserable pore. Like I'm going to try to steal that jerk of a husband of hers."

Isabella was taken aback by the bitterness that had come into her voice. She glanced at Felicity and saw her own thoughts echoed on her face.

"I think she disapproves of everyone," she said, feeling even as she spoke that it was a somewhat lame response. "She certainly did of Jake."

"You're right, though, about that religion thing of hers," said Felicity, rather too quickly. "It's some real firebrand chapel she goes to. Hellfire and damnation for all sinners, that sort of thing. She probably thinks she's on some sort of crusade – she has to make us all repent of our iniquities."

"Or face the consequences," said Lin.

"The wages of sin are death," said Isabella, almost to herself.

Was that what had happened to Jake, she wondered? Had his sins caught up with him, and some self-appointed judge and executioner done what they saw as God's work for Him? It was an unpleasant thought. Or was it the other way around – perhaps Jake had been stopped before the fiery sword of journalistic justice exposed someone else's wrongdoings. It was certainly a more palatable notion, not least because it was probably the sort of dramatic exit that Jake would have wanted for himself. Albeit several decades later.

The trouble was, the implied martyrdom was meaningless unless people knew about it. In which case it was nothing less than her duty to discover the truth and reveal it to the world.

She wondered how Bubs was getting on with the laptop. She realised that, contrary to what she had been telling herself on the tor earlier, she didn't really know what she wanted. Part of her craved, more than anything else in the world, the release of knowledge. Yet another, growing, part of her feared it.

That was the trouble with seeking the truth. By definition you didn't know what you were looking for. So you didn't know whether you were going to like it or not until you found it.

She became conscious of Felicity's eyes on her, sympathetic yet curious. She gave an apologetic smile.

"Sorry," she said. "Miles away. What were you saying?"

"Just that it can't be easy for Abi. As far as I know Peter never goes to church - with her or anywhere else. So her religion teaches her to respect her husband, but it also teaches her that he is damned. So what's a girl to do?"

Isabella pondered. "I've never really thought about it like that, but you're right, it must be an issue for her. The Catholic Church is a bit more forgiving – so long as you make it to confession at least occasionally, you're all right. I suppose she just has to plug away at him and hope for the best. The sacrament of marriage is definitely sacred – a woman has to stick with her man."

"No matter what?" Lin turned to her and fixed her with her disconcertingly direct gaze. "Whatever he's like - whether he beats you, abuses you? Whatever sins he has committed, whether or not he is evil?"

It was strange to hear Lin, normally so down to earth, functional almost, use words that could have come straight from her mother.

She hedged. "I'm not talking about me – I'm saying that's what some people in the church would say."

"And infidelity? What if he was unfaithful? Are you supposed to stay with him then?"

Isabella smiled and shook her head. "You're asking the wrong girl now. I'm part Italian, remember? We put up with a lot but not that. I'd cut his balls off with a carving knife if I caught my husband screwing around. And I think Jake was well aware of that, don't you Felicity?"

She glanced at her friend and was taken aback by the expression on her face.

"Felicity? Are you okay? You look as if you're in pain or something."

Felicity shook her head as if to clear it. "I'm fine. Just a touch of cramp."

Isabella turned to Lin. "What about you, Lin? Would you stand by your man, no matter what he did?"

Lin nodded. "Oh yes. I can't speak for men in general. But I would definitely stand by Simon. Whatever."

"He's certainly devoted to you."

Lin gave a wry smile. "You could say that. Actually, it gets a bit claustrophobic sometimes." She looked at Felicity. "What about you? You'd stand by Hugh, wouldn't you?"

Felicity didn't speak for a moment, then she too nodded. "Yes," she said. "Yes, I rather think I would."

Isabella stared at them, puzzled. She couldn't quite put her finger on why, but something struck her as curious about the interchange. It was as if both women had asked each other a different, unspoken question, and found themselves in agreement.

Perhaps she was seeing too much. Perhaps she just felt excluded, a widow surrounded by married women. A foretaste of the years to come.

Suddenly Felicity shivered. "God – I hope they hurry up – my bum is going numb."

Everyone seemed to relax with the change of subject. Lin glanced up at the path.

"I can't believe they'll be much longer. That mist has come down even further. We'll be in it ourselves soon."

Isabella followed her gaze. She was right – barely fifty yards of the path was visible now. Her tor had disappeared from sight altogether. The mist seemed to have leached all the colour out of the already bleak landscape, and they now inhabited a monochrome world of featureless greys. And to make matters worse it was growing darker, implying that the cloud was thickening rather than the reverse.

"What shall we do?" she asked.

Felicity shrugged. "What can we do? We'll just have to wait for them."

The flashback was like a sickening blow to her stomach. Felicity's words, the staring out into the increasing gloom, reminded her of another time of waiting and watching. The mounting panic in the darkness, the feelings of helplessness and dread, the growing premonition that something was terribly wrong. God, was she condemned to relive that night forever?

The moment passed. There was nothing wrong here – just the English summer weather and the tetchiness that it induced in people.

Then the silence was shattered by the last sound she had expected to hear in the middle of the moor – a Mozart symphony as performed by a mobile phone.

"Christ, that made me jump," said Felicity, fumbling in her backpack. "I'm amazed there's any signal out here."

After a short conversation she put the phone away again. "They're on their way back," she said. "Ten minutes, he reckons."

She plunged her hands deep into her pockets and forced a smile. "Bloody weather, eh? Whichever idiot had the bright idea of holidaying in Devon anyway?"

Chapter 9

By the time they got back to the house it was pouring with rain. Isabella hurried in with the others, aching for a hot bath and a change of clothes. Before that, though, she had to know what, if anything, Bubs had found on the laptop.

To her annoyance she heard voices coming from the kitchen. Peter and Abi had got back before them, and Abi was discussing – or more accurately, instructing – Bubs on what the boys should have for tea. She turned as Isabella entered and gave her a quizzical look, as if challenging the intrusion into what she considered to be her territory.

Isabella ignored her.

"Hi Bubs," she said in as nonchalant tone as she was able. "How's it going? Had a good day?"

"Not so bad," came the reply. "Big shopping trip this afternoon – stocked up for the next couple of days."

Meanwhile, over Abi's shoulder she gave a regretful shake of the head.

"It gets busy now, though – the boys' teas and your dinner to get ready. I'll be looking forward to having some spare time in an hour or so."

Interpreting this as 'sorry, can't talk now, but I didn't find anything anyway –let's catch up later,' Isabella smiled and left, aware of Abi's curious stare following her out of the door.

So, Bubs hadn't found anything. But there was something about her manner that had struck Isabella as odd – a hesitancy, perhaps, or even nervousness. It might simply have been awkwardness at Abi's presence, but it was not as if either of them had said anything remotely suspicious sounding. And Bubs was normally the epitome of jolly, self-assured, confidence. Isabella went back to her room puzzled, and slightly disturbed, by the encounter.

*

Later, a little before the hour now officially prescribed for cocktails, she came downstairs, and was surprised to find a hum of conversation coming from the drawing room. She tried sneaking past but Felicity caught sight of her and called out.

She stuck her head through the doorway. The entire party was there, except for the boys. More stage management, she thought.

Felicity was holding a champagne bottle, looking solicitous. "We thought we ought to mark the anniversary, not just in mourning, but also to celebrate his life some way. Drink a toast or something. So as this was his favourite tipple…"

Isabella tried to hide her impatience. "That's a really kind thought. But I just need to check something with Bubs. Won't be a sec."

She went into the kitchen. Bubs was putting the finishing touches to a bowl of what appeared to be trifle. She looked uncomfortable when she saw Isabella.

"Hi there," said Isabella. "Everything okay? I know you're still busy but I just had to know. Did you find anything?"

For answer Bubs wiped her hands and picked up a loose folder lying on the dresser.

"Here you are," she said. "I've copied out the relevant bits from all the files we didn't look at yesterday. None of it makes much sense to me, I must say – in most cases it seems to be a collection of circumstantial bits of evidence that someone may have done something wrong. Nothing really copper-bottomed as far as I can see anywhere. And on top of that everyone is identified by just one initial."

Isabella flicked through the stack of papers with growing dismay. Jake thought he had evidence, though it looked pretty flimsy to her, that someone identified only as 'G', obviously some sort of official, was taking backhanders. There was a suggestion that 'P' might be cheating on his wife with another man. And an 'S' had taken over all of their joint business when his partner had died in a suspicious car accident.

It was garbage. No wonder he never got anything published if this was as good as it got. So the laptop had been a dead end. She didn't know whether to laugh or cry.

"Is this it?" she asked. She looked up to find Bubs staring at her.

"What?"

Still Bubs said nothing.

Isabella felt a cold, hard, lump forming in her chest.

"What is it?" she insisted. "You found something else, didn't you? Tell me."

Bubs shook her head, but not in denial. "I didn't know what to do. I even thought of deleting it, not showing you, but that didn't seem right somehow."

"What is it?" Isabella struggled to control her alarm. She just couldn't imagine, after everything else they had found on the laptop, what could cause the reassuringly down to earth and practical Bubs to react like this.

"You'd better see for yourself."

Bubs led her into the library and starting typing into the laptop. Then she pushed it towards Isabella.

"I'm sorry," she said. "Of course, it could be fiction. But it doesn't really read like it."

Isabella sat down in front of the laptop and started to read.

'For possible future use as 'First Person Experience' article – Sunday supplements, women's mags etc. Change names obviously!!!'

The exclamation marks were Jake's little joke to himself – she had seen him use the technique before. Her heart sinking, she read on.

It was in diary format; a description of an affair, written in the first person, with someone called 'F'. The first entry started with their respective backgrounds, the relationships between them and their respective partners, and how they had first become involved - after an encounter at a school quiz evening. Then their meetings were covered, in a fair amount of detail, from which she deduced that Jake had been fairly pleased with how things had gone.

After that the entries had grown shorter – F, to Jake's outraged astonishment, had ended the affair. The file ended with the cryptic *'Poss. rethink ending.'*

So Jake had had an affair. And it was very obvious from the detailed descriptions who with. There could be no doubt that 'F' was anyone other than Felicity.

The room reeled around her. She lurched back, sick to her core.

"I'm sorry," said Bubs.

She nodded briefly, then rose to her feet. Her rage gathering by the second, she stormed towards the drawing room.

Felicity was standing in the middle of the room, the champagne bottle still in her hand, a worried look on her face.

"There you are," she said. "We were about to send off a search party. Have some..." Then she registered Isabella's expression. "What on earth's happened? What's wrong?"

"You were fucking him, that's what's wrong!" She was aware of other people in the room, of gasps of surprise and protest, but she ignored them. "You two-faced bitch - how can you just stand there and ask me what's wrong?"

Felicity had gone very pale. "No!" she said.

"You deny it? Really?" Isabella stepped closer so that her face was almost touching her friend's. "Look me in the eyes then, and deny it properly. Go on."

Felicity shook her head and slumped back into an armchair.

Isabella moved forward until she was standing over her. "You bitch. All that talk this afternoon about best friends." Tears began pricking at her eyes. "And all the time you knew that you'd..."

"It wasn't like that!"

"What was it like then? No – don't tell me." The tears were now flowing freely down her cheeks. "I just can't believe it – you of all people – fucking my husband and laughing at me behind my back. And what about everyone else? Did they all know as well?"

"No!" Felicity was crying now as well. "No-one else knew – I swear. Ask them."

Isabella looked around the room. Simon seemed to have gone into deep shock. Peter had gone nearly as pale as Felicity, while Lin was staring at the tableau in disbelief. Only Abi seemed to be enjoying the situation, leaning back in her chair and surveying the scene with an expression that was very nearly smug.

Isabella wanted to punch her.

"I knew," said Hugh.

All eyes turned to him.

Felicity gaped. "You did? How? And why didn't you say anything?"

He nodded slowly, as if considering the matter. "Because I loved you."

He leaned over and took her hand, then kissed her gently on the cheek. Sobbing, she buried her face in his shoulder.

Isabella looked at the pair of them and wanted to scream. She was the wronged party and Felicity the one screwing around, but it was Felicity who was being comforted, like she was some sort of victim. There they were, having their tearful, loving reconciliation. But she couldn't do the same with Jake, even if she'd wanted to, the lying, adulterous bastard.

Because some fucker had murdered him.

It was all so fucking unfair. Everything and everyone – even her supposed best friend – had conspired against her.

Felicity turned away from Hugh's shoulder and fixed her with miserable eyes. "I'm so sorry," she mouthed.

A red mist seemed to descend over Isabella. She saw the champagne bottle, still grasped in Felicity's hand, and she realised that she wanted nothing more than to grab it and smash it into the blonde head in front of her, again and again and again, until there was nothing left but…

…a bloody pulp, lying in the soaking grass, under a rhododendron tree.

Appalled, she turned and ran upstairs to her room.

*

She lay on her bed, tears of rage and frustration drenching the pillowcase. Eventually the anger ebbed away, leaving a yawning black void of emptiness. One by one all the props of her life were being kicked away. She didn't think she had ever felt so alone.

There was a soft knock at the door. Someone evidently didn't want to disturb her if she was sleeping, or perhaps they were simply unsure of their welcome. She looked at her watch and was surprised to see that less than an hour had passed.

"Who is it?" she called, annoyed that her voice sounded so broken and weak.

"It's Hugh," came the reply from behind the still closed door. "Can I come in?"

She sighed. Part of just wanted was to be left alone. But she also wanted answers, and Hugh obviously knew a lot more about what had gone on between Jake and Felicity than she did.

"Be my guest."

She pulled herself into a sitting position and smoothed her hair as best she could. She knew she still looked a mess and didn't really care, but she hated appearing vulnerable.

Hugh came in and stood at the end of the bed. His mouth kept twitching, as if he was unsure whether to wear a reassuring smile or look suitably serious.

She gestured at the armchair impatiently. "For God's sake sit down – you look like one of those hospital consultants who's wondering how to tell you you've got three days to live."

This time he did smile.

"I just wanted to see how you were," he said as he sat down.

She snorted. "Well, what do you expect me to say? That I'm fine, thanks, having just heard that my best friend was shagging my husband?"

He shrugged. "Stupid question, I suppose." He paused for a moment and appeared to study his feet. "So how did you find out?"

She had expected the question, and had been racking her brains for a plausible answer. She shook her head in what she hoped was an offhand manner. "I was thinking about my book, just going over stuff in my head, some of Jake's old things, and suddenly everything clicked. You know, things Jake had said. It suddenly seemed obvious."

She studied his face for his reaction. It didn't sound very convincing to her, and she could tell he found it difficult to believe as well. Her only advantage was that he would have no idea how she could have found out otherwise.

Before he could think of a suitable reply she shifted back onto the offensive. "I must say you seem pretty calm about it all. Though I suppose you've had longer to get used to the idea. But two things. You still haven't said how *you* found out. And I still don't get why you didn't say anything."

He nodded. "It's only fair that you know. Until this evening I only knew part of the story – I didn't know the how or anything, just that there had been something. I'll come back to how I knew in a minute. Felicity has just filled me in on the rest."

Isabella listened intently as he ran through the conversation at the quiz evening, the lunch and the assignation at the hotel. It confirmed what she had already learned in all the major details, although there were interesting differences in perception of some things, such as the quality of the hotel (and, she got the impression, although Hugh was too tactful to say as much, of the sex.)

She didn't let on that none of this was new to her though. She knew she was going to have to work out something more convincing to explain how she knew about the affair, but she sure as hell wasn't going to tell them about the laptop.

Then he got onto the part of the story that she didn't know.

"It was when I got back from the States that I knew something had happened. She met me at the airport and took me out to dinner, which was strange enough in itself, but it was her manner that was really different. It was like going out with a girl again – affectionate, even lovestruck, but somehow diffident, as if she was unsure of how I felt about her. All the cynicism, the ennui of the Felicity I'd known over the last few years had gone." He paused and shook his head ruefully. "Of course it didn't last – a few weeks later she was back to normal, but that evening was really something special. She even told me she loved me."

He paused again, his eyes unfocussed, remembering. "And then, the next morning there was a letter telling me that she'd been having an affair. With Jake."

Isabella jerked upright. "A letter? Who from?"

He shook his head. "I don't know – it was anonymous. But what was really weird was that I'd been getting anonymous letters before – one a month or so for over a year. At first I thought it must be the same person, but the style was completely different. So it must have been nothing more than a weird coincidence."

Really weird, thought Isabella. If it was a coincidence.

She had briefly wondered why the police had found no indication that Jake had been having an affair when they swarmed over his last few weeks, but dismissed the matter as irrelevant. She'd thought that the only living people who had known of it were Hugh and Felicity, and it was hardly surprising that they'd kept their mouths shut. But now she knew that at the very least there was one other person who'd been in the know. So why had they kept quiet?

"What were these other letters about?"

Hugh shook his head again. "That's not important. The point is, you asked me why I didn't say anything to Felicity."

He leaned towards her, his expression taut.

"Of course I was furious when I first read that letter – furious and absolutely gutted. I was beside myself – I didn't know what to do. So I bunked off work for the day and went off to the park, and walked around, or sat, all by myself, all day, just thinking. And I came to realise two things. First, that the affair had most probably been over before I even knew about it. Felicity's behaviour that evening was exactly that of someone who felt enormous guilt and contrition, and desperately wanted things to be back the way they were. And the second was that I loved her and didn't want to lose her over something like that. Don't get me wrong, I'm not trivialising it, I was totally distraught. But did I want to lose her for something that was a mistake, that she already regretted? No. I didn't."

She nodded slowly. It sort of made sense. But somehow it also sounded too pat – like a prepared answer.

She put that to one side for now. "I'd still like to know what was in the other letters."

He sighed. "Okay. Since we're doing heart to hearts, I might as well tell you. Years ago I was in partnership with a friend of mine – Mark. The business was doing well, and we got an offer to buy it at a very attractive price. I was all for doing so, and using the money to move on and set something else up, but Mark wanted to stay with it. We fell out over it – it was stalemate. Then, while he was on holiday in Spain he had an accident – his car went over the side of a cliff. He didn't stand a chance, apparently."

He paused, glanced at his feet, then continued. "They never came to any conclusion over the cause of the accident – there were no other vehicles around, and it was a sunny late afternoon. Personally I think he'd had a bit too much to drink at lunchtime, but it's still open as a suspicious death. Anyway, I obviously had control of the business then and was able to sell up – his estate got its share, and I thought that was the end of the story – admittedly a rather sad one. Then a couple of years ago I started getting these letters alleging that I had somehow caused the accident."

Something clicked in Isabella's head. She grabbed the folder of Bubs' transcripts, which she'd been clutching like a lifeline throughout her confrontation with Felicity and had brought upstairs with her, and started flicking through them.

"Here we are," she said, passing him the relevant sheet. "Does this look familiar?"

He read it through quickly, then again at a slower pace. The he looked up at her, an expression of bafflement on his face.

"Where on earth did this come from?"

She shrugged. "Just some old papers of Jake's I was going through. Mostly rubbish."

He handed the sheet back to her and nodded grimly.

"Rubbish indeed. God knows how he got hold of it, or why. But at least we know now who sent me those letters. I suspected as much, oddly enough. I still can't see what he was trying to achieve, though."

He held himself stiffly but Isabella could sense his anger. She didn't blame him.

She suddenly felt as if the room had become freezing. She pulled her arms around her and shivered. "What did they actually say? Were they threatening?"

He shook his head. "No, that was the strange thing. They never threatened exposure – not that there was anything to expose, anyway – they didn't ask for money – nothing. It was as if he was just toying with me."

She took that in. Jake had just been toying with him. It had all been a game. Well, that sounded like Jake all right. But what a nasty game to play.

She wondered how many more revelations about her husband there were to come, how many more she could take. Her remembrance of him, only a little while ago a splendid monument growing stronger and more enchanted with each passing day, was proving to be nothing more than a rose-tinted illusion. A fragile edifice, becoming ever more so as brick after brick was pulled away.

She pulled herself together. There were still things that she didn't know, and that she had to find out, however unpalatable the answers might be.

"But this last letter was different, you say? You're sure about that?"

He nodded. "No question. The writing style was similar, but not quite the same, and it had a totally different tone. Not threatening in any way, and not at all gloating - more shocked, or outraged, if anything. It was as if the writer sympathised with me, was on my side."

"Did you keep it?"

"No. I threw all of them away as a matter of course."

"And you never said anything to Felicity? Or anyone else?"

"No. Not until this evening." He paused, twisting his hands together awkwardly. "You know what Felicity's like. She's impulsive and she gets bored easily, but she's a good person really. Sometimes she makes mistakes – we all do – but I took the view that she'd learned a lesson from this." He paused again and fixed a sad gaze on Isabella. "And she's genuinely very fond of you, you know. I don't think she's ever stopped regretting what she did – to both of us."

It was with difficulty that Isabella held her tongue. Not as much as I'm going to make her regret it, she wanted to say. But this was the wrong audience for that sort of thing.

It was a strange situation, she reflected – that she, the betrayed wife, was being comforted by the cuckolded husband might seem straightforward enough, but for him to be trying to convince her of his wife's good nature was bizarre in the extreme. And maybe Felicity had learned her lesson. It would certainly explain why she'd been so attentive over the last year.

While Jake, of course, had not had a chance to learn his lesson.

Boy, would she have taught him a lesson if he had been here. But he wasn't, and all of a sudden she felt sick of the whole thing. Sick, and exhausted.

There was still one thing left to clear up.

"You've absolutely no idea who sent the other letter?"

He paused in the act of getting to his feet. "I've had a few thoughts – nothing concrete though."

"Really? Who?"

He shook his head. "I wouldn't like to say without thinking it through some more. I've no evidence, after all."

Isabella felt her frustration mount. "Well, can you think about it, then? Really try. It's important."

He shrugged. "Sure. Anyway, I'd better get down to dinner. Are you coming down?"

She shook her head. "I don't think so. Can you get Bubs to bring something up?"

"Okay."

He turned towards the door, stopping when she continued speaking.

"It really is important, Hugh. Because that letter means that there's at least one other person who knows all about this, and that person has kept very quiet. And I'd like to know why."

*

Isabella stood by the window, staring out into the gloomy shadows of the woods and the moorland beyond. Its blackness matched her mood, and she fancied that in some way it helped calm the turbulence in her mind.

Despite her exhaustion, she was restless, and found she couldn't stay seated for more than a few seconds. She was toying with the idea of taking a shower when there was a knock on the door.

It was Simon, carrying a tray prepared by Bubs. She looked at its contents - warm asparagus followed by baked salmon, accompanied by a full bottle of chardonnay with one glass.

She gave a wry smile. "Good old Bubs – she doesn't want me to die of thirst, does she?"

He put the tray down. "Well, you're still on holiday – no reason to deny yourself what pleasures there are." Then he frowned. "I know I'm not your GP, but I was wondering if there was anything I can do to help? You've had quite a shock."

She heaved a sigh. "Thanks for the offer, Dr Rayner, but I don't suppose you've got any pills that will give me my husband and best friend back, have you? No? Didn't think so."

She threw herself into a chair and poured herself a large helping of wine.

"Why, Simon, why? That's what I want to know. Come on, you've known both of us for ever – how could she do this to me? She's supposed to be my best friend, for Christ's sake!"

He eased himself onto the edge of the bed. "I can understand how you feel. But why are you focussing on Felicity? It's not as if she's solely to blame, you know."

Isabella felt her jaw tighten. "Jesus, Simon, I don't need to be told the bloody obvious. Of course I'm mad at Jake too. He behaved like a complete shit, and if he was here now I'd probably murder him myself. But I don't know – I would genuinely have expected better from Felicity. I think I actually feel more let down by Felicity than Jake."

Simon's pleasant, open face betrayed his shock.

"That surprises you?" she asked.

He shrugged. "A bit, I suppose. It's just that…"

"The sanctity of marriage, is that it? Okay then, try this for size. He cheated on me, but she cheated twice – once on Hugh, and once on her supposed best friend. That's me, Simon. Do you know what she used to say to me? We'll stay friends forever, Isabella. Friends forever."

She was aware that her voice had risen and that she was beginning to sound hysterical, but she didn't care. She wanted to cry and she wanted to hit someone, anyone. She knew that none of this was Simon's fault, but she had to have some outlet for her rage and frustration.

It was just his bad luck that he was there.

He sat, staring at her mutely, and her anger subsided again.

"The thing is, you can't conceive of being unfaithful to Lin, can you? Or of her letting you down like that?" He shook his head. "She really can do no wrong in your eyes, can she?"

He coloured. "You make me sound naïve, but I'm not. In my job you see all sides of life. I know nobody's perfect, that you have to accept people as they are. But when you know someone that well, you trust them and they trust you... It's something very special. I'd do anything for her."

His words were an unsettling echo of Lin's that afternoon. These days it was unusual to find a couple so fiercely loyal to one another - and slightly frightening. She tried to remember if she'd ever felt that passionately about Jake. She didn't think so.

She looked down, twirling her wine around in the glass. "I know – you're both very lucky."

"Oh God, I didn't mean to..."

"Jesus, Simon!" she interrupted him. "Can you just stop pussy-footing round me for just one minute? You're as bad as Hugh – you don't all have to treat me as if I'm made of some precious crystal, you know. I knew what Jake was like. I knew what sort of person he was, and if I'm honest I probably knew what he was capable of. I just didn't know about this, and I need time to get my head around it, okay?"

He got up to go. "Fair enough. Will you be coming down later?"

She shook her head. "I really don't think I can face everyone this evening."

He hesitated. "You know you can't..."

She felt another flash of irritation. "Hide myself away forever?" she said. "I'm not a bloody child, Simon."

The anger dissipated as quickly as it had appeared. He was a good friend, only trying to help.

She sighed. "I'm fine, really I am. You go and have dinner with Lin. I'll be more sociable tomorrow – I promise."

It was probably her imagination, but it seemed to her that he couldn't get out of the room fast enough.

*

She had two more visitors that evening. Bubs came to clear away the empty plates, even more subdued than earlier, plainly feeling guilty for stirring things up. So she summoned up a smile, and told her that she had done the right thing, and that it was always better to know than not.

She almost believed it herself.

And Bubs looked relieved and went, leaving her on her own again.

Then, much later, when she was tucked up in bed attempting to read a book and thinking about whether it was worth even trying to get to sleep, there was a tentative knock on the door.

It was Lin. At first she said nothing, just came and sat by the bed and took Isabella's hand, staring at her with that strange intensity she had.

Isabella felt slightly embarrassed, uncomfortable even. "I'm not an invalid, Lin," she said.

Lin reddened and withdrew her hand, and Isabella felt instantly guilty.

She reached out and patted Lin on the arm. "Sorry, I didn't mean to be sharp. I'm just a little raw this evening."

Lin grimaced. "I'm not surprised. It was enough of a shock for us, God knows what it must have been like for you."

"Shocked would be a bit of an understatement, I think it's fair to say. How are the rest of them?"

Lin cocked her head. "Hugh and Simon are doing their English stiff upper lip thing – you know, trying to pretend that nothing's happened. A bit silly, really. Peter's being a bit strange – he seems to be sulking, as if he's the one with something to be upset about. I assume it's because he and Felicity used to have a thing going themselves once, but that was ages ago, wasn't it?"

She nodded. "Yes, it was. But the problem is, I think he'd still be interested now if he had the chance."

Lin appeared to consider for a moment. Then she sighed. "Poor Abi. I suppose that explains a lot."

It was an unexpected response, given what she had been saying about Abi that afternoon. But then, Lin was always full of surprises.

"What about Felicity?"

"I think the phrase is, she looks as if she wants the earth to swallow her up."

"Good," said Isabella. She was aware that she sounded petty but didn't care.

Lin eyed her for a few seconds before answering. "This is probably not what you want to hear, but you know that it was Jake who made the first move, don't you?"

She sighed. "Yes, I'm aware of that. Is it supposed to make a difference?"

Lin shrugged. "I'd have said so." Then, as if that concluded the matter, she continued, "Anyway, the only person who seems to be enjoying herself is Abi. She looks like she's just won the lottery."

Isabella smiled wryly. "I'll bet. Her God is a vengeful God – very Old Testament."

Lin looked puzzled.

"I mean Abi always likes to see sinners get their come-uppance."

Lin nodded but said nothing. She seemed lost in thought.

The silence grew. The thick walls and ceilings of the old house muffled any noise there might have been for downstairs. Isabella yawned.

Lin jumped to her feet. "Sorry, I'm keeping you up. I just wanted to check you were okay. And say, you know - I'm sorry."

Isabella managed a tired smile. "That's all right. Tell the others I'll be down in the morning, okay?"

*

After that she had spent a long time lying awake. Images kept revolving in her mind – Jake's shameless computer account of his adultery, Felicity's face when confronted, her conversation with Felicity about friendship on the moor – and then the rage would come back again, forcing the blood to pound round her head. Sleep was impossible.

Part of her said she was being unfair. According to Hugh, who had as much reason to be aggrieved as she did, Felicity had felt - how had he described it? - 'guilt and contrition' almost immediately. In any event, Simon was probably right - she should be feeling angrier with Jake than with Felicity. It was he who had made wedding vows to her, not Felicity. And of course, she would have been, had he been there – it was just that he wasn't, and Felicity was.

And some of the anger came not really from jealousy, she came to realise, but from the sense of humiliation, that Felicity – and Hugh, for Christ's sake! – had known for over a year that Jake had been cheating on her, while she had remained in not so blissful ignorance. They had known more about her own husband than she had – and that hurt.

But the biggest part of her said that none of this took away from the fact that Felicity – supposedly her best friend - had betrayed her. However bad she felt about it, however many times she said she was sorry, she'd still done it, and it was simply not acceptable behaviour. Screw around if you must, but you didn't do it with your best friend's husband. It just wasn't done.

Then her thoughts turned to Hugh, rerunning her conversation with him over in her mind. And the more she thought about it, the more she came to realise that there was something not quite right about it. He was too calm, too in control. After all, he was in much the same boat as she was – his wife had been unfaithful with someone who if not exactly his best buddy, was certainly someone he would have considered a friend of sorts. Yet while she was spitting with rage, he was, apparently, sitting down calmly considering his options.

It wasn't so much how he was now that bothered her – he'd had a year to come to terms with the situation and make his peace with his decisions. And as she knew herself even the sharpest of pains began to dull over that length of time. It was what he had told her about his reactions at the time that did not quite ring true. Was it conceivable that a man who became convinced of his wife's infidelity would be able to shrug it off as some sort of minor indiscretion, a mistake that she'd made and thought better of, like buying a dog on impulse, or painting a room the wrong colour? Didn't men feel, just as much as women, a sense of ownership of their partners, that would be outraged by someone else taking possession of them, even on a single occasion? Wouldn't Hugh feel unmanned and violated by the very idea of his wife with another man?

Mature reflection, it was true, might give rise to the sort of cold, logical analysis that Hugh had described. But not immediately. Not within hours of being told.

His immediate reaction must have been the same as hers. He would have wanted to do something. He would have wanted to shout and scream at Felicity, and make her feel the same pain and humiliation that he did. He would have wanted to confront Jake.

And he would have wanted to hurt him, just as he himself had been hurt.

That was the thought that chilled her blood, and made that room, so cosy in the summer sun, seem the most comfortless place in the world.

Either he was the coldest, most unemotional man on the planet, to be that clinically analytical so soon after discovering what for most people would have turned their world apart. Or he was a wimp, who would roll over and accept anything to avoid confrontation and jeopardising what remained of his relationship. Neither of these chimed with the Hugh that she thought she knew. It was possible, of course, that it was some combination of the two – a man so in love and so besotted that he quite calmly decided to accept a compromised marriage rather than none at all. It would be a lot to stomach, even – or especially? - for an old school Englishman like Hugh, but it was possible.

Or perhaps, he was a liar.

Chapter 10

The next morning Isabella awoke slowly from a deep sleep to the sound of heavy rain drumming on the roof of the conservatory outside her window. She came to with the vague feeling that something was wrong, and it took her several moments to remember. That jolted her fully awake.

She heaved herself out of bed and pulled the curtains open, peering out at the morning. She was greeted by a vision of low, rolling clouds, all but obscuring the moors in the distance. The woods and lawns of the lodge's grounds, all bright greens and golds only two days ago, were now a rain-lashed mishmash of varying shades of grey.

If ever there were a day for staying in bed, this was it.

But she had things to do. Far from explaining things, yesterday's revelations had just opened up new questions, and she needed answers. And besides, she didn't want the others to think that she still couldn't face them.

Correction: she didn't want Felicity thinking that she couldn't face *her*.

She took a long shower to sluice the cobwebs away. As she was drying her hair she peered out of the window again – it seemed to be raining harder than ever.

She pulled some clothes out of the drawer. It was lucky that she'd packed for a variety of different weather conditions; the temperature seemed to have dropped about ten degrees since yesterday. She chose jeans and a loose sweater – comfort over style today. And it was not as if she was likely to be venturing out of doors.

She could hear conversation coming from the dining room as she went downstairs – evidently she was, as usual, one of the last up. She took a deep breath, more nervous than she would have expected, and walked in.

The conversation died, then resumed more loudly with a chorus of excessively cheery greetings and enquiries about the quality of her night's sleep. Only Felicity dropped her head, staring desperately at her toast.

Despite the forced bonhomie the atmosphere in the room was about as relaxed as in a courtroom waiting for the jury to return. Isabella wasn't sure what they were expecting – her to launch herself at Felicity with the bread knife, perhaps? But that wasn't on her agenda for today. Today was for thinking – information gathering, and ice-cold, objective, thinking.

She smiled and muttered something meaningless, then fetched herself some coffee and cereal from the serving table. She sensed some of the tension drain away from them as she failed to cause the anticipated scene. Hugh waited until she was seated before giving her what she supposed was meant to be a sympathetic yet reassuring grin.

"How's it going then? Did you manage to sleep through the storms?"

"Storms? I didn't even know we had any. I slept like a log," she lied, conscious of the puffiness around her eyes.

"That's great," he said, keeping his expression neutral as he glanced at her. "The bad news is, though, the forecast says it's going to stay like this all day, so we're just talking about what we might do. Unfortunately it's likely that most of the moor is under fog, so that limits us a bit. Any thoughts?"

Evidently he was the elected, or self-appointed, spokesperson; a patently unthreatening figure who could understand how she was feeling. She wondered how much of that was really true. After all, what did she really know about the urbane, cultured man sitting opposite her? His background, public school and then a short stint in the army, was one that put a premium on discretion and doing the right thing. Yet it also bred a streak of ruthlessness, and taught its men to conceal their feelings. He could be genuine, or he could be hiding the most terrible secrets. Evidently Jake thought he was onto something. She just didn't know.

She decided to put aside her suspicions for now. She needed time on her own to think things through properly.

"I think I'll probably work on my book. I'm a fair weather walker at the best of times, but this rain is just ridiculous. How about the rest of you?"

Peter gave her a wan smile. He didn't look as if he'd slept well either. "Abi's decided that we should take the boys to Paignton Zoo."

"Well, we can hardly keep them cooped up here all day." Abi's voice reminded Isabella of a hectoring schoolteacher. "It would be all right for you – you'd just disappear somewhere and I'd have to look after them all on my own. I'm afraid that it's one of the consequences of going away to the middle of nowhere. Some people never seem to think of others when they make these decisions."

Hugh, Simon and Lin stared in disbelief at her crassness. Even Felicity looked up wearily for a moment, incredulity written all over her face.

Peter looked around the room for a moment, savouring the situation. "As I was saying," he said with heavy irony. "Abi's decided."

She glared at him and he returned her look sullenly.

It was evidently the continuation of a longstanding argument, thought Isabella. She wondered when the explosion would be. The malicious side of her hoped that she would be around to witness it.

At least one of her fears for this week, that she would feel excluded by all the visible and public displays of married bliss, was proving groundless.

"I'll go stir crazy if I stay in all day." Lin turned their attention back to the matter in hand. "Personally I'm going to read this morning and hope it clears up this afternoon, but even if it doesn't I'm going to go out later to explore the rest of the grounds."

Hugh nodded approvingly. "I'll tell you what I'm going to do – I'm going to try fishing that lake we've got here. I'll do the same as Lin – give it a few hours to clear up, probably pop down later. Anyone else fancy joining me? There are plenty of waterproofs and wellingtons in the back porch."

Simon shrugged. "Maybe – I'll see. I'm still pretty stiff from yesterday. I've got a few things to catch up on first anyway."

All eyes slowly turned towards Felicity, the last to declare her plans. She glanced up and shook her head. "Me? Oh I don't know – I'll probably just read here for a bit. I might pop into the shops later."

All her confidence, all her vivacity, seemed to have deserted her. She seemed to have aged ten years overnight. Isabella tried to feel sorry for her, but failed.

She hadn't tried that hard anyway.

*

After breakfast she popped her head around the kitchen door. Bubs, as she'd expected, was busy with the dishes and the preparations for the day ahead. She looked up and gave Isabella a friendly smile.

Isabella put a finger to her lips. "I'm going to be in the library all morning. Come and see me when you can – we've got things to discuss."

She found it more difficult than she'd imagined getting back into the book. It had only been the day before yesterday that she'd been sitting here, jotting down ideas, planning the structure, but so much had happened since then that it seemed half a lifetime ago. The whole premise of the book, the grieving widow looking back on her life with her now dead partner, and using those positive memories to begin making a new life for herself, suddenly seemed cringe-makingly naïve. All her own experiences and memories were now irreversibly polluted by what she had learnt.

It was just another thing that had been taken away from her.

She tried being stern with herself, telling herself that she wasn't the sort of person to wallow in self pity, but it didn't work. She was too tired and too confused – and too let down. After a while she just lowered her head to the desk and quietly wept.

It was in that state that Bubs found her. She came into the room, and seeing Isabella, simply pulled up a chair and put her arm around her.

"You know," she said after a while. "When you first told me about Jake, it was awful of course, and I felt terribly sorry for you, but it was just a story – like hearing something on the news. But now – now it seems horribly real all of a sudden. It's not a story, it's something that actually happened – is still actually happening. It's alive. I find that scary enough – God knows what it must be like for you."

Isabella pulled herself upright. "Sorry," she said, fumbling for a tissue. "I'm not normally like this."

"That's probably because you don't normally have to deal with this sort of crap every day."

She managed a weak smile. "I guess not. It's just – I don't know where to turn – who I can trust. I thought I could trust Felicity, then when I was talking to Hugh I started wondering about him. I've even got to thinking that Simon and Lin are acting weird. I don't know if it's me or if the whole world really is against me."

Bubs gave her a hug. "I'm not – you know you can talk to me."

"Until you turn out to be an axe murderer or something."

The weird thing was, Bubs was right – she did feel she could talk to the kindly, slightly plump, not especially pretty, girl sitting next to her. It was a strange feeling, and she didn't quite understand it. She'd always been a sociable person, but never one of those people who made friends – real friends – easily or quickly. Yet now she was readily sharing the most traumatic aspects of her life with someone she'd known for about three days. It had to be the shock, and the feeling of having the rug ripped away from under her.

Either that, or she was turning into a lesbian.

Unaware of her thoughts, Bubs nodded seriously. "Fair point. Meanwhile, though, do you want to tell me about it?"

She nodded and took a deep breath. "Okay. Perhaps you can make sense of it."

She ran through her conversations with Hugh and the others the previous evening. By the end Bubs was deep in thought.

"Well?" asked Isabella expectantly. "What do you think? It's obviously new information – part of me is wondering whether I should go to the police, but I'm not very keen to do that without something more concrete. Especially after last time." She shuddered at the memory.

Bubs looked up slowly. This time her face was genuinely serious.

"I think you're right – I think this opens up a whole new can of worms. And I think it could be even more important than you realise."

There was something in her tone that sent a shiver down Isabella's spine. "What do you mean?" she asked. For no apparent reason she suddenly felt uneasy.

Bubs spoke slowly and deliberately. "I mean, that we've now got three people who potentially had a motive for Jake's murder."

"Three?" repeated Isabella, appalled. "Good God – I'd only thought of one. Who else?"

"Actually, at least three – excluding you, of course."

"Thanks – that's good to know."

"I'm serious though – you talked about going to the police? If you did, all they would see was a big fat motive for you that they hadn't heard about before. They probably wouldn't believe that you didn't know about Jake's affair, and might not even bother to look any further than you."

Isabella shuddered again. "Okay, you've convinced me – no police. But who else then?"

"Think about it. Hugh, obviously, as you said. Then there's Felicity. If Hugh's right and she really did regret it and was fearful for her marriage, might she not want to get rid of the only person – that she knew of at any rate – who could ruin everything for her? Perhaps he'd already threatened her with exposure – we don't know."

Isabella nodded slowly. "I suppose that makes sense – potentially, anyway. There are still a lot of 'ifs' in there."

"Obviously. And then the final person is the one we don't know – the person who cared enough about the affair to write that letter to Hugh."

"*If* he's telling the truth about that," interrupted Isabella.

"Okay, but let's assume he is. After all, if he is innocent he'd have no reason to lie about that. So, who other than you and Hugh would be bothered by it?"

Isabella shrugged. "I've no idea. But why does it have to be someone who cares? Aren't these letters often just written by busybodies?"

"Yeah, but remember what Hugh said about it? The tone was shock, outrage, all sympathetic to Hugh, wasn't it?"

Isabella nodded.

"That sounds like someone who cares. So who could that be?"

Isabella sat back and took a deep breath. "I suppose the person most likely to be shocked would be Abi – she'd definitely disapprove of adultery and want people to suffer for it."

"I'd thought of her, too. How did she take it all yesterday?"

Isabella scowled. "I think Lin's phrase was, she spent the evening looking like someone who'd won the lottery."

"That would figure – but what about when she first heard? Did she look surprised?"

Isabella tried to remember. "I think so."

"And do you reckon she's a good enough actress to fake that?"

Isabella shook her head emphatically. "No. But maybe it wasn't surprise - maybe it was just delight at everyone else's discomfort."

"Hmm." Bubs doodled on a scrap of paper for a few moments, looking dissatisfied. "I suppose then we can't rule her in or out at the moment."

She paused again. "But there is someone else – someone actually more plausible, I reckon."

"Who?" asked Isabella, her heart racing. Part of her was amazed that her surprising new best friend seemed to have such insights into people that she'd only known a couple of days, part of her irrationally offended. But then again, maybe that was the advantage of detachment. Perhaps she herself was just too close to the whole thing.

"Peter," said Bubs quietly.

"Peter?" repeated Isabella, startled. "Why?"

"You said it yourself – he's got a soft spot for Felicity. Even I can see that – his eyes follow her around all the time. He looks like a hungry puppy. That's probably one of the reasons that Abi's so chipper, by the way – she must see it too, and I bet she's well pleased to see his idol cut down to size. But coming back to the point, if he's had a crush on her for years, how do you think he's going to react to seeing her get off with another bloke?"

Peter. It was possible, she supposed.

She had known Peter for over fifteen years. Back when they were students he had been almost the dominant member of their group – popular, entertaining, self-confident. He was the man most likely to succeed, but somewhere along the line it had all gone wrong. While the friendship had endured, he had somehow lost status in the group, mainly because he had lost his own self-respect. It obviously didn't help that he felt that all his friends were more successful than him. And, of course, he probably felt like a loser in the marriage stakes as well – always comparing Abi's plainness with Felicity's glamour and panache.

But murder? To the best of her knowledge Felicity never gave him the slightest encouragement for his yearnings. Could jealousy still be strong enough to drive an essentially decent, peaceable man to kill? And if that were the case, why had he not attacked Hugh before?

It was as if Bubs was reading her mind. "It would have killed his dreams," she said. "Perhaps part of him was still hoping that one day Felicity would come to her senses and run away with him? Maybe it was that dream that kept him going – anyone can see that he's not a happy man. And the most surprising people can be dangerous when their dreams are destroyed."

"Perhaps. I just can't see him committing murder – it wouldn't be in character."

"I see. So which of your mates do you think it would be in character for to commit murder?" asked Bubs wryly.

Isabella nodded. "True," she acknowledged. "I suppose I mean that I could maybe see him writing that letter to Hugh – though God knows how he found out about it in the first place – but I can't see him killing Jake. And don't you think that they would be sort of mutually exclusive? Either you write a letter like that to make trouble, or you take things into your own hands. You wouldn't do both. I don't think I would, anyway."

Bubs laughed. "From what I've seen, I don't think you'd do either – a face to face screaming match would be more your sort of thing. I see your point, though - and I suspect you're right more generally."

Isabella frowned. "What do you mean?"

"I mean that your argument doesn't just apply to Peter – for anyone to write the letter *and* kill Jake would be odd."

"So the letter's probably a red herring?" said Isabella in dismay.

"Not necessarily. That person obviously knew about the affair long before anyone else. They may also know something else – something would lead us to the murderer."

"If it's connected to the affair at all, that is. We don't even know that for sure."

They fell silent, each alone with their thoughts. "So what now?" asked Bubs after a while.

Isabella sighed. "I don't know. You're right, I don't think I should go to the police. But there are so many possibilities, so many permutations. This bloody affair might not be behind the murder, but it's the only thing we have to go on at the moment. I think the two most important things I could do are to find out whether Hugh is lying, or at least not telling the whole truth, and to see if we can narrow down who sent him that letter. In other words, I have to go and talk to Hugh."

"On his own, or with Felicity?"

She considered. Her instinctive reaction was to recoil against the very idea of talking to Felicity. She didn't think she was ready yet to sit down and have a civilised conversation with the woman who had betrayed her. But Felicity had been at the centre of the whole thing. There were things that she knew that no one else did.

"I don't know," she said at last. "What do you think?"

Bubs didn't hesitate. "I'd try and see them both together," she said. "They'll have to be more honest with you with each other there - unless they've already sort of agreed to gang up against you, which I don't think is very likely. And Felicity will be very, very keen to help you. She really does feel terrible, you know."

"Don't you start," she snapped. "I've had it about up to here with being told how badly poor Felicity feels. She bloody well ought to. Anyway, you've talked me into it – I'll go and see them now."

"Are you going to tell him everything we've been saying?"

"God, no! No, I feel the one advantage I have is knowing some stuff that they don't. That probably makes me paranoid, but so be it – I think I'm entitled to be after what I've been through. And anyway, if Hugh's innocent, I want to get his own impressions. I don't want him prejudiced with ours."

Suddenly she plunged her face into her hands. "God – just listen to me. *If* he's innocent! These are my friends - I can't believe we're talking about them like this."

Bubs put an arm around her shoulder. "I know what you mean. And you're really being amazingly brave. It's the right thing to do, though – you can't just bury your head in the sand for the rest of your life. You wouldn't be able to live with yourself."

Isabella blew her nose. "I know. It doesn't make it any easier though."

She'd started closing down the laptop when a thought struck her.

"By the way," she said. "When you said back there that there were at least three suspects we should consider, were you just keeping your options open with the at least bit, or did you actually have anyone else in mind?"

Bubs looked uncomfortable. "Nobody in particular, no."

Isabella felt the now familiar sinking feeling in her stomach. "Oh shit," she said. "I know that look. It means you're about to tell me something I don't want to hear. Come on, spit it out."

Bubs shook her head. "Like I said, it's nothing specific. It's just that, if Hugh is right and Jake was writing to him anonymously, based on those files we found in the laptop, then…"

Isabella felt the hairs on her neck begin to stand on end. "Go on," she said.

"Well, there were quite a few files like that, weren't there? So isn't it possible he was writing to other people as well?"

*

Isabella set off to look for Hugh and Felicity. She tried the drawing room first, and found Simon and Lin sitting in the bay window playing chess. They both looked up and smiled a welcome.

"Hi," said Simon. "Taking a break from the great opus?"

"Sort of," she replied. "Actually, I'm looking for Hugh and Felicity. Any idea where they are?"

Simon's face was a picture. What does he think I'm going to do, she wondered, stab them to death and then burn their bodies?

Lin seemed to have no such qualms. "I think they're in their room," she said, and turned her attention back to the game.

She slid a piece across the board. "Check."

Simon's attention snapped back to the table. As Isabella left the room she heard a muttered 'shit!'

She went upstairs and paused for a moment outside Hugh and Felicity's door. She could hear voices on the other side. They were speaking too quietly for her to make out the words but it was clear from the tone of the conversation that they weren't discussing the weather.

She knocked and Hugh's voice instructed her to come in.

She found them in an odd mirror of Simon and Lin's positions; both seated in armchairs, one on either side of the bay window. Even the rain sodden view was nearly identical, and she realised, even while thinking how thoroughly irrelevant the fact was, that this room must be directly above the drawing room.

Both had been reading, or pretending to. Hugh had a paperback thriller in his hand, while Felicity had a magazine face down on her lap. She'd been crying again, and she looked up at Isabella with a mixture of trepidation and hope on her drawn face. His face was tense, uncertain, as if unsure whether to welcome the interruption or not.

Isabella didn't bother with the pleasantries. "We need to talk," she said.

Hugh glanced at his wife, then nodded. "I agree," he said. He started to get to his feet. "Have a seat."

"I'm fine here, thanks," said Isabella, seating herself on the stool by the dressing table.

"Isabella?" Felicity's voice was little more than a croak.

Isabella raised a hand. "Later."

Felicity's face started to crumple.

Isabella looked at her impatiently, and was surprised to find that for the first time she began to feel the faintest thread of pity for her friend. "Sorry. I need to ask Hugh some questions."

Without waiting for an answer she turned back to Hugh.

"Listen, I've been thinking about what you said to me – how you found out about this, and what you felt, and what you did. And, to be blunt, some of it just doesn't ring true."

She'd caught him off guard. He'd obviously been expecting to umpire some sort of showdown between her and Felicity, not have his own conduct questioned. He reddened, and she saw his face tighten before he regained control of himself.

"I see. Can you be a little more specific?"

She matched his flat, analytical tone. "I can. Specifically, I find it difficult to believe that a red-blooded male such as yourself, who blatantly adores his wife, can react so calmly to the news that she's been cheating on you. And with someone who, I think it fair to say, you did not exactly hold in the highest esteem."

He glared at her. "Why? I don't see your problem. You said it yourself – it was because I loved her that I bit my tongue. I couldn't bear the thought of losing her."

Felicity snuffled and reached for a tissue.

Isabella was determined not to be distracted.

"Maybe. But you obviously didn't feel the same way about Jake. It defies belief that you could carry on with him as if nothing had happened – socialising, laughing at his crap jokes. Why didn't you want to rip his guts out? What's wrong with you?"

Hugh tossed his head impatiently. "Of course I wanted to rip his guts out! I wanted nothing more than to wipe that smirk off his face – to make him pay for what he did."

"So why didn't you?" She paused, then said in a quieter voice. "Or perhaps you did?"

Felicity looked up sharply. Her face had turned as white as the tissue she was clutching. "What do you mean?" she whispered.

Hugh put his hand on her arm to quieten her but she ignored him. "What are you implying?"

Isabella stared at her dispassionately. "I'm not implying anything, Felicity, I'm just asking a question. But I'm very interested in your reaction to it."

Felicity started to speak but Hugh got there first. "Stop playing games, Isabella, we all know what you're saying. You're suggesting that I killed Jake because he seduced my wife. Well, I can see why you might think that, but I didn't. I can't prove it, the only way that can be done is to find the real killer. Until then you'll have to take my word for it."

He spoke so matter-of-factly that his words had the ring of sincerity. But his expression had hardened, and she sensed controlled anger beneath the surface. Although, who wouldn't be angry at being accused of murder, whether innocent or guilty?

If he was telling the truth and he hadn't killed Jake she could understand why he'd keep silent after his death – by that stage there was nothing to be gained by speaking out. But in those long weeks between his finding out about the affair and that damned concert at Kew? She still couldn't understand how he could have stayed so controlled. It wasn't human.

"I want to believe you, Hugh, I really do. But I just find it hard to imagine you rolling over and taking this so lightly."

They stared at each other for a long while. Felicity looked anxiously from one to the other, as if she wanted to say something but was not sure whether she should. Eventually Hugh nodded to himself as if he had come to a decision.

"God, you're stubborn, Isabella. All right, I'll be honest with you. Maybe I should have been from the start." He paused and Isabella felt herself stiffen in anticipation.

"I was going to do something to Jake."

Felicity gasped and grabbed at him. He shook her off. "I just didn't know what. Nothing so crude as murder, but yes, I was going to get my own back somehow – ruin him professionally, expose him for something else, I wasn't sure. If you must know, I was planning to hire a private eye to get some dirt on him, but I never got round to it before – you know. Meanwhile, the reason I was able to carry on as if nothing had happened, as you put it, was that I was savouring the knowledge that he was still in blissful ignorance of what was going to happen, while I knew he was going to get his come-uppance. And that's the honest truth."

It made sense – more so anyway than his previous protestations of virtuous martyrdom. At least it was human. But Hugh was an intelligent man – if he had killed Jake he might well reason that he had to give her something like this to get her off his scent. At the end of the day there was not a jot of what he'd said that could either be proved or disproved.

She'd think about it some more later. For now she decided to move on.

"Okay – let's put that to one side for the moment. You said you'd suspected that it was Jake sending you those letters – why?"

"Because they stopped after his death."

Of course. That would be something of a giveaway.

"But you didn't suspect before then?"

"Like I told you – I did wonder. But it's not exactly the sort of thing you expect your so-called friends to do, is it?"

Something in his tone – contempt, or disdain perhaps – hit a raw nerve. This was after all her husband he was talking about.

"I think we've all had to get used to our so-called friends providing us with nasty surprises, haven't we?"

Felicity sobbed and Hugh's mouth tightened, but her mind was racing ahead.

"But you didn't think the last one was from him? And you're completely sure about that?"

"I told you last night – the style was completely different." He was beginning to sound exasperated again. "And anyway, even if we're sure that the early ones were from him, it's obvious that this one couldn't be – he'd hardly be likely to shop himself, would he?"

Of course he was right. Whatever was happening to her? She was normally razor sharp, and here she was having to have the most blatantly obvious things pointed out to her. Unless…

"Unless he was trying to get back at Felicity somehow. It was you who ended it, wasn't it?"

She nodded. Too eagerly for Isabella's liking. As if that was going to help.

"And how did he take it?"

Felicity grimaced. "Not well. He did actually threaten to tell Hugh if I didn't carry on."

Isabella felt herself cringe at her words. Hugh's face darkened as well, though in his case it looked more like anger.

"He was just being an idiot," Felicity continued hastily. "I don't think he really meant it. Once I'd pointed out that you wouldn't be that impressed either and that he'd be out on his ear as well he shut up about it. He made a few stupid threats after that, but that was just to get back at me. I'm sure he wouldn't have written that letter."

"Then who did?" persisted Isabella. "Someone did. Who could have seen you?"

She shrugged. "Anyone who happened to be in the right place at the wrong time. I certainly didn't see anyone I knew. Although…"

"Yes? Although what?"

"The time at the hotel – I seem to remember Jake saying something like 'how strange, that looks just like…', as if he'd seen somebody he knew. But he never said a name. I'd definitely have remembered if he had."

Isabella stamped her foot in frustration. "What about you, Hugh? Have you got any further thinking about who sent it yet?"

He took his time replying. "I have been thinking about it, as it happens. I've got some ideas."

"And?" She wanted to shake it out of him.

He shook his head. "I'll tell you later, but I need to sort it out in my head properly. I don't want to go off half cock."

"Hugh! You've got to tell me. We're talking about the person that might be able to lead me to Jake's killer."

He stared her down. "That is exactly why I want to be sure before I say anything to you. I think you've thrown around quite enough unsubstantiated accusations for one day, don't you?"

She turned and left the room. She still didn't have the faintest idea whether she had been talking to an ally or to her husband's murderer.

*

As she went downstairs she was surprised to hear raised voices. She followed the sound into the rear porch, where she found Abi, Peter and the boys struggling out of their coats.

"Hi," she said. "I thought you guys were going to the zoo – what happened?"

Peter glanced up at her. His face was thunderous. "Bloody car, that's what happened. I'm not sure exactly what's wrong, but it started straining like anything, so we turned back. I'm going to try to get the AA out to have a look at it. I think it might be the clutch, and the last thing I need is to break down completely in the middle of the moor."

Abi gave a humourless laugh. "As if you know anything about cars." She turned to Isabella. "I told him to take in it for a service before we came down here, but could he be bothered? Too busy faffing about with one of his hare-brained schemes. And now the boys have missed their trip to the zoo." She started helping Tom with his boots.

"Oh yeah, and it would've been completely impossible for you to have taken it in, wouldn't it? With your busy schedule of lunches and coffee mornings and crap?"

Clearly Isabella had landed in the middle of a major row. "Oh well, it's probably just as well to be on the safe side," she said in as neutral a manner as possible. "And there's always another day." She smiled encouragingly at Sammy.

"Easy for you to say," said Abi. "Just stand still, will you, Tom? You haven't got to entertain these two in the rain for the rest of the day."

Charmless was the word, Isabella decided. Abi was one of those people who were utterly charmless. And right now she just couldn't be bothered with her.

She turned back to Peter. "So what's the plan now?"

He shrugged, and Abi barked another short laugh. "What are you asking him for? He'd be happy enough settling down with the drinks trolley for the rest of the day. While what we've got to do," she said, gathering her two sons to her, "is get some biscuits and juice for my two big boys here, haven't we?"

She dragged them off to the kitchen, leaving Isabella and Peter alone in the sudden silence.

He looked embarrassed. "Sorry you had to see that."

She shrugged. "It's all right. Even I remember that marriages have their ups and downs."

"Yeah, but, you and Jake…" His voice tailed off.

"Me and Jake what?"

He stared at her for a moment. It looked as if he was wondering whether he should say what was on his mind. Then he sighed.

"It's just that I always got the impression that, although you argued a lot, and sometimes you looked as if you couldn't stand the sight of each other, deep down you and he actually wanted to be together."

And you and Abi don't, she thought. It didn't really need saying.

"I guess so," she said. "Though I'm having to revise my ideas rather rapidly at the moment."

He shuddered. "I know – it must be awful for you. The idea of them together…" He shuddered again.

She knew exactly why the vision of Jake and Felicity together bothered him, and it was not sympathy for her. She was suddenly impatient with his self-pity. "The act itself is something I choose not to dwell on," she said briskly. "And I'd advise the same for you. I'm not your mother, Peter, but at some point you're going to have to live in the real world. And you're going to have to realise that everything you do, or say, has consequences."

Like Felicity has discovered, she thought. And Jake.

His reaction startled her. He recoiled from her as if she had physically slapped him, and his face, as open and guileless as a child's a moment ago, seemed to close down.

"I have absolutely no idea what you're talking about," he said, and turned and marched into the hallway.

So what was that about, she wondered?

Chapter 11

The rain continued unabated for the remainder of the morning, and it was an irritable, restless group that gathered for lunch.

Isabella had once again tried to settle to her book, but she found it impossible to concentrate. Her thoughts kept returning to her conversation with Hugh, trying to analyse every word, every nuance of expression, to give her some clue as to the truth.

Eventually she realised that she was in a logical bind; everything that he'd said – the reluctance to admit what he'd really planned, the outrage at the implied accusation - was perfectly consistent with him being innocent. Equally, it could have been lies from start to finish. And there was nothing tangible, nothing at all, to help work out which it was.

For once she was not the last into the dining room, though the moment she got there she wished she were. Abi was seated at the far end of the table with the boys, trying to persuade them to eat their lunch. They had taken a dislike to Bubs' homemade soup, and Isabella resigned herself to a meal punctuated by tears and whining. Peter was sitting seemingly as far away from them as possible, moodily dunking chunks of bread into his bowl and eating them. None of them took any notice of her as she went over to the sideboard and started helping herself.

She was relieved when Simon and Lin entered. Not that she really wanted company, but if she were forced into it she'd prefer something a little more congenial than fractious children and sulking parents.

They made idle conversation for a few minutes until they heard Hugh and Felicity making their way downstairs.

Hugh came in first, nodded brusquely at Simon and Lin, and marched up to the buffet. He ignored the rest of them, which suited Isabella just fine. Felicity followed, attempting a weak, haunted smile at no one in particular.

Simon and Lin were both looking at her in concern, and Isabella too found herself curious as to what had happened to her erstwhile best friend. She had never thought of Felicity as particularly thin skinned, rather the opposite. Sure, it was an unpleasant situation, but it was not great for her either, and she hadn't crumbled into something resembling last night's soufflé.

"Are you okay, Felicity?" asked Simon when they had sat down.

Felicity nodded tiredly. "I'm fine, thanks. Just a bit run down. I'll be better for a meal."

"Not if you're eating this, you won't be." They turned to see Tom staring up the table at them mournfully. "It's horrible."

"Just get on and eat it," snapped his mother. "You're not getting any pudding until it's gone. And that goes for you, too," she said, turning to Sammy. Tom started bawling.

"Oh, for God's sake, why don't you let them eat what they want?" Peter slammed his cutlery down. "Bubs said she'd cook them sausage and beans, didn't she?"

"They're not eating that rubbish," retorted Abi. "You'd think a proper cook would know better."

Isabella felt the need to stick up for Bubs. "She's only trying to help," she said. "I'm sure she'll prepare anything you want."

Abi sniffed. "She never seems very helpful to me."

"You might find she responded better if you tried speaking to her like a human being rather than a servant," said Hugh.

Abi stared at him. "But she is a servant, isn't she? She's paid to do it. She's just not a very good one."

Her expression was a strange mix of belligerence and incomprehension, thought Isabella. She genuinely doesn't understand what he's getting at.

Hugh seemed to be struggling to contain his temper. "Well, if the cook that I've provided for us isn't good enough, feel free to pay for someone else, or maybe even do it yourself. But just stop bloody complaining all the time!"

Abi pursed her lips. "I've told you before. I don't like swearing in front of the children."

The room went silent. Even the two boys stopped their complaining and listened, sensing that something big was imminent.

Hugh sat back in his seat and stared at her, nodding his head slowly. "So you have, so you have," he mused. Suddenly he leaned forward and smashed his fist down on the table. "So why don't you just fuck off then, if you don't like my language? Eh? Just fuck off."

Abi went pale. She rose to her feet and pulled her two sons up with her.

"Come on boys," she said. "We'll finish our food in the kitchen." She swept out of the room.

Peter also got to his feet, wiping his mouth on his napkin. "Nice one, Hugh," he said. "That's really going to help."

"And you can fuck off too," said Hugh conversationally, and returned his attention to his food.

Peter followed after his wife, shaking his head as he went.

The most extraordinary thing to Isabella was that Felicity hadn't intervened in the exchange. She had a mischievous streak, and had been known to wind people up before now just for the pleasure of watching an argument develop. But she'd normally have regarded it as her duty to ensure civilised behaviour at any table where she was the de facto hostess. Today it was as if she'd barely registered that her husband was hurling abuse at their guests. Nor, despite her earlier comment, had she done more than pick at her food.

Lin had noticed, too. "Are you sure you're okay, Felicity?" she asked.

"She said she's fine," snapped Hugh. "Just upset." He shot a meaningful look at Isabella.

Isabella felt her hackles rise and had an overwhelming urge to throw the contents of her plate across the table at Hugh. The nerve of the man, accusing her of upsetting Felicity. But she had determined not to get into another slanging match with either Hugh or Felicity, especially in front of any of the others. With difficulty she held her tongue.

She saw that both Simon and Lin had bridled at Hugh's words as well.

"She was just asking how Felicity was," said Simon stiffly. "There's no need to take that tone. Whatever's got into you today, Hugh?"

Hugh's eyes narrowed. "Nothing's got into me. I'm just saying that Felicity's upset. And I'll thank you to leave it at that."

"Uh, hello, she's not exactly the only one to have had the odd upset in the last couple of days," said Lin, with a sympathetic glance at Isabella.

He looked at her coldly. "There's two sides to every story, Lin. And before you start having a go at me or Felicity for upsetting people you might want to look a bit closer to home."

Simon glanced at his wife, shaking his head in bewilderment. "And what the hell is that supposed to mean? You keep coming out with this crap, Hugh, but I have to tell you I don't have the faintest bloody idea what you're on about."

"I think you do. Maybe you both do." He got to his feet. "You know what? I'm fed up with the bloody lot of you. You can go to hell for all I care."

They heard him stamping up the stairs.

It seemed to take a few seconds for Felicity to notice that he'd gone.

"I'm afraid my husband has been under a bit of a strain these last couple of days, "she said, pulling herself wearily to her feet. "I'd better go after him." And she too left, shutting the door behind her, leaving just the three of them.

Lin looked at her husband and raised her eyebrows. "What the hell…?"

Simon shrugged. "I've no idea," he said. He looked across at Isabella. "You?"

For a moment Isabella toyed with the idea of unburdening herself of her suspicions but dismissed the notion. It wasn't the right time. She shook her head.

"I've given up to trying to make sense of things. There doesn't seem a lot of point."

After that nobody spoke for a while. There didn't seem much to say.

A few minutes later Peter stuck his head around the door.

"Ah, the coast is clear," he said. "Hurricane Hugh has passed."

He came in and sat down. Abi followed but remained lurking in the doorway, disapproval still etched into every line of her face.

"What was that all about?" he asked.

"I've not a clue," said Simon. "It obviously wasn't personal, though – he's had a go at all of us."

Peter shrugged. "It's odd. I mean, if he'd just found out about it all, you'd understand – but he's the one who's known all along."

"I know. And why he should have a go at poor Bella here... Mind you, Felicity does look pretty ropey."

Lin suddenly leaned forward conspiratorially. "But you know what I think? I think..."

She broke off at the sound of footsteps coming down the stairs, accompanied by the muffled sound of Felicity's voice. Then they heard Hugh, louder, a sharp 'No!'

The door opened and Felicity stood there. She looked embarrassed.

"He's gone down to the lake to fish. It'll do him good – calm him down."

Isabella glanced out of the window. Unnoticed in all the excitement, the weather had started to improve – patches of lighter sky were evident, and the rain had slowed to a drizzle.

Lin followed her gaze. "Oh, good, it's clearing up – I might go out myself in a while."

Felicity smiled nervously. "I'd probably steer clear of Hugh though. Just for now." Then, almost as an afterthought, she added. "By the way, he gave me a message for you, Isabella. He said to tell you, he doesn't want to talk to you now, but he'll catch you later."

A silence fell across the room as all eyes turned to Isabella. She felt herself redden.

"Sounds awfully melodramatic," said Peter, staring at Isabella curiously. "What's that about then?"

Isabella, her mind racing, shook her head. It presumably meant that Hugh had worked out who had sent him the note, but she was damned if she was going to let that on to everyone else – not until she knew who it was, anyway. She mentally cursed Felicity for blurting out the message in front of everyone else.

"Nothing important – just something I needed for my book that I thought he might know."

She looked around, conscious that every pair of eyes in the room was still staring at her. "Actually, I might pop down and see him now."

Felicity looked her in the eye and held her gaze for the first time since their confrontation the previous evening.

"I wouldn't do that, Isabella," she said. "I really wouldn't."

*

The remainder of lunch passed mainly in uncomfortable silence, punctuated by the occasional lacklustre exchange. Nobody wanted to stray onto potentially dangerous territory and provoke another outburst.

There had been general agreement that the improvement in the weather might not last, and Peter and Abi had decided to take the boys out for a game of hide and seek before the rain returned. The others all politely declined the opportunity to join in. Simon and Lin announced their intention of going for a walk on the moors, assuming they could find the lodge's private gate, reputed to be somewhere on the far side of the grounds, beyond the lake.

Felicity went back to her room and Isabella retreated to the library, insisting that there was something she wanted to finish writing. While there were indeed a few ideas that had occurred to her over lunch that she was anxious to get down while she remembered, she had another, stronger reason for wanting to escape the others. Although she was desperate to get out of the house and into some fresh air, it was only if she could do so on her own. She found she couldn't stand the idea of walking with anyone else, even the relatively unthreatening Simon and Lin.

She wondered whether this apparent inability to spend long amounts of time in others' company was a permanent part of her make-up now. But it wasn't the company per se that she had become allergic to – it was the seemingly inevitable rows that accompanied it.

She sat staring out of the window. She saw Sammy and Tom haring across the lawn towards the woods, and heard Abi calling some instruction or other after them. The bickering had started before they had even left the house – something about wet weather clothing, from what she'd heard, although she had tried to ignore the whining complaints of the boys and the sharp, impatient, responses of their mother. From the look of them, Abi had won – all four were well wrapped up in wellingtons, long waterproof coats and hats. All they needed now was a lifeboat.

Now, down by the edge of the woods, there seemed to be a fairly animated discussion going on – presumably setting out the ground rules for the game. Eventually the boys ran off, followed at a slower pace by Abi. Peter, apparently the first seeker, waited a full minute, then set off after them. From his body language he could think of things he'd rather be doing.

As soon as he'd disappeared into the trees - were they deliberately waiting, to avoid any chance of being drafted into the hide and seek? - Simon and Lin strode into view. Similarly clad in anonymous, all-encompassing wet weather gear, they bounced along purposefully.

She watched them out of sight then sighed and turned her attention back to the notebook in front of her. She'd found that even though she could now access the laptop, and had even set up her own username for the purpose, she couldn't bring herself to use the wretched thing. She was always too conscious of what else it held; its hidden mischief and corruption sapping her energy, deadening her inspiration.

Not that she could concentrate especially well now. She could jot down her ideas well enough, but she seemed totally incapable of following them through or refining them in any way. She was never at her best straight after lunch - something to do with biorhythms, someone had once told her – but today she was particularly useless.

She looked at her watch. It was a quarter to three – she'd been in the library on her own for nearly an hour. If she wanted to get out and get a walk in before it started raining again she'd better get on with it.

She poked her head out of the door to check the skies. Sure enough, overhead was clear blue with the odd patch of fleecy white, but towards the west an ominous wall of grey surging forwards promised change ahead.

She went to get changed. She could hear Bubs bustling around in the kitchen, to a pounding accompaniment of loud music. It was nothing she recognised, and she briefly felt old. It didn't seem that many years ago that she knew, or at least knew of, almost every contemporary band there was.

All the wellingtons that would even remotely fit her were gone. Cursing under her breath, she put on her walking boots, still caked in mud from yesterday, and pulled on a waterproof jacket.

Before setting off she stuck her head around the kitchen door. Bubs looked surprised to see her.

"Oh, hi," she said, turning down the volume. "I thought you'd all gone out. I wouldn't have had this so loud otherwise."

"That's okay – thick walls. I hadn't even noticed it. I'm just popping out for a stroll."

Bubs gestured towards her boots. "Looks like quite a stroll you're planning."

"The wellies are all gone. And anyway, I might go as far as the moor – I haven't decided yet."

"Fair enough. How are you feeling?"

Isabella shrugged. "As well as. Whatever it is, it's catching though. Most of them are like bears with sore heads. It feels like I'm having to calm everyone else down now. Weird, to say the least."

Bubs gave a wry smile. "I think weird sums up this house very well."

*

Isabella set off, following the path that Simon and Lin had taken into the woods. They should be far enough ahead by now that there was no danger of catching them up, and she found the idea of roaming the moors on her own very appealing at the moment. Just her, the fresh air and the wind, and her thoughts.

When she got near the lake she slowed down. She wasn't sure where exactly Hugh would be fishing, and although she was itching to find out what he wanted to tell her she guessed that barging into him, unannounced, would be counter-productive. Nor did she think she could bear yet another scene just now. There would be time enough to talk to him later, when he'd calmed down.

And part of her, the part that wondered if there was really any point in hearing whatever story he'd thought up this time, also wondered whether being on her own with him in the wilds was exactly a good idea.

Finally she spotted him. He was at the far end of the lake, casting into the pool formed by the entry of the stream. Either he was so absorbed that he hadn't noticed her, or he was ignoring her. She hurried on, head down, suddenly anxious for her solitude again.

Lin had told her that the path to the moor was beyond the lake, and curved away uphill to the left. It would be a pretty arduous climb, she'd warned her, going all the way from the bottom of the valley to the beginnings of the high moor, but that was what Isabella wanted right now. Stiff physical exercise, to purify the soul.

She found the path easily enough, a narrow but well-defined passage between the trees and bracken, and began to breathe more easily as she climbed away from the lake and Hugh.

The silence was divine – just the occasional birdcall and the soft drip of the morning's rain falling from the high canopy of the woods onto the leaves below. She could physically feel the tension beginning to ease from her neck and shoulders. Soon her mind would clear as well and she could start to think things through. Properly.

The path became steeper and muddier. The bracken and ferns grew higher and closer, narrowing the path until it was barely wide enough for one person. It got darker as the trees became denser, as if they were squeezing the daylight out of the woods. She would have doubted that she was on the right path if it weren't for the obviously recent boot prints in the mud ahead of her. As it was she was glad of her waterproofs; even though it wasn't raining the wet undergrowth pressing in on her on either side would have drenched her.

Lin hadn't been exaggerating about the length of the climb. It seemed to go on forever, and she was beginning to wonder whether it was worth the effort when the gloom suddenly lifted. The path opened out again, and a dry stone wall with a rusty gate came into view. Beyond it she could see open moorland, treeless except for the occasional scrubby patch of gorse. With a sigh of relief she went through the gate and leaned back against the wall to catch her breath.

She seemed to have three possibilities. There was a track that followed the line of the wall, uphill to the left, downhill to the right. Or she could take the path that set off straight ahead, climbing onto the moor proper. She was just contemplating her choices when she heard a cheery greeting and turned to see Simon, striding up the path towards her from the right.

He reached her, red-faced and out of breath.

"Hi," he said. "You decided to chance it then."

She shrugged. "I just needed to get out of the house for a while. Where's Lin?"

He waved his arm in the direction of the central path. "Oh, up there somewhere. We set off onto the moor – you get some amazing views once you get over that crest – and Lin saw a tor that she wanted to climb. She's amazingly fit, that girl. Anyway, I'm not, so I decided I'd had enough fresh air and came back on my own. Rather than coming back the same way I could see a bridge over a stream down there on the right that I reckoned would take me back to this path. Bit muddy but here I am." He paused and breathed deeply for a few moments. "So what are you planning? I'm about done but you might be able to catch Lin on the way down if you want company."

There was nothing farther from her mind but it seemed impolite to say so.

"Oh, I don't know," she said evasively. "I think I'll just rest here for a minute or two then go and see what there is to see."

He smiled, as if he knew exactly what she really meant. "Fair enough. Better watch out for the weather though. Anyway, I'm heading back to what counts for civilisation around here. Though I might join Hugh for a bit of fishing first."

She raised her eyebrows and he laughed.

"Oh, you know Hugh – it'll all have blown over by now."

She wondered.

He disappeared down the path. She waited until he was out of sight, then set off up the track that hugged the wall to the left. For a while she trudged doggedly along through the mud, then as she crested a small hill the moor opened up in front of her.

She'd been out on the moors several times in her short stay, but even so, the sight still took her breath away. To her left the path snaked away, still running alongside the wall until it mundanely joined a small road that she recognised from the day before. To the right she could see now see the tor Simon had spoken of, lonely and bleak against the cloud-strewn sky. As she looked a figure emerged from behind it and started down the hill. The distance was too great to be sure, but something about the gait convinced her that it was Lin.

Ahead of her the moor rolled, majestic in its desolation, wave upon wave unfolding to the purple grey misty peaks in the far distance. She knew that what she was seeing was a trick of perception, the tops of hills that concealed valleys with roads, villages and farms, but the illusion that she was alone in front of some vast expanse extending to infinity was a powerful one.

A shadow passed over her and she glanced behind. The rain clouds were getting closer, darker and more ominous than before, and she had to decide what she was going to do. On the one hand she knew the sensible thing was to turn back – getting caught on the moor in a really heavy storm would be no joke. On the other, she felt she had been cooped up inside for too much of the day already, and was reluctant to return to the claustrophobic atmosphere of the lodge. The cobwebs had not yet been properly blown away.

She decided to take a leaf out of Lin's book, and set herself the manageable but at least slightly challenging task of getting to the pile of rocks she could see at the top of the first hill in front of her. She had no idea of the distance; she found it impossible to guess on the moors, but unless there was some sort of raging torrent at the bottom of the valley between her and her goal she thought she should be able to make it. She set off determinedly along a faint path that seemed to be going in roughly the right direction.

She walked fast, forcing herself to concentrate on each step lest she trip in some treacherous pothole or catch her foot on one of the many roots that laced the path. She was aware that she was doing this not just to beat the rain, but also partly to prevent herself thinking too much – yet. There was plenty of thinking for her to do, but she needed her mind totally focussed before she could start making the decisions she knew she had to make.

Other than the odd swampy patch of ground in the dip between the hilltops she met with no obstruction on her short hike and soon she was standing, out of breath but triumphant on the top of her tor. She sat down, and then, finally, allowed herself to think.

It wasn't surprising that she was making heavy weather of it, she realised, because the ideas that she was struggling with were, quite literally, the unthinkable. It was what she had been so furious with Bubs for suggesting – could it really have been only the day before yesterday? She wondered now whether her anger at the time was because she herself had subconsciously suspected the same thing but suppressed it, but she thought not. Although, as she had told Bubs, it had crossed her mind, she had never really contemplated it as a serious possibility. It just wasn't what you thought – that one of your best friends would murder your husband.

But then, you didn't really think that another of those friends would sleep with him, either.

Now that she did give her thoughts free rein, though, she discovered what her subconscious mind had been doing while she was walking. What had started out as a ludicrous idea, then turned to suspicion, had finally become near-certainty. There was no running away from it any more. Of everyone, Hugh had the strongest motive for killing Jake. He'd had ample opportunity – she remembered vividly him wandering off that night at Kew, supposedly to search for Felicity. He would have had plenty of time to track down Jake, lure him into the bushes, and kill him. It might not even have been premeditated – he might just have bumped into him and taken his chance. Or perhaps he had confronted Jake and been angry at the reaction he had got – knowing Jake, he might easily have just laughed in Hugh's face, driving him into a rage. Not that there was much point speculating. Unless Hugh volunteered the information, she would never know. It didn't really matter, anyway – the fact was, he had done it.

And Felicity knew. That was the missing piece of the jigsaw that she had only just figured out. Why it hadn't occurred to her earlier she couldn't imagine, but it now seemed blindingly obvious. How long her erstwhile friend had had that knowledge wasn't clear – perhaps she'd always suspected but wasn't sure – but now that she knew that Hugh had always known of the affair she would be certain. It explained her attitude since the revelations had started, the misery that went way beyond contrition and embarrassment. It was guilt – not guilt at infidelity, which Isabella suspected Felicity would consider a fairly trivial matter, but guilt that she had caused a death.

And turned her husband into a murderer.

A wave of anger came over her. Who were these people who had destroyed her life so cavalierly, disposed of her husband like some piece of inconvenient garbage, and then had the nerve to carry on pretending they were her friends? How could people behave like that?

The anger felt good, and she briefly marvelled at how little anger she had felt in the last few days – the odd explosion, yes, but nothing on the scale that might have been expected of her. It was the shock, she supposed, and bewilderment. Her mother had a proper Italian temper, and had explained to Isabella as a child that anger cleansed the soul, and allowed a person to get on with their life again.

Not that it seemed to be working today, though.

She realised she was shivering, and stood up. The wind had got up and the chill from the stone seemed to have seeped into her bones. The rain was probably only minutes away. It was time to get back.

She started walking, head down against the wind. She knew, with as much certainty as she was ever likely to get, what had happened to Jake. She knew why. What she didn't know was what she was going to do about it.

She'd already confronted Hugh and he'd denied the crime. Unconvincing bluster, yes, but if he hadn't cracked at the surprise of the first accusation – as Felicity had – he was hardly likely to if she tried again. On the other hand, if she went straight to the police without any new evidence – hard evidence – they would simply dismiss her suspicions out of hand. She didn't even know who to go to now that the miserable DCI Gormley had gone. All she knew at this stage was that whatever she did it was going to turn everybody's lives upside down, including her own. Again.

She wondered briefly about her own safety. Staying in the same house, in the middle of nowhere, as a murderer who knew that you knew of his guilt was not really, on the face of it, a very bright thing to do. But she thought he was unlikely to make a move on her. His whole strategy was one of denial and distraction – hence the message about 'knowing who it was'. She had nothing on him, while the one thing that would definitely draw police attention to him was an attack on her, whether successful or not. Ergo, so long as she had no hard evidence, she was safe.

So as things stood, she seemed likely to stay safe for a very long time.

As she approached the rusty gate the rain started.

Big, wet, drops. Sporadic at the moment but heralding the downpour to come. It was a good metaphor for her life.

She hurried down the path. By the time she reached the lake the rain was bucketing down again. Some summer, she thought. No wonder Devon was so green.

Instinctively she glanced towards the other end of the water, where Hugh had been standing earlier. There was no sign now; he had obviously gone in before the rain had got too heavy.

She got back to the house and peeled off her waterproofs. She was chilled through, though her clothes were still dry underneath.

She decided a cup of tea was in order and went into the kitchen. Bubs greeted her with a smile, which faded when she saw Isabella's face.

"What is it? Has something happened?"

Isabella shook her head wearily. "I'll tell you later. I can't talk now. Right now I need a cup of tea."

"I'm just making one for everyone else — they're all back now, except Hugh. He's still fishing I expect."

Strange, thought Isabella, but dismissed the matter. He must have moved further upstream.

"I can't face the others now. I don't suppose you could be an angel and bring it up to my room?"

"Of course. You go and rest."

*

After her tea she lay on her bed. She must have dozed, because when she glanced out of the window the sky was clear again, but the shadows were much longer. She had slept through to the early evening.

She gradually became aware of what must have woken her - a woman's cries, indistinct but growing louder. Then the sound of a door crashing open and the cries gained definition. It was Felicity's voice screaming.

Then there was a pounding up the stairs. Her door flew open and Felicity stood there, dishevelled and panting, her perfect hair tangled, her eyes wet and wild.

Isabella had barely a moment to take all this in before Felicity launched herself at her, hands outstretched to Isabella's throat, howling like a wounded animal.

"You killed him, you bitch, you killed him! And now I'm going to kill you!"

PART III

Chapter 12

Detective Chief Inspector Ireland of the Metropolitan Police took his glasses off and rubbed his eyes. The volume of paperwork attached to his job just seemed to get bigger and bigger every year. Either that or he was turning into one of those grumpy old coppers who were always complaining about how much better things were in the old days. Of course, it could be both.

He put his glasses on again and continued reading. The glasses themselves were yet another unwelcome reminder of the onset of middle age. He, who used to have perfect eyesight, was now reduced to scrabbling around in his pocket before he could even make sense of a restaurant menu. It wouldn't be so bad if he didn't keep forgetting the damned things. Perhaps he would have to do as he knew a number of his friends had - own about twenty pairs and just leave them lying around in different places.

And his sight wasn't the only thing that was beginning to go downhill. Nothing too serious, and at forty eight years old it was only to be expected, but the signs were there – the belt buckled out that extra notch, the hair that was not just greying but so thin at the front that he had to worry about sunburn *above* his hairline. Only his eyes themselves never seemed to change – the same penetrating grey, albeit somewhat deeper set than they used to be.

Thank heaven for small mercies.

The phone call when it came was a welcome diversion. At least, he thought it was going to be until he picked up and heard the voice of his boss, the appropriately named Bellow. Or, as he enjoyed reminding Ireland, Detective Superintendent Bellow.

But Bellow's tone was uncharacteristically subdued.

"Dave, glad I've caught you. Can you pop up here for a minute? There's a bit of a situation I need your help with."

His curiosity piqued, Ireland made his way up to Bellow's office.

It was about five times the size of Ireland's own. It had real leather furniture and walls lined with certificates and photographs of the man himself with various bigwigs. Best of all, it also had natural daylight and a view from a real window.

And Ireland wouldn't have swapped, if it meant taking Bellow's job with all its committees, meetings, and politics, for all the tea in China.

Bellow was leafing through a weighty file, his face troubled. He looked up as Ireland came in.

"Ah, Dave, take a seat. You remember the Chester murder last year?"

Ireland frowned and eased himself onto the chair in front of his boss's desk. It was what he supposed would be called 'contemporary' and looked both fragile and uncomfortable.

"Chester? Last year? Vaguely - I never had any involvement in it myself. It was never cleared up, though was it?"

"Too damned right it wasn't. And going through this file, it's no bloody surprise. The investigation's got more holes in it than my granny's tights."

Pushing that thought aside as quickly as possible, Ireland struggled to remember what he could about the case.

"It was at Kew Gardens, wasn't it? A mugging? And old Tom Gormley was the SIO."

Tom Gormley. Now thankfully retired, and not before time. He'd been known as an old-school copper, which in his case meant a stubborn insistence on sticking to the way he thought he remembered being trained forty years ago. Trouble was, his memory wasn't even that good.

He was a decent enough bloke, and nobody really disliked him. But he was a lousy detective.

"Exactly," said Bellow grimly. "I can't believe I didn't spot all this at the time. But you remember how it was last summer."

Ireland did indeed. A combination of a sudden upsurge in violent crime, a nasty summer flu which seemed to lay low half the force, and holidays (many of which ended up being cancelled) had led to near chaos in the division. With every team working at full stretch and more, there was little chance to look out for what might be going wrong on somebody else's patch.

"Are you saying we missed something then, sir?"

Bellow glared at him. "What I'm saying is, that from this file there's no bloody way of knowing! There's even references to complaints about the investigation from the widow. Nothing official, of course."

Ireland wriggled on his chair. "That's not so uncommon in these situations, is it?"

"No, but she's a high-powered lawyer of some sort."

Even more likely then, thought Ireland, but he knew what his boss was getting at. A lawyer, having at least in theory a better understanding of the due processes of law, should perhaps have less gratuitously unreasonable expectations of the police.

'Perhaps' being the operative word.

"So what's made this crop up now?" he asked. "Is there some new evidence?"

Bellow pursed his lips. "You could say that. There's been another murder. One of the party that was at the same picnic that night."

Ireland was confused. "Well, that's obviously very unfortunate and all that, but are we assuming that they're connected? Because…"

"We're saying there's a chance they might be," Bellow interrupted him. "It's exactly the same group of eight people, sans Chester himself of course, on holiday in some country house in Devon, and one of them turns up dead in a lake in the garden, having been hit on the head first. The day after the anniversary of Chester's death."

Ireland whistled. "Jesus," he said. "I see what you mean." It sounded like something out of an Agatha Christie novel. "And Devon and Cornwall CID have asked for our help?"

Bellow snorted. "Yes, like that's going to happen. No, it's not quite that simple. They insist that this is their case, and they only want what we've got on Chester as background. Reading between the lines, it was only with gritted teeth that the SIO managed to put in the request to us at all. He's obviously one of those."

Ireland knew exactly what he meant. You didn't 'call in the Yard' any more, but a lot of regional detectives were still a bit chippy when it came to dealing with their counterparts from the Met. As if the Met didn't have enough work of its own, without traipsing around the country, nicking other people's.

"So what do we do?" he asked.

Bellow eased his bulk back into his chair, causing the leather to creak in protest.

"I've been thinking about that. Obviously, if there is a chance of getting this one cleared up I don't want to miss it. But the last thing we need is Devon making a big deal out of Gormley's cock-ups and rubbing our noses in it by sorting it out on their own. We obviously can't send a senior officer of our own down to sit on their backs, even if we could afford the manpower – that would be like a red rag to the proverbial. So what I propose is to send them a liaison officer – someone nice and junior and unthreatening – a sergeant maybe. Devon won't be able to object to that, and then whoever it is can report back to you."

He jabbed a plump finger at Ireland. "In other words, Dave, I want you to take over the Chester case. Consider it live again."

Ireland's heart sank. Another case – albeit a cold one. That was all he needed right now. But he knew better than to argue.

"Fair enough, sir. But which sergeant? Who worked with Gormley on the original?"

"Hambledon. Who, if you recall, subsequently left the force to go and save turtles, or some such nonsense. He was no great loss, anyway. No, I thought it might be a good opportunity for our newly promoted Sergeant Chu. She's young, bright, and knows when to keep her mouth shut and her eyes open. She shouldn't scare the folk down in Devon too much. Assuming of course, that they've ever seen a Chinese person in the flesh before."

He paused, and a glimmer of mischief came into his eye. "And you won't mind working with her again, I daresay."

He threw the file across the desk at Ireland. "You'd better read this through before you talk to her."

Ireland was halfway to the door before Bellow spoke again.

"And Dave?"

Ireland turned back to face him.

"Let's not have any cock-ups this time. You know what I mean."

*

Eventually Isabella could stand the claustrophobic atmosphere of the house no longer. The police had instructed them not to leave 'the property', a term she interpreted as including the grounds as well as the lodge itself. So she waited until she was reasonably sure that nobody would see her leave, and sneaked out the back door across the lawns.

She stole a glance towards the woods. The vast police circus had largely moved on now. The vans, and the scores of men and women in white suits who had picked their way around the crime scene with meticulous care, had all gone. But although from here the woods seemed just as serene and peaceful as they had on the day of their arrival, she knew that inside the lakeside remained sealed off with blue tape, and plastic sheeting still stretched over the crime scene itself. She shuddered and continued on her way.

It was seclusion she craved. Since Hugh's death she didn't feel as if she'd had a waking moment to herself. From the moment Felicity had burst into her room, accusing her of killing her husband.

Simon had followed Felicity up the stairs that day and dragged her off a still dazed Isabella. Unable to get any sense out of her, they'd all gone down to the lake, where they found Hugh lying face down in the water. He wasn't moving, and he had an ugly gash on the back of his head.

They'd hauled his sodden body out of the lake. Simon attempted to revive him but it was no good – he was dead. And so the police were called and the grounds around the lake sealed off by the men in white suits, and the whole horrible circus had begun.

They were herded into the drawing room, where they were cooped up for hours together. Occasionally one of them would be pulled out for more questioning, otherwise, after the initial banalities, they'd sat in silence.

It had been suggested, at first gently, then with unequivocal plainness, that they should stay at the house while the police enquiries were proceeding. The message couldn't have been clearer; they were all suspects. When Abi protested, forcefully, that it was no place for children and that she must take the boys home she was told, no less forcibly, that it was out of the question.

So the next morning Abi's mother, a mirror image of her daughter, mouth tight with disapproval, had arrived and whisked the boys back to London. That left the six adults, plus Bubs. The atmosphere couldn't have been more strained or poisonous if they had been picnicking on a toxic waste dump.

Now, two days on, Isabella's mind was still a whirl. She had convinced herself that Hugh had killed Jake; now someone had killed Hugh. Had Hugh indeed murdered her husband, and then provoked a similar end for himself? Or was she wrong about him, and the same person had killed them both? There was no doubt about what Felicity believed. It was even possible that the others all believed the same as well. She was, after all, the only person who knew for absolute certain that she hadn't hit Hugh over the head and pushed him in the lake.

It wasn't a very comforting thought.

Earlier in the week – it seemed a hundred years ago – she'd found a stone bench, standing on its own in a small suntrap of lawn hemmed in on three sides by tall holly bushes. She hurried to it and sank onto it with relief, oblivious to its unyielding cold. In fact the weather had perked up in the last day or two, and in another world today, with its light breeze scudding the fluffy clouds across the deep blue sky, would have been ideal for a hike on the moors. Unfortunately, though, it wasn't another world.

As the long hours had passed the similarities with the events of a year ago had grown and grown, to such an extent that she felt herself becoming disorientated, wondering whether it was all just a bad dream. At first, she'd felt oddly detached from the whole thing – she was involved, of course she was, but she wasn't the prime mover, the centre of attention. Not at the beginning, anyway.

By the time the police had arrived Simon had given the hysterical Felicity some sort of sedative. So she was resting in her room when they began their interrogations, and were obviously annoyed at Simon's refusal to disturb her until she'd had a chance to calm down. With ill-concealed impatience they had taken statements from the rest of the group, including her – alert, boring into her with their eyes, seeking to probe into her soul, it had felt like, but basically routine stuff. Where had she been that afternoon, who had she seen and when, what had she been wearing, especially on her feet.

Isabella had wondered whether she should tell them about Jake, and what she'd found out about from the laptop and her suspicions about Hugh, but something held her back. All of it would come out in due course anyway, and she would doubtless be given the third degree. For now though she wanted as long as possible to think things through.

She didn't get very long for that. Everything changed once they'd seen Felicity. She'd marched into the room where they were all being held, shot one, icy look at Isabella, then retreated to the window seat. There she shrugged off all offers of sympathy and refused to speak a word.

There had then been a hiatus of some time before Isabella was summoned, the first of the group to face a second round of questioning. With a dread feeling in her stomach she'd followed the silent constable back to the dining room, which the detectives had requisitioned for the purpose.

There was a palpably different atmosphere in the room this time. She'd felt that their interest in her had intensified, that they were metaphorically – if not literally – leaning further forward over the table to interrogate her. She sensed hunger, as if she were surrounded by predators.

She also sensed something else, a tension between the detectives that hadn't been there before. It seemed that the time since they'd finished questioning Felicity hadn't simply been used for a tea break; there had been some sort of disagreement between them.

There were two of them. A grizzled Chief Detective Inspector called Lark, who seemed anything but. He had a broad Devon accent and an air of having seen too many slippery characters talk their way out of trouble to believe a word anyone said. When he'd heard that she was a London lawyer he had not bothered to hide his contempt, although she thought she detected a certain wariness creep into his manner. At least he would be playing things by the book, she thought to herself.

It was scant comfort.

The other detective was younger, in his early thirties perhaps, with an educated voice and a manner that suggested that he may once or twice have been further east than Taunton. Detective Sergeant Harris, he'd introduced himself as. It would be an overstatement to say that he seemed exactly sympathetic to her, but she at least felt that he was someone who was on vaguely the same wavelength. She ventured a small smile in his direction when she went into the room for the second time, and was rewarded with a curt nod.

In the first interview, they'd behaved like a team, albeit an ill-matched one. In the second, though, there was clearly some undercurrent. Lark ploughed ahead with his questions pretty well as if his subordinate hadn't been there, while Harris had taken on the brooding, truculent air of someone who knew they were right but was no longer allowed to argue his point. She wished she knew what the disagreement had been about; it might have been something she could have used to her advantage.

It became clear fairly early on that Felicity had told them what she thought about Isabella, as well as providing a lot more detail about the events leading up to Jake's death than she or any of the others had. What was a lot more alarming was that Lark appeared to share her suspicions.

He kicked off belligerently. "It seems there were quite a few things you didn't bother to tell us first time round."

She shrugged as nonchalantly as she was able.

"I answered your questions, that's all. I'll happily answer any more you have."

He raised his eyebrows and nodded. "Happily, will you? That's good. That's very good. So," he leaned forward and glared at her. "Can you *happily* tell me what made you think that Mr Hugh Guthrie murdered your husband?"

She tried to remember what she had said, either to Hugh or Felicity. As far as she could recall, she had never actually accused him of Jake's death. She'd discussed it with Bubs, yes, but surely Bubs wouldn't deliberately land her in any more trouble than she was already in?

Best to be on the safe side, though. She made a mental note to try to catch Bubs on own her own as soon as possible.

Meanwhile she contrived to look surprised at Lark's suggestion.

"Whoever told you that? Obviously I've never stopped trying to work out who could have killed my husband – wouldn't you? But I never said that I thought he'd done it. On the contrary, I thought he might have some information that might help. He was going to tell me but never got the chance. Ask Simon and Lin – they heard Felicity – Mrs Guthrie - pass the message on at lunchtime."

She had the satisfaction of seeing a flicker of uncertainty cross Lark's heavy face. He can't really just go on the rantings of a recently bereaved widow, she thought. She remembered with bitterness how little notice the London police seemed to have taken of her own opinions a year ago.

But he came back out fighting. "It was quite a pretty scene last night, by all accounts. Seems that Mrs Guthrie was lucky to get away with her own life from what I hear. Got a bit of a temper on you, have you?"

And so it went on, Lark trying to provoke her, she trying to stay calm and hold on to the fact that there was no evidence against her because *she hadn't done anything*.

Eventually, clearly dissatisfied, he had let her go again, with instructions not to leave the property. Then, as she was leaving, he turned and spoke to Harris.

"Please yourself if you must. Get on to them. But I'm not having them on my patch, do you understand?"

He sounded irritable. She wondered whether he had meant her to hear, or simply didn't care. But she did wonder who 'them' might be.

And if Lark was so hostile to them whether they might be a bit more sympathetic to her.

*

Ireland walked down the stairs to his own office slowly, leafing through the file as he did so. He'd need to go through it in detail, of course, but he was curious. These inter-force diplomatic missions, with their tiptoeing around and niceties of etiquette, normally bored him rigid, but this one looked a lot more interesting than most. For one thing, he would be working with Karen Chu again.

Chu. He'd worked with her on two cases previously, both before her promotion to Detective Sergeant, the latter of which involved a complicated – and murderous – financial fraud in a City bank. Since then he'd seen her around the building on various occasions, and exchanged nods, but they hadn't actually spoken. She was intelligent, hard working, and intuitive, and he suspected she had a very bright future ahead of her.

She was also absolutely stunning.

There had been a time when he thought something might happen between them. That moment had passed, but the memory was fresh enough in his mind to cause his pulse to quicken at the prospect of seeing her again.

He had to admit that Bellow's parting words had given him a bit of a shock. It may be that all his superior was doing was making a generic reference to his partiality for attractive girls - though even that would be alarming enough in its way. But surely there was no way that Bellow could know what had taken place late one evening in a deserted City wine bar.

He got himself a coffee and settled back in his chair to study the file properly. He quickly realised what Bellow had been getting at. It wasn't as if there were any glaring errors that jumped off the page, rather just a general air of sloppiness, of not following things through. It was as if Gormley, having tried to pin the murder on each of the picnic party in turn, had given up when none of them had crumbled under his questioning and concluded therefore that it must be some random mugging. Which was unlikely enough in itself, Ireland knew, let alone when the man's valuables had not even been taken.

Well, now it looked as if they had another bite at the cherry.

He picked up the phone and dialled the number he had written down.

"Is that Detective Sergeant Chu? I don't think I've congratulated you on your promotion yet."

"Sir? Is that you sir? Thank you very much."

He was cheered to note that she sounded pleased to hear from him. And that she obviously recognised his voice, even after several months.

"It was well deserved. Now, I've got a job for you. Direct orders from Bellow – you're off whatever you're doing. Where are you? Can you pop over to my office?"

"No problem. I'm stuck on desk duty. I'll be right over."

Ireland had to swallow hard when she walked into his office five minutes later. His memory hadn't deceived him – she was gorgeous. She was dressed in a smart navy suit with a white open shirt, businesslike enough without concealing that there was a very good figure underneath. It made Ireland acutely conscious of his own sagging grey suit, holding in an equally sagging middle-aged body. She'd also styled her hair differently, in a sort of bob rather than her previous ponytail. It had the effect of making her look more sophisticated without losing any of that girlish charm that had first attracted him.

He gave himself a mental cold shower.

He smiled and gestured her to the seat in front of the desk.

"Interesting one, this," he said, handling her the file. She eyed it curiously for a moment before turning her attention back to him. "You'll be working a cold case," he continued. "Or rather, not working it."

He saw the look on her face. "Don't worry – it's not as strange as it sounds."

He explained the situation, stressing the sensitivity of the whole thing. "Devon will be quite within their rights to send us packing at any time," he said. "And that's the last thing we want - you know how Bellow feels about his clear-up rate. Charm and tact are what will be required – that and a good feel for when it's going to be worth sticking your nose in."

He saw that she still looked unsure.

"You okay with all that?" he asked.

She shrugged. "I suppose so. I'm just trying to think it through. Don't get me wrong – it sounds really interesting, and thanks for giving it to me. It's just that it's so unlike anything else I've done I'm not too sure where to start."

He nodded. "I think the best thing will to keep a low profile to start – give them what they want but don't ask for too much yourself at first. But do try to get to sit in on any interviews that you can, especially with Chester's widow. And above all," he paused for emphasis. "Make sure that if there's any shit headed in our direction, you know it and let me know about it."

She looked puzzled. "Is that likely?"

He smiled wryly. "I think when you've read the file, you'll realise that there were one or two – how shall I put it? - shortcomings in our investigation. Anyway, I think you should stick with the sergeant on the case." He consulted his notes. "Harris is his name – you'll be able to catch up with him at Torbay. According to our man who dealt with him his boss was all for keeping us out altogether, but Harris talked him into it. So if you've got any allies at all down there, he's your man."

He leaned back in his chair. "It's very important that you realise that this is at least in part a damage control exercise. Don't worry too much if you don't feel that it's taking us any closer actually solving Chester's murder – we all know it's a long shot. Just do your best in that regard. It may even turn out that this one really is the random intruder, and that there's no connection, though I somehow doubt that. Anyway, if you need any advice just give me a call. And make sure you check in with me daily in any event."

He beamed at her. "So, on your way, and good luck, sergeant!"

*

Isabella got back to the house feeling somewhat calmer. She was still a million miles from understanding what had happened here, let alone the implications for her own situation, but at least there was the possibility that a new police investigation might make some progress where the previous one had failed.

She was in for a rude awakening. The moment she entered the hall Lark was there, almost snarling with rage.

"Where the hell have you been?" he said. "I told you not to leave the premises."

Taken aback, she just stared at him for a second. "I didn't," she said eventually. "I just went for a walk in the garden. That's part of the premises."

His eyes narrowed. "And I don't suppose it occurred to you to tell anyone where you were going, did it? I was about to put out an all points search."

She shrugged. "Sorry, I just wanted to be on my own for a bit. Anyway - I'm here now."

He nodded. "Aye, you are. But not for long as it happens. I want you to come into the station for some more questions. In Torbay."

She felt as if her knees would buckle. "Torbay? But why? You've already questioned me twice. And I can answer any more questions here, can't I?"

He smiled nastily. "Because I want to question you in Torbay, that's why. If you don't like it," he paused meaningfully. "I can always arrest you if you prefer."

Her shoulders slumped. So that was the way things were heading.

She contemplated making the customary demand to see her lawyer. It was the smart thing to do, and with her contacts she knew she could get hold of some of the brightest criminal defence brains in London. But in the end she decided to say nothing for now. This whole thing was a stupid mistake, and she didn't want to escalate matters further. If the situation deteriorated she could get someone down tomorrow.

"That won't be necessary," she said.

He nodded. "Best get a few things," he said. "You might be there a while."

Chapter 13

Bubs stood with Simon, Lin and Peter on the front steps and watched the police car drive away, an ashen-faced Isabella seated in the back. When it was out of sight she turned and faced them.

"Well?" she said. "What are you going to do?"

Simon started as if being roused from a reverie.

"What do you mean?" he said.

She rolled her eyes impatiently. "About helping her, of course. That inspector is a complete yokel – he'll just go for the first thing that he sees under his nose. He's not going to look for stuff that's going to get her off, so you'll have to."

None of them said anything.

It took a few moments for Bubs to get it. "Christ, you don't believe she actually did it, do you? For God's sake, how can you? She's your friend!"

Simon spoke slowly, as if to a child. "Bubs, someone has just killed another of our friends. Another. That's two now. I don't know what the hell is going on, and it's obviously possible that some stranger got into the grounds without any of us knowing, but there's got to be some likelihood that it's one of us – one of the six of us left. All I do know," he said, putting his arm around Lin protectively. "Is that it's not either of us."

He drew Lin into the house. Peter looked after them and shrugged. "All we want to do is get back to London. I can't believe they still won't let us go."

Then he too went inside.

Bubs stood seething on the steps for a moment or two. With a muttered imprecation she followed them in and went off to the only place she still felt comfortable, her kitchen.

From the moment they'd got back to the house after finding the body the house party had seemed to degenerate into some sort of ghastly reality TV show. She knew that times of stress tended to make people more tribal, but she'd never witnessed anything so extreme before. On one side was Felicity, implacable in her belief that Isabella had killed Hugh. Her natural ally from the word go was Peter, with Abi seeming to follow his lead without much resistance. At the other was Isabella. She'd seemed to Bubs to be something of the odd one out all week; Hugh's death only served to increase her isolation. And Simon and Lin, naturally disoriented by the whole thing, initially trying to play the diplomat, bridging the divide, becoming increasingly drawn towards Felicity's camp.

Which left Isabella with only one ally - Bubs herself.

She made herself a cup of tea and sat down at the long wooden table to try to think. Simon was of course right – it had to be one of them. With everyone in the house straying all over the grounds that afternoon it was inconceivable that none of them would have seen an intruder. She personally was convinced that it wasn't Isabella, and she thought she could rule out Felicity, so that left four – Peter and Abi and Simon and Lin.

She felt the now familiar shudder as she realised that she was trying to work out which of the nice, ordinary seeming people in the next room was a cold-blooded murderer, and understood that this, only many times worse, must be what Isabella had had to cope with every day.

The police didn't seem likely to be much help, she decided. Focussed as they were on Isabella they wouldn't be looking at anyone else. Then she checked herself – she was probably being unfair. They might regard Isabella as their strongest lead at the moment, but that didn't mean that they wouldn't be following up on other stuff as well. There would be a huge mass of forensic evidence from the lake for sure, and some of that might exonerate her. It certainly couldn't incriminate her, as she'd sworn to Bubs that she hadn't been up to that end of the lake until she'd raced down with the others, and Bubs believed her.

And if that inspector had seemed like a yokel, as she'd put it to Simon, the same couldn't be said for his sergeant. He seemed pretty cool. Fit, too. Perhaps he would help her prove her friend's innocence.

She heard a noise and looked up to see Abi standing in the doorway, looking pointedly at her mug of tea.

"I came to see if we were all able to get one of those," she said.

Bubs strained with the effort not to make some sort of sarcastic retort.

"Sure," she said, getting to her feet. "I'll make a fresh pot for you."

Abi seemed reluctant to let go. "It is your job, you know."

Bubs spun round suddenly, causing Abi to back away in alarm.

"I know my job, thank you very much. I've just been a bit pre-occupied thinking about how to get *your* friend off a murder rap. Which is more than I can see any of you doing."

Abi advanced into the room again. "How do you know she didn't do it, eh? Someone did, you know. It might as well have been her as anyone else."

Bubs held her ground. "Because although I only met her a few days ago, I reckon I know her pretty well. It could be any of you for all I know, but I know for a fact it wasn't her."

Abi's eyes narrowed unpleasantly. "Yes, you have spent a lot of time with her, haven't you? It's been noticed, you know. We've all wondered what you two were up to. So what did she tell you to make you so certain, eh?"

Bubs realised she was in danger of letting on altogether too much. "Nothing much," she backtracked. "It's just I know what she's like, and what she's been through. It's not the sort of thing she'd do."

Abi stared at her for a moment. "Yes, well," she said eventually. "When you're a bit older you might realise that appearances can be deceptive."

She turned to go, pausing in the doorway.

"And some biscuits would be nice."

*

Chu had decided to drive down to Devon. The train would have been quicker, but when she realised that the local CID headquarters was in Torbay, the Incident Room in some tiny village called Chudleigh, and the crime scene in some place on Dartmoor so obscure that it didn't even feature on her map, she realised that it was going to be essential to have her own set of wheels. Somehow she didn't think the locals were likely to offer her a police driver.

She had read the file thoroughly the previous evening. She saw what Ireland and Bellow had meant – there were no obvious howlers, just an overall laziness that she hadn't seen before on any of the cases she had worked. It was as if Gormley had ended up simply tossing it into the 'too difficult' basket.

And so now it was down to her – her first murder as SIO. Of course she wasn't really, Ireland was, but stuck on her own in Devon she was going to have to make her own decisions pretty much all of the time. She just had to hope she didn't screw up.

She really, really wanted to impress Ireland on this one. If she'd stayed in uniform she'd have made sergeant at least a couple of years ago, but she'd been set on CID. As it was the promotion had come through quicker than she might have expected – due in part, she was sure, to Ireland's influence.

He'd made it very clear that he had been pleased with her police work on that last case. He had made a few other things pretty clear as well, which had come as a bit of a surprise to her at first, although she'd decided after a while that she didn't mind too much. He'd been very sweet about everything, not at all aggressive, and studiously avoiding playing any power games with her. She'd actually been quite tempted – it wasn't as if her love life was exactly in overdrive at the time - but she'd turned him down in the end, just because she didn't really want that sort of complication so soon into the job.

And if they did have a relationship, and it became public, there would be those that said she only got on because she was shagging the boss. She knew that wasn't the case, she knew she was going to be a bloody good detective. But it was the sort of hassle you didn't need.

Not when you were as ambitious as she was.

She wished she knew more about Chester himself. She had often heard Ireland say that the solution to most murders lay in the character of the victim. She knew it was hardly an original sentiment, just common sense really, but that didn't make it any less true.

Chester was a reporter, and she knew that reporters often made enemies. Not that it looked from the file as if he was exactly a hardcore investigative journalist, but he might have stumbled onto something dangerous. There had been the usual attempts to reconstruct his life over the weeks leading up to his death – computer activity, phone records, etc., but nothing there looked even remotely suspicious. Still, it didn't look as if the wife had been questioned much on that subject – Gormley had been too busy pursuing her as a suspect at first, and after that it looked as though relations had been somewhat strained between the two of them. Chu resolved to ask Isabella about his journalistic activities when she got the opportunity.

And then there was the new evidence of the affair, which Harris had told her about. That certainly provided a few motives, not least for Guthrie and the widow. But if either of them had killed Chester, why on earth would they draw attention to themselves now, in her case by confronting Felicity Guthrie, or in his by admitting to the knowledge? It didn't make sense.

She had spoken to Harris before setting off and agreed to meet him at the local headquarters in Torquay. She parked in a public car park and walked the last few hundred yards, relishing the chance to stretch her legs. It was late afternoon, the sun was warm, and she was – more or less – at the seaside. In other circumstances she might even enjoy herself. Today, though, all she felt was trepidation.

She announced herself at reception, then sat down to wait – just like a civilian. After a few minutes Harris appeared, with a friendly but businesslike smile, and shook her hand.

"Hi - I'm Gerry."

"Karen," she replied, matching his manner.

"Let's go and catch up in one of the interview rooms," he said, leading her away. "There've been a few developments since we spoke."

She had formed a mental image of him from his voice on the telephone, and she was childishly pleased to discover that her ideas had been almost spot on. He was a bit shorter than she had expected, and a little younger - barely older than her in all probability - but the slim, athletic build was there, as was the short fair hair. Well-dressed for a copper, too. Maybe they'd get on.

She'd shed her normal city office look in favour of anonymously casual jeans and tee shirt, and she was amused to see him covertly checking her out as well. He got them both coffees and they sat down on regulation plain plastic chairs, either side of an even plainer Formica table.

He didn't beat around the bush. "We're a bit surprised London sent anyone down at all, to be honest. All we wanted was the file for background. You can do a lot with phone and email these days, you know."

She shrugged. "We've got an unsolved murder, this seemed to be a chance to put it to bed. And you know how it is – sometimes things strike you when you're there on the ground that wouldn't come out from a report, however good. I'm obviously not here to try and muscle in on your case, though, if that's the worry."

He nodded. "You better not be. It's not me, you understand. I was trained recently enough to know that colleagues, even those from the wild fringes of civilisation like London, aren't always a threat. Sometimes they can even be of some help."

"But your boss…?"

"Is old school. Don't make the mistake of underestimating, him, mind. Just because he's not got a fancy accent doesn't mean he's not a bloody good copper – he is. But he doesn't like interference. He's already got the Major Crime Investigation Unit lot all over the case, and he's not in the mood for any bright sparks from the Met starting to play silly buggers. I've got orders to keep you away from him, basically."

"But I'll be able to talk to the witnesses, right?"

He shook his head. "Only with me there." He grinned. "That's not so bad, though, is it?"

She smiled back. "So you're my nursemaid, eh? Fair enough."

It was as good as she was likely to get. And he seemed a decent enough bloke. One thing was absolutely plain, though – without his help, she was going to be frozen out completely.

"So what are these new developments you mentioned?"

His face clouded. "The boss's idea. He's hauled the Chester woman in for questioning – going to give her the third degree. He's letting her cool her heels for now – soften her up."

Chu recalled what she had read about Isabella in the file. From what she had read she didn't sound the type to soften up in a police cell – rather the reverse.

"But why? Everything from our original investigation – I know it wasn't the best, but I happen to believe this bit – tells us that she didn't kill her husband. So why should she kill Guthrie? Do you think there are two killers?"

He shrugged. "Like I told you on the phone, there's evidence that she'd started to believe Guthrie killed her husband, so maybe she killed him in revenge. That's the theory, anyway."

"But you don't believe it?"

He gave her a hard look. "I don't *not* believe it. It's just totally circumstantial, that's all. And we're going to get a whole lot of forensic evidence, so personally I'd rather wait and see what that tells us before coming down heavy." He shrugged again. "But it's not my call."

She thought for a moment. It was possible. It still needed Guthrie to have been colossally stupid in volunteering a motive for the Chester murder. Unless, of course, Isabella had killed him in the belief that he was her husband's murderer, when in fact someone else altogether had been responsible.

Now there was a thought. And not a very nice one. It would mean in all probability that her cold case would be officially closed, but with the wrong man being blamed.

"Can I see her?" she asked. "I'd love to sit in on the interview."

He shook his head, a look of exaggerated wonderment on his face. "Have you listened to a word I've been saying? There's not a cat's chance in hell old Lark'll let you do that. No, the best we'll be able to manage is to sneak you in after him."

He rose to his feet, adding as a grim afterthought. "Assuming, that is, that we haven't released her for lack of evidence."

*

That left Chu with the prospect of at least several hours to kill. She decided the first thing to do was check in at her hotel, if the small inn she had found surfing the net yesterday qualified as such.

She'd taken the view that, since she was likely to be spending quite a bit of time driving between Torbay and

Dartmoor, she'd be better off staying slightly out of town rather than in the main tourist zone. Now, as she struggled out through the summer traffic, she was having second thoughts.

But when she got there she was pleasantly surprised. Sure, it was on a main road, but it was not that noisy by London standards, and her room, while small, was clean and well furnished. A tiny dining room and cosy bar completed the picture. Perfect – everything a girl could need.

She toyed with the idea of staying in and eating, but decided it would be best if she wasn't too far from the station, in case Harris suddenly summoned her. Also, the sea air seemed to have roused a craving for fish and chips. So she unpacked, showered, and headed back into town, this time heading for the sea front.

It was not at all what she had expected. It was much classier than her idea of the typical English seaside resort, with its ornate white buildings and yachts bobbing in the marina. The hotels and restaurants were much more upmarket than she had imagined, as well. She wasn't really in the mood for sitting on her own having a four course meal with starched white linen and silver cutlery. But eventually she found what she wanted.

She'd half hoped that Harris might have suggested dinner, but of course he was busy with his boss, interviewing Isabella Chester. Perhaps another night. But she was probably going to have to get used to spending quite a bit of time by herself.

It was gone nine when he called. He sounded exhausted yet somehow relieved, as if he'd at last dealt with something that had been bothering him.

"We've let her go," he said without preamble.

"What? But you said…"

"Something came up, we couldn't justify holding her, so we've put her in a car back to the house."

"So what was it?"

She heard him hesitate for an instant. "Tell you what, why don't I explain it to you over a drink? You've not seen much of our traditional Devon hospitality yet. Where are you?"

She explained where she was, and a few moments later they'd agreed to meet in a pub a few hundred yards away. Somewhat to her surprise, he was already there when she arrived.

He saw her expression and laughed. "Never keep a lady waiting, that's what my old dad always says. I cheated though, I'm afraid – I was already in the car heading in this direction. What'll you have?"

"Why don't I try one of your good, wholesome, local bitters? You chose one for me."

"You got it. Pint or half?"

She gave him a pitying look. "How long do you think I'd last in CID drinking halves?"

A few minutes later they were each clutching a pint of Gargoyles Humbug.

"Is that really its name?" she asked, suspecting she was being wound up.

He nodded. "Really."

"Blimey – what a mouthful." She took a long swig that caused him to raise his eyebrows. "Good beer, though. I needed that. So, what explains your boss's sudden volte face?"

He leaned forward and lowered his voice. "It's the first report from forensics on the footprints from the crime scene. Makes very interesting reading."

She was puzzled. "But I thought you said it was all a mess – that they'd all dashed down when the body was discovered – natural enough behaviour – but that it had ruined any evidence there was."

He nodded. "That was what we thought. But it turns out that where they first saw the body, and where they dragged it out, wasn't the same place that it was pushed in. So they've got much cleaner data from there."

Chu whistled softly. "Well, that should nail it then, shouldn't it? If I remember rightly it had been raining heavily that day – you should be able to get a perfect match, right?"

He grimaced and shook his head. "Not that simple, I'm afraid. There are still quite a few prints. All from wellington boots. All the same make, too – but lots of different sizes."

"Bit of a coincidence, isn't it?"

"Not really – they keep a stock at the house, apparently, for the guests to use. Obviously bought a job lot. But the problem with that is, you can't tie any individual pair to one person."

"So how does that get Isabella off the hook? I don't understand – if you can't make a positive id, how can you make a negative one?"

"Guess which is the only member of the household who wasn't wearing wellies that afternoon?"

"Isabella?"

"Isabella. Apparently she was the last out and all the wellies of her size had been taken, so she wore her walking boots. Very distinctive prints, plenty of 'em found where she said she was, none at the scene."

"Lucky for her. And it's verified that that's what she was wearing?"

He nodded. "The cook, this Bubs person, apparently saw her just as she was setting off and commented on it."

Chu must have looked surprised because he continued a little testily. "There's no need to look like that. We do know how to take evidence down here, you know."

"Sorry – I didn't mean… That's good work, though. So what next?"

He shrugged. "Back to square one, I guess. Old Lark will be nagging forensics for more detail on the prints that they did find, but I know those boys – if there was any chance of getting anything useful they'd have told us."

She thought about that for a moment. Sometimes forensics could point the detectives in the right direction, even if they had no actual evidence that would stand up in court. But equally, drawing tenuous conclusions from inconclusive facts could send them off on a wild goose chase, wasting valuable time. Harris's 'boys' were right to be cautious.

"In other words, everyone's in the frame except Isabella now, is that right?"

He shrugged again. "The boss says it doesn't even completely rule her out – you know, just because you don't find a print doesn't necessarily mean the foot wasn't there. But even he's got to concede that she's a much less likely prospect now. Definitely not enough to hold her."

She nodded. "So when do I get to meet everyone?" she said.

He looked up from his beer. "Tomorrow. Old Lark has got to go to Plymouth for a meeting, won't be around until after lunch. So I can take you up to Harracombe Lodge in the morning and you can join the house party. And good luck to you - they're a right bunch." Then his face broke into its grin again. "But that's for then. Why don't we talk about something more interesting now? Let's start with you."

*

By the time Isabella got back to Harracombe Lodge it was late, way past dinner time. She'd called ahead to Bubs to tell her that she would be back that evening and to ask her to keep some food for her, but beyond that she'd not told her anything about the day's events. She couldn't be bothered.

Exhaustion vied with rage for control of her emotions. It had been a long day, and it was not as if she had slept well the last few nights. The interrogation itself had not been excessively aggressive, but the sheer strain of being in police custody, even just for questioning, took an enormous toll.

The main thing that kept her going was the adrenaline provided by her anger - not anger that she was being questioned, but anger at *why*. She was there because her friends had put her there. All of them. It wasn't just Felicity, although it was her who had made the accusations in the place. But the others had all had the chance to put different points of view to the police, to put Felicity's comments in context. But they hadn't.

If even her friends of many years believed her to be guilty, how could she blame the police for believing the same?

They had all gathered in the hall to meet her. They knew she was coming back but not the reason for her release, and the expressions on their faces betrayed their feelings on the matter as clearly as any words – Felicity's sullenness, Simon and Peter's awkwardness, Abi and Lin's frank curiosity.

For a moment they all stood in silence and stared at each other.

Eventually Simon stepped forward and put his arms out to give her a hug.

"Good to have you back," he said. Several of the others murmured a sort of assent. "What happened? Was it awful?"

She sidestepped his arms and smiled frostily. "I'm tired now – I'm going to my room. I'll tell you all about it in the morning."

Let them sweat.

*

By the next morning Isabella felt better. She'd had a nice long chat with Bubs while eating her supper from a tray, and getting things off her chest had helped calm her down and allowed her at least some decent sleep. She decided there was no point in holding grudges – they were all in this together. Fighting would only make it worse.

She made her way downstairs. There was desultory conversation coming from the dining room. It faded away as she walked through the doorway.

She tried a bright smile that she knew must have come out forced, but it was enough. She could feel the tension in the room, at breaking point when she made her appearance, ease like a spring uncoiling.

"How're you feeling this morning?" asked Simon, not bothering to hide the relief in his voice that she wasn't going to launch at them all. He'd always been one of those people that hated confrontation.

"Much better, thanks. I expect you all want to know what happened?"

Nods all round, except from Felicity, who continued studying her muesli intently.

She took a few moments to get herself a coffee from the side table and sat down. By now all five faces were gazing at her expectantly.

"You'll be pleased to hear," she began. "That the police have released me because they have decided that I am almost definitely the only one of us who *couldn't* have killed Hugh."

As she had expected, a stunned silence greeted her words. She glanced at Felicity – her face was pale, her expression unreadable.

Simon cleared his throat nervously. "That sounds quite a tall order. How have they done that?"

She explained about the wellington prints, and her own position as the only wearer of walking boots. "None of you wore your own boots, right? You all wore the ones that live in the house, which are all the same make?"

Simon, Lin and Peter nodded. "The boys had their own," said Abi. "We didn't bother bringing ours – we thought we were going on a summer holiday." She gazed out of the window miserably. She must be missing her kids, thought Isabella, with a momentary pang of sympathy.

"But surely they must be able to say something about size, if they've got prints," argued Peter. "That would narrow it down further, wouldn't it?"

"They think not. There are so many of them, you see. They can identify them as wellingtons but nothing else." She looked around at them. "So, as I said – I'm in the clear."

The emphasis she put on the final 'I' was unmistakeable. She saw curiosity give way to doubt, speculation turn to dread as the full impact of what she'd said sank in.

Her good news was everybody else's bad news. The temperature in the room seemed to drop as they looked at each other, shrinking away from each other. Wondering which of them might be a murderer.

*

It was another fine day, and after breakfast – conducted mainly in an uncomfortable silence after her revelation – Isabella made her way down to the stone seat behind the holly bushes. She was beginning to regard it as her private place, her refuge, where she could be alone with her thoughts – or, as was the case today, a book of Sudokus.

Despite the early hour it was already warm in the sheltered corner, and soon she was down to a singlet and shorts, wishing she'd had the foresight to bring enough cushions to allow her to lie down on the cold stone and sunbathe properly. She was just contemplating risking the grass, superficially dry but surely still damp underneath from the previous rains, when she heard a rustling sound coming towards her.

It was Bubs. Isabella's annoyance at the interruption faded when she recognised her. Then she saw the expression on her face.

Bubs gave an apologetic smile. "Sorry. I wouldn't have, but it's the police. They want to talk to you again."

Her heart sank. "You've got to be kidding! After yesterday? What the fuck is it now?"

Bubs raised a calming hand. "I know, but look – it's not Lark, it's the cute one, Harris, and a woman detective from London. A Chinese girl. It's her who wants to see you by the sound of it."

Cross, Isabella started gathering her things together. "Well, that's all right then," she grumbled. "They can't get me for Hugh, so they're going to have another go at fitting me up for Jake. Bloody brilliant."

Bubs wrinkled her nose. "I hope not. She doesn't seem like that, anyway. Almost human."

*

Isabella found Harris and Chu waiting for her in the tiny library. Her first surprise was that the emissary from London was so young; she supposed she had expected someone more senior looking. In a bizarre sort of way she felt short changed. The second surprise was that she saw immediately what Bubs had meant. Chu greeted her in a sympathetic, very nearly friendly, fashion, and explained that she was there purely as an observer, in case anything turned up in the course of the current investigation that had any bearing on Jake's murder. For once Isabella felt that she was being treated as a witness, even as a victim, rather than as a suspect. Even Harris seemed more at ease than he ever had in the presence of Lark.

It was a relief not to be starting the conversation already battling against a barrage of preconceptions, but Isabella remained on her guard. She reminded herself that while this briskly efficient woman, who looked more like an off-duty banker than a detective, might seem to be on her side, she was not. She played for the other team. They had their own loyalties, their own agenda, their own rules. And, just as in court, if they wanted to put you at your ease, it was only to get you to lower your guard. It was simply another device to get you to condemn yourself out of your own mouth.

Her reservations obviously showed.

"The last couple of days must have been awful for you, I know," said Chu. "But you must want to find out what happened to Jake even more than we do. You must have thought about it – what do you think happened?"

She shrugged. "I don't know. Of course I've thought about it, but I know no more than you do." She paused. "I'll tell you what I do think, though – it definitely wasn't some sort of random mugging, whatever your lot say."

To her surprise, Chu nodded. "I have to say I tend to agree. So, you think it must have been a member of your picnic party?"

"Not necessarily. Or at least – I used to think it must be some enemy Jake had made, that I didn't know about. He did sometimes make himself unpopular, you know." A faint nod of understanding from across the table. "Maybe he bumped into someone like that? But since Hugh…"

"Yes?" prompted Chu.

"Well, it would be a bit of a coincidence, wouldn't it? Two members of the same group, struck down in unrelated incidents, exactly a year apart?"

"Some of your friends think that's what happened, though," broke in Harris. "An intruder in the grounds here, perhaps?"

It was the first time he'd spoken apart from to introduce Chu, and his tone was subtly different to before – less blunt, less confrontational. As if he was really interested in her views, not just catching her out. Perhaps without Lark's baleful presence he felt that he too could relax and be a human being.

Or perhaps it was just another police tactic.

She swatted his comment away impatiently. "Of course they want to believe that. We all would – it'd be so much more convenient, wouldn't it, than having to believe that one of your best friends is wandering around, bumping you off one by one. But wanting something to be true doesn't make it so. I think we all know that," she ended bitterly.

"Is that how you think of it?" picked up Chu. "That someone is killing you off one by one? That would be pretty scary, wouldn't it?"

Isabella considered for a moment. "Actually, no, I don't think that's it – I don't really know why I said that. If it was the case, there'd have been so many other opportunities. No, my guess would be that if the two are connected, which I suspect they are, something specific must have happened to prompt Hugh's murder."

"Makes sense," said Chu, nodding her agreement. As did Harris, Isabella noted with interest.

"Which begs the question," continued Chu. "What could that specific something be? What's happened this week that's new?"

Isabella's mind turned guiltily to the laptop. That was certainly new, but no one knew about it except her and Bubs.

And she'd decided - that was the way it was going to stay.

She saw a flicker of interest in Chu's almond shaped eyes. She's sharp, this one, thought Isabella – the hesitation had been minute, yet she'd picked up on it.

"I can't think of anything," she said with more force than she intended. She saw Chu's eyebrows rise slightly at the overreaction. "Honestly. I've been racking my brains, and there's nothing."

Chu stared at her for a long moment, her eyes expressionless. She doesn't believe me, thought Isabella. She felt a small stab of panic. Shit, here I am, for the first time with a fuzz that seems even faintly sympathetic, and I'm pissing her off. Smart move, Isabella.

Bu Chu seemed disinclined to pursue the matter for now.

"Okay," she said, and Isabella breathed a little easier. "Tell me a bit about your friends, from your own point of view. I know you won't want to be disloyal, but you're a lawyer – try and do it from a lawyer's perspective – as dispassionate and objective as you can."

Isabella had a wild impulse to say that the Detective Sergeant seated opposite her had obviously not seen many lawyers in action if that was what she thought they were like, but she suppressed the urge. Hysteria was not going to help.

She set about addressing the question seriously.

"Well," she began. "There's Felicity."

She broke off. This was going to be tougher than she'd thought.

"I'd have always said that she was my best friend. You know, the one that's always there in the background, not the sort you see all the time. Family, almost. But then she goes and does something like – well, you know. And you wonder whether you ever knew them at all."

"It was just the once, wasn't it?" asked Chu gently. "And it wasn't her that instigated it?"

Isabella's hackles rose. "And that makes it all right, does it?"

"Just that people make mistakes. I see that all the time in my work – you too in yours, I'd guess. Anyway," she continued more briskly. "That's not really my business. I suppose I'm asking if she might have regretted her infidelity and feared for her future so much that she might have killed Jake. After all, he was the only person – or so she thought – who could expose her."

Isabella shrugged. "I've wondered that as well. I don't think it's her style, but I suppose it's possible. She'd never plan it like that, but if you were going to pick one word to describe Felicity it would be 'impulsive'. But what about Hugh? Why should she kill her own husband? He's been a complete saint."

Chu nodded and consulted the file lying open on the table in front of her. "Fair enough? What about Peter and Abi then?"

Isabella sighed. "Poor Peter. Nothing ever seems to have gone right for him. He sort of drifted into teaching because he couldn't decide what he really wanted to do, and he hates it. He met Abi at teaching college – she was a pretty little thing then, you wouldn't believe it now. They married within months – it was the one quick decision he's ever made in his life, or maybe it was all Abi's doing, I don't know. But he's probably spent most of his time since wishing he hadn't."

"Why?" interrupted Chu. "What's the problem there?"

Isabella shook her head. "They're just too unlike. He's got the most amazingly quick mind, too quick, maybe, like a butterfly – he can never stay on one thing for long. But he needs to be around others like him. Abi though – she's just dull. Solid, basically a good person – she's a complete religious nut, you know, though sometimes that comes out as a nasty judgemental streak – but really, really dull. And it's only got worse since she had the kids."

"So why did he marry her?" asked Harris.

The same old question. The one they'd all asked each other so many times. "I think, at the end of the day, Peter's a fundamentally weak character, and one of the things he liked about Abi was that she was no challenge. It was a lazy choice, and obviously one that he's come to regret. And, of course, he's always comparing her with

Felicity. That's never going to be a very flattering comparison."

"Why Felicity?" asked Chu, looking puzzled. "Why not you, or Lin?"

"Oh, he's always had a thing for Felicity. They were an item for a while at uni. Nothing serious, but he never seems to have quite gotten over it."

She saw the two detectives exchange glances, and realised how they were interpreting what she'd just said.

"Why wasn't this mentioned before?" asked Harris sharply.

"Because it's not relevant. Look, I'm just telling you this so you have the complete picture. It doesn't mean that I think that Peter had anything to do with this. It's been a standing joke for the rest of us for years, the only person it bothers is Abi. And she's just being stupid."

Chu's voice was very serious now. "Fine, but that was when there was a status quo. You don't think that discovering that the object of your affections, not content with marrying someone else, also goes and has an affair with one of your friends, might tip you over the edge?"

Isabella ran her fingers through her hair, desperately trying to think straight. "Well, yes, obviously. But that's the point – he didn't know about the affair, did he? None of us did until this week."

"But that's not right, is it?" said Harris. "Someone wrote to Mr Guthrie to tell him about it. Couldn't that have been Peter?"

"What? Of course it could have been, I suppose. Or it could have been Simon, or Lin, or Abi, or the bloody Archbishop of Canterbury. We just don't know, do we?"

"Okay, okay," Chu broke in. "So you don't rate him as a candidate, am I right?"

"No. I don't."

But always the nagging follow up, the echo of Bubs's question – so which of your five close friends do you think is a candidate for double murder?

Chu was pressing on. "And Abi? We've talked about her a bit, but could she have any motive for either murder? That we haven't heard about?" she added, almost as an afterthought.

Isabella shrugged mutinously, and stared out of the window. The square of sky visible above the trees was bright blue and cloudless. How she longed to be out there, away from murder and its cast of suspects, witnesses and police.

"Only that she hated Jake, disapproved of everything that he stood for. But she was probably just happy at the thought that he was going to burn in hell forever – I don't see why she'd especially want to accelerate the process. And other than that last lunch, when Hugh had a go at her, I can't see any reason for her to attack him."

She looked at Chu. The detective's eyes were boring into hers, probing, not in an unfriendly way, but one that was unnerving nonetheless. She'd seen counsel with that ability in court – to make witnesses feel that their very soul was being stripped bare, layer by layer. It was a powerful disincentive to lying.

But I'm not, she told herself. So I've nothing to worry about.

If only she believed that.

"Okay," said Chu eventually. "Simon and Lin?"

Isabella tried to gather her wits again.

"The sensible ones," she said. "He's a doctor, always been rather studious and serious, met her when he was working in Thailand. Absolutely dotes on her. She's smart, had no education out there, but has learnt quickly. Pretty well dotes on him too. They had a big row with

Jake – he wrote a stupid article about them – but it was more hurt feelings than anything else."

She paused to consider. "I suppose they're the dark horses – there's definitely hidden depths there, but I can't for the life of me think what would push either of them into killing Jake or Hugh."

She sat back and gave what she knew was a rather brittle smile. "So there you have it – none of 'em did it. It needs the plucky detective to ferret the obscure motive out of the distant past and prove it, in a momentous denouement in the drawing room."

Chu wasn't smiling. "Unfortunately, this is the real world. Rabbits don't come out of hats quite that easily." Then she did smile, a genuine, unforced smile. "And I don't think that I've ever been called plucky before. But you're right about one thing, Mrs Chester – we are going to get to the bottom of your husband's murder this time."

The two detectives rose to leave the room and Isabella followed, her spirits suddenly lifted. For the first time since Hugh's death she began to feel that there might be a way out of this mess, that this time the police might actually do their job.

Then, at the door, her fingers already resting on the brass handle, Chu turned. "I would say one thing to you, though, Mrs Chester. If you're right that someone killed your husband, and then a year later – when they must have believed themselves to be safe by now - did the same to Hugh, there can only be one explanation. They must have thought that Hugh knew something. They killed him to shut him up. And if that person begins to think the same thing about someone else, that they have potentially incriminating information – even if in fact they're wrong about that – then they might well kill again." She paused. "So if I were you I'd be careful."

Isabella's spirits crashed down to earth again.

*

After the interview Harris went off to make a telephone call. Chu waited for him in the hall.

He'd promised to show her the crime scene, not that she expected to learn much from it. It had after all been crawled over by literally dozens of specialist officers, and everything that was conceivably relevant had been tagged, photographed, bagged, or some combination of the three. For some reason, though, she never felt fully involved in a case until she'd gone through the ritual of visiting the scene itself. Even though she usually hated them when she got there.

After a minute or two Harris reappeared, a cheerful grin on his face. "Off we go, then."

The pair of them walked slowly across the lawn towards the woods.

"What was that last bit about, then?" he asked when they were well out of earshot of the house.

She frowned. "Didn't you feel she was holding out on us about something? I did. I'm not sure what, but there's definitely something she's not telling us."

He looked surprised. "Not really, no. I thought she was pretty candid, to be honest, considering yesterday." He grinned. "I put that down to your calming influence."

She smiled back. "I'm quite sure you can turn on the charm when you want to." Then the smile faded. "It was when we were talking about Felicity."

He shook his head. "I wouldn't have thought there would have been too much love lost there at the moment. Do you think we were wrong about her then? Letting her go, I mean – do you think she could still be in the frame, then?"

Her immediate instinct was to say no. She had liked Isabella, and everything she had said – except for that one, jarring instance – rang true. And she'd been taught by Ireland to trust her instincts, to look at the psychology of a murder as well as the hard evidence.

But that was the point. It was as well, not 'instead'. She'd had her wrist slapped, quite correctly she had to concede, a couple of times for getting that balance wrong. It wasn't the sort of mistake she supposed Ireland would ever make.

And how well could you get to know someone in a half hour police interview, anyway? Particularly someone like Isabella, a lawyer, who would understand what to say and what not to say, where to seem open and where to show reluctance.

Following your instincts could only take you so far.

"I don't know," she said. "I don't think so. If it was just Jake we were looking at, yes – she had the opportunity, and there would have been plenty of motive if she'd known about the affair."

"You had no idea of that at the time of the original investigation?"

She shook her head. "I wasn't involved, but there's not the faintest inkling of it in the case notes. But in any event, you always come back to two things with her – the physical evidence of the bootprint, and the fact that it was apparently her who stirred up the whole thing again in the first place. Why do that and risk everything? It's not as if the others were pushing her to do it – quite the opposite, by the sound of it."

"Unless Hugh had cottoned on to her somehow."

She shrugged. "But there's no evidence for that at all. And if that was the way his mind was working, wouldn't

Felicity have had some idea? In which case you can bet she'd have passed that on to you as well."

"You're right there. Pure vitriol, she was, that first day. Anyway, here we are."

They had been walking along a broad path through the woods, the soft greens broken by golden shafts of light where the sun peeked through the leaf canopy. They now reached the edge of a small lake, so still that Chu could see the tops of the trees on the opposite side clearly reflected. It was fed by a broad stream from the right, slow and sluggish at this time of year. She could just make out a faint gurgling sound in the otherwise silent woods.

He gestured towards a small wooden jetty, hemmed in by blue and white tape. "That's where the body was found, and he'd obviously been fishing off that jetty for a while, but he actually went in the water a few yards upstream. Come on, I'll show you."

They forced their way through the undergrowth a few yards behind the path, avoiding the tarpaulins still pegged down to protect whatever evidence the mud might be holding.

"Just here," he said.

There wasn't much to see. The stream was about eight feet wide at this point, and didn't look very deep, even in the middle. Long green tendrils of weed writhed lazily on the muddy bottom. She couldn't see any fish.

"Not that I know much about it, but it seems an odd place to fish doesn't it? When you've got all that lake back there. And I'm surprised the body even carried down, the water's so shallow."

He nodded. "Remember though that this was just after some really heavy rain – the stream would have a been a fair bit deeper, and faster. But you're right about the fishing – it doesn't seem as if he was actually casting here. Maybe he was just exploring, looking for something better. He doesn't seem to have had much luck at the lake."

"He didn't have much luck here, either," she said, half to herself.

He looked at his watch. "It's nearly lunchtime," he said. "What do you reckon? There's a decent pub just a few miles away on the edge of the moors. I can show you a bit more of our beautiful Devon scenery."

For the last sentence he put on an accent so broad that she could barely make out the words, but she got the general gist.

Lunch in a country pub, on a gorgeous summer's day. Plus the chance to carry on talking shop with Detective Sergeant Harris.

"Sounds good," she said. "Lead on."

Chapter 14

Isabella had watched the two detectives amble across the lawn deep in conversation. They seemed to get on very well, and she found herself wondering if they allowed themselves to think about each other as members of the opposite sex, or whether it was business all the way. She supposed they did, at least now and then – even detectives were human. It was an odd thought.

She waited until they disappeared out of sight into the woods, then turned and walked slowly back into the house. Simon, Lin and Peter were all sunbathing on the far side of the patio area. She had no idea where Abi and Felicity were.

She went into the drawing room and slumped into one of the armchairs with a sigh. The interview had exhausted her. Even though this time the questioning had been very consciously not hostile, she still felt that she had to keep a guard up the whole time, watch every word she said. God knows what it would be like if you were actually guilty of something. She sensed a movement in the room, and her eyelids, which had started to droop, snapped open warily.

It was Felicity. She looked terrible – as if she'd aged ten years over the last few days. There was something else, though, a difference from only a few hours ago. It took Isabella a few moments to work out what it was.

The anger in her face had gone. It had been replaced by long overdue grief for her murdered husband. But now that her features were no longer animated by that rage it was as if all the life had drained from her - as if the anger was the only thing that kept her going. Now that it was gone she looked literally like the living dead.

She stood in the doorway uncertainly, than gave a weak smile.

"Hi," she said, gesturing towards one of the sofas. "Do you mind if I…?"

Isabella shrugged. "Be my guest," she said.

She watched as Felicity seated herself carefully in the far corner of the nearest sofa. It sent, she thought, whether consciously or not, a distinct message. Felicity wanted to be close, but didn't want to crowd her.

She was intrigued. "So?" she said, raising her eyebrows. "Sun too hot for you?"

Felicity took a deep breath. "I owe you an apology. Several apologies, really."

Isabella waited. There was nothing to disagree with there.

"The thing with Jake," Felicity continued. "There's nothing I can say or do now, I know – it was an awful thing to do." She kept her eyes fixed on her hands, which were fiddling with each other nervously in her lap. "But what I said about you and Hugh. I wanted to explain."

Isabella remained silent. Part of her couldn't help feeling moved by her friend's distress. But the shock and hurt she'd suffered at Felicity's hands over the last few days were too recent and too raw to allow her to reach out to her yet. There was still a gulf between them, a chasm of betrayal and mistrust. Perhaps there always would be.

Felicity didn't seem to be expecting any response though. She took another deep breath.

"You see, the reason I immediately jumped to the conclusion that you'd killed him is that I'd thought the same thing. As you, I mean."

Isabella stared at her. "I'm not quite sure what you mean?"

At last Felicity lifted her head and met her gaze. "I though it possible that Hugh might have killed Jake. In revenge. I'd thought it for a long while."

"But..." Isabella was bewildered. "You didn't know that Hugh knew. Or was that a lie as well?" She felt her colour rise alongside her temper.

"No, no! I had no idea that he really knew. I'd always had this feeling – that if he'd somehow found out, and taken matters into his own hands. But I didn't know, I swear. It just seemed that he was acting strangely around then, that's all. But then later I wondered if it had just been me feeling strange, if you know what I mean."

Isabella continued to stare at her. "But if you knew, or even suspected, all that time, why didn't you...?"

The question froze on her lips, too stupid to articulate. Of course Felicity wouldn't have said anything to the police, or anyone else, with her suspicions. Telling the whole world, including Hugh, if he hadn't already known, about her adultery. Wrecking for sure the marriage she was so anxious to protect.

"So you just assumed that I'd come to the same conclusion and taken matters into my own hands, as you put it?"

Felicity nodded miserably. "I know. It was an awful thing to do. But all those questions you'd been asking – and I was so shocked, and numb. And it was a way to avoid thinking about my own guilt, I suppose. But it was all my fault, I can't run away from it forever. I'm so sorry, Isabella!"

And she burst into tears; great, racking, sobs that seemed as if they would tear her thin body apart.

She was not conscious of willing it, but Isabella found herself rising to her feet and moving over to the sofa. She sat down next to Felicity and put her arm around her friend's bony shoulders.

"It's not all your fault. Some of it, yes, but not all. It's at least as much Jake's. I know that."

It felt strange, saying those words to Felicity. Twelve hours ago it would have seemed inconceivable to her. But her friend's grief was genuine – and she could remember all too well what it was like to lose a husband.

She gripped Felicity more tightly. "But what I also know is this – whatever you did, or whatever Jake did, the person who's really to blame is the bastard who killed them. If I ever get my hands on them…"

Her voice trailed away, her eyes fixed on a point above the fireplace, wondering. She felt Felicity begin to relax as some of the tension drained from her body, and the weight as she leaned into Isabella's shoulder.

Two best friends. United by near enough the worst tragedy that can befall a person, but divided by betrayal and accusation and bitterness. The memory of those things could fade, but they could never be undone.

She sighed. For the second time that morning, she had felt a small glimmer of hope. One of the things in her ruined world had been restored, at least in part. But she was too pragmatic a person to imagine that things could ever be the same again between her and Felicity.

It was just another thing the murderer had stolen from her.

*

Chu and Harris went in his car, driving with the windows open, some local radio station alternating cheesy pop with adverts that sounded like they'd been made by the local amateur dramatic society.

At first the narrow road they were on climbed between high walls, fields one side and woods the other. Then suddenly they rattled over a cattle grid and the moorland opened up in front of them, green and purple hills and grey rocks, rolling away as far as the eye could see.

Chu gazed around her, taking it all in. "It's amazing," she said.

He smiled at her like an indulgent parent. "This is your first time up here, I take it?"

"I like walking, but I normally only get to the countryside near London. This is different – much less..." She searched for the right word. "Cultivated."

He nodded. "Certainly is. Though it's deceptive. It looks from here like it's solid moor, but in lots of the valleys there are little villages and farms hidden away. Here on the edge, anyway. The middle is different."

As if on cue the road narrowed and then dipped, then started snaking down possibly the steepest hill that Chu had ever travelled on wheels. She prayed they didn't meet a bus coming the other way.

They passed through a tiny hamlet, no more than a few farms and houses and a village shop in someone's barn, then climbed up the hill on the other side of the valley.

"I see what you mean," she said. "Whatever do these people do when it snows?"

"They stay at home. Here we are."

The pub was right on the edge of the moor, and benches and tables were set out with views that swept across what seemed like mile upon mile of wilderness. They were high, and there was a stiff breeze that made her glad she had a jacket.

They got their drinks and a ploughman's each and sat down at one of the tables. They were early, and there were only a handful of other customers, all hikers by the look of their footwear and rucksacks. She wondered what they made of her.

"Are there many places like this, then?" she asked.

He shook his head. "Not actually on the moors, no – the pubs are mainly in the towns and villages. There's one famous one called the Warren House, which is fun, but it was a bit far for us to go today. But when you get to the real heart of the moor there's nothing - no roads or houses or anything. Just sheep and army firing ranges."

"You seem to know your way around very well."

"Well, being brought up where I was, we used to come out here quite often, hiking and stuff. Still do, when I get the opportunity. While you're here you should come out with me one day, Karen, if we get the chance."

There was a hint of diffidence, almost shyness, in his tone. Sweet.

"Sounds fun," she said. Then she looked down. "I'd have to find some more suitable footwear first, I suspect."

She'd enjoyed her evening with him yesterday. They hadn't stayed long – the beginning of a murder case wasn't really the time for a major session, and both of them were driving. But he was easy to get on with, and there was that feeling of being able to relax and not worry about what someone thought about your being a police officer. You never got that with civilians.

She'd learned that his family had lived around Exeter for generations, and that he'd been the first of them to go away to university. His mother had been worried that he'd stay away, but he couldn't see himself in a big city like London. She'd half seriously tried to sell him on it; all the bars, restaurants, clubs, venues that were there for people their age to enjoy, but he wasn't interested in that sort of thing, he said. What are you interested in then, she'd asked, and he'd said he'd show her tomorrow. And so he had.

But they still had a murderer to catch.

"What about Felicity, then?" she asked. "She's an interesting character."

He barked a laugh. "That's one way of putting it. Came in to us, all guns blazing. Sold Lark on it being your mate Isabella immediately."

"So it seems. Does he always got for the obvious?"

He bristled. "I don't know about in London, but down here about ninety per cent – maybe even more - of violent crimes are committed by the obvious suspect."

"Fair enough," she conceded. Harris was clearly loyal to his boss and there was no point in antagonising her only ally in Devon. And he was right, of course. She often wondered why it was that she always seemed to overcomplicate things. Whether it was work or in her private life.

"But if we now assume for sake of argument that it wasn't Isabella, what chance Felicity?"

He shrugged. "I think you summed it up well earlier. You can see why she might want to get rid of Jake, particularly if he'd started making a bit of a nuisance of himself. But her own husband? After the way he took her fooling around like that?"

"But maybe that's just what he was saying in public," she answered slowly. "Think about it, Gerry – he sounds quite an uptight sort of bloke. Supposing he could put up with it when he thought he was the only one who knew about it, but how would someone like that respond to it becoming public knowledge? Maybe he felt humiliated, and threatened to divorce her?"

"So she killed him to stop him divorcing her?" He sounded sceptical. "I don't think people do that sort of thing nowadays, do they?"

"Well, maybe she knew that he knew that she'd killed Jake and was worried that when they weren't married he'd let on?"

Even to her it sounded lame.

Harris turned, drink in hand, and raised one eyebrow.

"Good trick," she said, pointing at the eyebrow.

"And is that your central thesis, Miss Detective Sergeant from the Met?" he asked.

She smiled. The sarcasm was soft-edged.

"Just brainstorming," she said. "Got to look at all the possibilities, haven't we? So what about the others?"

He took a few moments to finish chewing a large chunk of bread and cheese before answering. "I agree with the Chester woman that the Rayners are dark horses, but there's nothing tangible to tie either of them to either killing. You'd have to have a pretty short fuse to snap like that over the sort of arguments we're looking at here, and your lot didn't find any history like that for either of them. So they're not top of my list right now."

"Agreed," nodded Chu. "Which leaves…"

"Peter and Abi Willis." He pushed his empty plate away and looked at her, a serious expression on his face. "Now there we did learn something new. That's the first we've heard about him having a thing for Mrs Guthrie, and I reckon it puts a whole new complexion on things. That's what I was doing on the phone back at the house just then, telling my boss the story. And I can tell you, he was very interested to hear it."

"But you heard what Isabella said about him? And he didn't know about Jake's affair with her until this week."

"So he says. How do we know that's true? We haven't even asked him yet. No, I think DI Lark will be having a very serious conversation indeed with Mr Willis."

They made their way back to the car in silence, Chu trying to sort out her ideas in her mind. Harris was right, of course. With this new information they had about Peter they had no choice but to bring him in.

But her thoughts were elsewhere. The hesitancy, or evasiveness, she had detected in Isabella hadn't been when they were talking about Peter, it had been earlier in the conversation. And it couldn't have related to his obsession with Felicity as Isabella had volunteered that information quite happily later on - until, that is, she'd belatedly realised how her comments were going to be interpreted. So there was something else that she wasn't telling them.

And it was surely a basic tenet of detective work, that what you weren't told was always more interesting than what you were.

What if Hugh really did know, or had found out, some information that could identify the killer? And what if that information was the same thing that Isabella was concealing, possibly without even realising it? That was what she had been getting at with her final comment to Isabella.

If she was right, Isabella herself was in danger.

*

The companionable silence in the car was shattered by the shrill sound of Harris's mobile.

"Do you mind?" He gestured towards the open storage compartment between the front seats.

Chu roused herself from the reverie into which she'd slid during the short journey back form the pub and reached into the pile of coins, sweets and miscellaneous debris to grab the phone. She glanced at the name on the display.

"It's your boss," she said.

Harris grimaced. "Probably wondering where we are."

"Hello," she said. "DS Harris's phone."

"Who the fuck is that?" the unfamiliar voice said. "And where the hell is he?"

"It's DS Chu, sir. We're just a few minutes away – we popped out for some lunch."

Lark snorted. "Well, I'm kicking my heels here, so tell him that if he could hurry up and finish his pudding we've got work to do."

He hung up before Chu could correct him. Which was probably exactly what he'd intended, she reflected.

Lark was sitting in his car, barking into his phone when they arrived. They stood, waiting patiently beside the car until he had finished his conversation. Then he got out, glared once at Harris, before fixing his gaze on Chu.

"So you're our liaison officer from the Met," he said, eying her up and down. "You here to do anything useful, other than dragging my officers away from their duties?"

She knew better than to rise. "As I'm sure you'll understand, sir, we're very keen to get some sort of result on the Chester murder," she said diplomatically, laying the faintest of emphases on the name. "Our conversation with the widow this morning was very useful in that regard."

He grunted. "Yes, well, that's what we need to talk about. Get in the car – no, I'm fed up with being cooped up. Come over here towards the trees. That lot in there have probably got their ears pressed against the windows."

They followed him across the lawn. He was much as Chu had expected. Typical middle-aged DI going no further, drank a bit too much, probably smoked. A drooping body crammed into clothes that had once been smart, and if you went back far enough, maybe even been fashionable. Apart from the broad West country accent, he could have been any number of officers she had come across in the Met and elsewhere. But also like so many of them, one glance at his face showed her exactly what Harris had meant. Ignore the truculence and the bloody-mindedness; it would be a mistake to underestimate this man.

He came to a halt next to a rose bed in full bloom. Chu's senses were assailed by summer; the scent of the flowers, sunlight, birdsong. She couldn't help reflecting on the incongruity between all that and the matters that Lark had dragged them across to discuss.

If Lark had such sensitivities, he kept them well hidden.

"Right, Gerry, run me through what the Chester woman said about Peter Willis. Seems like he was holding out on us."

Harris duly obliged. By the time he'd finished his economical précis Lark was rubbing his hands with glee.

"Very good, very good. There's more than enough there to bring him in. And it sounds like it wasn't just him holding out, either – the rest of them seem to have been just as tight-lipped. Why they'd want to cover up for a double murderer, though – it's beyond me. Londoners, I suppose – sticking together," he finished with a meaningful look at Chu.

She'd resolved to keep her mouth shut, but she found she couldn't help herself.

"With respect, sir, I don't think they were deliberately covering anything up – Mrs Chester came out with it quite openly. I think they just never saw it as relevant."

Lark's expression of pleasurable anticipation evaporated in an instant. He stared at Chu with distaste, as if she was something with too many legs at the zoo. She half expected him to come out with some sexist or racist remark, but if he was going to he thought better of it.

"Well if that's what they thought, if, they're fucking stupid, then aren't they? A man has a clear motive for both murders and they think it's not relevant? Give me a break!"

He leered at her. "Motive for both murders, Sergeant, remember? If you're really lucky we're going to clear up your year old case for you in, what, four days?"

She took a deep breath. "Again, with respect, sir, they're all agreed that Willis didn't know of the affair at the time. He was just as shocked as the rest of them to find out this week."

Lark's face, red at the best of times, now turned puce. "So he says, so he says. Jesus wept, if you lot believe every fucking word a suspect tells you no wonder you never get anything solved. Now come on, you," he turned to Harris. "We're taking him to Torbay."

He set off across the lawn, leaving them to trail in his wake. "You," he suddenly swung round to face Chu. "I want you out of the way. You've got no official standing here, understand? I'll let you know if I ever want to see you again."

He stormed off again, muttering 'fucking liaison' under his breath.

Chu looked at Harris. His mouth was set as he rolled his eyes. The message was unmistakeable – you've blown it big time.

She thought she could have worked that one out for herself.

*

Lark was not one to stand on ceremony. He marched into the house, shouting as he went. "Mr Willis? We need to speak to you."

Peter's startled face popped out of the dining room door. Behind him Chu could see the other members of the house party sitting over the remnants of their lunch, staring through the doorway anxiously.

Lark halted inches from Peter's face and drew himself up to his full height.

"Mr Willis, I'd like you to come down to headquarters with me to answer a few questions about the deaths of Mr Hugh Guthrie and," he paused for effect. "Mr Jake Chester."

Peter's face assumed a petulant scowl. "And if I don't want to?"

Lark grinned at him happily. "I'm asking you to come with me voluntarily, so of course you can refuse." He waited just long enough for Peter's expression to begin to relax before he continued. "But then I'd have to arrest you. Your choice."

Peter paled. The others had by now crowded out of the dining room behind him and for a moment they all stood as if in some tableau – Lark, with Harris, Chu and two uniformed officers facing Peter and his friends.

Then Peter nodded once, and without a backwards glance started walking towards the front door.

Abi started wailing, a formless, animal sound of distress and pain.

At the door Peter turned, and, ignoring his wife, addressed Lark. "I want you to know now, that whatever she," he nodded towards Isabella. "Has told you, I've done nothing." Then he turned again and went out of the door.

Without warning Abi launched herself at Isabella, catching her off guard, and nearly knocking her to the floor. Fingers clawed at her hair. "What have you done now, you witch?"

The uniformed officers, one a WPC, grabbed Abi and pulled her away from Isabella. Lark surveyed the scene with disdain. "Get her sorted out," he said to the WPC. Then he turned to Chu. "And you – you can do something useful and help."

He turned and went after Peter. With an apologetic glance in Chu's direction Harris followed suit.

*

Chu shut the bedroom door behind her and sighed with relief. She and the WPC had taken the hysterical Abi up to her room and spent several minutes trying to calm her down. When they eventually succeeded in reducing her screams to a low keening, Chu had left them to it. There was nothing she could do there for Abi.

Feeling suddenly claustrophobic, she went downstairs and out to the patio, gratefully drawing in great lungfuls of fresh country air. After some moments she became conscious that she was not alone, and turned to find a bikini-clad Lin lying on a sun lounger a few yards away. She was eyeing the new arrival with interest.

"Hi," said Chu.

Lin nodded back. "So you're the detective from London? Yours is the first oriental face I've seen since we've been down here."

Chu smiled. "You should come to Torbay – there's a few more there."

Lin stared at her. "I'd love to go to Torbay," she said wryly. "Except we're not allowed off the premises."

Chu was surprised. It seemed a bit draconian even by Lark's standards to keep the entire party confined for so long. "Sorry – I hadn't realised. Still, there are worse places to be cooped up," she said, looking around her.

"True," said Lin, following her gaze down to the woods and the moors beyond. "Though I can't stand being stuck any one place for long – I'm a real outdoors person. That's why I love this country so much – even in London you never feel shut in. Not like Bangkok." She turned back to Chu. "You were born here?"

Chu nodded. "My parents came from Hong Kong."

"So you had all the education and everything? You're lucky." She sounded bitter. "People take you seriously."

Chu shrugged. "I guess. You don't feel that?"

Lin likewise shrugged. "Oh, I don't know. I can't really complain – it's better than being in Thailand at least – I never want to go back to that. I'm probably just on edge. This whole thing is just awful." She looked at Chu accusingly. "It's as if you people are persecuting us."

"Lin, two people have been killed. Don't you think we should try and find who did it?"

"Yes, obviously. But why does it have to be one of us?"

"Of course it doesn't have to be. We're just trying to see who's most likely, that's all."

Lin shook her head. "I just hate it," she said, standing up.

As she turned around Chu was surprised to see a colourful tattoo of a dragon covering most of her lower back.

"Interesting tattoo," she said. "Does it mean something?"

Lin shrugged. "I was told it was supposed to bring luck."

"And has it?"

Lin stared at her for a moment. "I don't know yet."

She went into the house.

Chu stood and looked after her for a while, then feeling suddenly depressed, made her way round the outside of the house to her car. Her place was not here.

*

Isabella sat in the drawing room with Simon and Felicity. Nobody seemed to feel much like talking.

She heard a car start and rose to look out of the window. It was Chu, presumably going back to Torbay to take part in the dismemberment of Peter.

Lin came into the room, looking fed up, followed by Bubs. For the few seconds the door was open they could clearly hear the sound of Abi sobbing upstairs.

Lin sat down on the sofa next to her husband. Bubs took an upright chair in the corner and stared round at them all.

"So what now?" she asked.

Nobody seemed to think it strange that the young cook was talking to them in such a peremptory manner. Perhaps they were so punch drunk they didn't even notice.

Simon stirred himself. "We wait, I suppose. Again. That's something we're all getting used to."

Lin scowled at him. "You may be getting used to it. It's doing my head in, just sitting around, being picked off one by one."

She turned to Isabella. "What did happen, anyway? Did you shop Peter, like Abi thinks?"

Isabella shook her head wearily. "No, I didn't shop him. I just told them what we all know." She recounted her interview that morning. "I didn't think anything of it. Then that sergeant must have told Lark, and he jumped on it. Just like he did me."

No one spoke for a few moments, then Lin sighed. "I wish we could all just go home."

Bubs shook her head decisively. "I think that's just got a lot less likely. If Lark decides he's definitely got his man then maybe, but I'm guessing that from his point of view what's just happened totally vindicates keeping you all here. I reckon he still sees you all as liars, all potentially guilty. He won't be letting you home any time soon."

Felicity pulled a face. "The bloody rental's up in a few days, what's he expect us to do then?"

Simon laughed. "Somehow I rather doubt that's his top priority," he said.

Lin shivered. "We might as well all be down at the police station anyway."

Isabella gave a grim smile. "Oh, I can assure you it's quite a lot nicer here," she said.

There was an uncomfortable silence, broken eventually by Felicity.

"But seriously, it does now feel as if we're all under arrest. He seems to think we're all guilty of something."

"Perhaps we are," said Simon. "Just like in Murder on the Orient Express? Perhaps we all did it."

Felicity glared at him. "Not funny," she said.

Simon reddened. "Well, someone did it. And unless it was Peter, it was someone in this house. One of us four, or that snivelling old bat upstairs. That's the fact of the situation, Felicity."

Lin suddenly turned on him.

"Why are you so sure of that? You keep saying that sort of thing, but how can you be so certain?"

Isabella had never heard her speak to her husband in that tone of voice before. He seemed surprised, as well.

"Surely it's obvious, Lin? Just how likely is it that there are two separate murderers in a group of eight people? I mean, one is unlikely enough, statistically, but two?"

"Statistically? Statistically? Two of your friends are dead and you want to talk about fucking statistics? The fact is, we can't be sure about anything. The police originally thought that Jake was killed by a mugger, so how can you know that there wasn't an intruder in the grounds here? Look at the place – it's enormous, in the middle of nowhere – there could be fifty people out there now and we wouldn't have a clue."

She paused for breath and Simon patted her hand.

"I know you always like to think the best of people," he said. His voice was almost cloyingly gentle. "It's one of the loveliest things about you. But we have to face up to reality, you know."

She ripped her hand away from him. "Stop bloody patronising me!" she exploded. "I'm not an imbecile and I don't always 'think the best of people'. I just don't see why you always have to assume the worst. Look," she gestured wildly at Isabella. "Yesterday you were all convinced that she'd done it – don't deny it – and yet now you know she hasn't. So how can you be sure of anything?"

"I never thought she had," broke in Bubs.

Isabella hid a smile but Felicity flushed angrily.

"Okay, if you're so brilliant, who did?"

Bubs shrugged, unfazed. "Quite frankly, I don't know. But I bet the police are going to find out. Maybe not Lark," she raised her hands against the murmurs of protest. "I agree he's a complete tosser. But the girl from London – she's smart."

"I think you're right there," said Isabella reflectively. "The problem is, though, it's not her running the show – it's Lark. And like I said - he just seems to go for the first thing that's put in front of his face. Today it's Peter, yesterday it was me."

She paused and looked around at her friends. All of their faces were showing the strain now, telltale lines of tension etched between the eyes and the mouth. None of them looked like they were on their summer holidays.

"And tomorrow – tomorrow it could be any one of you."

Simon's jaw set. "Maybe. Or maybe it really is Peter. We just don't know."

Nobody seemed inclined to argue the point. Then Felicity spoke, her voice dreamy, her eyes unfocussed.

"Of course, Simon, you know who Hugh always thought had killed Jake, don't you?"

He stared at her. "No. Who?"

"You."

There was a shocked silence, then Simon laughed. It was a brittle, mirthless, sound. But then it wasn't really a laughing matter.

"Me? Why? What on earth made him think that?"

"Because he pissed you off. Worse, he pissed off Lin," she answered calmly. "And we all know how," she paused delicately, as if seeking the right word. "Protective you are of her."

Now it was his turn to redden with anger. "Complete bloody nonsense," he said. "If I'd…"

"Oh, for God's sake, shut up the lot of you!" Isabella leapt to her feet. "What's happened to us? We're just going round and round in circles, accusing each other. I can't stand it any more."

She wrenched open the door and walked quickly through the house and out on to the patio area. There she stood for a moment breathing deeply. She felt as if she had been suffocating. Perhaps they all were – drowning in their own fear and bile. It was becoming intolerable.

The garden, with its birds and sunshine and tress waving gently in the breeze, seemed to be mocking her. It was as if she was trapped in a nightmare, except that in a nightmare the horror was in your mind and reality was the refuge to which you longed to return. Here it was the other way round – the dream was this idyllic garden on this perfect summer's day. And the reality was the horror crouching in the dark corners inside.

She heard a step behind her and spun around, ready to scream with rage. Why couldn't people leave her alone? But it was only Bubs.

Her shoulders slumped and she breathed again. "It's you," she said, unnecessarily. "God, I don't know what's the matter with us."

She moved over and sat down on one of the wooden benches.

Bubs followed her and perched on the arm of the bench.

"I should say it's a thoroughly normal and predictable reaction to a situation of extreme stress. You've all had a terrible series of shocks, and in not knowing which, if any, of your friends is a killer, you've had one of the foundations of your whole adult lives, your trust in your friends and your support networks, ripped away. Plus, you're all trapped in a highly claustrophobic environment. It's classic."

Isabella looked at her with sudden aversion. "Is that all it is to you? A fucking psychological experiment? We're not a bunch of your poor sodding lab rats, you know."

She knew even as she was speaking she was being horribly unfair. None of this was Bubs's fault. Her only crime was being there.

Bubs stiffened. "Sorry. Speaking out of turn again. I'd better go and clear up lunch." She made to go.

"No," Isabella grabbed her arm to prevent her leaving. "I'm sorry. All I ever seem to do is have a go at you, and you're only trying to help. Please – sit down for a bit."

Bubs hesitated only for a moment, then eased on to the bench next to Isabella. For a while the pair sat, like an old couple at the seaside, staring straight ahead of them at nothing in particular.

"Trouble is, you're right," said Bubs. "I do see things like that – I can't help it. But it doesn't mean I don't feel really bad about everything."

Isabella sighed. "I know. It's just sitting in there, you can't help wondering, which of you... I feel so alone."

Bubs squeezed her arm and half smiled. "At the end of the day we're always alone, and at the same time never alone. It's a paradox."

Isabella stared at her. "Is that a quote from somewhere?"

Bubs shrugged. "Don't know. It's true, though, isn't it?"

Isabella nodded. "Too damned right. That's exactly how it feels. Physically, I can't get away from them, yet I feel totally isolated from them."

Silence fell again.

"So you rate the girl from London, do you?" asked Isabella after a while. "I didn't know you'd spoken to her."

Bubs shook her head. "I haven't properly. But just seeing how she reacted to things – to you, to Lark – she seemed okay. What did you think?"

"Better than Lark, I suppose, but that's not saying much. So would Stalin be, probably."

"No, but she didn't seem the type just to go for the obvious, did she? Didn't you think you could trust her?"

Isabella snorted. "Trust her? She's police, Bubs. At the end of the day they're all the same."

"But you're a lawyer – surely you don't really believe that, do you?"

She looked genuinely shocked, and Isabella was reminded how young she was. She had a lot to learn.

Isabella sighed. "No, I suppose not. But when you've just been through what I have, it does shake your faith in things a bit. Of course you're right – she is better than the others. But what can she do on her own?"

Bubs hesitated. There was something in her manner that made Isabella look sharply at her.

"What?"

"I was just thinking." Her voice was tentative, almost childlike. "Maybe you should show her the laptop?"

Isabella was aghast. "The laptop? You're kidding!"

"No, listen." Bubs's voice was urgent. "You want to find out what happened to Jake. She's from London, that's her main interest. That's what she told you, they want to clear up their cold case, right? So don't you think you should do anything you can to help her?"

"What's the point? We know what's on it. What can she do?"

"I don't know, but they're the experts – maybe they can find something we missed. It's worth a try, isn't it? What've you got to lose?"

"For one thing, it would give Lark another excuse to haul me in and have a go at me for withholding evidence. And I don't want him pawing all over Jake's stuff."

She knew she sounded stubborn and peevish but what she said was no more than the truth – she couldn't bear the thought of sitting opposite Lark, his leering face reading out Jake's account of his romps with Felicity.

But Bubs wasn't going to let go. "Tell her so then. Tell her that this is new evidence for the Jake investigation and that it's for the Met's use only. She won't mind – you can tell she hates Lark as much as you do."

Isabella was unconvinced. Her faith in the police had taken such a pounding that she found it hard to believe that any of them would keep their word or respect her wishes. Even someone as apparently human as Chu.

"I still don't know. Maybe. I'll think about it."

"But…"

"I said I'll think about it, okay? Just leave it for now."

Bubs left it.

Isabella shifted her position. Her eyelids felt heavy, and if the bench had been less uncomfortable she might well have dozed. As it was the heat of the sun and the call of some songbird, repeated almost hypnotically every few seconds, were almost enough to send her off. And if she slept, she could forget…

"So what do you really reckon about Peter?" Bubs's voice broke into her reverie.

She sighed. "I just don't know. Maybe. Probably not. I'd never have said he was capable, but who knows what anyone's capable of anymore?"

Bubs looked at her. "Then we just have to hope the police get it right."

Isabella returned her gaze. "Do you believe they will?"

Bubs shrugged. "Got to, haven't you?"

"I suppose. Lark doesn't exactly fill you with confidence, though, does he?"

"Perhaps if they had the laptop…"

Isabella had to smile. "You don't give up, do you?"

Bubs grinned back. "So various ex-boyfriends have complained." The she looked serious again. "But no, not when I think something's important."

Isabella rose to her feet wearily. "Okay. You win. Let's give her a call."

Chapter 15

Peter's interrogation went on all afternoon and well into the evening. Lark had been reluctantly persuaded by Harris to allow Chu to sit in on the interview, on the basis that he was now the prime suspect for both murders. He had conceded with ill grace, motivated, she suspected, not so much by some newly discovered spirit of inter-force cooperation as by the prospect of putting one over the Met in front of their own officer. Even then, she still had to put up with a lecture on what she was and wasn't to do that wouldn't have seemed out of place in a convent boarding school. Put simply, she was to sit in a corner, not move a muscle, and keep her mouth shut.

The interview room was no better and no worse than she would have expected from a tiny box, deep in the bowels of a large building, in the middle of July. Stiflingly hot, claustrophobic, and, after holding four bodies for several hours, very smelly. She found herself thinking longingly of the garden at HarracombeLodge, and the cool breezes that came off the moors.

The conditions could have been designed to fray tempers from the outset, let alone with an officer like Lark in charge. He was ebulliently confident. Another hour or so and I'll have broken this little sod, his body language seemed to say. Chu lost count of the number of times she had to bite her tongue in the face of his abusive, ranting, interviewing technique. But Peter's repeated rebuffs of the accusations, and his failure to rise to Lark's provocations, seemed in the end to wear the detective down rather than the other way round.

Peter admitted his obsession with Felicity readily enough, and gave the appearance of answering all Lark's questions – about their shared history, his feelings about her marriage to Hugh and his own to Abi – in a straightforward enough fashion. His description of his rows with Jake at the quiz evening and elsewhere corresponded exactly with the records on file of what he'd said the previous year. But he was adamant that he'd never lifted a finger against either Jake or Hugh, nor that it had ever occurred to him to do so

"So. Peter. You've admitted that you thought Jake Chester was a useless little shit. Can't say as I disagree with you there. He took the piss out of you all the time, and we know of a number of times that you lost it with him completely. You even threatened him on at least one occasion, didn't you?"

Peter sat with his head cradled in his hands, staring at the table. The sweat was pouring off him but his voice was steady.

"I was drunk," he said. "I didn't mean it. I never touched him."

"But that was just at a bloody school quiz evening, wasn't it? I mean, how bad can something like that get to make a man lose his rag, eh?" Lark's expression conveyed total incredulity at the very idea.

"I told you, I was drunk," repeated Peter.

"But you were also drunk at the Kew evening, weren't you? Lose your temper with him there as well, did you?"

Peter continued staring at the table and said nothing.

"And then there's Guthrie. What I'm not sure of is whether he somehow found out that you'd done in old

Chester, or whether you just saw this as an opportunity to see off another rival. Or perhaps it was a bit of both?"

Peter shook his head. "You've got the wrong bloke – I never touched either of them."

Lark raised his eyebrows. "Really? I don't think I've got the wrong bloke, Peter. I don't think so at all."

He let the silence develop before a few moments before continuing. "The trouble is, your mate Jake Chester knew how to press your buttons, didn't he? He made you feel like a loser – not that that's too hard to do, I expect. But you couldn't have liked that, I imagine?"

He leaned right across the table so that his face was inches from Peter's. "So what I ask myself is, if he could wind you up that easily, how must you have felt when you found out that he was knobbing the love of your life? The woman you always wanted, and couldn't have. And now the man you hated had slipped into her knickers," he clicked his fingers. "Just like that."

He sat back in his chair again and narrowed his eyes. "I think we know the answer to that, Peter. You'd have wanted to kill him – of course you would. Anyone would. So when you got the chance, you did."

Peter looked up, a defiant expression on his face. "No," was all he said.

Lark carried on as if he hadn't spoken. "I don't expect you planned it, of course. You probably bumped into him, just the two of you, and you had a go at him about it. Then perhaps he taunted you, told you how good a lay she was maybe, and you just lost it."

Suddenly he slammed his hand down on the table, making them all jump. "Is that how it happened, Peter?"

Now Peter leaned forward, his face flushed and desperate. "I've already told you, why won't you fucking listen? I never touched him. Or Hugh," he added as an afterthought.

Then he slumped to the table again. "Why won't you believe me?" he moaned.

And so it went on.

By the end of the day Lark was a very frustrated detective indeed. But he was obviously still convinced that he had the right man - it was just that cracking this particular nut was going to be a bigger job than he'd anticipated. So with an instruction to keep Peter in overnight, and the promise of a resumption of hostilities in the morning, he stomped off to marshal his energies and his arguments for the next day.

"And get bloody forensics to pull their sodding fingers out! If he was there he must have left traces – he wasn't bloody Tinkerbell, flying in and out again. Tell them to find me something."

Chu couldn't make up her mind what she thought. Peter had had plenty of time to put together his own story. And he was no street thug, that you could catch out on some minor detail and use that to unpick the entire catalogue of lies. On the other hand, everything he said was consistent, both internally and with the character of the man as she was beginning to understand him. There was really no indication at all that things weren't exactly as he said they were.

And yet. There was something, some underlying evasiveness, not an outright lie perhaps, but something that he wasn't saying. She felt it, time and again, and she knew that Lark did as well. He wasn't stupid, after all – just a bloody-minded pain in the backside. But on this occasion she couldn't really disagree with the decision to detain Peter. She only wished she could figure out exactly what it was that bothered her so.

She was so exhausted by the day's events that she declined Harris's offer of a quick drink and a bite, and decided to go back to her coaching inn for a much-needed bath and some room service. Besides, she still had to check in with Ireland, and update him on developments.

She had turned her phone off in the interview, to avoid giving Lark any excuse to banish her completely. She settled into the driver's seat of her car and turned it on again.

She had two messages. The first was from her mother, reminding her that her uncle and aunt were coming for lunch on Sunday, and to make sure she was there. She sighed. Her mother simply could not understand how anyone could let the demands of a job come before family duty. What do you mean, you're in Devon on a murder enquiry? Your uncle is expecting you.

Sometimes it did her head in.

She debated whether to call back now, or whether to risk aggravating the situation by putting it off until the following day.

She still hadn't made her mind up when the second message put all thoughts of her uncle from her mind. It was from Isabella.

*

Her voice was tense, barely above a whisper. She was obviously wary of being overheard.

"Sergeant Chu? It's Isabella Chester here. I wonder if you could give me a ring on this number? There's something I want to give you – something of Jake's. And please, please don't tell anyone else about this until we've spoken. Thanks."

Intrigued, as much by the urgency in Isabella's tone as by the message itself, Chu pressed call return. The call had been made hours ago, and she hoped she was not too late.

"Hello?"

"It's Sergeant Chu here. You wanted to talk?"

The voice at the other end of the line changed – it became alert and businesslike – artificially so, to Chu's ears.

She heard Isabella say 'the office – I'll take it upstairs', then a pounding sound as Isabella ran upstairs. Then a door shutting.

Isabella's voice, slightly breathless now, barely above a whisper.

"What's happening down there? I was hoping you'd have called this afternoon."

"Sorry, I've literally only just got your message. We've been interviewing Peter."

"How's that going?"

"Lark's keeping him in overnight."

"I see." Isabella, fell silent, presumably thinking through the implications of that.

"Something of Jake's…?" Chu prompted her.

"Yes." She suddenly sounded reluctant. "It's an old laptop of his – I didn't think he'd ever used it, and I brought it down to do some work on, but then I found it was full of his stuff."

She paused. "Odd stuff. Some not very nice. But there's various files about people, some in code, and we – that's Bubs and me – thought there might be something that would help find his killer. Anyway, we can't see anything, and you've got more experience of this sort of thing and maybe special equipment, so we wondered if you'd like to take a look."

"Well, obviously." Chu's mind was racing. "Are you saying the police have never seen this before? Not in the investigation last year?"

"No – I told them it was unused and they never bothered. It was a genuine mistake."

She sounded anxious, but Chu knew that the real mistake wasn't hers. How the hell did detectives investigating a murder come to take someone else's word over something as important as a victim's laptop?

"Of course. And you've not told anyone down here? The local police, I mean?"

"No. The only other person who knows about it is Bubs. And regarding the local police," her voice suddenly grew more assertive. "I want to be very clear – I am surrendering this to you as new evidence for the Met's enquiry into my husband's death, and that's where I want it to stay. As far as I'm aware it has no bearing on Hugh's death, therefore the Devon police have no jurisdiction over it. I don't want Lark to even know that it exists. Do you understand?"

It sounded like a prepared speech, the arguments carefully thought out. Chu knew exactly what she was saying, she just wasn't sure she could agree to it.

"You're putting me in a very difficult situation, Mrs Chester. Police forces are supposed to cooperate on murder enquiries. Supposing there is something relevant to Mr Guthrie's death? After all, you were only saying this morning that the same person was responsible for both deaths. I can't promise not to show DI Lark evidence pertinent to his case."

"So is Lark fully cooperating with you, sharing everything with you?"

Fair point. But she had to play the party line. "Inspector Lark…"

"Of course he's not," Isabella interrupted her. "Look, I'll make a deal with you. You treat it in the first instance as only relating to Jake's death. If it helps identify Jake's killer and that leads in some way to Hugh's then of course you can tell Lark. And in the highly unlikely event that it has nothing to do with Jake but does have a *demonstrable* bearing on Hugh's death, then again you can let Lark in. But until then it remains secret. Now, do we have a deal?"

There was something about lawyers. She sighed. "Yes, we have a deal."

Isabella sounded pleased. "Good. So when do you want to collect it? I'd drop it over myself only your friend doesn't allow me off the premises."

The light-hearted tone didn't disguise the resentment. Chu looked at her watch.

"How about now? I'm going to be tied up with Mr Willis again in the morning."

"Now?" Isabella sounded surprised. "I suppose so. But listen, I don't want the others to know anything about this. Why don't you stop down the drive out of sight of the house and text me? Then I can pop out to you with it. A bit cloak and dagger, I know, but I really can't face a whole load more questions here. I think they're all a bit suspicious of me anyway, and Abi definitely blames me for this thing with Peter."

She suddenly sounded exhausted, and Chu remembered the strain she was under.

"No problem," she said. "I'll be there as soon as I can."

She turned the ignition and sighed again. That bath had just got a lot further away.

*

Once she was out of Torbay and on more open roads she called Ireland. She needed to update him on developments anyway, and she wanted to bounce her agreement with Isabella off him. She still wasn't entirely happy that she was doing the right thing, and she wanted to make sure she'd get some backup if it all went horribly wrong.

He sounded pleased to hear from her.

"Karen? I was wondering when you were going to find time for me. How's it all going?"

"Interesting, guv. There've been several new twists today."

She quickly ran him through their discovery of Peter's infatuation with Felicity and his subsequent interrogation, including her own misgivings.

He was not amused. "Jesus, how did Gormley miss that one? We're going to look bloody stupid if Lark's right about this. You'd better stay close on this one, Karen. What a disaster."

She was tired and was having to concentrate on road. A hands-free phone was all well and good, but it was a bit harder to disengage your mind from the conversation. "But it's not our fault, surely, if there were failings in the original investigation?"

An exaggerated sigh came down the phone. "Christ, Karen, I thought you were supposed to be intelligent? Of course it's not our fault, but that's not going to help much when the Super hits the roof over all the 'Met incompetence' headlines, is it? No, if this is our man I'm going to really have my work cut out covering Bellow's backside for him." He sighed again. "God, what a howler. Anyway, just do your best, okay? Anything else I should know?"

There was an obvious answer to that. It was just that she wasn't sure that she wanted to be the one to tell him.

"I'm afraid there is, guv."

"Shit. What this time? Come on - out with it."

She told him about the laptop. His reaction to the news of yet further evidence of the shortcomings of DI Gormley and his team was predictable, and he let Chu know in graphic terms what he's like to do to the whole lot of them. And she'd not expected a particularly enthusiastic reaction to her 'deal' with Isabella. But there she was in for a surprise.

"She said that, did she? Good girl!" He was positively chortling with delight. "Well, we can't let members of the public down, can we?"

"But guv, supposing there is something…"

"Like the lady said, *if* we find something, *then* we can help out our colleagues from Devon. But right now we've got the first decent chance we've had to get out of this without egg on our faces."

Then his voice grew serious. "You're right, though, you'll have to handle this carefully. Now, time is of the essence by the sound of it. I suggest you give this laptop a good going over on the ground first, see what you can get out of it. If you can't find anything, we'll get it couriered up here, see if the geeky boys can do better. How's that sound?"

Her heart sank. "Fine, guv, but when am I supposed to do this? We're interviewing Willis again at nine in the morning."

"Well, you've got," a pause while he presumably consulted his watch. "Just over eleven hours, then, haven't you? And phone me first thing in the morning with whatever you've got – this is very high priority for us, remember that. "

"Right." And she was supposed to sleep, when?

"Good." Then he paused. "And Karen?"

"Guv?

"Be careful, okay? This is getting messy, very messy indeed. I don't want any more deaths."

*

Harracombe Lodge was a lot harder to find in the dark. There were no street lights at all in the little country lanes, and she found on a couple of occasions that she'd driven straight past a road sign before she'd even seen it. By the time she got there she estimated that the journey had taken nearly twice as long as it had that morning.

She inched along the drive with the car's lights off, anxious not to do anything that would disturb the household. It was a clear but moonless night, and her only guidance came from the faintly paler tinge of the gravel. Without it she would have had no chance of negotiating her way through the narrow, shrub-lined way without crashing into something.

As soon as she saw that the path was widening out into the garden proper she killed the engine and texted her message to Isabella. The she got out of the car and walked the few yards until she was clear of the bushes.

The bulk of the house loomed into sight across the lawn. Both it and the garden looked completely different in the starlight. In London it was never completely dark; here the blackness was near absolute. The house itself was simply a darker shape against the sky, exaggerating the pitch of the roof and the steepness of the gable. The only variation in tone came from the muted puddles of light spilling around the curtains from several ground floor and one upstairs window. Set against the Stygian gloom of the woods the whole effect was surprisingly sinister. Despite the warmth of the summer evening Chu realised she was shivering.

The silence was broken only by the strange little rustling sounds that woods always seemed to be full of at night, and she found herself wishing that Isabella would hurry up. She decided to take her mind off things by picturing the look on Lark's face if he knew what she was doing.

After a minute or two she sensed, rather than actually saw, a presence advancing across the lawn towards her.

"Isabella?" she whispered. "Over here."

She was surprised to find that not one, but two figures emerged from the darkness.

"Is that you?" she asked in alarm. Isabella hadn't said anything about anyone else.

"It's all right," she recognised Isabella's voice with relief. "Bubs insisted on coming with me to protect me."

"Well, what do you reckon, Sergeant?" Bubs sounded remarkably cheery. "Do you think wandering around the garden on your own, here, in the middle of the night, is a smart thing to do?"

"Probably not, in the circumstances. Have you got it?"

"Here you are." Isabella passed her a small case. "The username is JC, the password Bernstein. As in the journalist."

"Or pianist," broke in Bubs.

"JC, Bernstein," muttered Chu to herself. "Right. So what sort of stuff is in there? You've obviously had a look but you were very cagey on the phone."

"Yeah, well…" Isabella's voice tailed away.

"There's loads of files about people in there," picked up Bubs. "No names, and it mainly looks pretty innocent, but we wondered whether he might have got a bit too close to something dodgy. We made some notes – they're in the case."

"Fair enough," said Chu. "Anything else?"

There was a pause, then Bubs continued. It seemed that she'd become Isabella's official spokesperson.

"Nothing relevant. There's a tacky little piece about him and Felicity – she's the 'F' if you need a clue – and some very dodgy pics. They look like internet downloads, though, nothing he took himself."

"Right." Sounded like she had a great night ahead of her. "I'd better be off, then. Thanks."

She turned to go, then stopped in her tracks. She motioned for the others to be quiet.

"What?" asked Isabella. "What's the matter?"

"Sh!"

They all stood silent for a few moments, but the only sounds of movement were far away in the woods. "Didn't you hear that?"

"No." Isabella's voice was suddenly fearful. "I didn't hear anything. What was it?"

"I don't know. Footsteps maybe?" She peered about her, trying to make out anything untoward in the shadows.

"Can't see anybody," said Bubs. "Some animal, probably."

"I guess," she said, still uneasy.

She turned to go again but Isabella grabbed her arm. "You will keep your promise, won't you? You'll not say anything to Lark? Or his sidekick?"

"Of course." Then as an afterthought she added. "And by the way, I wouldn't mention it to anyone else yourself. Just to be on the safe side."

*

It took Chu a lot of persuasion to get even a sandwich out of the hotel kitchen at this late hour. That, and the not very subtle use of the phrase 'Detective Sergeant', something she normally hated doing. But, as they said, a girl's got to eat.

At least the bar was still open. She took her cheese sandwich and bitter up to her room and settled down at the tiny desk for her night's work.

While the machine was starting up she munched her sandwich and flicked through Isabella's notes. Her initial impression was disappointment – if this was all it contained the laptop might be a testament to the expansiveness of Jake's imagination, but its contents could hardly be described as a smoking gun.

If, of course, was the operative word. There might be other stuff that wasn't obvious. She summoned up her limited computer skills and did a few quick checks to see if there was evidence of much that had been deleted. If there was she wouldn't be able to access it here, but at least she would know that she wasn't wasting her time by sending it off to the Met's own specialists.

Nothing. She found no evidence of tampering whatsoever. The internet history had expired, but it didn't look as if it had been shredded or anything, and would be easily recoverable if necessary. Jake had obviously not thought it necessary to cover his tracks at all. And there was no email account. So if she was to find anything useful here, it would be in one of these files.

The trouble was, she had no idea really of what she was actually looking for. Something that was so awful that it was worth killing to keep it from coming out, was what it came down to. With a hollow feeling in her stomach that the cheese sandwich hadn't really done much for she started going through the files, one by one.

Most she was able to dismiss with in a few seconds, but there were a few that seemed to contain some vaguely serious allegations. She made a separate note of them, and after an hour or so she had a sort of priority list of a dozen or so accusations of various types of murder, mayhem or malpractice, against person or persons unknown. Or, more accurately, person or persons identified only by an initial. Which, according to Isabella's notes, wasn't even necessarily the right initial – in the file on Hugh's alleged murder of his partner, he was titled 'S'.

She checked her own records – Hugh Timothy Guthrie. Not an 'S' in sight.

She decided to look at it the other way round; ignore names and initials altogether, and see which of her more serious cases *could* involve any members of the house party. With most of them she drew a blank – the descriptions, skimpy as they were, just couldn't be of Isabella, or Peter, or any of the others. But there was one that could, and she reread the relevant file with growing excitement.

It concerned a doctor. And Simon Rayner was a doctor.

Like all the others, it was short on fact and long on speculation. Anything useful, like names of people or places, were identified only by initials, and she found herself cursing Jake Chester and his paranoia. But there were dates, and they looked uncoded. If this did relate to Simon, the dates should make everything verifiable, even without the other names.

She yawned and looked at her watch. It was past one – no wonder she was tired. She tried to concentrate.

The doctor in the file was referred to as 'H'. That was funny; Hugh was identified as S, while the person she was hoping was Simon was referred to as H. Pity it wasn't the other way around.

Suddenly she jerked awake. Surely it couldn't be that simple? The oldest code in the English language? But there was no reason why not. Jake hadn't really been serious about computer security, that much was obvious just from spending a couple of hours roaming around the laptop. The coding was simply another of his games.

Quickly she pulled a blank piece of paper towards her and wrote out the alphabet in a line across, then underneath wrote it out again backwards. She was right – using this most elementary of coding systems H corresponded to S and S to H. She had cracked Jake's code.

She sat back on the uncomfortable desk chair and admired her handiwork. It was, she reminded herself, probably just a bit early to break out the champagne. Featuring in one of Jake's conspiracy theories was no guarantee of guilt. Hugh had done so, after all, and although they only had his word for it that it was all a pack of lies, the fact that he himself was now dead was pretty compelling support for his argument. There was a good chance that even if this did relate to Simon it would prove to be another dead end.

But it was worth checking out, though, and she set about decoding the rest of the file. The hospital now began with an 'M', while the dead child had the initials CT. The date was reasonably precise, April 1996. If she phoned in first thing in the morning Ireland should have no trouble checking whether a Dr. Simon Rayner had worked at a hospital beginning with M at that time. And if so, what had happened there.

She wondered if there was anything else she should do before trying to grab several hours sleep. She spent a few minutes decoding the other files on her priority list, but nothing jumped off the page at her. In particular she looked for any items that could refer to Peter Willis, but there were none. She was done.

She turned the computer off and started getting ready for bed. She was too tired even to take her bath.

*

The next morning Chu arrived at Torbay headquarters with minutes to spare before Peter's interrogation was due to resume.

Harris was already there, clutching a beaker of coffee and looking anxious. He spotted her and his face broke into a smile, which quickly changed to an expression of curiosity.

"You okay? You look really knackered."

"Gee, thanks. No, I just didn't sleep well. Going over stuff in my mind, you know? Trying to figure things out."

It wasn't really a lie, she'd just left a few things out. Like the laptop, and getting up early to report to Ireland and get the investigation into Simon under way.

He nodded unconcernedly. "Yeah, I know. I really don't think you needed to bother, though. My boss reckons he's got it all figured out. He's absolutely convinced your mate Peter Willis is his man."

"Hmm." Chu was still not convinced herself, but there didn't seem much point in arguing the point now. Not with the interview just about to start. "Anyway, why are they always my mates?"

"Because they all like you up there. You're the nice cop, we're the nasty ones. Well, DI Lark is, anyway."

There was no argument there.

"Which is why," Harris was continuing. "He's given you and I a little task."

He stood there, an expectant grin on his face.

"Go on," she said, suddenly suspicious.

"Oh, it's nothing to worry about. It's just that, if Willis did know about Jake and Felicity, he must have found out somehow – either seen them, or been told by someone who did. So he wants us to go and have a chat with the lovely Felicity, see if she can help. If we can prove that he knew then it'll blow his defence right open."

"If we can," said Chu. "It's quite a big if, you know. I thought you'd already asked her if she'd any idea who wrote to her husband. Why do you think she's got any more to tell us now?"

He shrugged. "We don't. Worth a try, though, isn't it?"

*

They found Felicity sitting on the patio with the others. They were all reading books except Lin, who was lying on a sun lounger, and Abi, who was simply sitting, staring into the distance, chewing her fingernails. Some contemporary rock music, unfamiliar to Chu, drifted through the kitchen windows.

She stole a glance at Simon, but his expression was its usual bland self. She wondered what was going through his mind, if he was as unperturbed as he seemed, or whether the sight of the police would have produced a brief, reflex, moment of panic.

Before they had a chance to speak Abi leapt to her feet and confronted them.

"When am I going to be allowed to see my husband?" she demanded of Chu.

Chu looked at Harris. His turf, his problem.

Harris squared his shoulders. "As you are aware, Mr Willis is being held for questioning in connection with a serious offence. However, I am sure that you will be able to speak to him if you present yourself at the station."

She looked taken aback. "Well, last time I asked I was told that none of us were allowed off the premises."

Harris looked surprised. "Really? They shouldn't have…"

"And if she is to go, one of us will have to go with her," interrupted Isabella. "Abi has no car. So unless you are going to arrange police transportation for her one of us is going to have to give her a lift."

Her voice was cold, clinical. Chu imagined it was her professional lawyer's voice. She looked around the group and was surprised to see a similar blank hostility on every face. It was as if the group had somehow closed ranks against the common enemy.

So much for the good cop.

Even more interesting, though, was what it implied. Abi was a separate case, of course. But as far as the others were concerned, if she and Harris were now the enemy it meant that they all believed - or perhaps in the case of one, pretended to believe – that Peter was the murderer.

She wondered if Harris had noticed.

But his mind was obviously on other matters. "Look, what I was going to say was, of course you're allowed to leave the premises. We'd like you to continue staying here, as in not going back to London, for a bit longer, but that original instruction was only meant for the first day. I'm sorry. There's obviously been a breakdown of communications here."

Five pairs of eyes stared at them.

"Thanks for telling us," said Abi, her voice heavy with sarcasm. "Just as well we asked, isn't it?"

So their charge sheet now had 'police incompetence' added to it, to go alongside 'harassment'.

Harris was plainly irritated at being wrong-footed. "Anyway, that's not why we're here. Mrs Guthrie, we'd like a word please."

Without waiting for a reply he marched into the house and into the library. Chu and Felicity followed him, and silently took their places, next to and opposite him respectively.

He seemed to be waiting for a while before speaking. Chu guessed he was trying to work out how to get the interview onto a cooperative footing after such an unpromising introduction.

Felicity got there first.

"So you think Peter did it? Killed both of them?"

Her voice was flat, but a faint quaver gave away the depth of emotion behind the simple questions.

Harris pursed his lips. "We have to see it as a possibility. But for him to have had a motive for killing Mr Chester he must have known about your relationship with him. He denies that, of course. So that's what we want to talk to you about – how he might have known."

She sighed and dropped her eyes to her lap. "We've been over all that. I didn't think anyone knew – not until Hugh told me about that letter. And the only time I can think that we could have been seen was outside that hotel – you know, when Jake seemed to think he'd recognised someone. But I've got no idea who he thought it was, and I can't see how racking my brains any further is going to help."

She was near to breaking point, thought Chu – not surprising after all she'd been through. But they needed her to stay together a bit longer.

"I know it's a long shot," she said gently. "But we've got to try. And if it isn't Peter we've got try even harder to find out who it is."

Felicity looked up sharply at that, then gave a weary nod.

Harris took up the running again. "What we want is dates and places of every time you met Mr Chester. Not just that day, but any time you met him alone, that could give the impression…"

"Of an affair," Felicity finished for him. She gave the faintest of smiles. "Not difficult – we only met twice. Both times midweek, during the day, so we were home well before evening. There was the time at the hotel, that was the 21st June. I don't think I'll ever forget that date. It was at a grotty little hotel at the top end of Baker Street – the Cleopatra. And we had lunch at a country pub exactly a week before, so that would have been the 14th. The Star at a village called Downey, in Surrey."

He noted down the details. "Could anyone have seen you there?"

She shrugged. "I can't imagine so. There were a few people there, not many, and I certainly didn't know any of them."

"What about on the way there or back. Did you stop for petrol, for instance?"

She considered. "Once, on the way down, on the A3 just south of the M25. I suppose someone might have seen us then. But I can't see how you're ever going to find out if they had."

Nor did Chu. She couldn't help feeling they were just going through the motions here.

Harris was looking dispirited. He obviously wasn't relishing reporting back to Lark with the pitiful amount of information that Felicity had given them.

He got to his feet. "Well, if you think of anything else…" He didn't even bother to finish the sentence.

On the way out they passed Isabella, hovering in the hall. Harris glared at her, presumably imagining that she had been trying to eavesdrop on the interview. Chu guessed, though, that she would have liked a word alone with her, to see if she'd got anywhere with the laptop. She shook her head very slightly, and Isabella turned away, looking disappointed.

When they got outside they both stood, blinking in the strong sunlight.

"Well?" asked Harris. "Any great insights from the Met on that?" His voice sounded bitter.

She shrugged. "I don't know what you were hoping for," she said.

"Something! I was hoping for something, anything. And that was bugger all. What am I supposed to tell Lark now?"

He strode off angrily towards the car.

She waited until she was in the passenger seat before replying. "There is one thing we could do. It's another long shot, but…"

He turned to look at her. "Spit it out, then."

"Willis is a teacher. He should have been at school both those days, it was term time. Schools keep attendance records, staff as well as pupils. I can get our people to check with his school for those dates, and if the records show he was there all day we'll know that it couldn't have been him who saw Felicity with Jake."

He stared at her. "And that's your big idea, is it? When Lark asks what we found out, all I've got for him is that we've successfully put his pet suspect out of the frame? Great. Thanks."

She was suddenly fed up with the whole investigation; the picking up the pieces after other people's cock-ups, the politics, the egos. Above all with Devon and Cornwall CID.

"So what do you want to do?" she blazed. "Cover up any fact that's inconvenient for your boss's case, let someone get banged up whether they're guilty or not, just so Lark can get a result? No wonder you don't like having outsiders around if that's the way you do things."

His hands clenched on the steering wheel. "Is that what you think of me?" he said through gritted teeth.

"No," she admitted. "I don't. But your boss seems – I don't know, always trying to twist things. And that's how mistakes get made. Bad ones."

There was a strained silence for a few moments, then he started the car.

"Just make your bloody phone call," was all he said.

She did. And then the rest of the journey was conducted in silence.

Chapter 16

Their trip to Harracombe Lodge had taken no time at all, and it was barely past mid morning when Chu and Harris arrived back at Torbay. They were told that Lark's interrogation of Peter Willis was still going on, so they made their way to the interview room and Harris poked his head around the door.

Lark interrupted his questioning to come outside and debrief them. He looked as if he could do with a breather.

"Well?" he demanded, mopping his brow with a dank handkerchief.

Harris briefly relayed what Felicity had told them. "In other words, sod all," he said, glaring at Chu, as if it were somehow her fault.

She knew she should keep her mouth shut, but she was getting fed up with this man, superior officer or not.

"Not necessarily, sir. Since there are only two relevant dates, we may be able to establish at least who *couldn't* have seen the pair of them. Willis, or anyone else we're looking at. Surely that's got to be useful?"

He shoved his face inches from hers. She could smell his sweat, and stale coffee on his breath. It was all she could do not to recoil.

"None of it proves anything," he breathed at her. "Even if he wasn't there himself, this anonymous letter writer could've written to him too. And get it into your pretty little head - we're not looking at any one else."

He disappeared back into the room, followed by Harris. Well, I am, she said to herself as she followed them in. I bloody well am.

*

Peter looked a mess. His hair looked unbrushed, he hadn't shaved, and he looked as if he hadn't slept. A glimmer of hope seemed to flicker in his eyes as he registered her presence, as if she might somehow bring relief, only to fade again as she took her seat in the corner without speaking.

Lark resumed his bullying, haranguing, questioning. After a while he moved on to asking Peter about anonymous letters, whether returning to a line he'd been pursuing earlier, or perhaps because of what he'd just heard, she didn't know. But what interested her was Peter's reaction. His previously determined manner, answering Lark clearly if wearily, seemed to crumble. He became evasive, and appeared to be avoiding eye contact. He was a poor liar, she thought.

Lark sensed a change as well, and threw her a triumphant glance before leaning forward to press home his advantage.

And it was at that precise moment that her mobile phone chose to ring.

Lark glared at her, Harris raised his eyebrows in disbelief, Peter seemed to breathe a sigh of relief. She looked at the display – it was Ireland.

With a muttered apology she stumbled from the room, hearing Lark's ironic voice echoing after her. "Eleven fifty four am – Detective Sergeant Chow leaves the room."

Bastard did it deliberately.

She answered the phone. "Sorry, guv – was in the Willis interview. What's up?"

His voice sounded crackly. "Willis, did you say? Very appropriate. That's what I wanted to talk to you about. We've paid a visit to his school. I'm there now, in fact."

She was surprised. "Already? Blimey, that's quick."

"I told you, this is very high priority for us. You should enjoy it – it may be the first and last time in your career that you get what you ask for the moment you ask for it. But seriously, you'd better listen carefully to this. Got a paper and pen handy?"

She listened, gob smacked, to what he had to say. It went far beyond what she had hoped for. The line was so bad that she made him repeat it all, but by the end there was no doubt about it.

"Make sure you call me back, let me know what's happening as soon as you can," he cautioned. "The Super will be waiting to hear."

She returned to the interview room and stuck her head around the door.

"Excuse me sir, but there's something I think you should hear."

Lark's face turned beetroot red. "What the…" he began, but Chu wasn't in the mood to be bullied.

"I said, I really think you want to hear this. I've just heard back from London – it's important. Sir."

It was the nearest she'd ever got to outright insubordination. It felt good.

She saw Lark's eyes narrow, then his mouth twitched in a small smile. Presumably imagining what he'd do to her if her information wasn't up to scratch.

"All right," he said, getting to his feet. "But this better be bloody good."

He suspended the interview and he and Harris followed her out to the narrow corridor. He stood with his arms folded. "Well?"

She took a deep breath. "My guvnor has been to the school where Willis teaches. He wasn't there the day that Chester and Mrs Guthrie went to the hotel – the 21st

June. He was supervising a school trip – to the Planetarium."

Lark's eyes lit up. "Was he indeed? And where the fuck is the Planetarium when it's at home?"

She paused, savouring the moment. "It's in the Euston Road. Just a few hundred yards from Baker Street."

*

The three of them marched back into the interview room. Peter looked from one to the other of them, fear plainly visible on his face. He wasn't stupid; he'd have realised from Lark's body language if from nothing else that something momentous had happened out in the corridor.

"Tell me, Mr Willis," asked Lark, his voice menacingly silky. "Where were you exactly on the 21st June last year?"

"I've already told you – it was a school day." He was pale and sweating – far more so than the heat of the room would warrant. "I'd have been at school."

"I know you've told us that, but we've been doing a little checking with your school."

Chu noted the 'we' with a mixture of fury and amusement. No matter – Ireland knew the score, and he was the only one who counted in her book.

Lark had paused to let the implications of what he had just said fully sink in. And from the expression on Peter's face, that's exactly what they were doing.

"So, now you know that, would you like to check your memory again?"

Peter shook his head. "It was last year, for God's sake. You can't expect me to remember what I was doing on every single day."

He was blustering, desperately hoping that they were bluffing. And Lark knew it, and was enjoying it every bit as much as a fisherman enjoyed playing a lively salmon.

"But you might remember what you were doing," he suddenly lunged forward towards Peter, causing him almost to fall off the back off his chair. "The day you saw the woman you loved coming out of a hotel with a man you detested!"

Peter's jaw dropped. His mouth seemed to struggle to form words, but nothing came out.

"You saw them, didn't you?" Lark was relentless. "You saw them and it ate you up, so you wrote to Mr Guthrie so he would stop it. But nothing seemed to happen, and you were still eaten up, so when you saw your chance you killed him. That's what happened, isn't it? Peter? Come on, now – tell me. The game's up now, you know."

"No!" Peter's voice was little more than a wail. "I didn't kill anyone. You've got to believe me. Okay, I was there, and you're right, I was furious and wrote that letter. But that was it. I didn't kill anyone, I swear."

Lark gave a triumphant smile and sat down, taking his time in doing so. "Peter, I don't think swearing's going to do you much good. We've caught you out – I reckon the CPS will think we've got more than enough to charge you now. Double murder, Peter, double murder. You're going away for a very long time. Now, why don't we make this easy…"

Chu heard Lark's voice droning on, but the words washed over her. She was watching the face of a man whose world has come to an end. And wondering why, having got the result she was sent to Devon for, she felt so empty inside.

*

Somewhat later, in the comparative freshness of the station lobby, she was drinking a cup of life-savingly cool water. Lark had decided that they should take a break, and let Peter sweat for a while on his own.

She'd phoned Ireland and told him the news as soon as Peter had been dragged back to the cells. He had been delighted, extravagant with his praise of her conduct, and announced that he would be coming down the next day to interview Peter himself. It should have cheered her up, made her feel good about the whole thing. But somehow she still felt flat.

She jumped as a hand clapped on her shoulder. It was Harris, a broad grin on his face.

"The boss has decreed a small celebration down the pub. Are you coming?"

She shrugged. "Sure, if I'm welcome."

"Of course you are. Look, I've always said to you, he's not that bad really. He just gets a bit stressed when there's something big on. Now you've helped him get his result he'll be all sweetness and light with you, I promise."

Helped him get *his* result, of course. That was the key.

"It's not actually a result yet, Gerry. Willis hasn't confessed, remember?"

He stared at her in amazement. "You're kidding, right? Surely you don't believe he's innocent, do you? Think of all the lies we've caught him out on."

"Yes, I know, but…"

Her voice tailed away. The truth was, she had no idea what was bugging her. Of course Harris was right, Peter had spent hours denying any knowledge of the affair, and only admitted to knowing about it when he'd been backed into a corner. Of course he'd try the same trick with the murders themselves.

Harris was looking at her more sympathetically now. "Look, I know how you feel. He seems like a nice guy and you don't want to get it wrong. But think about it from the opposite point of view. If he is guilty, he's a very calculating killer. Okay, the first murder might have been a sort of crime of passion, but Guthrie was his mate, who he got rid of just to save his own skin. Isn't this exactly how someone like that would play it?"

She didn't answer, so he put an arm round her shoulder and started leading her out of the station. "Come on – you're tired and it's been a bloody tough couple of days for you. So Doctor Harris is prescribing you a large, cold, glass of something with a funny German name. How's that then?"

*

They went to a traditional old boozer not far away, mercifully devoid of tourists. It was clearly a regular haunt for Harris. A few officers were already gathered at the bar. Chu recognised none of them, bringing it home to her the extent to which she had been kept away from the main body of the investigation. Though from the looks on their faces, they knew exactly who she was.

Lark arrived a few minutes later, looking cheerful. He nodded in her direction, a curt nod, but at least it was an improvement on his customary sneer whenever he saw her.

After exchanging a few jokes with his colleagues Harris took her off to a corner table.

"To teamwork," he said, raising his glass. "I think we made a bloody good team, don't you?"

"Absolutely," she said, raising her glass in reply. "Teamwork, and inter-force cooperation."

He looked at her closely. "Cheer up," he said. "You look more as if you're at a funeral than at a celebration.

It's not going to do the Met's reputation much good with the boys, you know, if they think you don't know how to party."

That made her smile. "Oh, I know how to party, believe me. Though, to be fair I don't normally do it at lunchtime." She shook her head. "I'm sorry, I don't really know what's wrong with me."

"You not really still wondering whether we've got the right bloke, are you?"

"No. Well, not as such. It just seems a bit – obvious, I suppose."

He sighed. "Karen, we've already had this conversation. Just because something seems obvious doesn't mean it's wrong. Quite the opposite. Things don't always have to be complicated, you know."

"Don't they?" Perhaps it was just her experience that they always were. She made an effort to pull herself together. "No, of course not."

They sat in silence for a while.

"So I suppose you'll be heading back to London soon?" he asked eventually.

"Not sure. My guvnor's coming down tomorrow, but he didn't say anything about staying. So we could be off as quickly as Sunday, I suppose." Making it theoretically possible for her to get to her parents' for lunch with her uncle. Another cheering prospect.

"That's a pity. No time for me to show you the moors properly."

She was about to reply when Lark arrived at their table. Her heart sank when she saw his face.

He stood, leaning over her, deliberately invading her space. "I've just had a very strange phone call, sergeant," he said. "From Dr Simon Rayner. Wondering why I've been, as he put it, stirring things up, asking questions about him at his old hospital. Now, I don't know anything about that, so it occurred to me to wonder whether it had anything to do with you? And if it did, why you hadn't had the courtesy to tell me about it?"

Chu swallowed hard. Harris was staring at her strangely, his expression tightening by the second as he realised that his boss wasn't just having a go at her but this time really did have something to complain about.

Lark didn't wait for a reply. He nodded to himself.

"As I thought. Well, it's all academic now, anyway – we've got Willis so it doesn't matter what you've been up to on the side. It saved me a phone call as it happens – I was able to tell him that him and the rest of his mob are now free to bugger off back to London – as I guess you should be doing very soon." He paused to take a swig of his own beer. "I have to tell you, though, I don't like being embarrassed like that, on my own manor. I shall be having a word with your superior officer tomorrow."

He left. Chu turned to see Harris, stony faced, staring at her.

"Any chance of telling me what that was all about?" His voice was as hard and cold as groundfrost.

She took a deep breath. "I can explain."

She told him about the laptop; how Isabella had insisted that Lark did not know of its contents, but that she'd agreed that if anything relevant were found of course it would be shared with them. She left out Ireland's involvement, and tried playing the whole thing down as tying up loose ends. She was conscious that her tone was wheedling, almost pleading, reeking with guilt, but she couldn't help herself. She did feel guilty about it.

He heard her out in silence.

"I would have told you if anything had come up – honestly I would," she finished.

He stood up. "What was it, inter-force cooperation, and teamwork? Nice. Well, as the boss said, it doesn't matter anymore."

He walked over to join the others at the bar, where he stood with his back to her. Miserably, she finished her beer in one gulp, then slipped out of the door to head back to her hotel.

*

Isabella was roused from a dreamless sleep by Bub's voice, calling them all to lunch. She rolled off the bed and went to splash some water on her face to wake herself up properly. These last few days she seemed to have fallen into the habit of not being able to sleep at night but having constant short naps throughout the day. It was the boredom of being cooped up here, she supposed. She didn't know how much longer she'd be able to stand it.

She wandered downstairs and into the dining room. Felicity and Lin were there, as was Abi. She looked in a shocking state. Never one to worry too much about appearances at the best of times, since Peter's sudden departure yesterday she seemed not to have either changed her clothes or brushed her hair. It had been agreed that Felicity was going to take her into Torquay later that afternoon to visit Peter. They'd have to think of some tactful way to get her to tidy herself up – it wouldn't do much for her husband's morale to see her looking as if it were she who'd spent the night in the cells, rather than him.

"Where's Simon?" she asked Lin.

"Just finishing a phone call – he'll be down in a minute." She helped herself to some soup from a tureen on the side table. "He said not to wait."

They followed suit, and a few minutes later they heard a clattering of feet down the stairs.

Simon appeared in the doorway.

Isabella took one look at his expression. "What?" she said.

He went across the room and sat down next to Abi, putting his hand gently on her arm. His bedside manner, thought Isabella. This is not good news.

"I've just been on the phone to the police," he said. "I'm afraid that Peter's admitted to knowing about the affair. It was him who wrote that letter to Hugh. So now they know he had a definite motive."

He paused. "They haven't charged him yet but it was pretty clear that it's only a matter of time."

Abi leapt to her feet, spilling soup across the table. "No!" she howled. "He didn't do it – they've got it all wrong! Oh, God, what am I going to do now?"

Felicity went over to her and put her arm round her, trying to comfort her, and Bubs rushed into the room, looking concerned. "What's up?" she asked Isabella.

"Simon's just heard from the police – Peter knew about the affair all along. He reckons they're going to charge him."

"Shit."

Abi had slumped back into her chair, and was now sitting there, sobbing. Isabella met Felicity's eye, and saw her friend shrug ever so faintly. What do you say to someone whose husband has quite possibly murdered yours? There was nothing about that in the etiquette books.

"I think it would be best if you went and had a lie down for a while," said Simon. Between them he and Felicity ushered an unresisting Abi out of the room and upstairs.

"Thank God for Simon," said Isabella after they'd gone. "He's always brilliant at times like this."

"It's his training," said Lin. Of all of them she had displayed the least emotion at Simon's bombshell, simply sitting there and staring at Abi. "He's probably completely panicked inside." She smiled bleakly. "It's just like being in a horror film, isn't it? Just when you think things can't get any worse, then – out jumps the next thing."

"What's the difference between being arrested and charged, anyway?" asked Bubs. "It's still not the same as being convicted, is it?"

"Basically, when they arrest you, they have grounds for thinking you might have done it. Then, when they've convinced themselves and the Crown Prosecution Service that you actually did, they charge you. Then they have to convince a jury. So no, it doesn't mean that Peter is definitely guilty. But..."

She couldn't bring herself to finish the sentence. After all the nightmares of the last year, culminating in this week's onslaught, she should be ready for anything. But the idea of Peter, one of her oldest friends, as the brutal killer of her husband, just wouldn't lodge in her brain. Somehow when she didn't know exactly who the killer was, even though logic insisted it had to be one of them, she could avoid the issue. Her mind could sort of slide away from the idea that it was any one person when it got in danger of being too real, on to the next, in a sort of never ending mental game of pass the parcel. But now the last layer of wrapping was off the parcel. And there, exposed, was Peter.

"If he's innocent he'll be all right," said Lin matter-of-factly.

Isabella looked at her. "You think so?"

"Of course." She sounded surprised at the question. "I have faith in this country. You English – you don't know how lucky you are. Where I come from – in so many other places – there is corruption. People are destroyed for things they never did. Here, things are different. You should have belief in your criminal justice system."

Simon and Felicity came back into the room and sat down. "I've given her a mild sedative," he said. "Help her rest and calm down. There's no point in her going to see Peter when she's like this."

"What exactly did the police say?" asked Isabella. And, though she didn't say it, why did they choose to make their announcement through you?

He shook his head. "They didn't say much. Only what I already told you, that they'd charged him with both murders. And that he's admitted to seeing Jake and Felicity together, and sending Hugh that letter. Old Lark sounded pretty pleased with himself, I can tell you." He gave a short laugh. "He seemed to think that I ought to be happy to hear it as well." He shook his head again. "But he did say we were all free to go now."

"Thank God," said Lin, visibly brightening. "We can go today, then?"

He shrugged. "In theory."

"But we can't just leave Abi here on her own," protested Felicity. "Look at her – she's hardly in a position to cope."

"I'll be here," said Bubs. "I can look after her."

"That's very sweet of you, dear, but I think she'll need her friends. At least for a day or two."

She saw Lin's face and continued. "Look, I know you want to get the hell out of here, we all do, but we simply can't just abandon her. Let's all agree that we'll stay until tomorrow. We should have got more of an idea by then. And it's not as if we're under house arrest any more, anyway – you lot can all go out on the moors this afternoon if you want. I don't mind staying with her."

It was as if the old, imperious, Felicity had suddenly returned, taking control and issuing edicts. Isabella wondered what had prompted that – whether it was the burden of uncertainty being removed, or perhaps the sense of crisis, the need for someone to take a lead. Though what she said made perfect sense.

"I think that sounds like a good compromise. Personally I'd love to get out on to the moors one last time – it seems that the only days I managed it before it was pouring with rain."

Lin looked at Simon, who nodded. "Fine by me. Okay, the three of us will go out." He paused. "There is one other thing, though." He stared at Isabella intently.

"It's very odd. You see, the police didn't call me - I called them. An old friend phoned me this morning to say that the police had been asking questions about me, about an – incident - that happened in a hospital where I was working some years ago. Very insistent, they were, apparently – very concerned to know if there had been any allegations of negligence on my part."

"I never heard anything about that," broke in Felicity. "What sort of incident?"

Simon waved her question aside. "That's not important. The point is…"

"Is that why you left the country in such a hurry that time?" Felicity interrupted him again.

Simon reddened. "Christ, Felicity, will you give over?" Then he gave a deep sigh. "Look, in a way it was. There was an accident in an operation, and a child died. It really was just an accident, one of those awful things, but the parents kicked up a stink, so there had to be a full enquiry. That concluded quite categorically that no one was to blame for it, but it was still bloody upsetting, and that's why I left the country in a hurry, as you so nicely put it. But not because I'd done anything wrong, okay?"

He paused for a few moments. When he resumed his voice was calm again. "Anyway, I phoned up Lark to find out what the hell he was playing at, and – so this is the odd part – he didn't sound as if he knew anything about it."

"That's certainly weird," agreed Felicity. "What do you think happened, then?"

He shrugged. "I can only assume it was the London police's doing, not this lot at all. Something to do with that girl. Which begs the question, how did she know anything about this?"

Isabella was beginning to feel uncomfortable. "Why are you staring at me, Simon? I don't know."

"Because it strikes me that there's been quite a bit of new information around this week. This, for example. And you never really did explain how you found out about Jake and Felicity."

Felicity put her head to one side and frowned. "You know, he's right, Isabella. All you said was something about 'some stuff of Jake's'. But what stuff of Jake's could possibly tell you that? I never gave him anything."

Isabella looked desperately at Bubs. She wasn't sure what she was hoping for. But Bubs kept her eyes resolutely fixed on the table in front of her. This is your business, these are your friends, she seemed to be saying. You have to deal with this one on your own.

It was probably time to come clean about the laptop. It surely couldn't do any harm to do so now. She took a deep breath.

"I brought an old laptop of Jake's down to use for my writing. I thought it was unused, but it wasn't. He used it for his secret stuff – his conspiracy theories, and notes on people he knew. There was some stuff about Hugh, do you remember I told him about that?" She looked at Felicity, who nodded noncommittally. "And there was a sort of journal about the affair – that was really obvious, he barely even bothered disguising your name. And," she added, looking around at them deliberately. "He used it to look at internet porn. There's God knows how many files of pictures on there. I glanced at a few and that was quite enough. So now you understand why I wasn't exactly keen to advertise it."

Four faces stared back at her. She briefly met Bub's eye and received a faint smile of encouragement, but the others were blank, whether from astonishment or hostility she wasn't sure.

"Okay, I understand that much," said Simon. He didn't sound happy about it though. "But are you saying that all that crap about me at the hospital came from this laptop? Because if so, how did the police get hold of it? Did you tell them?"

"No! I didn't know there was anything about you on it. I had a look around it, as I said, but everything was in code, I told you. I just gave it to her because as far as I was concerned it was new evidence that might help find Jake's killer. You know how they crawled all over his stuff at the time, including his pc. Well, they would have done this, as well, if they'd known it existed. All I was doing was trying to find out what happened to my husband. I didn't know they were going to start hounding you, Simon."

To her horror, she found she was fighting back tears. Just as they should all be coming together, in shared mourning for the loss, in different ways, of so many of their loved ones, she found that she was once again the outsider, the enemy. And all the shocks and the stress had taken their toll. She just had no reserves left.

"It's all right, don't cry." Felicity's voice was soothing. "We just wanted to know what happened, that's all. But you could have told us, you know."

"She couldn't tell us because she thought one of us was the killer," said Lin. Her face was impassive and she spoke in an entirely emotionless tone, but Isabella could see her hands trembling. "Isn't that obvious? Come on, you've all spent the entire last few days suspecting each other. Well, now you've got what you want – one of your friends is going to jail. So can we please, please stop going on about it and ripping each other's throats out? It's over."

She stood up so abruptly that Simon nearly toppled sideways off his chair. "Come on, you two. If we're going to go for a walk on the moors, we'd better get on with it."

Chapter 17

Chu arrived back at her hotel room with a sandwich she had picked up in Torquay and little idea about how she was going to spend the rest of the day. There was plenty of paper work connected to the case she could be getting on with, but right now the prospect of returning to Torbay police headquarters seemed about as enticing as root canal surgery. So she sat down with her sandwich in front of the tiny hotel television, flicking between channels and wondering what sort of moron actually watched this drivel on a regular basis.

Her mobile bleeped a message.

Don't worry about laptop keeping laptop secret, cat out of bag here now. Not taken well. Isabella.

That bloody laptop. Presumably the same thing had happened to Isabella as to her — an irate Simon demanding to know what the hell was going on. She could well imagine that the assembled party at Harracombe Lodge would not have been too impressed to find out that Isabella had been holding out on them. It wasn't as if it had held anything of relevance in the end anyway — just the sordid detritus of a short, sad, sick, little life.

She decided to have one last scan of its contents. She didn't really expect to find anything new, but it would make her feel that she was doing something useful, and was better than watching another televised car boot sale. And maybe it would sort of vindicate her, if she could find something on there about Peter.

She looked through the files again, in part marvelling at the fertility of Jake's imagination, but more often wondering how someone of obvious intelligence could waste his time with such stuff. There was nothing particularly outrageous; it was just in the main either utterly bonkers or cringingly banal.

Jake had obviously hoped that some of his research had the makings of a good piece of blackmail, though what he'd actually attempted in that line wasn't clear. He'd got as far as writing to Hugh, though that seemed to be for making mischief rather than money. She found herself wondering how someone like Isabella had ended up with such a miserable apology for man.

The one part of the computer she hadn't explored properly was the picture files. A superficial inspection the other evening had quickly made it plain what sort of things Jake liked to look at, and she hadn't felt the need to explore very far. Now a sudden compulsion for completeness drove her satisfy herself that she hadn't missed any vital evidence, that there really was nothing here.

She discovered that Jake had a particular interest in pictures of girls, especially oriental ones, in poses of degradation or pain. No pretty air-brushed teenagers smiling into the camera here – it was hardcore action all the way. Often with more than one man, at least once with a dog.

She scrolled through the images file by file, looking for some pattern, anything, that might be of relevance to the case. But after a while she realised she was wasting her time. This wasn't the business part of Jake's computer; it was his entertainment section.

She closed the picture set she was looking at and sat back, staring at the vast list of files Jake had stored. Did he go back and look at them all, she wondered? And if so, how did he find the one he wanted? They all seemed to have meaningless jumbles of letters and numbers for names, nothing that seemed to describe their contents. Perhaps he was happy to treat it as a sort of lucky dip.

She scrolled down the page again, then something caught her eye. Not all the files had gibberish titles; there was one here that bore the hallmarks of Jake's special interest. 'The Story of O!!!' it was labelled. Wasn't that some old dodgy book?

Curious, she clicked the file open again. At first glance it seemed nothing out of the ordinary - in this context at least – just some poor oriental girl being used, simultaneously, by three black men. So why had Jake singled it out?

She was going through the file, picture by picture, when her phone rang.

It was Ireland.

"Karen?" he said. "I thought I'd better let you know where we've got to with Simon Rayner. We've spoken to his hospital."

"Yes, I know. What did they tell you?"

The call didn't take long. When it was over she sat, heart racing, with the phone in her hand, her eyes still glued to the images on the laptop.

So now she knew what had happened. And she knew what she had to do.

*

"Gerry? It's Karen. You've got to come over. We have to go up to Harracombe Lodge."

"I'm busy right now." His voice was distant. "It'll have to wait until tomorrow."

"It can't wait, Gerry. This is really important." Silence at the other end of the phone. "Listen, I'm sorry I held out on you, but you have to trust me on this."

She waited, rigid with impatience. She'd like to have him along, she had the feeling his presence could be important, but if he wouldn't help, she'd go on her own.

"At least tell me what it's about."

"It'll take too long on the phone – I'll explain on the way. Please – it'll be quicker."

She heard a sigh. "Okay. But I'll have to clear it with the boss first."

She almost ground her teeth in frustration. "You can't do that, Gerry, it will take too long. Think about it – Lark's never in a million years going to approve you going off to help me. But if we don't get up there fast it could be too late."

Still he hesitated.

"Gerry, I'm trying to do you a favour here. These people will be going back to London soon, do you want it sorted out there rather than down here? I want you along, but if you don't come I'm warning you I'll do it on my own. On your manor. And I'm willing to face the consequences."

At last, that seemed to convince him. "Okay. I'm on my way. But you'd better be right on this."

*

She waited for him in the hotel car park. Her little room was beginning to feel claustrophobic, and besides, it would be quicker this way.

After what seemed an eternity she saw his dark blue hatchback turn in at the car park entrance. Without even giving him a chance to turn off the engine she hopped into the passenger seat.

"Thought you could drive – you know the roads and it will be faster."

He grunted and swung back onto the road.

"So," he said. "Are you going to tell me what this is all about?"

She told him what she had discovered. He frowned as he thought it through.

"I can see your point – it provides a pretty strong motive. But it's still not evidence. It's no stronger a case than we can make against Willis."

"No, but I've also checked a few things in the files from last year. They stack up. Admittedly it's still circumstantial but it all points the same way. That's why we've got to do this now – while we've got the element of surprise."

"Still seems like a bit of a gamble to me."

She smiled, more confidently than she felt. "You know how it is – nothing ventured, nothing gained."

*

When they arrived at Harracombe Lodge Chu was relieved to see that there were still several cars in the drive, though she had the impression that there was at least one missing. She prayed that they were not too late.

Felicity emerged from the front door, evidently surprised to see them. "I heard the car and wondered who it could be," she said from the top of the steps. "What do you want this time? I hope you're not here to hound poor Abi – she's resting. She's been through quite enough for one day."

She seemed much more together than when Chu had last seen her. She guessed this might be nearer the real Felicity – bossy, proprietorial. Someone who was used to getting her own way.

"No, it's not her we want to see, Mrs Guthrie. Are the others here?"

"No, they're out on the moors. Since we're all hoping to be going back to London tomorrow they thought they'd get one more trip in. I'd have gone too but someone had to stay with Abi, so Simon and Lin have taken Isabella."

Chu mentally cursed. "Do you know where they've gone?" she asked.

Felicity shrugged. "I know they're starting at Haytor, that's all. Isabella's never seen it. They've not been gone long."

"Haytor?" Chu thought she recognised the name but had no idea what or where it was. She turned to Harris. "Where's that? Do you know how to get to it?"

He smiled. "Of course. Everyone knows Haytor. It's a massive rock, not far from here. People even use it for mountaineering practice, the sides are so high and steep."

She stared at him. "Shit," she said after a moment. "I've got a bad feeling about this. Come on – let's go."

*

Isabella was panting by the time they'd climbed to the top of the long path that led up to Haytor Rocks, but she was fresh as a daisy compared to Simon. He trailed up behind her and Lin, red-faced and wheezing, his chest heaving with the exertion.

"Jesus!" he said, collapsing onto a rock. "I'm too old for this."

"Are you all right?" asked Isabella. "Perhaps you ought to see a doctor?"

"Ha bloody ha," he said. "I don't know what's the matter with me though. I don't smoke, I'm not that overweight, and look at me. God knows what I'll be like when I'm fifty."

"It's because you spend your entire life behind a desk," said Lin. She'd barely broken into a sweat during the climb. "You need to get out more, exercise more."

"Yeah, well, that's easy for you to say," he grumbled.

Isabella was staring at the huge pile of rocks in front of them. "At least there are steps," she said. "I was wondering how on earth we were going to get up that."

"Oh, it's a piece of piss from this side," said Lin, following her gaze. The colloquialism sounded odd coming from her.

She looked down at her husband. "For us, at least. Are you up for it, or do you want to sit it out and wait for us down here?"

"What a very good idea," he said. "Why don't you girls bounce on up to the top and admire the view and I'll see you when you're done?"

The climb was actually much easier than it appeared from below. A series of steps had been part cut, part worn into the shallowest face of the massive rock. There was a small leap from one section of the outcrop to the other, but apart from that it was not much harder than walking upstairs.

A family of brightly-clad tourists waited politely at the top for them before smiling and starting their way down the narrow path, and soon Isabella and Lin were standing on their own on the broad, flat, summit.

Isabella turned around slowly, taking in the amazing panorama.

"I see what you mean about the views," she said. "It would have been a shame to come all the way down here and miss this."

She started walking towards the back of the summit. It was much windier up here, and she found herself edging her way gingerly as she realised how exposed it was. The rock simply ended, leaving a sheer drop of dozens of feet to the moor below.

A sudden gust made her lurch forward, and she backed away hastily.

"Careful." Lin's voice, inches from her ear, caused her jump. "We don't want any more disasters on this trip."

"No," she said, wandering back towards the centre of the platform. "That we most definitely don't."

For a moment the majesty of the view had almost taken her mind off the events of the last week. Almost.

She sighed.

"Perhaps we should never have come," she said. "But Felicity and Hugh meant well. It was all for me, you know. So in a way it's all my fault. Poor Hugh."

"Poor Hugh," echoed Lin. She had moved back to the south side of the rock, and was now staring intently at the sea glittering in the distance. "You never did find out what he was going to tell you that day, did you?"

"Not from him, no. But we know now it was Peter."

"Yes," said Lin so quietly that Isabella could barely hear her above the wind. "So it seems. It was Peter."

"Not the murder," said Isabella. She realised that Lin had misunderstood her. "I mean, yes, I suppose Peter did that as well, though I still can't really believe it. But that wasn't what Hugh's message was about – he didn't have any more idea about who the actual killer was than I did. All he was going to tell me was who he thought had sent him that anonymous letter."

There was a gasp, and Lin seemed to stagger. Then she recovered herself.

"Are you okay?" asked Isabella in concern.

Lin turned to face her, moving slowly, like a sleepwalker.

"I just felt faint." She attempted a smile. "It must have been the climb. I'm obviously not as fit as I thought I was."

"Why don't we sit down for a bit?" suggested Isabella. "I wouldn't mind resting my legs myself."

The two sat side by side, gazing across the moors. They were so high that everyone else seemed like ants, busy in the car park far below, or toiling up the path to the rocks. For some reason, despite the good weather, there seemed to be comparatively few tourists out today, and the scene was of near complete tranquillity.

How different from what was really going on in the world, thought Isabella. How different even from her own thoughts – and those presumably of the woman seated next to her. Death, destruction and betrayal should not be visited upon a place like this.

"What will happen to that laptop of yours now?" asked Lin suddenly. "Will you get it back?"

It seemed a strangely banal question in the circumstances. But of course, for Lin, the laptop was new news.

"I guess so. There's no reason for the police to keep it – it's not evidence." She shuddered. "Though with all that – stuff – on it, I'm not sure I want it back. I'm certainly never going to use it."

"I need a laptop," said Lin. "If you don't want it, why don't you wipe everything off it, and I'll buy it off you?"

Isabella stared at her in surprise. The suggestion struck her as bizarre, to say the least. But perhaps for someone of Lin's background it would be inconceivable to let a valuable item go completely to waste. She still wasn't sure she was very comfortable with the idea, though.

"Maybe," she said. "I'll think about it."

Lin seemed pleased with the answer. She smiled at Isabella and patted her on the arm.

"Good," she said, as if everything had been settled.

*

Chu and Harris arrived at the car park at the bottom of the hill in record time. She stared up at the steep path stretching in front of them in dismay.

"We've got to climb that?" she said. "Isn't there a road up?"

He shook his head. "If I was in a Landrover I'd give it a go, but we wouldn't get ten yards in this. There's nothing for it but to do it on foot. I hope you're fit."

They started out at a jog, but quickly dropped back to a fast walk. Even so, by the time they were close enough to recognise Simon leaning back contentedly against one of the myriad of smaller rocks surrounding the main outcrop they were both dripping, and so out of breath they could barely speak.

He had recognised them too, and was watching their scrambled approach with ill-disguised suspicion.

"Where – are –your – wife – and – Mrs Chester?" panted Chu.

Wordlessly he pointed towards the summit, and they set off again, this time at a more sedate pace. A sprained ankle wasn't going to be much help.

Chu looked up and saw the two women's silhouettes outlined against the bright blue sky. They seemed to be sitting down, deep in conversation.

"There they are," she said, mainly to herself. "Thank God."

They were in time.

*

Isabella and Lin both turned at the sound of feet pounding up the stone steps. A familiar face appeared, followed by another.

"Sergeant Chu?" She stared at the detective in astonishment. "And Sergeant Harris. What on earth are you doing here?"

Lin leapt to her feet and backed away from the newcomers, a look of alarm on her face. Isabella also got up, and stood waiting for an explanation.

For the time being both police officers seemed unable to speak. Chu was standing with her hands propped on her knees, her shoulders heaving as she struggled to get her breath. Her colleague didn't seem in much better shape; he stood, hands on his hips, gulping in air. His eyes never left Lin.

"You okay, Isabella?" Chu got out eventually.

"Of course I am," she snapped. "Why shouldn't I be? What's going on?"

Chu sort of nodded, then turned her attention to Lin.

"It's over, Lin," she said. "I've seen the pictures. I know what happened."

Lin shook her head, too emphatically, and backed away from them. "I don't know what you're talking about."

"I'm talking about the pictures on Jake's laptop, Lin. The ones he found on the internet of you. Was he blackmailing you? Was that why you had to kill him?"

"What's going on here?"

No one had heard Simon's approach. Now he too clambered on to the summit and stood, staring at the tableau in bewilderment.

"I'm sorry, Dr Rayner," said Chu. "We're here to talk to your wife about the deaths of Jake Chester and Hugh Guthrie."

"Lin? What nonsense." His eyes flickered between his wife and the detectives. "Lin wouldn't hurt a fly, would you, darling?"

"Perhaps she wouldn't normally, but Jake was blackmailing her about…"

"Shut up! Don't listen to her, Simon. She's making it up."

"I'm not, Lin, and you know it," said Chu, taking a step towards her.

"Don't come any closer!" said Lin, backing further away.

She was getting dangerously close to the edge. Isabella saw Chu look around. There was no way for Lin to escape without getting past her and Harris. She took a step back and raised her hands in a calming gesture.

"Okay," she said. "Let's just talk, though, shall we? Jake had these pictures of you, from your past life, before you met Simon…"

"What pictures? Where?" interrupted Simon.

He looked completely baffled, and Isabella shared his feelings. Was Chu really saying what she thought she was?

"Pornographic pictures," answered Chu calmly. "You were much younger, of course, and your hair was different then, but it's definitely you. It was your tattoo I recognised first, in fact. The photos weren't really concentrating on your face."

Simon jerked to attention. "Your tattoo?" he said. "That time in the pub, with Jake…"

"Shut up!" screamed Lin. She turned back to Chu. "So he had pictures – so what? There's no proof of anything else."

Chu shook her head almost sadly. "I checked our old files for Jake's phone calls," she said. "In the weeks before his death there were quite a number to your husband's surgery – where you work as receptionist, I believe? Nobody thought much of it – you were known to be friends, after all. But they weren't to your husband, were they? Did you talk to Jake much on the phone at that time, Dr Rayner?"

"Me? No." His tone was dismissive. "He knew better than to call me at work." Then as if he had just realised what he'd said he turned to his wife. "Lin? Is this true?"

She said nothing – just stared at him. It was a look of extraordinary intensity.

"What did he want, Lin?" asked Chu gently. "Was it money?"

Something appeared to snap in Lin. Her shoulders slumped and all the life seemed to drain from her face.

"Money? God, no. He got that from his wife, didn't he?" Her tone was bitter, contemptuous. "No, he wanted sex. He said he'd tell Simon about my past if I didn't go to bed with him. You should have heard the things he said he wanted to do to me. He spoke to me like I was an animal."

Isabella felt her flesh crawl as she listened to Lin's words. This was her husband she was talking about, the man she had pledged to spend her life with. But the worst thing about them was that they held the ring of truth.

Simon must have sensed it too. "But why didn't you tell me?" His voice was barely more than a whisper.

Lin's face twisted in agony. "Tell you? How could I tell you? That was what he was holding over me! You had me on this pedestal, thought I was some sort of saint. How would you have reacted to finding out that your precious little china doll was nothing more than a cheap whore?"

"You could have told me – I'd have understood…"

"You've never understood anything! How could you - any of you - understand what it's like?" She was almost having to shout to be heard above the wind. "To have nothing, nowhere to turn, so when your parents get ill and you have five brothers and sisters to feed you have to sell your body because that's the only thing you've got that's worth anything? And then how it feels when a miracle happens, and someone comes along who thinks you're wonderful, just because you're you, and takes you away from all that pain and squalor?"

She looked around at them desperately, willing them to understand. "But then, just when you are allowing yourself to believe that it isn't all a fairy tale that's about to end, that life has for once given you a decent break, some bastard comes along and threatens to take it all way from you. Just for his own sick pleasure. What would you do?"

No one spoke. They all stood like statues, each, Isabella guessed, in their own way stunned, appalled, saddened by Lin's stream of revelations.

"And you know the funny thing?" she continued, her face contorting in a parody of a smile. "I didn't even realise until this week that I wasn't that special, that he'd already had a go at Felicity. I wasn't even his first choice!"

She sounded close to breaking point.

Simon simply stood, staring at her as if at a stranger.

"So your saw your chance to end it at the picnic?" Chu's voice was calm, authoritative. "I'm guessing it wasn't premeditated?"

Lin nodded. "That's exactly it. We bumped into each other; he was drunk and got nasty, threatening to tell Simon right there in front of everyone else. So I saw my chance and I took it. Just like he did. And you know what? I don't regret it."

She turned to Isabella with an apologetic shrug. "I'm sorry, but there it is. You're better off without him – he was a shit."

"But Hugh Guthrie wasn't, was he?" Harris spoke for the first time.

Lin's face, which had grown more animated as she'd sought to explain herself, seemed to die again.

"No," she said. "That was wrong. It was a mistake. I panicked. If I could change that, I would."

"You thought he'd somehow identified you as Jake's killer?" asked Chu. Lin nodded, and she continued. "But he hadn't, had he? He hadn't seen the pictures. But when Isabella told you all about the laptop you thought she must have seen them, so you brought her up here to get rid of her as well. Is that right?"

Lin's head snapped up. "No!" she cried. "No – I was never going to do anything to her." She turned to Isabella. "You've got to believe that. I could have, couldn't I, if I'd wanted to? I could have pushed you off earlier. But I just told you to be careful."

Isabella nodded mutely.

Chu looked unconvinced. "But weren't you worried that she had seen the pictures? Why else are you up here?"

"I knew she hadn't seen the pictures because I heard what she said to you when she gave you the laptop. I was there that evening."

Isabella remembered Chu's sense that there was someone else in the garden. She'd been right.

Lin was continuing. "I only brought her up here because I wanted a chance to talk to her. I wanted to see what was going to happen to that laptop - make sure those damned pictures didn't do any more damage."

Chu turned to Isabella. "Is that right?"

Again Isabella nodded.

Simon seemed to regain his voice. "Lin! What are you saying? Stop it –

stop it now!"

She smiled at him bleakly. "It's too late for that, Simon. Perhaps it always was. You see, I've never been the person you thought I was. I tried to be, and maybe without Jake it would have worked. But that sweet, innocent, waitress you fell for was just an act. I'd have slept with you for twenty dollars if that was what you'd wanted – just like I had the previous day with someone else. But you wanted something different and I was happy to try and give it to you."

"But you were…"

"You saw what you wanted to see, just like you always do. Even now, when I've just spelled it out for you, you're standing there denying it. How could I expect you to still want me when Jake had made you realise what I really was?"

He looked at her imploringly. "But I love you – of course I'd have understood. It would have been hard, but … Why couldn't you trust me?"

She shook her head sadly. "Don't you see? I just couldn't take that chance."

Chu cleared her throat and took a step forward again. "Mrs Rayner, you're going to have to come with me now."

Lin responded by taking another step back, until she was right at the edge of the precipice.

The wind had been rising steadily, and a sudden gust made her sway alarmingly. Harris made to move towards her, but Chu stilled him with a gesture.

"Lin," she called out. "Don't do anything stupid."

Lin squared her shoulders and looked Chu calmly in the eye. "Stupid? What's stupid? Why do you think I killed Hugh? It was because I couldn't bear the thought of going to prison. I have to be free, to be able to come to places like this. Prison would kill me. I wish I hadn't done it – he was a good man, and it's made no difference anyway. But I still can't go to prison. I just can't."

She turned to her husband. "I'm sorry," she said. "But always remember, I did it for us." She gave him one last, lingering look, then turned to Isabella. "And tell Felicity I'm sorry."

What happened next seemed like a slow motion blur to Isabella. Someone, she thought Simon, screamed. Lin glanced behind her, then took the last, irrevocable, step backwards. Harris and Chu both launched themselves towards her.

But when they got there, all their clutching hands could grasp was empty air.

*

The sun was settling low in the western sky when the last of the emergency vehicles drove away. Lin had been pronounced dead at the scene. Harris had gone with a distraught Simon, who had insisted on accompanying his wife's crumpled, broken, body back to Torbay. Chu was to take his car back, dropping Isabella off at Harracombe Lodge on the way.

The phone calls had been made, Ireland informed. A subdued Lark had returned to police headquarters to deal with Peter. Now, for the time being at least, Chu had nothing to do. Apart from Isabella she was alone with her thoughts.

The two of them sat in silence on the same rock that Simon had rested on earlier. The few remaining tourists were making their way home and the daylight colours of the moor, the greens and golds, purples and whites, were turning to more sombre tones. Its chill desolation did nothing for her spirits, and she found herself looking forward to Ireland's arrival tomorrow. His at least would be a friendly face. Or at least she hoped so.

After a while Isabella turned to look at her. "You okay?" she asked.

Chu thought about the question. Was she okay? She'd been vindicated – her analysis was right, and Lark's wrong. Two murder investigations were now closed, beyond all doubt.

But another person was dead. No wonder success felt so much like failure.

"I don't know," she said eventually. "I keep going over it in my mind – could I have done things differently?"

"You can't allow yourself to think about it like that," said Isabella. "I know that's easier said than done, but it's not going to do anyone any good. You did what you thought was best – that's all there is to it."

Chu gave a hollow laugh. "That's not how the inquiry is going to see it, believe you me." She sighed. "But yes, of course I had my reasons."

"Okay," said Isabella, suddenly businesslike. "I won't pretend it's my field, but if you're going to have to justify yourself like that, why not run it by me? I'll see if it stacks up."

Chu shrugged. "Sure. Well, there were two principal reasons why I felt I had to corner her up here, which is how it's going to be presented. The first is that I knew I had to use shock tactics, to confront her and get a confession before she had time to gather her defences. After all, she was right – there was no hard evidence against her. Even the phone records were purely circumstantial."

Isabella frowned. "That works, I guess. Though I think I might be careful about using words like 'shock tactics' when talking about dealing with a vulnerable suspect at the top of a mountain. What was the other reason?"

"You," said Chu simply. "I was always nervous that the killer, whoever they were, might come after you if they thought you were getting too close. So when I heard that the two of you were on your own at the top of a sheer cliff, I was downright terrified."

Isabella sat silent for a moment, staring into the distance and chewing her lip.

"Not too sure what to say to that," she said after a while. "Thanks, I suppose. It's hardly the sort of argument I can have a problem with."

Then she gave a wry smile. "Though, of course, it does make me feel just a bit like it's all my fault. Again."

"None of this was your fault," protested Chu. "You've not killed anyone."

"But what made Lin kill in the first place? It all started with Jake, and what he did. Perhaps if I'd…"

"What Jake did was nothing to do with you," Chu interrupted her, gently but insistently. "A lot of people ended up as Jake's victims in this, one way or another. Jake himself, Lin and Hugh, Felicity – and you. You're a victim too, you know – don't forget that."

Then Chu's mind back to the photographs, and the toxic cocktail – poverty, lust, callousness, hypocrisy – that lay behind them.

"But you know what I think," she said. "It all started a long time before Jake. Back in Thailand. With the misuse and exploitation of a young girl who wanted nothing more than to look after her family. How many other lives are destroyed like that, I wonder?"

She shivered, and got up, stretching her tired limbs as she did so.

"Come on," she said. "It'll be dark soon. Let's get the hell out of this place."

The End

Acknowledgements

Many people have helped me with my writing career over the years, but I would particularly like to mention Elena Forbes, Richard Holt, Cass Bonner, Gerry O'Donovan, Kathryn Skoyles, Margaret Kinsman and Broo Doherty - and most of all, my wife, Pui Kei.

About the author

Keith Mullins spent over two decades working in the financial markets before deciding that there must be more to life than watching small numbers flickering over a screen all day. His love of crime fiction led him to try his hand at writing, and 'Cheating Truth' is his second published novel, his first, 'The Rector's Husband', is also available on Amazon. He lives in Surrey.

Printed in Poland
by Amazon Fulfillment
Poland Sp. z o.o., Wrocław